D0294771

The Dictator's Muse

www.penguin.co.uk

Also by Nigel Farndale

FICTION

The Road Between Us

The Blasphemer

A Sympathetic Hanging

NON-FICTION

Haw-Haw: The Tragedy of William and Margaret Joyce

Flirtation, Seduction, Betrayal: Interviews with Heroes and Villains

Last Action Hero of the British Empire: Commander John Kerans 1915–1985

The Dictator's Muse

Nigel Farndale

doubleday

TRANSWORLD PUBLISHERS
Penguin Random House, One Embassy Gardens, 8 Viaduct Gardens, London SW11 7BW
www.penguin.co.uk

Transworld is part of the Penguin Random House group of companies
whose addresses can be found at global.penguinrandomhouse.com

First published in Great Britain in 2021 by Doubleday
an imprint of Transworld Publishers

A CIP catalogue record for this book
is available from the British Library.

ISBNs 9780857527172 (hb)
9780857527189 (tpb)

Typeset in 11/14.25 pt Goudy Oldstyle Std
by Integra Software Services Pvt. Ltd, Pondicherry

Printed and bound in Great Britain by Clays Ltd, Elcograf S.p.A.

The authorized representative in the EEA is Penguin Random House Ireland,
Morrison Chambers, 32 Nassau Street, Dublin D02 YH68.

Penguin Random House is committed to a sustainable future for our business, our readers and our planet. This book is made from Forest Stewardship Council® certified paper.

1

To Mary

There is, indeed, a problem in getting the facts straight about Riefenstahl. My secondary sources may have been defective on three points but they're still more reliable than Riefenstahl herself.

Susan Sontag, responding to criticism of her essay 'Fascinating Fascism' published in the *New York Review of Books* in 1975

Nothing fixes a thing so intensely in the memory as the wish to forget it.

Michel de Montaigne

TIMELINE

7 June 1934: British Union of Fascists rally at Olympia, London
5–10 September 1934: 6th Nazi Party Congress (Nuremberg rally)
1–16 August 1936: Berlin Olympics
4 October 1936: Battle of Cable Street
9–10 November 1938: Kristallnacht

SELECT FILMOGRAPHY FOR LENI RIEFENSTAHL

1932: *Das blaue Licht* (*The Blue Light*)
1933: *Der Sieg des Glaubens* (*The Victory of Faith*)
1935: *Tag der Freiheit: Unsere Wehrmacht* (*Day of Freedom: Our Armed Forces*)
1935: *Triumph des Willens* (*Triumph of the Will*)
1938: *Olympia – Fest der Völker* (*Olympia – Festival of Nations*)

PART ONE

ONE

Winter, 2005. Somewhere in Bavaria

As she tried to close the car door a second time, Sigrun Meier sensed that someone was watching her. It was no more than a woollen scratchiness across her nape, but it made her feel uneasy and on her guard. A dangling seatbelt, she realized, was the cause of the obstruction. When she tucked it back inside the door frame, her actions felt false, as if she was engaged in a performance for the benefit of unseen eyes.

Only now did she look up at the house. Made of wood and glass, it had a heavy, gently sloping roof and wide, well-supported eaves set at right angles to the front. Large sliding glass doors, blotchy with dust and rain, led on to a second-floor balcony. From the outside, there were no clues as to the identity or notoriety of its recent occupant, yet the building seemed stupefied, naked in the cold morning sun.

The property, built on the shores of Lake Starnberg, had not changed since Sigrun's last visit, three years earlier on her twenty-ninth birthday – and as this thought struck her, she felt a pang of remorse. She had not been entirely truthful with Dieter, her boyfriend, when she had told him that she wasn't sure where Pöcking was exactly, before adding, 'I know it's in Bavaria somewhere.' She had not wanted him to know the true extent of her fascination with Leni Riefenstahl, partly because it went all the way back to her childhood, when her terminally ill mother had given her a book on the 1936 Berlin Olympics for her birthday. Dieter would, not unreasonably, find that weird.

On either side of the glass-panelled front door, sitting in terracotta urns, were rubber plants with spiked leaves, like guard dogs warning visitors to keep their distance. Without taking her eyes off them, Sigrun pressed the key fob in her hand. When the car failed to make a locking sound, she turned towards it, cursed, and used both her thumbs on the device. This time the hazard lights flashed in unison and the car *ping-pinged.* The thin layer of white that had settled on the roof overnight was still clinging on, more ice than snow.

As if bracing herself for what was to come, she gripped her shoulder bag and strode towards the front door, ignoring the 'guard dogs' and sidestepping a puddle of slush. Before knocking, she checked her reflection in the bevelled glass and gathered her hair into a loose knot. Its chestnut colouring looked natural in the flat, winter sunlight, even if the bright red streaks added to it did not. They matched her lipstick, the same shade favoured by the woman who, for the past decade, had been her subject, the focus of her academic research, the wraith who haunted her dreams.

But she now regretted wearing a leather jacket, denim skirt and biker boots over thick woollen tights. The dark, vampish nail polish, the ring on her thumb and the Sanskrit tattoo on her wrist would all give the wrong impression, too. She needed this job.

'Is it what you expected?'

Sigrun made an involuntary backward movement, a half-step, and turned to see a middle-aged man standing five yards away in the drive. The formality of his dress – a three-piece suit with a silk handkerchief in the breast pocket – made Sigrun feel even more self-conscious about not looking the part.

'I'm sorry,' the man said in a nasal voice, his breath pluming in the cold air. 'I didn't mean to startle you. I'm Wilhelm Becker; we spoke on the phone. Thank you for coming out all this way.' They shook hands. His were doughy and damp. 'Have you been to Pöcking before?'

Sigrun smiled and shook her head at the same time, the one gesture cancelling out the other.

'Is it what you expected?' His accent was Bavarian.

'Where . . . Were you waiting for me in that car?' Sigrun pointed at an olive-green Audi parked across the road.

'Yes. I suppose I could have waited inside but . . .'

But what? Sigrun wondered whether he was afraid of being left in this house on his own.

'Is it how you imagined it to be?' Becker pressed.

'The house?' Sigrun looked up at it again. 'I don't know what I'd imagined.' She tucked her hair behind her ear. 'How long did she live here?'

'We're not sure. A couple of years? Half a century?' He smiled. It was a smile that contradicted the coldness of his eyes, which were small behind thick lenses. 'She was a hundred and one when she died.'

'I know,' Sigrun said with a trace of impatience.

Becker seemed to be enjoying her discomfort and gave the impression that he had rehearsed this moment. Perhaps he got a kick out of bringing visitors here, watching their reaction as they absorbed the atmosphere and satisfied their morbid curiosity. 'Everything is as she left it,' he added as he reached the door and tried to find the correct key from a rattling bunch. 'The place is like a museum, which is how it will stay until the nieces, nephews and distant cousins can stop squabbling and reach an agreement about the estate.'

Becker stood to one side to allow Sigrun to enter first, but she remained where she was, peering inside. A draught from the door disturbed particles of dust, making them spiral languidly above a sun-bleached Persian rug. The items of furniture in the hall had white sheets draped over them, like children playing at ghosts.

Sigrun felt the prickle again, this time at her temples. Her reluctance to enter was inscrutable, even to herself, more a feeling than a resolution. It was as if to enter was to be lured by Leni into a fate she had been avoiding. Yet she felt her entire life had been leading to this moment – every seemingly random action, every decision made with apparent free will, as if she had had no choice in the matter.

When Becker prompted with a throaty noise, Sigrun squared her shoulders, stepped inside and sniffed. The air was sour. Curdled milk, perhaps. Or catfood. The hallway did indeed have the appearance of a museum, or perhaps a shrine, bearing totems of a long life lived at full charge, from a mountaineer's ice-axe to an African tribal mask mounted above two crossed spears. But this was a museum that had had its prize exhibits taken away to be stored in vaults. There were unfaded squares of wallpaper and the only picture still hanging was a framed certificate confirming the award of a Gold Medal for Leni's *Triumph of the Will* at the 1937 World Exhibition in Paris. Almost seventy years after it was made, it was still against the law to screen the film in Germany.

Sigrun put her head around the door and saw what appeared to be the sitting room. It was dominated by four 1970s-style copper-coloured leather chairs surrounding a coffee table on which were stacked some large art books. And there, on a side table, was the Meissen porcelain alarm clock Sigrun had only ever seen pictures of before. She moved forward to touch it, and the thought that Hitler's fingers had also once touched it – it had been a sardonic present from him, because Leni was always late – caused her to flinch.

She looked up. Taped to the cornice was a cluster of dusty, deflated pink balloons, the number 100 visible on the shrunken rubber. Sigrun had sent Leni a birthday card for the occasion. Had the old lady even opened it? A smell of mothballs and camphor overpowered the sour scent in here.

'Were you expecting to see swastikas draped across the wall?' Becker asked, unable to disguise the note of amused satisfaction in his voice.

Sigrun ignored his question. 'You mentioned on the phone that your firm was acting on behalf of her family,' she said.

'Such as it is. She had no children.'

'As far as we know,' Sigrun replied. 'She was a great believer in the use of smoke and mirrors. I should know: I helped write her obituary for *Der Spiegel*.'

'I believe that she was married for a brief time to a Wehrmacht officer during the war, and that she may or may not have remarried a month before she died. There doesn't seem to be an official record of this, however.'

'His name was Horst Kettner. The second husband. He had been her cameraman since the nineteen sixties.'

'Did you know he was forty years her junior? Good going, huh?' This time Becker caught her peeved expression. 'Yes, of course you knew. Well, anyway, she also had a brother, who was killed on the Eastern

Front, but not before he'd fathered a couple of children, and so there have been all sorts of legal complications. Not so much the triumph of the will as the tragedy of the will, you might say.' He seemed pleased with his joke. Once more it sounded rehearsed.

Sigrun leaned forward to examine a framed photograph on a shelf. It was one she knew well, a self-portrait Leni had taken in 1934 using the Agfa colour film she had helped pioneer. Across the bottom was a dedication scrawled in black ink that had faded to brown – 'Liebe, Leni Riefenstahl'. Sigrun smiled. Only Leni would display a signed photograph of herself in her own home. She picked it up carefully, as if afraid it might crumble. The greatest female film-maker of the twentieth century looked gorgeous in this photograph: an icy intelligence in her eyes, her ruby-painted lips half open, as though she were holding back some secret thought.

'I wonder what it feels like to live that long,' Sigrun said, almost to herself. 'She was so full of life. Did you know she took up scuba-diving in her seventies? She lied about her age to the instructor. She was still doing it in her nineties.'

Sigrun had a fleeting impression of her own features reflected in the glass covering the photo, as if superimposed in a double exposure. Her chin was a little too strong and the dimple at its centre made it look too masculine, but there were similarities. At thirty-two, Sigrun was the same age as Leni had been in this photograph. 'Where are the films?' she asked.

'In the basement. She had a screening room. There is a projector already set up.'

'I would rather take the films away for analysis at the university,' she said, 'if that's OK.'

'I'm afraid the family don't want them to leave the house,' Becker said carefully. 'I did ask.'

'So the films are still in her safe?'

'No. We took them out. They're on a table in the basement, but still in their canisters. Should we have left them in the safe?'

'They should be fine down there, assuming it is dry.' She turned to face Becker. He was tugging his hair as if trying to prove it wasn't a wig. 'Has anyone looked through them yet?'

'No. Miss Riefenstahl gave very clear instructions in her will that no one was allowed to touch the contents of the canisters – except you.'

Sigrun felt a lurching sensation in her stomach. 'What? She asked for me specifically? Why?'

'I'm told you're an expert in film restoration and that you wrote your PhD thesis on Miss Riefenstahl. Is that not correct?'

Sigrun nodded but she was feeling dazed. It was correct. It would also be correct to say that her thesis had been the subject of a faculty board of inquiry, following accusations by the external examiner that she had 'taken liberties' with her research. Her justification was that there was 'psychological truth' behind the disputed sections; that they were based on evidence from letters and diaries and Sigrun had merely joined up the dots and ironed out Leni's discrepancies to give it a consistent narrative arc. She had wanted to say that she had 'channelled' her subject – who had a flexible approach to the truth herself – but she suspected that that would not have helped her cause. In the end, after the 'unsourced' research had been extricated, the doctorate was awarded. She had sent Leni a copy of her thesis, but had received no acknowledgement. She wondered if Leni had ever read it.

'I never met her,' Becker said. 'Did you?'

'In later years she refused most requests for interviews, because she said people only ever wanted to talk about the Nazis. I had heard her house was somewhere in Bavaria, but I didn't . . .' She trailed off. The lies were turning to rust on her tongue. Sigrun had been here, to this very house, several times, but Leni had never opened the door to her. On one occasion, she had spent almost two days in her car, waiting for her subject to leave, but had given up. Apart from a question she had once managed to ask at a press conference, the closest she had come to direct contact with Leni was when she had posted her latest interview request halfway through her door before it got stuck. As she was walking away she heard a metallic rattle and turned to see the letter disappearing inside.

'Do you believe in ghosts?' Becker asked suddenly.

'No,' Sigrun replied, puzzled by his question. 'They are a biological impossibility. But I do believe in guilt. We Germans love our guilt.

When I was at school we had lessons in it. You know, maths, geography and double guilt – or "history" as it was more formally known.'

'Guilt about the war, you mean?'

'Of course.'

'Do you think Leni ever felt guilty?'

'Not really, no,' Sigrun said. 'But she should have. Her Nuremberg film helped invent the Hitler myth. She presented him as a Wagnerian hero. She should have accepted some of the blame for that. But I also think her side of the story never came out. Perhaps these films will tell us more.'

'Well, good luck,' Becker said with an ironic shrug. He was examining a clapperboard. 'But I'll need you to sign a non-disclosure agreement regarding the contents of the films that were in the safe. The press has been sniffing around. There is talk of a . . .' He tucked the clapper under his arm and made the air quote gesture with his fingers. '. . . "director's cut" of *Olympia*.'

'What do they think is in the films?' Sigrun asked.

'Not what,' Becker said with a cold smile. 'Who.'

Sigrun raised her eyebrows. 'Eva Braun's husband?'

Becker did not seem to like it when other people made jokes. 'There were always rumours that Hitler *did* shake hands with Jesse Owens at the Berlin Olympics,' he said primly. 'Just not on the honours stand.'

'And you think that Leni—' She checked herself; the first name familiarity she had fallen into whenever she thought about her subject seemed inappropriate here. 'You think Miss Riefenstahl might have filmed the moment?'

'Who knows? Maybe. It would certainly spoil the myth about the Jesse Owens handshake snub if she did.'

Sigrun took a Handycam from her shoulder bag and checked the battery light.

'Afraid not,' Becker said, leaning over and tapping the camera. 'The family don't want there to be any copies.' He gestured towards a spiral staircase at the end of the hall. 'After you.'

Sigrun descended the stairwell cautiously, feeling her way in the listening darkness. When she reached the bottom step, she groped with her hand until she touched a door. She heard the tentative whisper of her own fingers on the latch, and then she was inside, feeling for the light switch. Becker insinuated himself into the room behind her and she became aware of his smell – car upholstery and cigars – and felt not nervous exactly, more a sense of disquiet.

As the fluorescent strip lights in the ceiling flickered on, Sigrun saw that the basement, Leni's inner sanctum, was divided into three adjoining rooms without doors. When she saw the first was lined with shelves containing hundreds of small canisters of films, she gave a small gasp.

In the second room were two Steenbeck editing tables and a projector. As Sigrun ran her fingers over the latter, she nodded. It was a collector's item, a 1950s Bolex reel-to-reel. And then a cold tingle ran down her spine as her eyes found the objects on the table: two large, rusty metal canisters, the size of wheel hubs, much bigger than the cans on the shelves, with black Gothic lettering stencilled on the side: *Olympia: Festival of Nations* and *Olympia: Festival of Beauty*. They would not contain the reels for the entire film, which was four hours long and would need at least a dozen cans, so presumably these were out-takes.

'There was a Cartier gentleman's wristwatch in the safe with them,' Becker said. 'And a starting pistol dating back to the nineteen thirties.'

Sigrun felt a hollow thudding in her chest as she picked up a pair of white cotton gloves and slipped them on. 'I wonder when this was last opened,' she said as she lifted up one of the canisters. 'There might be air trapped inside that hasn't been disturbed for seventy years.' The lid was stiff at first but, with a scrape of corroding metal, it came free.

Inside there were dozens of numbered offcuts: celluloid of various lengths, all loosely coiled and giving off a strange vinegary smell. Sigrun pulled out one, roughly sixty-four frames long, and held it to the lightbox, emulsion side up. She then dusted it before carefully threading it through the projector sprocket. There was a hair on the lens, she now noticed. She removed it with tweezers and placed it in a small, plastic film container. If the hair was one of Leni's it would be useful, should a DNA test ever be needed. She had a friend at the university who could help with that.

She flicked the on-switch, the projector whirred into life and there they were: athletes on parade for the opening ceremony. The images were a little grainy, with the odd white dot and scratchy line, but the condition of the film was surprisingly good. After four seconds, the screen went blank again and there was a clicking sound as the reel continued to spin.

'Was that it?' Becker said.

'The clips vary in length,' Sigrun explained. 'Some will only be a few seconds long. There is a longer one here.' She unravelled it and nodded to herself. 'This should be about four minutes.' As she watched it, she heard the blood pulsing loudly in her ears. It was of Leni herself. She was wearing flared trousers and a white polo-neck. Her ever-disobedient hair was blowing in her face and she pushed it back by lifting her sunglasses to the top of her head. She then stepped on to a camera trolley and put her hand on her hip as it was pushed along. This clip must have been staged for publicity purposes, Sigrun thought, because in normal circumstances Leni rarely got in front of the camera. After a few yards, the man pushing the trolley stopped and the group all held the pose for a few seconds before Leni turned to the cameraman and raised her thumb. She looked slightly cross-eyed as she stared directly down the camera lens; then she gave her wide smile, revealing the tiny chip in her front tooth. Sigrun felt a melting sensation in her chest. Such a vital, irrepressible, unapologetic woman, she thought. Ballsy, too. When Goebbels had ordered her to edit out all the black athletes from her film, she had simply defied him.

Over the next half-hour, Sigrun looked through dozens more clips while Becker nodded in the corner, his head heavy with the desire to sleep. At one point, he jolted upright with a grunt, checked his watch, and asked: 'Would you like a coffee?'

Sigrun was distracted. Hidden underneath all the loose film clips was a small metal container, not much bigger than a CD. She looked over her shoulder to see whether Becker had noticed it. Apparently not. 'Please,' she said. 'I take it black. No sugar.'

She waited for Becker to leave before opening the can. There were four clips coiled up inside it. She held one up to the light, then threaded it into the projector. Jesse Owens was preparing for the long jump, limbering up, rolling his neck. Behind him, on the edge of the shot, was a tall, striking athlete with fair hair parted to one side and a smoothly muscled body. 'Definitely haven't seen *you* before,' Sigrun said to herself. The man was wearing a white vest with two grey bands across the chest, one darker than the other. The British colours, she was sure.

When the clip ended, Sigrun took out another one. As the frames of celluloid stuttered through the gate of the projector she saw the same British athlete walking around, talking to his coach, collecting his jumper, warming up, seemingly unaware he was being filmed. Leni had clearly taken a shine to him, whoever he was. She always did have a lively appreciation of male pulchritude.

Sigrun felt her fingers tingling with anticipation as she threaded the next clip: a shot of the British athlete in tight close-up in the starting position, filmed from the side. The film then cut to him pounding down the track and cut away again as he hit the take-off board, this time switching to a head-on shot. The camera stayed on him as, silhouetted against the sky, he leapt, folding his legs, stretching his arms in front of him and landing in an explosion of sand.

The fourth clip seemed to be of Jesse Owens doing practice long jumps again but, as before, the British athlete featured in the background. This time, as the camera turned to him, he raised his arm out in front of him in what was either a Nazi salute or a wave to the person behind the viewfinder – which was Leni, presumably. The man had a sculpted mouth and a shy, off-centre smile that seemed endearingly boyish and innocent.

When Sigrun clicked the dial to the reverse position so she could watch the clip again, something odd happened. As he moved backwards, the athlete seemed to look straight down the lens at her. In that moment, Sigrun experienced a thrilling jolt of connection. It was as if she was seeing through Leni's eyes.

A noise upstairs made her look away from the screen. She glanced at the door, then pulled the film from the reel, rolled it up tightly, slipped it into a small plastic canister and pressed the pliant rubber lid firmly shut. She listened again, holding her breath. What if Becker searched her on the way out? Seeing his shadow approaching down the stairs, she turned and shoved the canister under the waistband of her denim skirt, into her underwear. Only as she removed her hand, turned back to face the door and smoothed down her skirt, did she realize she had become a thief.

Still picturing the unknown British long jumper with the strange and engaging smile, she whispered under her breath: 'Who are you?'

PART TWO

TWO

Summer, 1933. London

The cry carried through the air like the sharp flick from a towel. It had come from the broad-jump pit. Kim was thirty yards away, sitting with his long legs stretched out in front of his bent torso. While other athletes ran over to find out what was happening, he remained in this stretch position, his fingers holding his toes for a count of ten. As the numbers in his head subsided, he replayed the cry, hearing again its single report, like a starting pistol that leaves smoke and a buzzing silence in its wake. And into this emptiness other London sounds now flowed – the stutter of a motorbike, the hiss of a sprinkler, a smoker's cough. He could also make out a distant whining, born of frustration this time rather than pain. Kim felt sorry for his team-mate, for he knew all about that whine. A similar one had escaped his own lips the previous year when a hamstring injury meant him losing out on a place in the hurdles at the 1932 Los Angeles Olympics. He was not going to let that happen again. He was not going to let his whole athletic career be rendered meaningless by something as small and trivial as the fibre that connects bones to other bones. He had invested too much.

He bent his knees and after removing the sand-filled pouches strapped to his ankles – weights to help build up his strength – he massaged his calves to prevent cramping. Rising to his feet with a lightness that belied his height, he collected the garden trowel he used to dig the starting holes in which he planted his feet and headed over to join the crowd gathering at the broad-jump pit.

Kim was a softly spoken young man with a calm and measured demeanour that made people want to listen to him. But when he asked one of the other athletes what had happened, his question was met with a distracted shrug. His team-mate was still lying prostrate where he had fallen, face down, his fist slowly pounding the sand.

The arrival of the team physiotherapist was met with an expectant hush. After a brief examination, the man nodded, looked up at Mr Riley, the head coach, and mouthed the word 'knee'. He did not need to say the words out loud, not in front of the victim. The athlete's anterior cruciate ligament had clearly snapped – he would have heard the pop himself and, in that fraction of a second, would have known his chances of representing his country in the British Empire Games the following year had all but slipped away. Even if surgery worked, he would be unable to train for months and would then struggle to regain his form, always knowing that the selectors would be nagged by doubts about whether it might happen again.

Mr Riley, whose first name no one seemed to know, was a broken-nosed Irishman with a florid complexion and a vivid turn of phrase. He always wore a boater on his head, indoors and out, and it was said of him that even his own mother addressed him as Mr Riley. Noticing Kim standing on the edge of the crowd, he said: 'Can you bring the stretcher, please, Mr Newlands?'

Kim jogged back to the tunnel where, hanging on the wall, was a stretcher with wooden handles worn to a smooth shine from decades of contact with sweaty palms. There was a date stencilled on its sun-bleached canvas: 1915. Kim had often glanced at it on his way out to the track, wondering if the stretcher had seen action in the Great War, if those dark stains spoke of spilled blood. Picking up a clean towel from a rack, he dabbed his brow before draping it around his neck and lifting the stretcher from its mounting.

Back at the pit, Kim laid the stretcher alongside his team-mate and helped roll him on to the canvas. The injured jumper's knee was raised at an awkward angle and he was covering his eyes with his hand, perhaps to hide his tears. Kim helped carry the stretcher to the changing room, where Mr Riley pressed an icepack against the injured limb. Kim took a step back and rubbed his own knee, feeling once more the grain of the penultimate hurdle, which he had grazed with his trailing leg. It had been a good session. In his final runs his closing speed had been consistent and he had clocked 23.8 seconds.

Nevertheless, he knew he needed to shift his balance forward more to remain on the balls of his feet and that he had to work on his rhythm so that he could make the approach step at the same distance from each hurdle. Behind him, the other coaches were whispering and a single phrase interrupted his thoughts:

'. . . we don't have any subs.'

The phrase echoed in Kim's head as he reached the shower room and held the door open for a moment. He was diverted by the sight of his reflection in a mirror and said the words out loud: 'We don't have any subs.' In other words, the team did not have any substitute broad jumpers.

As a hurdler, Kim had always wondered if he might have the height and speed required for success in the broad jump. And if he had a third discipline – he also ran in the 4 × 110-yard relay – it would increase his chances of being picked for the Berlin Olympics in three years' time. He pictured himself coming away with not two but three medals to show to his mother – or at least to take along with him when he went to visit her grave in Southsea.

To distract himself, Kim gripped the door frame and did a chin-up, feeling the burning sensation in his muscles as he held the lift. Although he was broad across his shoulders and his chest was deep, Kim's frame was sinewy, his stomach ridged like corrugated iron. His jawbone was angular, his nose straight, his eyes deep cobalt blue – and his hair was still as blond as it had been the last time his mother saw him. At twenty-one, Kim was in peak physical condition. He was also confident, ready and ambitious. Instead of showering, he headed back outside to the track.

For once, the White City Stadium did not look to him like a giant discarded eggshell; in the velvety blue twilight, it seemed more like a coliseum. The other athletes, all those over-privileged varsity men with their languid postures and their private incomes, were calling it a day, talking in huddles about the injury and what it meant for the British team. Let them, Kim thought. I'm not done yet.

He walked towards the broad-jump pit, considered it for a moment, then picked up the rake and smoothed down the sand, erasing the impression left by his fallen team-mate. He had often watched the jumpers and, having tried it himself several times, knew he had some natural ability. With a glance over his shoulder, he paced out twenty yards from the board, then took a run and a jump. The attempt was non-committal. He raked the sand again, walked back and had a second go, this time with a faster run-up. On his third attempt, he found a better rhythm, with longer strides, and accelerated without apparent effort, holding his form steady, his upper body straight.

'Try pivoting from the hip more.'

It was Mr Riley. He must have been watching.

'And keep your centre of gravity forward,' the coach continued, walking towards the pit. 'Concentrate on your form and try to generate as much velocity as possible before you hit the board. How long is your run-up?'

The athlete locked eyes with his coach. 'Twenty paces.'

'Try it from twenty-two. The greater the speed at take-off,' Mr Riley said with a sibilant 's', 'the longer the trajectory of the centre of your mass.'

Kim knew he had the speed needed for a successful jump; it was just a question of whether he could also achieve a high enough leap, and the right angle.

His next attempt was better. The coach paced out a distance from the take-off board and placed a white handkerchief at the side of the pit. 'The world record is twenty-six feet two inches,' he said, tipping his boater to the back of his head. 'I've marked it. Be sure to keep your feet flat to the ground on take-off. And don't jump off your toes, it decreases stability. When you make contact with the board, keep your torso upright and move your hips forward.' He raked the sand and watched with folded arms as Kim rocked back on his heels in preparation for his next attempt. 'Know what I like about you, Mr Newlands?' the coach added. 'You have the tender gallantry of a subaltern in Flanders fields.'

Kim wondered if Mr Riley, a decorated veteran of the trenches, was being sarcastic, but decided he was not. Sarcasm required a sense of humour that the coach lacked. He tried again and this time he felt he was moving more smoothly, his arms pumping in rhythm, his gait more natural. This time he hit the board at full stride, without looking down, and left the ground at an angle of twenty degrees. For a full second he was in the air, but it felt split into smaller fragments of time, like frames in a moving strip of film.

The sound of clapping now. With his spikes still planted where they had landed – about two feet behind the handkerchief – Kim looked around and realized that the applause was coming from Connie, his girlfriend. She was walking towards the pit, her short, strawberry-blonde hair rippling like honey under the floodlights.

'Thought you were a hurdler,' she said in a crisp, patrician voice that always made Kim want to click his heels and stand to attention.

'He is,' Mr Riley said, picking up the rake again. 'But it seems our Mr Newlands has been hiding other talents.'

'Clever boy,' Connie said. 'Come on, then, if you want a lift.'

Ten minutes later, Kim emerged from the changing rooms, still towelling his hair, and looked around for Connie's car, a convertible Wolseley Hornet. It was parked by the entrance gate and Connie was sitting in the driver's seat, looking at her reflection in the rear-view mirror as she puffed on a cigar.

'Since when do you smoke cigars?' Kim asked as he walked towards her, frowning in an amused manner.

She let a wisp of smoke curl from her mouth, removed the cigar and picked a shred of tobacco from her tongue. 'Since now,' she replied.

Kim sat in the passenger seat and drew his legs up so that he could fit them into the small well.

Holding Connie's hand to his mouth, Kim said: 'Have I told you that you drive me crazy?'

Connie extracted her hand and angled the rear-view mirror so that she could reapply her lipstick, then nodded towards the glove compartment. 'Have a look in there.'

Kim opened it and stared in disbelief at a pistol half wrapped in a handkerchief. His mouth formed a word, but no speech came.

'Stole it,' Connie said.

Kim picked up the gun, holding its muzzle between his finger and thumb. 'Stole it from where?'

'From a kitbag. That's where I found this as well.' She waggled the cigar.

'It's a starting pistol,' Kim said, realizing now that the items must have come from Mr Riley's kitbag, because he was a cigar-smoker. 'Why would you want a starting pistol?'

'So we can rob a bank. You can be Clyde, I'll be Bonnie.'

'Who are Clyde and Bonnie?'

'Don't you read the papers?'

'Yes,' Kim said.

'I don't mean the sports pages.'

'Just because I didn't go to university, doesn't mean I don't read newspapers.'

'Don't be so defensive,' Connie said.

'I'm not being defensive.'

'Yes, you are. I can tell. You get a little frown just here.' She tapped his forehead and puffed on the cigar, then started to cough. 'Disgusting,' she said. 'Why do people smoke these things?'

When she threw the cigar away, Kim climbed out of the car, ground it out with his shoe and tossed it into a hedge so that the coach wouldn't find it. As he lowered himself back into the car, Connie pressed a button and the engine started.

Kim crossed himself as they set off, a running joke of theirs because she much preferred the accelerator to the brake.

'OK,' Connie shouted. 'Which bank do you want to hit first?'

THREE

Berlin

From the first-floor window, looking down Unter den Linden, Leni could count thirty-one individual flags rippling in the breeze; sixteen down one side of the avenue, fifteen down the other. After this, they coalesced into a single angry blot of red at the vanishing point. Each was thin and tall and appeared to be untethered, the poles supporting them mostly hidden from her view. She closed one eye and framed them using her fingers and thumbs, imagining what they would look like foreshortened by a 600-mm telephoto lens: the nearest out of focus, with the spidery black symbols becoming an aesthetically pleasing blur.

Keeping her arms in front of her, she rotated through 180 degrees and, with one eye still closed, framed objects dotted around the room. An antique globe. A leather-bound ledger. A Bakelite telephone on the desk. And, on the wall, a calendar with today's date, 14 June 1933, circled in red ink. Underneath this, also in red, was her name. Not Leni Riefenstahl. Just Leni. Dr Goebbels's presumption of familiarity annoyed her.

A man was now mowing the strip of lawn that surrounded the giant fountains below. The grass around him steamed under the mounting sun and she could hear the rattle of his cutters above the distant hum of trams and cars. She inhaled deeply and held the breath until the pressure in her lungs made her body begin to pitch back and forth and her vision grow dim. The sickly smell of smoke that had been lingering for the past month – since the students had had their little book bonfire in Opernplatz – had all but dissipated. Foaming columns of water jetted up into the blue sky before tumbling back into the basin of the fountain. As Leni shifted her weight to her other hip and contemplated them, she became mesmerized, overwhelmed by a bone-deep feeling that in this moment, in this place, she was at the centre of things.

'I am Berlin,' she whispered and then looked over her shoulder in case anyone had entered the room and overheard her. Once this meeting was over she would take a taxi out to Potsdam and go for a swim in the lake. She had a new swimsuit. Perhaps she could put on a show for the other bathers. She thought back to her days on the stage, before a knee injury had curtailed her career as a dancer. She had been uninhibited, provocative, experimental. 'The German Isadora Duncan' they had called her.

Maybe she should go right now and forget this damned meeting. It was not too late to escape. In a moment of irrationality, she leaned forward to see how far the drop would be if she left through the window. She could easily climb down. But no, people might see her. She might be photographed dangling from the window ledge, and that would make her look ridiculous. Besides, she was wearing a skirt. Even though she was a few inches taller than Goebbels – who could not be more than 5 feet 5 inches – she had wanted to wear high heels today so that she could tower above him. She had made an effort with her make-up too, in order to annoy him, because he had decreed on billboards across the metropolis that: 'THE GERMAN WOMAN DOES NOT NEED MAKE-UP'.

She had also attempted to tame her wild hair, spending at least twenty minutes on it before she came out. A mischievous part of her enjoyed driving the Little Doctor crazy with desire. And she had to admit that she was sometimes flattered by his attention, by his constant telephone calls and letters. He had become a powerful man since they first met, when she was a motion-picture star and he a mere local government official. Indeed, he had boasted to her at their last encounter, when he had turned up at her apartment unannounced, that he had become the 'invisible string-puller' in the Reichstag. 'I make the puppets dance,' he had said.

Where was he? Was she being punished for being late for their appointment? She had kept him waiting, so was he now doing the same to her? Typical. Psychological games. That would be his way.

As she waited, Leni remembered Goebbels bragging that night. He had been following her around her kitchen, unable to keep up because of his club foot, the result, so she had heard, of osteomyelitis in his childhood. Then his mood had changed. 'I need you,' he had said. 'Without you my life is a torment.' With this he had knelt down and begged her to be his mistress. Such melodrama. It had been a pitiful sight and Leni suspected her refusal had only increased his ardour. Perhaps he enjoyed being humiliated by her. When she had turned her back on him, he had grabbed her ankle. After this, she had lost her temper and ordered him to leave, opening the apartment door and stepping forward to press for the lift. Without glancing at her again, he had left, his head bowed as though he were a naughty schoolboy.

Their next encounter had hardly helped improve relations between them. In a bid to intimidate her, no doubt, Goebbels had turned up at her production office with a couple of his henchmen and had called her a 'treacherous bitch' in front of her staff. He had also called her a 'mongrel' and a 'mad dog'. And when he had asked her, rhetorically, what she had to say for herself, the unexpectedness of her answer had made a couple of those present splutter with laughter: 'Woof?'

There had been several phone messages from his office since, and she knew she could not go on ignoring them, because that would be dangerous. She might not have wanted him as a lover, but that did not mean she wanted him as an enemy. Besides, she felt it might be easier to meet him here, in his office, surrounded by photographs of his blonde and statuesque wife. She looked around, and, unable to see any pictures of Magda, bit her lip and gazed once more through the open window.

Something was wrong. It seemed too quiet. She looked outside and saw that the man who had been mowing the grass had finished. Yet it was more than that. There was a conspicuous lack of ambient noise: no birdsong, no footsteps, no traffic.

Leni thought for a moment that she could make out the smell of fresh grass cuttings carrying towards her on the breeze. Realizing the odour was coming from inside the room, her attention turned to an arrangement of heavy-headed dahlias flaming and drooping in a pot on a small table to the right of the window. It seemed an improbable choice of flower for the Reich Minister of Public Enlightenment and Propaganda.

Where was he? She checked her wristwatch and flinched as a slight movement of something, or someone, was reflected in it. When she spun around, she realized Goebbels had been standing behind her, no doubt studying the seams in her stockings and the curve of her hips. He had entered the room in silence, barely moving the air around him.

'I hope I didn't startle you,' he said. He was wearing a pinstriped, double-breasted suit with a gold swastika pendant on the lapel that glinted at her like an interrogator's lamp.

'No, I was just . . .'

'You were admiring the flowers,' he said. 'You must have them.' As he stepped in front of her to scoop them out of the pot, she smelled his sharp cologne. 'They are beautiful, are they not?' he said, handing them to her.

Here we go, she thought. 'Actually, I find flowers creepy,' she said. 'It's the way they carry on blooming after they are picked, as the nails on a dead man are said to keep growing.'

'Tea or coffee?' Goebbels asked after a short pause. 'I seem to recall you prefer tea.'

She requested coffee and, as he pressed a buzzer on the wall by the door, she tried to appear calmer than she was feeling. She felt such an idiot now for accepting his invitation.

'As you know,' Goebbels began, pulling back the seat behind his desk and directing her to sit in the chair opposite him, 'the Führer has put me in charge of the alignment of cinema, theatre, art, radio and press.'

He wants to sit down so that our height difference isn't so noticeable, Leni thought as the almost untranslatable German word for alignment, *Gleichschaltung*, joined *Dummkopf* circling in her head. Serves him right. I will remain standing.

'I wanted to talk to you, therefore, about your future film projects,' he said. 'I think I'm right in saying that you have been commissioned to do a motion picture that deals with espionage. What other plans do you have?' He leaned back and regarded her with cold eyes and a thin smile.

So he is being businesslike, Leni thought. Again, this was good. This she could deal with. She finally sat down. Drips of water from the flowers in her lap began to soak into her skirt, cooling her skin.

'I would like to play Kleist's Penthesilea,' she answered carefully.

A servant arrived and Goebbels ordered coffee. 'That would certainly be a good part for you,' he said. 'I can imagine you as an . . .' He paused to lend suggestive weight to his words. '. . . Amazonian queen.'

'I'm not *that* tall,' she said sharply.

He was staring at her, as if trying to hypnotize her, his eyes cast in shadow, giving his face a skull-like appearance. 'Now,' he went on, 'I hear you want to visit the Führer to discuss your plans with him?'

So, the Little Doctor did not know about her most recent encounter with his boss. She could use this to her advantage. 'Did Adolf not tell you about our meeting the other day?' she asked evenly. She was sure that, unlike her, Goebbels was not allowed to refer to the Führer by his first name.

A pause from him. Then: 'Of course, though we have both been very busy and have not had time to discuss the matter in detail. What did you talk about?'

He is trying to establish how close I am to Adolf, Leni thought, pressing her fingertips together. He considers me a rival. 'I mentioned that I wanted to work only as an actress and not as a director,' she said. 'I directed *The Blue Light* purely as a stopgap, because I did not have the money to hire a director.' She was speaking more correctly now, aware that, when Goebbels had taken her by surprise a few minutes earlier, she had slipped back into the reedy Berlin accent of her youth. The studio had insisted she take elocution lessons when she made the transition from silent movies to talkies, but she sometimes forgot to practise what she had been taught.

'It's a great pity you do not want to cultivate your talents as a director,' Goebbels said. 'Because I have a wonderful project for you, and that is what I wished to discuss today.' There was something false and ingratiating about his tone. He was talking in a singsong that seemed too loud, as an adult might talk to a child. Leni studied him uneasily. 'It's a film about the Führer,' he added.

Before she could reply, Goebbels launched into a monologue about how the next Nazi Party rally, to be held in Nuremberg in the autumn, would be the greatest ever and perhaps she might be the right director to make a film about it. The prestige and the financial reward for whoever was lucky enough to get the job would be huge.

The coffee arrived and he poured her a cup with a slightly trembling hand as he continued with a talk that he had clearly rehearsed in advance of their meeting. An oily sheen was making his weak chin and prominent forehead glisten.

'I would do a scenario and finance the production. You could work directly with me, if you play your cards right, and are chosen for the job.'

Was he trying to bribe her? A favour for a favour? 'But I know nothing about politics. I would . . .' She trailed off, then said: 'You should ask Walter Ruttmann.'

Goebbels shook his head: 'Out of the question. Ruttmann is a communist. We couldn't possibly consider him.' The tension in his gaunt face seemed to lift momentarily. 'I like the fact that you have a mind of your own, Leni. And I like that you have physical courage. I know you scaled glaciers without safety ropes for one of your films, and climbed barefoot in the Tyrol one summer to toughen your feet.'

'It was nothing,' Leni said, feeling a tightness in her throat.

'You survived being buried alive in an avalanche, emerging from it still in character, with the cameras continuing to roll. Was that nothing also? I know all about you.' He stood up, went around the desk, and perched on one side of it, facing Leni. 'You know, in 1926, I stood outside the Ufa Palace, at the premiere of *The Holy Mountain*, hoping to catch a glimpse of you, like a crazed fan.' He laughed in anticipation of his own joke. 'You probably pushed me out of the way, and I probably felt honoured to be pushed.'

'Flatterer,' Leni said, but she felt uneasy and thought about her most notorious silent role from that time, the film she not only regretted but now denied ever having been in. She had appeared bare-breasted in *Ways to Strength and Beauty*, wielding a fan in her role as handmaiden to a Greek noblewoman. The little masturbating creep was bound to have watched that one.

'You're an unusual woman,' Goebbels said. 'You see the world in different colours.' Pause. 'And you know I desire you.' Another pause. 'I will never stop fighting for you.' With this he leaned towards her and his open hand hovered over her chest. Was he about to grope her? Is that what he did with his starlets? As she stared at the hand, time seemed to hesitate.

Then she tapped his fingers to one side and stood up. In one quick movement, he grabbed her arms and pinned them to her flanks. Though he was stronger than he looked, so was she. Wrestling herself free, she made a dash for the door. He caught up with her before she could reach it and, this time, he pinioned her against the wall and pressed his hard lips against her mouth.

Leni resisted as best she could and edged herself sideways along the wall until she was able to push her back against the buzzer. Goebbels let go of her, straightening his tie and checking his hair before the servant arrived. As soon as the door opened, Leni hurried out, without looking back or saying goodbye. She did not wait for the lift but instead took the stairs two steps at a time.

It was not until she was outside, by the fountains in Pariser Platz, that she stopped to catch her breath. She looked back at the building's brutalist façade. Goebbels was standing in the window, watching her. A minute later she hailed a taxi to her villa in the Grunewald.

Back home, Leni closed the front door behind her, stripped off her clothes and turned on the shower. She remained standing under it for a quarter of an hour, and then, with her hair wrapped in a towel, she lay on her bed, staring at the spinning blades of the ceiling fan. Eventually, she poured herself a schnapps, lit some candles and, not wanting to be alone, rang one of her lovers, Hans Schneeberger, a cameraman. When there was no answer, she remembered he was away filming in the Dolomites. She tried Anderl Heckmair, a fellow climber. He picked up.

An hour later, when she opened the door to him, her eyelids were pink and swollen, her cheeks streaked with mascara. 'I'm drunk,' she said, slurring the words as she thrust a glass of schnapps into his hand. 'You have some catching up to do.'

FOUR

London

As they strolled along the King's Road on an overcast afternoon, Kim kept glancing at Connie. She looked graceful in her cloche hat and fur stole and he longed to hold her hand. It had been her idea to go to Sloane Square, to see if the new department store being built there was finished. 'You're dedicated to sport,' she'd said. 'I'm dedicated to shopping.'

The building was like a wall of glass and when they cupped their hands around their eyes and pressed them against the windows, they could see carpenters still at work with hammers and saws, and sparks being sent up from a grinder. They turned to face one another at the same moment and their noses almost touched.

At 6 feet 3 inches, Kim sometimes felt self-conscious around women, but Connie was also tall. With her he felt comfortable. More than that, when reflected in her wide green eyes, he felt admired and unstoppable. Although he had never been in love before, he knew that's what this was now. There wasn't anything about Connie he did not like – from her face and voice to her unpredictability. Above all, he appreciated the ease with which she laughed, and made him laugh. And he missed her when she was not around – the Connieless world seeming greyer, more banal, less fun.

A woman about their age was approaching, her long skirt swirling around her in ironed pleats. The moment Connie recognized her, she grabbed Kim's sleeve and marched him across the road, holding up her hand to slow an oncoming car. When Kim turned and followed the rolling motion of the woman's hips with his eyes, Connie punched his arm.

'Hey,' he said with a laugh as he rubbed his arm to exaggerate the injury.

'Well, you shouldn't have been staring.'

'Who was she?'

'No one.'

'A friend of yours?'

'Not really.'

Kim narrowed his eyes playfully. 'Why won't you let me meet your friends?'

Connie looked away; then her eyes snapped back. 'Why won't you talk about your background? You've never told me anything about your people. You must come from somewhere.'

'Must I?'

It was a familiar stand-off and they both fell silent as they continued walking across Sloane Square, Connie's heels giving reproachful little clicks on the pavement. Kim took her hand in his, but when a passer-by tutted in disapproval at this public display of affection, he let go.

They had been courting, after a fashion, for two months. She had been the one who pursued him in the first instance, having seen him in action at an Amateur Athletics Association Championship at White City. She had come along with two friends who, dressed as she was in a party frock and strings of pearls, seemed to have come across the event by accident, on their way to somewhere more glamorous. Afterwards, as youngsters formed a huddle around Kim and his fellow athletes to ask for autographs, Kim had noticed Connie noticing him. She was carrying a glass of champagne in one hand and a cigarette holder in the other, which she pointed in Kim's direction before leaning towards one of her friends to whisper something. A short while later, she came over and asked him where and when he did his training. Two days after that she had turned up at one of his sessions, and had asked him to take her to the pictures, which he duly did – *She Done Him Wrong* starring Mae West and Cary Grant. She had also been the one to initiate their first kiss. 'Come on, then,' she'd said, 'we both know you're going to kiss me, so you may as well get on with it.'

He was flattered by the attention but also puzzled by it. What did someone like Connie see in him, beyond his sporting prowess? Part of the attraction, he suspected, was that he must seem enigmatic to her – he'd told her almost nothing about his family and his received pronunciation gave nothing away, so he aroused her curiosity.

As they approached the Lyons Corner House, Connie said: 'You don't say much, do you? The silent type.'

'I do talk,' Kim said. 'When I have something to say.'

'I never shut up. That's what everyone tells me.' Half a minute passed before she spoke again: 'Bored now.'

'What would you like to do?' Kim asked.

'Don't know. Harrods?' She asked this lightly, as if Harrods were a place that Kim might frequent.

He did not want to go because it would mean spending money. Having never had to worry about pounds, shillings and pence, Connie did not seem to appreciate that other people might have to. 'Let's walk a bit longer,' Kim said.

'Maybe you should marry me,' she said.

Her words prompted a floating sensation in his stomach. Did she say marry, or carry? When she added 'It could be part of your training', he realized, with a cut of disappointment, that she had said 'carry'. He wrestled for a beat too long with the idea of saying something about carrying her across the threshold, but the moment had gone.

They walked along, gazing at the shop windows, and then sat under an awning outside an elegant café that would have looked at home on a Parisian boulevard. Kim wondered whether he should order a glass of champagne for Connie, but having never tried alcohol himself, he was not sure whether he had enough cash to cover the expense. Besides, Connie would ask, as she always did, why he wasn't joining her in a drink. He didn't want to explain to her that it was because his father was an alcoholic, just as he didn't want her to know that his late mother, who had been an asthma sufferer, was the reason he didn't smoke.

Connie pushed a cigarette into her holder and waited for Kim to light it. 'I'll have a Manhattan Dry,' she said, slowly exhaling a column of smoke.

'What's that?'

'Why don't you try one? It won't kill you. It's what they're all drinking in New York this season. Did I tell you I'm going to New York?'

Kim tried to sound nonchalant. 'No, I don't believe you did.'

'A cousin of mine is out there. He's inviting everyone. It will be a hoot.'

When the waiter arrived, he said he didn't know how to mix a Manhattan Dry, so Connie ordered a gin and tonic instead. Kim asked for a glass of milk, a drink that reminded him of his mother, then asked Connie: 'Do many of your family live in America?'

'No, just that cousin.'

So far, Kim hadn't met any of Connie's family, but he had heard from someone at the South London Harriers that there was an older sister, that her father was a peer – Lord Dalton – and that Connie was an 'Hon'. 'The Honourable Constance Lavinia Emily Dalton', he had since discovered, featured regularly in the society pages of *Tatler*, but not with him by her side. He had never been invited back to the townhouse in Mayfair where she lived, even though, from what he could gather, she seemed to have the place mostly to herself. Her parents spent the majority of their time in 'the country', at the family seat in South Wales.

A week earlier, Kim had offered to call by her house before they went out. She had said, 'I'd rather you didn't, not yet, it would be too shame-making,' and he had winced. When she saw his crestfallen reaction, she quickly added: 'I'm ashamed of who *I* am, silly, not of you . . . Not that you ever tell me much about yourself.'

After that awkward moment, Connie had reluctantly told him a little more about her past: that she had been expelled from a school called Roedean and that she had been engaged twice. Kim had already assumed he was not her first lover, but news of these betrothals had come as an unwelcome surprise. He imagined her former suitors would have come from good families and would have attended the right schools, not a grammar like the one he went to. They would have owned country estates, golden retrievers, signet rings.

Kim knew he was not Connie's equal socially, but there were other things to recommend him. He was a quick learner and a keen reader – he got through at least one library book a week – and he did have prospects. If his ambitions were realized, in three years' time he would be stepping off the podium in Berlin with a laurel wreath on his head and a third gold medal around his neck: one for the 220-yard hurdles, one for the relay, and one for his new discipline, the broad jump. And although Connie didn't know it, as of six months ago, he was also an apprentice clerk at an insurance company, Pickering, Turnbull & McCann Ltd in Holborn. The job did not pay much but it was enough for him to cover his rent and have a small sum left over each week for food, clothes and two shillings' worth of cinema tickets. He had been told that, if he worked hard, he could expect to be made a clerk within three years, though he guessed that wouldn't impress Connie much. His ultimate ambition was to become an insurance broker for Lloyd's, specializing in shipping, as that, apparently, was where a man could make his fortune.

For now, though, Kim had a problem. He was not likely to win any Olympic medals unless he trained more, and he could not train more because he needed an income. What he lacked was a patron: someone prepared to sponsor his Olympic bid without compromising his status as an amateur. He couldn't ask Connie – she would think less of him, and he less of himself – but after approaching the Rotary Club, the Salvation Army and even Lipton tea for financial help, all to no avail, he was running out of ideas.

'You *are* going to win a gold medal at the Olympics, aren't you?' Connie said now, intruding on his thoughts. 'I've told all my friends you are.'

'You've told your friends about me?'

Connie gave him a mock serious look. 'Course I have, silly.'

'When am I going to meet them?'

'I'll organize a big party,' she said. 'And you haven't answered my question. Are you going to win a gold?'

'Yes,' Kim said, momentarily surprising himself. 'Three, in fact.' He had fantasized about it often but never said it out loud.

'What are they doing?' Connie said, distracted, pointing across the square at two men standing either side of a spikey Gothic arch. Above it was a Union flag rippling on a halyard attached to an angled pole. The building was made of bricks blackened by years of exposure to London smog and was four storeys high, with a double-gabled roof that mirrored the spike of the arch. Connie suddenly pushed back her chair and started walking towards it, so Kim signalled to the waiter and quickly paid the bill before catching up with her. The two men, he now realized, were sentries. Both were wearing black uniforms and kept their hands behind their backs in the 'stand easy' position, their feet apart, their eyes fixed on a point in front of them.

'They must be Blackshirts,' Connie said. When Kim did not respond, she added: 'Oh, I forgot you only read the sports pages.'

'I know who the Blackshirts are,' Kim said with a roll of his eyes. Seeing two posters on either side of the entrance, he moved closer then read one out loud: '"Fascism is practical patriotism".'

Connie read the other: '"Fascism for King and country", I should say so!'

They looked at one another and laughed, but Kim felt uneasy.

'I know a couple of people who have joined,' Connie said. 'Country members. It's all the rage among the hunting set.' She looked up. 'This is the old teacher-training college. These Blackshirt chaps must have commandeered the place. Are they allowed to commandeer things?'

'It would appear so,' Kim said.

'I'm going to have a look around.'

'Don't be ridiculous.'

'Why not?'

'Because the Blackshirts are trouble. Don't *you* read the papers?'

But Connie had gone over to one of the sentries and was inspecting the well-ironed creases in his trousers. 'Don't mind if we have a look around, do you, old boy?'

The sentry remained impassive, staring straight ahead.

'It's OK,' Connie said to him. 'I know Sir Oswald.'

At this, the sentry directed a sideways glance at his fellow guard, who gave a barely perceptible shrug.

'Come on, Kimothy,' Connie said.

'I'm not going in there,' Kim said, frowning.

Connie plucked at her jacket, as if it were a source of discomfort. 'Suit yourself. Wait here for me.'

'All right, all right, I'm coming,' Kim said. As he passed the sentry, he felt obliged to explain to him in an undertone: 'And my name's not Kimothy.'

The entrance led on to a gloomy hallway that smelled of disinfectant and bore a sign at knee-height with the words 'The Black House' painted on it in Gothic lettering. Walking along it at a brisk pace, they soon reached a quadrangle where they found two military-looking trucks with loudspeakers on the back, and some men in white vests who were lining up in front of a wooden vaulting horse. Other white-vested men were lifting weights or boxing, their arms pale, their muscles modest.

'There you go,' Connie said with a sweep of her arm. 'Just like your athletics club.'

'This is nothing like my athletics club,' Kim said.

'Well, it smells like your athletics club.'

'Can we go now?'

'Not yet.' Connie opened a door but, seeing that it led into what looked like a chapel, she closed it again. She tried another, beckoning Kim to join her. Inside was a hall with chairs set up facing a stage on which there was a table covered with a Union flag. The room was chilly and, as they stood in silent contemplation of the flag, Connie shivered in an exaggerated way. She then marched up to the stage and draped herself across the table. 'Let's do it on here,' she said. 'Come on.'

'Connie!' Kim said in an urgent whisper. 'This is not funny.'

Connie opened her arms in invitation and gave him a sulky pout.

'Get off there! Someone's coming!'

Connie rolled off the table and crawled under it, hidden by the flag, as Kim stepped back behind a stack of tea chests. An echoing clunk broke the silence and a beam of light illuminated the stage. There was the slap of leather soles on floorboards as a figure climbed up to the stage, fanned sheets of paper out on the table and stood in the spotlight. The man was tall, with a neatly clipped moustache and a strong chest visible under a tight black shirt. His fingers raked his backswept hair, then he folded his arms and turned his head slowly, as if taking in an imaginary crowd. He nodded to himself and cleared his throat.

'My lords, ladies and gentlemen. This . . .' He stopped, scribbled something on the paper, put his hands on his hips and paused.

'This great meeting is gathered tonight to hear the policies of fascism,' the man continued in a sonorous aristocratic voice. 'If you think the present system . . .' He paused again and made a hacking noise to clear his throat. 'I come to you with a revolutionary . . .' Another pause. 'I come to you with a *virile*, revolutionary idea.' He made a fist and shook it. 'I come to you tonight with a virile, revolutionary, *new* idea! Fascism is a thing of the spirit! It is a thing of civilization! It is a thing of equality between rich and poor!' He thumped his fist into the palm of his hand. 'The corporate entity of fascism embodies the finest aspirations of the human mind and spirit in superb sacrifice to a sacred purpose.' He stopped again. Made another note. 'To a sacred and *noble* purpose . . .'

A bugle sounded somewhere in the barracks. The man checked his watch, gathered his notes and loped down off the stage. He left the hall via a side entrance.

'I think that was Sir Oswald,' Connie said in a half-whisper as she poked her head out from under the flag. 'I recognized his voice.'

'Why didn't you say hello to him, then?' Kim asked.

'I don't *really* know him,' she said, jumping down off the stage and dusting off her hands. 'Not properly. My parents invited him to dinner once. I had to sit next to him and he kept putting his hand on my knee. He's notorious for that. We talked about hunting, and real tennis, and making marmalade. He was wearing his black uniform rather than a dinner jacket, and, I have to say, he did look rather dashing in it.' When she reached Kim she gave him a peck on the cheek and added: 'But don't worry, he's not as dashing as you.'

Back outside in Sloane Square, Connie turned to Kim and said: 'Well?'

'Well what?'

'Well, should we join?'

Kim smiled, but then realized she was being serious. 'No. Of course not. We don't know anything about them.'

'Look, everyone has to be either a fascist or a communist these days, and how will you know which you are unless you try both of them out?'

'Everything's just a game to you.'

'Come on. Where's your sense of adventure?'

Kim watched her march back across the square to the entrance of the Black House. He hesitated, then followed reluctantly. When he found her in the courtyard, she was standing admiring a group of female Blackshirts practising drill, their arms swinging out of time to the skirted stride of their legs. They were wearing the same style of black shirt as the sentries at the entrance. Behind them, half a dozen male Blackshirts were fencing with foils, their blades making ticking noises as they connected.

Connie marched straight up to a drill sergeant and tapped him on his shoulder. 'I say,' she said, 'where does one sign up?'

The sergeant pointed at a green wooden door.

Kim could do nothing but follow.

A quartermaster, sleepy-eyed and with Brylcreemed hair, was handing Connie a form. 'Your uniform costs seven shillings and sixpence, but you get this for free,' he said, pushing a badge across the desk. 'About a third of our members are ladies.'

'Looks like a bundle of sticks,' Connie said, picking up the badge and examining it.

'It's a representation of the *fasces*,' the quartermaster explained in a bored voice. 'Italian. Symbolizes that a single stick might be broken but a bunch cannot be.'

'All right, enough of this nonsense,' Kim hissed to Connie.

'And you have to pay a monthly subscription of a shilling if employed,' the quartermaster added. 'And fourpence if you're unemployed. Are you employed?'

Connie gave a playful frown. 'Goodness no, never have been and hopefully never will be. Is that it? Don't you want some proof of identity?'

'No need,' the quartermaster said. 'A candidate simply has to state that he, or she, is loyal to King and Empire. *Are* you loyal to King and Empire?'

'Most of the time.'

'Then you're in.'

'My friend here is the one you want,' Connie added, patting Kim on the back. 'He's going to represent Great Britain at the Berlin Olympics. The hurdles, the relay *and* the broad jump. Three gold medals.'

The quartermaster sat up straighter, clearly impressed. 'You should have a dekko at our training facilities here then, young man. We have all the latest equipment.' He reached into a drawer for a packet of cigarettes. 'Do you smoke?'

'We're not joining,' Kim said, gently treading on Connie's foot.

'I smoke,' Connie said.

'Try one of these.' The quartermaster pushed the packet across the table. It was black. 'Blackshirt cigarettes: they're good for your throat. Medically proven.'

Connie took one, put it to her lips and, as usual, waited for Kim to light it. She then transferred her cigarette to her left hand and saluted the quartermaster in the British Army style with her right: long way up, short way down.

'We don't salute like that here, miss,' the quartermaster said. 'We do this.' He raised his arm straight out in front of him.

'Come on,' Kim said, linking arms with Connie, 'we're leaving.'

With the cigarette sticking out of the corner of her mouth, Connie turned towards the quartermaster as she was being led away and held up a clenched fist – the communist salute.

FIVE

Autumn, 1933. South Wales

The Black Lion was known as a miners' pub. Located at the lower end of the Rhondda Fach, the smaller of the two valleys, it was the nearest one to the colliery and, when the shift ended there on a Friday night, the publican would line up dozens of glasses of beer along the bar. To mark the end of their working week, the miners would go straight to the pub without washing first and, their eyes white and wide against their still-blackened faces, they would always drink their first pint in silence. Then the talking and joking would start. Sometimes, as part of this unwinding, punches would be thrown.

The brawling was the reason Alun Pryce preferred to drink there on a Saturday night, when the miners came back in a less confrontational mood, after a day of rest or an afternoon watching their teams play football in Swansea, Newport or Merthyr Tydfil. Their skin would be scrubbed clean and they would be wearing starched white scarves over collarless shirts and polished shoes rather than hobnail boots.

As he sat on his own in the corner of the pub, nursing the only pint he could afford, Alun took a sip to fuel his courage for what he had come here to do: he was about to jump on the table and make a rallying speech that could spark a revolution.

A sinewy twenty-two-year-old with a Trotsky-style beard and pale, angular features, Alun was not a miner himself, but he felt a great affinity with the mining brotherhood. For him they epitomized the phrase 'the dignity of work'. He had contemplated going down the pit himself at one stage, but his eyesight had let him down. Even with the round, wire-rimmed spectacles he habitually wore, in dim light people simply blurred into shapes. It had been suggested at one stage, though not by him, that he might follow his father into his profession instead, that of a milk-delivery man. 'Pryce the Milk' was what everyone in the valleys called his father and whenever Alun heard that name he winced.

Slight of build, freckly of skin and reserved of nature, his father had failed his army medical and so, unlike many of the men in the valleys, he had not fought in the Great War. He didn't even drink, having for years been indoctrinated every Sunday in chapel by temperance propaganda. The son did not share the father's interest in religion, just as the father did not share the son's in politics. Alun's mother, shy and prematurely aged by malnourishment, was the same, finding consolation for the hardship of her life in this world with the prospect that the next might prove more agreeable. She worked as a scullery maid at the big house, Dalton Hall, and seemingly had no ambition to improve her lot. There was never anything that could pass for intellectual conversation in their house. There weren't even any books.

A teacher had spotted Alun's academic potential when he was ten and, without consulting his parents, had arranged an interview for him at the County Grammar School in Port Talbot. He had been asked to sit an exam that day and a free place had followed. The school was a thirty-five-minute train journey away, which meant he lost touch with his old classmates from Rhondda and his sense of alienation began. From there, after being moved up a year, the seventeen-year-old Alun had won an exhibition to read history and law at Cardiff University. Late-developing acne had knocked his confidence for a while – he had found it especially hard to make eye contact with women – but it had cleared up eventually, and he had found a social life through student politics, joining the university Labour Party and, in his third year, serving as its president. That role had helped hone his skills as a public speaker, as he learned how to structure and present an argument, starting slowly and building towards a passionate climax. Though this office had interfered with his studies, he nevertheless came away with a first-class degree. Not only was Alun the first in his family to go to university, but, as far as he knew, he was also the first person in his small community to have done so.

Not that it had helped him much. After graduating in the high summer of 1931, when the country was being driven off the gold standard and unemployment doubled, he had been unable to find work befitting his education; his strong Welsh accent and acerbic witticisms always let him down in interviews. He decided instead to work his way up from the ground floor at a brewery in Birmingham, only to be made redundant after two months. He was laid off from his next job, at Austin Motors, also in Birmingham, after only one month. Moving north, he took a job as a shop steward at the Crewe locomotive works. He lasted only one week in that role, his attempt to take the workers out on strike having gone unappreciated by the management. He had taken his case for unfair dismissal to the head office of the Trades Union Congress in Swansea but even they seemed to regard him as too much of an agitator, especially after he lost his temper and told the general secretary that he was a 'fat-fingered capitalist lackey'.

After that, Alun had decided to embrace the class struggle through direct action and during the mass trespass organized by the Young Communist League on Kinder Scout in 1932, he had been involved in a violent scuffle with gamekeepers that had led to him being arrested and sentenced to six months in prison. He had put a brave face on the experience, but it had been frightening and for the first month he had cried himself to sleep every night. It was the sound of the cell door slamming shut that he could not stand. It had to be closed that way because there was no handle on either side, but there was no sound like it: heavy steel finding its frame; the clunk of turning locks. And then there was the silence that followed, a deadness that permeated the air.

For several months after his release Alun was unemployed and then he was offered a job as a chargehand porter in a railway goods depot in Swansea. He was diligent and managed to stay out of trouble, but the end result was the same. In the summer of 1933 he was out of work again. Eventually he had returned to Rhondda to live with his parents. When not looking for work there he spent his days reading books and feeling lonely. He had still not managed to kiss a girl, and never would, he felt, unless his circumstances changed.

As he sat in the corner of the pub, Alun took another sip of his pint and prepared his speech in his head. He wanted to call on the miners to join the fight against the new government policies on tighter means testing. Miners in employment had to show solidarity with those, like him, who were unemployed through no choice of their own. He wanted to tell the miners that the government minister who had recently announced that the unemployed should be expected to live off five shillings and a penny ha'penny a week was himself on a salary of eighty pounds a week. The minister did not understand what it meant to live in poverty.

A national hunger march was being planned that would pass through almost 150 towns across the country, including Rhondda, which was why Oswald Mosley and his Blackshirt thugs were planning a visit. They wanted to stir up trouble and disrupt the march, but they would fail.

Alun felt his radical young heart racing as he steeled himself to stand up now and make his speech. The bosses, like Lord Dalton who owned the local colliery, were only interested in profit. In every sector, men were being asked to do more work for less money and any who refused were being sacked. He was just thinking about the colliery owner when he overheard two men sitting at the next table talking about how there had been a pheasant shoot on Lord Dalton's estate that day and they had been beating for it.

'How much does that pay, then?' a man on another table asked, leaning back on his chair.

'Good money,' the older of the two beaters said. 'Sixpence a drive. And soup and bread for lunch.'

'I talked to one of the men who was loading,' the younger beater said. 'His man had two shotguns on the go and the barrels were red hot, they were. Never seen so many birds come down. I swear to God, there must have been two thousand pheasants in the wagons at the end of the day.'

'What did they do with them all?' Alun asked.

The beaters turned to look at him.

'They can't eat them all,' he continued. 'Do they sell them?'

'They bury them, boyo, don't they,' the older beater said.

'Bury them?'

'They're sitting up there around the back of Dalton Hall right now, a great big pile of them waiting to be buried.'

Alun felt a throb of indignation. He had no objection to people killing animals for food or to protect crops, but it seemed immoral that pleasure could be part of the equation. If these creatures had to be killed it should have been done with dignity and humanity, not as a means of showing off to your parasitic, monocle-wearing friends. And if you were going to end the lives of these birds, then you should at least have the decency to eat them, especially when half the country was starving.

'That's obscene,' Alun said. 'Why don't they give them to the poor?'

The beaters looked at him for a moment, then laughed.

But Alun wasn't joking and, instead of making his speech that night, he went from the pub to the stable where his father kept his cart and horse. Sunfell seemed to know the way to Dalton Hall, clip-clopping past the giant wheel suspended above the pit shaft and then three and a half miles up the gentle hill out of the valley. When they reached the gatehouse, she turned in of her own accord and Alun realized that the hall must be on his father's milk round. They continued up through the avenue of limes that lined the drive, crossed the humpback bridge over the southern corner of the ornamental lake and moved on past the boathouse.

The columned front of the hall hove into view, on its roof the silhouettes of dozens of chimneystacks like spines impaling the night sky. The contrast between the delicate beauty of this architecture and the brute ugliness of the colliery that had paid for it, Alun thought, could not have been greater.

He saw a mound and assumed it was the pheasants but, as he drew closer, he saw it was earth. The hole had already been dug and half a dozen spades had been left in the ground around it. Behind this mound there was a second one formed of pheasants. Alun could smell the cloying, sweet smell of blood.

As he got to work loading the pheasants on to the back of the milk cart, he calculated that he would need about two hundred. He was going to strike a blow for social justice by draping a brace of them from every front doorknob on his terrace, all the way down the hill. When his neighbours woke up the following morning, they would find their evening meal waiting for them.

The horse now snorted and began raising and lowering its head, making its bridle and bit rattle noisily. Alun stopped and looked around. Had a fox spooked it? They would no doubt be after these pheasants. He began loading again but then he froze. He had never smelled gun oil before, or heard a shotgun being cocked, but when he smelled and heard both now he knew instinctively what they were. The barrel that was pressing into the small of his back confirmed it.

SIX

Spring, 1934

Although Connie wrote one letter a week to Kim every time she went away – to her family's country estate in Wales, visiting her cousin in New York, skiing in Austria – her letters were gossipy in tone and superficial in content. She seemed incapable of taking anything seriously, including their relationship. Because she had still not introduced him to any of her friends or family, Kim wondered if there was another man in her life, a Household Cavalry officer perhaps, or some Old Etonian playboy with a title and a yacht.

That would all change, he felt sure, once he came back from Berlin with three gold medals. Her family and friends would be begging to be introduced to him then. And it was starting to look like a real possibility. His hurdling was improving by the week. Mr Riley had taught him to lead with his left leg when jumping in order to stay closer to the inside of his lane around bends, and to run with his hands in loose fist shapes – not tightly clenched – to keep his body from tensing. These things had already knocked half a second off his personal best. His coach had also shown him an unorthodox technique for reducing strain when waiting for the starting gun. He kept his head down while his rivals looked ahead.

But he was not finding it easy to keep up his strict training schedule while holding down a job. He ran five miles before work, did a hundred press-ups in his lunch break and spent three hours every evening at the track or in the gym. All this left him feeling permanently tired, so much so that on more than one occasion he had nodded off at his desk, waking with an exclamation that made his colleagues jump. In some ways, though he missed Connie when she was away, he was almost relieved that her social life was as hectic as it was, because if he'd had to fit in seeing her as well it might have finished him off.

Unlike the athletes with private incomes who could train as much as they liked, Kim needed financial support. He'd already tried several avenues and was becoming increasingly frustrated. So, as he often did when faced with a dilemma, he went to visit his mother. She always seemed to help him clear his head. On the train to Portsmouth he closed his eyes in the hope of finding her voice. It was usually the same phrases of hers that he came back to, like a tongue returning to the tender cavity left by a recently extracted tooth. In his head he soon heard her response when he'd won a scholarship to Portsmouth Grammar School. 'This is the proudest day of my life, Kim,' she had said.

As the train swayed gently, he remembered the honey tang of her breath and the licked hanky she had used to clean his face with before taking him straight round to the school outfitters. There she had bought him a uniform she could ill afford: grey cap, grey shorts, grey socks held up by gaiters with red tassels, and a beautiful grey jacket with red piping and the PGS crest on its breast pocket. When he had protested about the expense, she had said: 'Nonsense. I have only one child. I am allowed to spoil him.'

He nodded at this memory, then his brow puckered as he pictured himself two years later, on his thirteenth birthday. By then his school uniform was already too small for him.

Because he had been wearing an old pair of his mother's spectacles that day, with the lenses taken out and the 'good eye' side taped up to force his 'lazy eye' to do the work, he had not noticed the fairy cake on the bedside table; not straight away. It was next to the glass of milk that was always waiting for him when he got back from school. He recalled taking a step closer to the cake but not picking it up. Written on it in blue icing sugar was the number thirteen. When had his mother found the time to bake it?

Having purposefully blocked his memories of that day for years, Kim now found them creeping back in bright, shimmering colours. He remembered how the sight and smell of that cake had twisted his gut, but that he had resisted taking a bite because he wanted to share it with his mother when she got home.

With his eyes still on the number thirteen, Kim had taken from his satchel the maths and Latin homework he had been given. By the time he had completed the algebra part, it was getting dark and so he found a candle and, by its light, read the sheet of paper he had been given by the speech lady.

Every Tuesday morning his mother would press seven shillings and fourpence into his hands with the words 'Don't tell your father' and every Tuesday afternoon, after school, Kim would hand the money over to the speech lady. She had also given him homework that day. He had to practise softening what she called his 'plosive consonants' to help with his stammer. He stood up straight, loosened his shoulders and, with his head tilted upwards in order to open his throat more and relax his vocal cords, he began:

'B-B-B. Bin. P-P-P. Pin. T-T-T. Tin.'

When he heard a noise at the front door downstairs, he stopped his vocal exercises and listened. It was a false alarm.

There was no point in going to bed before his father came home. Even if he did fall asleep, he would be woken by the shouting. His mother's as well as his father's. It would not last long. She would be silenced, as she always was, by his fists. Kim would inch down the stairs and, with his hands covering his ears, would watch them through the keyhole. The shouting and the fighting would end with his mother struggling for breath on the floor, a bluish colouring around her lips. Kim had inherited her asthma. His tangled tongue and lazy eye were all his own.

The speech lady had told him that the way his voice had started to go deep one moment and high the next was a sign that it was breaking. As he looked in his bedroom mirror now, Kim could see that there was a moustache of milk over the line of downy hair that had recently appeared above his mouth. He licked it off and sucked in his cheeks to make his already sharp features look more angular. His fair hair was cropped short at the back and sides and always seemed to be itching.

He'd been scratching so much in his elocution sessions that the speech lady had asked if he had nits. She'd also asked if he was getting enough to eat at home. 'I get plenty at school,' he'd said by way of avoiding her question. He hadn't told her about the fleas in his bed, or the hard-skinned insects that came out of the hole behind his cupboard. He hadn't told her it was his thirteenth birthday either.

When he finally came downstairs, Kim could smell paraffin from the oil lamp. His mother must have come home quietly and lit it before falling asleep on her chair. She had not taken off her coat, or the scarf she tied over her hair, like a turban. She called this her 'uniform'. 'I'm a member of the RAC,' she liked to joke, 'the Royal Auxiliary of Charladies.' Her extra cleaning job, the one she went back to after coming home and putting out Kim's glass of milk, was also one of their secrets. 'If your father knew about the extra money, he'd only spend it down the pub.'

Her breathing as she slept was laboured. Kim sat on the floor next to her and gently placed her hand on his head, staring at the white cracks in the pair of leather boxing gloves hanging from a hook on the door. The clock on the mantelpiece said it was 9.30 p.m., an hour before closing time. Next to the clock was the picture of his father taken on the day in 1915 when he won the Royal Navy boxing cup. He was a big man, over 6 feet 2 inches, and had heavy-lidded eyes and a blond, waxed moustache that curled up at the sides. His mother said his father had been happy when he was a rating and that he'd wanted to stay in the navy after the Great War was over, but they wouldn't let him. His first job after being demobilized was selling boxes of matches on street corners. Then he'd found work at the Singer sewing machine parts factory before going to work on the docks, loading and unloading ships.

Kim could not remember his father ever being happy. His first memory of meeting him was when he was six. That was when he'd come back from sea. A stranger had arrived one day and tried to take over Kim's role as 'man of the house', fetching the coal scuttle for his mother as well as carrying the shopping and the laundry. Soon the stranger was trying to teach him the 'art of boxing' and, when his patience ran out, he would tell Kim he was 'weak' and 'clumsy', and that he would 'never amount to anything'. When Kim had started wetting the bed, his father had started taking off his belt to beat him. And that was when his stammering had begun.

He looked up at his mother's sleeping face. If only I could protect you, he thought. If only I could build up my strength by eating properly. He lifted his mother's hand from his hair without waking her, got up quietly and went into the kitchen, but the only food he could find there was a plate of corned beef. It was grey and fatty. Remembering the cake, he went back upstairs. For what he was planning to do, he would need some nourishment.

An hour later he heard his father trying and failing to lift the latch-tongue on the front door. It meant he was drunk again. Kim could hear stumbling and cursing.

'Put up your fists,' Kim whispered without stammering as he raised his own to his reflection. He rubbed his arms to get rid of the goosebumps and then gritted his teeth. He would be able to defend himself by shielding his face and body with his arms. The pain was bearable, he thought, once you accepted that it was inevitable. A nose bleed would not kill you. Bruises would not kill you. Only cowardice killed you, from the inside out.

With those words circling in his head, Kim took two handkerchiefs from his drawer and, as he wrapped them around his knuckles, he stared again at his reflection and nodded. It was time to be a man.

'Mum . . .' Realizing he had said this out loud in the train, Kim opened his eyes and looked around. None of the other passengers seemed to have heard him. He touched his brow. It was damp with sweat.

His mother had said she wanted him to have all the things she had never had: all the experiences, the opportunities, the dreams. That was another reason she'd paid for him to have speech and elocution lessons. 'You could be a doctor one day, Kim,' she'd said. 'Or an insurance broker. Or, I don't know, an Olympic gold medallist.' Harold Abrahams had won a gold medal for Britain in the Olympics the previous year and it had made a big impression on her. He remembered now the curious way she had always referred to Harold Abrahams as 'the Jewish athlete Harold Abrahams'.

The train had reached its final stop.

Kim's mother was buried at the Jewish cemetery in Southsea and it was only recently, nine years after she had had an asthma attack, lost consciousness and died, that he had been able to pay for a proper gravestone. Like the surrounding gravestones, it had inscriptions on two sides. On the side facing the road the inscription was in English and on the back it was in Hebrew. The rabbi had explained to Kim that this was a local custom: when viewed from the street it gave the impression that this was a Christian burial ground. The gravestones could, he said, be 'taken as a metaphor for the assimilated Anglo-Jewish community in Portsmouth': wishing to be seen as English and integrated on the outside, while maintaining a discreet Jewish identity on the inside. At the time, Kim hadn't understood what the rabbi meant, but he did now. Before that day, Kim hadn't known his mother was Jewish.

New graves had been dug in open ground, beyond the shadow cast by a tree. Two had fresh flowers on them. No headstones yet, not until the earth settled. The jangling bells of a nearby church stopped with a humming abruptness as Kim placed his own flowers – another Christian assimilation – then stood back and bowed his head.

He recalled how the synagogue had made all the arrangements for her funeral and had done everything so quickly – the next day, as was the Jewish tradition – that there had been no other mourners present, not even his father, who had disappeared on another drinking binge. When they brought out a seven-branched candlestick he realized he had seen one before, when exploring the cupboard under the stairs. His mother must have kept it hidden there.

For almost eighteen months after the funeral, Kim had barely spoken. But his father had begun drinking less and there was usually some food to eat, though they did not have their meals together. Mostly they avoided each other around the house. Then one day Kim came home to find a note from his father saying that he had 'gone back to sea' and that an aunt who Kim had never heard of before would be coming to look after him. When, after three days, the aunt had not arrived – but the rent collector had – Kim went to see the rabbi, who arranged for him to be taken in by foster parents, a retired couple.

His asthma remained but the attacks became less frequent and severe, and they didn't seem to affect his ability on the athletics field. In the space of a year, as he moved between two other sets of foster parents in the Portsmouth area, one Jewish, one gentile, Kim had gone from winning school championships to junior county cups. A year after that he had moved to London – his board and lodgings paid for by the synagogue – and he was competing in the nationals. For a time, he read the Old Testament and, in a flirtation with the faith of his ancestors, he tried praying. But each time he did so, he was reminded of the fact that his mother had hidden that aspect of her life from him, and the memory became too painful. Eventually he let religion slip from his life.

The last communication from his father had been that note left on the kitchen table.

Kim looked around him now at the gravestones. All these people, all their stories buried in the ground. He had not found the answers he was looking for, but as he left the cemetery and headed back to the station, he did feel more determined to do something that would make his mother proud.

On the train back to London he flicked distractedly through a copy of *The Times* that a passenger had left behind. Then he sat upright, his attention caught by a photograph of a man in a white fencing jacket holding a foil in front of his face. He read the accompanying article, stared in an unfocused way at the rushing scenery beyond the window, then read it again. It felt like a sign.

SEVEN

One month later. London

When the bell above the door made a single dull clunk, Alun looked up from the newspaper he was reading, pushed his spectacles further up his nose and looked down again. Having flicked through the latest edition of *The Blackshirt*, he was feeling annoyed with the world.

On the cover was an Aryan-looking athlete with hair cropped close at the sides and an arrogantly raised chin. He was striking an heroic pose, hands bracing his hips, staring into the middle distance as if taken by some profound thought. Fat chance of that, Alun surmised. This idiot didn't look as though he had ever had a profound thought in his life. Even worse, he was wearing a white running vest that was clearly intended to show off his muscles. The photograph was taken at the Black House, presumably, judging by the Blackshirts prancing around behind him like a chorus line of demented boy scouts.

The customer who had come in and disturbed his reading was now seized by a coughing fit. Alun looked up again and, as he fixed his eyes on him, he could feel his teeth begin to grind. With his trilby hat and watch chain, the customer looked like a Tory spiv who'd never done an honest day's work in his life. There was a cigarette sticking out of the corner of his mouth, one that he was not removing to allow himself to cough more easily. As he coughed he continued browsing through a rack stacked with communist pamphlets.

'That's a bad cough,' Alun said. 'Not that I know what a good cough sounds like.'

The man gave him a blank stare.

'Looking for anything in particular, are we?'

'Do you have any books here that aren't about politics?'

'No,' Alun said. 'This is a political bookshop.'

'So nothing on cricket?'

'I refer the honourable gentleman to my previous answer.'

'Eh?'

'No.'

The doorbell made the same dull clunk as the man left. Alun watched as he headed across the cobbles of Covent Garden towards a flower stall. Addressing the bust of Lenin on the counter he said: 'Bet you didn't have to put up with any of this nonsense, did you, boyo? You'd have had all the time-wasters put up against a wall, you would.'

The bell made its thunk again and a tall man wearing a beret lumbered in, giving a perfunctory clenched-fist salute. 'Comrade Pryce,' the man said in an expressionless voice. Despite the warmth of the afternoon he was wearing a buttoned-up donkey jacket.

Alun raised his own fist in salute, looked down at his newspaper and said, 'Comrade Herzl.'

'Still not got the bell fixed, then?'

Alun's eyes remained on the paper. 'I have not.'

'I suppose you think a tinkling sound is too capitalist.'

'Doesn't everyone?'

As Martin Herzl never tired of pointing out to Alun, he, unlike most of the comrades in the Communist Party of Great Britain, had once been to Mother Russia, to see how things should be done. Alun, meanwhile, always enjoyed reminding Herzl that when not freeing the world from the yoke of capitalism, Herzl was supposed to have another job, working as a tailor for his cousin in Spitalfields.

There was something familial about the way the two comrades liked to undermine one another, and the age and height difference between them – Alun was a wiry 5 feet 9 inches and the bulkier, middle-aged Herzl was five inches taller – added to the impression that they were father and son. In fact, Herzl was a second-generation immigrant from Hungary.

The CPGB bookshop was on the ground floor of the Party headquarters in Covent Garden and, along with their other duties, the two comrades ran it together. This meant they also served as gatekeepers to Harry Pollitt, the General Secretary of the Communist Party. Any members of the executive attending meetings upstairs tended to pass through the bookshop rather than using the main entrance on Bedford Street, and this meant that Alun and Herzl could monitor the comings and goings and work out who was in favour and who was not. That members of the public were also able to wander in off the streets and browse the bookshop made the arrangement even more convenient, in so far as it made the work of the Special Branch and MI5 surveillance teams who followed senior CPGB figures everywhere harder.

'How's business?' Herzl asked, retrieving an orange from his pocket and digging a thumbnail into its peel.

'Had a bloke in here a few minutes ago looking at *Das Kapital*.'

'And?'

'Didn't buy it. Wanted to know if we had any books on cricket.'

Herzl finished peeling his orange, pulled off a segment, and put it in his mouth. 'What you reading, then?'

Alun held up the copy of *The Blackshirt*.

'Any good?'

'Of course it isn't any bloody good!' Alun said. 'It's *The Blackshirt*!'

'Why you reading it, then?'

'To know your enemy, you must become your enemy.'

Herzl took the newspaper from him and flicked through it. 'You have to admit, the enemy has done a nice job with it. Very professional.' He ran his thumb over the cover. 'Feel that quality. Why can't *we* do something like that?'

Alun levelled another peevish stare at his comrade: 'Because General Secretary Stalin hasn't sent us any money in five months?'

Instead of reacting to the stare, Herzl bobbed around like a log on the ripples of tension he was creating.

'Well, good luck to the Blackshits, I say. How's our petition going?'

Alun nodded at a sheet of paper tacked to the wall. It read: 'Sign below if you think Britain should boycott Hitler's fascist Olympics.' There were five signatures, including Alun's and Herzl's.

'I've heard Mr Hitler is letting Jews compete now anyway,' Herzl added.

'No.' Alun took a slow, steadying breath through his nose. 'Mr Hitler is not letting Jews compete. He is letting local athletics clubs decide . . .' He stopped when he realized Herzl knew this already and was trying to provoke him.

'Probably wouldn't make much difference anyway,' Herzl said.

'How so?'

'When was the last time you saw a Jew in a pair of running shoes?'

'Harold Abrahams was Jewish!'

Herzl puckered his lips and nodded. 'Good point, Comrade Pryce. Very good point.'

Alun distracted himself by flicking through the newspaper again. He wished his comrade, who was Jewish himself, would take anti-Semitism more seriously. 'Says here the Blackshits have managed to recruit record numbers of female members,' he said, talking at a rapid pace, as was his way. 'Why can't we recruit record numbers of women?'

'Obvious, isn't it?'

'Go on then.'

'It's the uniforms,' Herzl said. 'All the girls love a uniform.' He prised the newspaper from Alun's fingers. 'You have to admit the tailoring is beautiful, though,' he said. 'Maybe *we* should have uniforms.'

'I've told you before, uniforms are . . .' Too late, Alun realized that Herzl was teasing him again. This was how they liked to pass the time in the bookshop, each looking for a crack in the other's psyche, preferably one that could be amusingly crowbarred into an open wound.

They had been working together for more than six months now, ever since Alun had been offered a job in London after spending a fortnight sharing a prison cell with Harry Pollitt in Wales. Alun had been arrested for stealing pheasants from Lord Dalton. Harry had been charged with sedition after giving a speech that was so fiery it had provoked someone in the crowd to smash a shop window. As they awaited their respective trials at the Swansea Assizes, they had talked night and day about the need for a socialist revolution in Britain. The judge was satisfied that Alun was telling the truth when he said he'd intended to give the pheasants away to the hungry rather than sell them, especially after the gamekeeper who 'arrested' him admitted under cross examination that the plan had indeed been to bury the birds. Both men were given cautions and were bound over to keep the peace. By then, they had come to regard one another as brothers in the class struggle.

'Anyway,' Alun continued, scratching his thin beard. 'It says in this paper that the Blackshits are planning a rally at Olympia, bigger than the one they had at the Albert Hall. Twelve thousand people this time.'

'Oh good,' Herzl said, rubbing his large hands together. 'So what's it to be, then?' His eyebrows were raised expectantly now, like two dark clumps of untended foliage. 'Same as last time? Chanting and holding up placards? That'll hurt their feelings.'

Alun knew what Herzl was referring to, in his heavy-footed way. The Albert Hall rally in April had been considered a great success for the Blackshirts, and a great failure for the anti-fascist protestors, who were barely mentioned in the press reports the following day. The Reds were losing the propaganda war.

'I'm serious, comrade,' Alun said. 'This time we disrupt from the inside. Two thousand of us.'

'Excellent,' Herzl said, before adding with a frown: 'How do we do that, then?'

'Look.' Alun turned to a page of *The Blackshirt* he had folded over. 'We apply for tickets. I'm going to put it to the Committee tonight. I know Harry will approve.'

'And what are we, sorry, *you* going to do when you're inside Olympia?'

Without answering, Alun flipped the door sign around to 'Closed' and slid the bolt into its fastening. 'Come and have a look at what we've been stockpiling upstairs.'

Behind the counter was a door leading to the back stairs. They ascended in single file past the noisy first-floor room where the secretaries were answering telephones, printing leaflets and typing letters, on past Harry Pollitt's office on the second floor and then past the meeting rooms on the third floor, where chairs were stacked alongside piles of unsold and out-of-date *Daily Workers* with dozens of red flags propped against the walls. When they finally arrived at the top floor, Alun opened a door and said: 'Look.'

Herzl was bent over, trying to catch his breath. When he eventually looked up, he saw dozens of empty bottles on the floor. 'You had a party and you didn't invite me?'

'They're for petrol bombs . . . and look at these.' Alun pulled back a rug covering a tea chest full of knuckledusters, blackjacks and punch-knives. 'The time has come to take the fight to the enemy. It's the only way. We have to use the newspapers to turn the British people against fascism and dictatorship, before it's too late. And take a look at these little beauties,' he said, reaching for a cigar box and opening it. 'Disposable razor blades.'

'We're going to shave the fascists?'

'No, we're going to throw potatoes at them. Potatoes with nasty little surprises embedded in them. They're known as "sharp murphys". Our brothers in the IRA have been using them.'

'But what if someone gets hurt?'

'There are always casualties in a war, Comrade Herzl. We have to stop wringing our hands and accept that reality.' Alun punched the air as he stirred himself up into a rhetorical fever. 'For the sake of democracy, we have to provoke the enemy into retaliating. It's the only way we can win.'

'So it's a suicide mission, then?'

'That's the whole point,' Alun said. 'We want to explode this myth about the Blackshits being disciplined and law-abiding. Can't you see the headlines? "Fascist thugs attack harmless catcallers".'

'Hardly harmless if you're throwing potatoes spliced with razor blades. I'd prefer a headline that went: "Fascist thugs reflect carefully upon what harmless catcallers have to say and then write them a strongly worded letter, setting out their differences and suggesting a reasonable way forward".'

Alun attempted a grin. 'I knew I could count on your support. And don't worry, I will see to it personally that your noble sacrifice is commemorated with a fine monument. You will live on in the hearts of your comrades.'

Herzl sniffed: 'I'd rather live on in my own house.'

'That's funny,' Alun said. When amused he was always more likely to say 'That's funny' than to smile.

EIGHT

A mile away, in the basement of the Ritz Hotel, Leni was handing over a suitcase for safekeeping. Inside it were four canisters of film. She had considered asking a bellboy to deposit the case for her in the storage room, but had decided against. This had to be done in person. She slipped the receipt into her handbag and went outside to find the taxi that was waiting to take her to Croydon Aerodrome. The film was an illegal copy she had made of *The Victory of Faith*, her documentary about the 1933 Nuremberg rally. She had needed it to accompany the speech she had delivered the previous day to students at the University of London, but she couldn't risk taking it back with her to Berlin in case Goebbels found out about it. Technically his Ministry of Propaganda owned the copyright.

Even before the Junkers had finished its deafening climb through the grey light of south London, Leni had popped the latches of the briefcase she was cradling on her lap and had started work on the contracts for her next film. Underlining odd words as she ran her pencil down the page, she tutted to herself and thought she was going to need a much more generous budget. This one would barely cover the cranes and dollies she had ordered let alone the towers she was intending to build in order to give her cameras loftier vantage points.

The financing for *The Victory of Faith* had been chaotic, even with the Ministry of Propaganda's backing. So much so that her brother had had to step in as producer at the last minute. Including herself, that had meant that her entire film crew had numbered only five. But the production side had gone relatively smoothly compared to the choreography. Rather than marching in tight formation, Hitler's Brownshirts had milled around in loose groups, half of them obscured by flags and banners, an uneven expanse of mismatched bodies – some short, some tall, some fat, some thin, but all chalky-faced and swathed in ill-fitting uniforms and kepis. Hardly the examples of Aryan superiority, discipline and manhood portrayed in Goebbels's newspapers. Some had even been waving rather than saluting.

While a few marshals at the front had linked arms to hold the Brownshirts back, others had run in a crouching position to head off a second column that was about to march straight into the first. Adolf had looked stiff and unnatural that day and had not been able to tame his unruly forelock – every time he flicked it back with his hand, he looked like he was having a spasm. As he had come level with Leni's camera rostrum he had looked directly into the lens, even though she had explained to him several times that he must try to ignore her cameras.

The Victory of Faith had, nevertheless, provided her with a useful template, and there were scenes from it she was planning to recreate for *Triumph of the Will*, the title-in-progress of her next project, a film about the upcoming rally in Nuremberg. She liked the moment a cat on a window ledge had stopped licking itself and looked up. This had been spliced with footage of Adolf's cavalcade passing, and there was no reason why she couldn't use that footage again in the same way. But for this second film she would have to be much tougher in her negotiations with the Little Doctor. If the Nazi Party wanted a decent documentary, they were going to have to pay for it. She also wanted her new film to make a more powerful statement artistically. It would be much more geometric, capturing the monumentality of physical forms. And the choreography had to be perfect. Balletic. No mistakes this time. She wanted symmetry. She wanted patterns that were almost abstract. She wanted viewers to experience something akin to aesthetic euphoria.

Leni had mentioned this in her talk to the London students, after she had screened *The Victory of Faith* for them. Their applause at the end of the lecture had been encouraging, if possibly a little sycophantic, given how amateurish her film had looked. In the question-and-answer session afterwards, one of them had asked her if she was also planning to film the Blackshirt rally that was due to take place in Olympia. Leni replied that she had to get back to Berlin, but would watch the news footage of the rally with great interest.

Her thoughts returned to *Triumph of the Will*. It would need a grand, unifying theme. As she felt a pressure in her ears, she looked out of the window. They were above the clouds now, at cruising altitude, and she could see the shadow being cast by the plane. Against the sea of cotton wool below, it looked like a slow-moving cross.

She gazed at it for several minutes, then clapped her hands, making the passenger in the next seat jump. That was it. She would open *Triumph of the Will* with footage of Adolf's plane flying over Germany on its way to Nuremberg. Its cruciform shape would introduce a religious mood, with Adolf taking on the role of a Wagnerian demi-god descending from the sky – the messiah come to save his people. The clouds would then part to reveal the spires and gables of Nuremberg.

Yes, she thought as she tapped her teeth with the pencil, and when Adolf made his speech she would film him from below, as if he were a priest in a pulpit. Yes, yes, this would work! And this time when he walked to the war memorial to do the salute to the fallen, he would be on his own. Her brow furrowed. No, better still would be two people walking behind him, on either side. Three of them, like the three men on Calvary. A triptych. The Holy Trinity.

At this moment, a steward in a white uniform interrupted her. Like all experienced fliers, Leni wore cotton wool in her ears to avoid having her eardrums perforated by the noise on take-off and landing. She removed this now and asked the steward to repeat his question. Would she like anything to eat or drink? Leni shook her head.

Of what had she been thinking? Yes, this year's film would be infinitely better than last year's. *Triumph of the Will* would be a work of art. When people saw it, they would forget *The Victory of Faith*.

In her gut now, a sudden hollowing anxiety. What if Goebbels found out about the illegal copy she had made? Because he, for his own annoying reasons, had not yet signed the licensing agreement necessary for general distribution, she had taken an unnecessary risk in not asking his permission to make the copy. At the time she had persuaded herself that, if she had asked him, he would have demanded a favour in return. She bit her lip as she imagined the worst. What if he had been quizzing her assistant in Berlin while she was away in London? What if he had got him to confess that he had made a copy for her? Goebbels would use it against her somehow: blackmail her into sleeping with him, perhaps.

Her anxiety resurfaced when, waiting her turn to step off the plane at Berlin's Tempelhof Airport, Leni spotted Goebbels standing alone a few yards beyond the wing. He was wearing a full-length, black leather coat and carrying a black trilby in one hand and a briefcase in the other. Had he come to arrest her? The passengers around her, all men, began whispering to one another.

After descending the short flight of steps, the other passengers filed past Goebbels like guests at a wedding reception. Feeling conspicuous as the only woman on the flight, Leni had placed herself at the end of the line and she now hesitated and looked back at the metal skin of the fuselage, as if contemplating running back inside. Goebbels saw her, put on his hat, then stepped forward and kissed her hand.

'To what do I owe this pleasure?' Leni asked as she removed the protective cotton wool from her ears.

'I have a surprise for you,' Goebbels said, looping his arm through hers as he led her towards a silver Mercedes-Benz. It was a two-door coupé and it looked new, its wings shimmering in the heat haze.

'What's this?' Leni said.

'A gift,' Goebbels replied, 'to show our appreciation.'

She had heard that Adolf had ordered a fleet of Mercedes saloons as staff cars, but not sporty convertible models like this one. It was beautiful: its running boards and windows forming sleek curves set off by white-wall tyres and pale leather seats.

'From Adolf?'

He smiled thinly. 'From all of us.'

As she tried to work out what this meant, an internal alarm sounded. Was Goebbels trying to take the credit for this gesture or, more significantly, did Adolf want Leni to think it a gift from the Party, for services already rendered and service yet to come? If she accepted the car, it would be tantamount to an acceptance that she was now one of them – 'our poster girl', as Goebbels had recently called her. Yet if she declined the gift and it emerged that it had indeed been Adolf's idea, that would be a tactical mistake on her part.

'She has eight cylinders,' Goebbels said, patting the bonnet. 'Only a handful have been made so far. Let's take her for a drive, shall we?'

The driver's door was hinged to swing open at its forward edge. As Goebbels grabbed the handle for her, Leni gathered her skirt and stepped in. He then clicked his fingers at a porter who had collected her case from the plane and was standing a few yards away, a signal for him to put the case in the small space behind the front seats. The Little Doctor then climbed into the passenger seat, ostentatiously removed a pistol from his leather coat and placed it in the glove compartment. 'Never go anywhere without it,' he said.

Leni put her foot on the clutch pedal and her hand on the ball mounted on top of the gearstick. Goebbels leaned forward with a creak of leather and pressed the starter button for her. Leni put the car in first and it set off smoothly, its engine purring like a sewing machine.

'Where to?' she asked.

'Head to the Grunewald,' Goebbels said. 'Those winding roads through the woods will show you what she can do. And they're on the way to your house, I believe. I can get a taxi from there.'

As she drove out of the airport and followed signs to the Grunewald, the weather began to change, the sun disappearing behind clouds. Leni kept darting glances across at her passenger. He was being uncharacteristically quiet. Eventually he asked: 'Your trip to London was a success?'

'Fine.' Then: 'How is Magda?'

He looked away. 'Fine.'

'Pregnant again?'

He nodded stiffly.

Leni thought about her last encounter with Magda, at a gala premiere of *Madam Butterfly*. Goebbels had rearranged the chairs so that he could sit next to Leni and, as soon as the lights had dimmed, she had felt his hand on her knee. When it had begun to move up her thigh she had scratched it with her nails and it had retreated like a wounded snake. Leni had glanced at Magda to see if she had noticed but, if she had, she was pretending to be oblivious, her opera glasses directed at the stage.

During the interval, Leni had fallen into conversation with Magda and, feeling sorry for her, had decided to stay for the second half. At least it was Puccini they had come to see and hear that night, not boring old Wagner. Leni liked Puccini.

'You look beautiful, Magda,' Leni had said. She meant it, too. In pearls and gold satin that crackled as she moved, Magda had looked radiant.

'So do you, my dear,' Magda had said. 'Gorgeous dress. Who made it?'

'Chéruit.' Leni had patted her stomach. She always felt too slim next to Magda, who, with her broad hips and pelvis, was built for child-bearing. 'Got it from Paris last time I was there.'

'I get my cosmetics from Paris,' Magda had said. 'Elizabeth Arden. I have a case full of little boxes and pots. They're simply wonderful. And I have to stay looking good if I want to compete with all these actresses who swarm around you-know-who.'

Leni had frowned. Was that a jibe? Was Magda aware of all the stories about her husband's infidelity? Leni had studied Magda's face in the red-shaded lights, but her expression had been unreadable. Not for the first time, Leni suspected that perhaps Magda did not care one way or the other about her husband's busy hands – her heart belonged to Adolf. Leni had sensed it especially on that day when the four of them had gone on a picnic excursion to Heiligendamm on the Baltic Sea. As Adolf had fussed over Leni, offering her sandwiches, cake and lemonade, there had been jealousy in Magda's eyes.

That night at the opera Magda had touched a satin-gloved hand to Leni's bare arm, leaned closer and confided in a whisper: 'Especially now.'

'Oh, why?'

'Have you not heard?' Magda said. 'I'm expecting another baby.'

Leni had acknowledged this with a clenched smile. 'How wonderful. Congratulations.'

Magda allowed herself a smile at this; then, with studied innocence, she asked: 'What about you? Have you ever thought about children?'

'Thought, yes, but I fear my schedule is too busy at the moment.'

'Well, don't leave it too late,' Magda had said. 'Time is the enemy and we all have to do our bit for the Fatherland.'

In the car now it had started to rain – intermittent fat drops that Leni could feel spattering on her brow. Snapping back into the moment, she pulled over and Goebbels climbed out and demonstrated how to put the roof up. He then flicked a switch that turned on the windscreen wipers and they set off again. It was raining heavily and puddles were forming on the road. As she concentrated on them, Leni felt an icy contraction across her scalp. His darkly circled eyes were on her again. 'Why are you staring at me?' she asked.

'I was looking at your badge.'

She looked down at the Golden Party Badge pinned to her lapel – a gold-plated wreath surrounding a ruby-red band with the words 'National-Sozialistische-D.A.P.' in gold lettering. This in turn surrounded a black swastika. The badge was colloquially known as the *Bonbon* and only a few thousand had been produced. They were awarded to the original Party members, the 'old fighters', with their membership number on the back. Adolf's was numbered '1', of course.

'You have joined?'

Leni shook her head. 'Adolf presented me with it.'

'Are you going to join?'

She shook her head again.

'Why not?'

'Because I'm not interested in politics, only art.'

Goebbels smiled. 'You disappoint me. Magda is a member.'

Leni gave him a patient look and said drily: 'Good for Magda.'

'And your architect boyfriend.'

Leni glowered at her passenger. 'Albert Speer is not my boyfriend, as you well know.'

'You should be careful,' Goebbels said. 'The Führer will not like it if you keep on refusing to join the Party. And you don't want to make an enemy of him.'

'Let me worry about that.'

For the moment, Leni had other things to worry about, such as Goebbels's straying hand. It seemed unlikely that he would have a specific seduction plan. She needed to undermine him somehow, cool his ardour, make him doubt himself. 'Who are Adolf's friends, would you say?'

'That's a ridiculous question,' he said in a gritty voice. 'The Führer does not need friends.'

'Everyone needs friends. Are *you* his friend?'

With another creak of leather, Goebbels folded his arms as he seemed to make a calculation. 'I have the utmost admiration for the Führer.'

'Does he address you as Joseph?'

'That would be disrespectful. He calls me *Herr Doktor*.'

'Correct me if I'm wrong but isn't it only medical doctors who are allowed to use that title? Or is that only in England and France?'

'A doctorate is a doctorate.'

Leni pursed her lips to suppress a smile. 'What was yours in?'

He looked away. Clenched his jaw. 'Nineteenth-century drama.'

Leni drummed her fingers on the steering wheel. 'Adolf calls Albert by his first name, you know. And Albert calls him Adolf. I've even heard that when Albert greets him with "Heil Hitler" he sometimes responds: "Heil Speer".'

'Who told you that?'

'Common knowledge.'

'What does the Führer call you, then?'

She gave her passenger a sideways glance. 'Leni, of course.'

Goebbels looked annoyed for a moment, but then his demeanour changed. 'Look,' he said in a friendlier tone, 'I think you and I got off to a bad start. All I've ever wanted to be is a friend to you. I like your spirit. I think you're hugely talented. And I'm not as bad as you seem to think I am. Some people have even been known to like me, once they've got to know me.'

Leni allowed herself a suspicious smile, to which he responded with a mischievously innocent raise of his eyebrows. It was true, the 'He-goat of Babelsberg' could be charming when he wanted to be. She was about to needle him again by asking if Adolf had given Albert a sports car too, but Goebbels interrupted her thoughts, asking about the subject of her lecture to the London University students.

'Oh, the usual things. My film career. German cinema.'

'Did they ask about *The Victory of Faith?*'

Leni felt palpitations in her chest, thinking of the copy hidden back in London.

'Not really.'

'Probably just as well. There may be a little change of plan with regard to its distribution.'

'What do you mean?'

'You'll find out in due course.'

'Tell me now.'

'All in good time.' Goebbels's thin smile indicated that he knew he had won back the upper hand. 'What do you think of the car? Powerful, yes?'

A few minutes later, as they reached the outskirts of the forest, he leaned forward to flick on the light switch. Leni was now cursing herself for having got into this vehicle, this bribe, and allowing herself to be bought so easily. Then, in a moment that seemed to expand as it unfolded, Goebbels leaned towards her and slipped his arm around her waist. In her surprise, Leni jerked the steering wheel violently, the car swerved from the road and she felt a jarring bump as its front tyres hit a mound of earth. The engine cut out.

The car was leaning at an angle, rain drumming on the canvas roof. Goebbels got out from the passenger side and shouted above the percussion of the rain: 'Try starting it.'

Leni started the engine and put the car in gear, but its back wheels spun without purchase and it stalled again. She climbed over into the passenger side and got out the same way Goebbels had. Despite the semi-darkness, she could make out that the rear axle was stuck in mud up to the running board. The headlights were still on and were directed like searchlights into the branches in front of them.

Leni became aware of two things at the same moment: that her high heels were sinking into the wet earth and that there was no other traffic around. They were alone together in the dark wood. She lost her balance slightly as she extracted one shoe. Goebbels took a frictionless step forward and, without breaking eye contact, raised his right arm slowly and silently, reaching for hers.

'We cannot be seen together,' she said, taking off her shoes. 'Think of poor Magda. You go that way.' She nodded at the road ahead. 'There is a main road a few minutes away and you can telephone for a taxi from there.' She remembered passing a tavern about a mile away. She would be safe there. 'I'm going back this way,' she added.

For half a minute, Goebbels did not move, but then he lowered his arm, nodded, turned up his collar against the rain, and limped off down the road. As she watched his shape lose its focus, she sensed the nocturnal dark thickening around her. She leaned back into the car, turned off the lights and removed the key before collecting her case from the back seat. Only then did she remember the gun in the glove compartment. It was a Luger, the texture of its scored wooden grip coarse to the touch. She was not sure how to check whether it was loaded but it felt heavy when she held it up and looked down its sights.

The walk to the tavern was further than she remembered and when at last she saw its lights through the rain she lowered her shoulders in relief. Inside were half a dozen men and they looked up from their tankards as she walked towards the landlord with muddy bare feet and asked if he could call a taxi for her. His smile suggested that he recognized her. Being a part of Adolf's inner circle had its advantages. He handed her a towel to dry her hair before disappearing into another room to make the call.

When he returned, she explained that her car had broken down.

'I have a friend who is a mechanic,' he said. 'If you leave your keys and tell me your address, he can bring it to your house in the morning.'

'That's kind,' she said. 'I live not far away.'

As his eyes kept sliding down to the Golden Party Badge on her lapel, she began to doubt whether he had recognized her at all. The badges were rare enough to guarantee a good table in a restaurant, first-class travel on trains and planes, and, it seemed, a free breakdown recovery service.

While she waited for her taxi to arrive, sitting next to a pot-bellied stove, Leni sipped a glass of steaming glühwein – which the landlord had handed to her with the words 'on the house' – and stared thoughtfully at her case, picturing the pistol it contained and fantasizing about emptying its entire clip into Goebbels's face.

NINE

Because the traffic had slowed to a walking pace, it was taking a long time to reach the Olympia exhibition centre at Earl's Court where the Blackshirt rally was being held. In the back of the taxi, Kim gave Connie a sidelong glance and took her hand. She was wearing her new uniform, the top half of which, with its black, shoulder-buttoned shirt, was identical to his.

Kim's decision to join the Blackshirts had not been easy, but after he had read that *Times* article on the train, about how Sir Oswald had once been an Olympic fencer, it had seemed providential. Despite his misgivings, he had wondered whether the BUF leader and he could come to some mutually beneficial arrangement.

'You have an appointment?' the Blackshirt had enquired when Kim had gone to the headquarters and asked to see Sir Oswald.

'I tried to make one by telephone,' he had said. 'But no one answered.' He had gone on to explain that he was an athlete hoping to take part in the next Olympics. The receptionist had looked him up and down, then risen from her chair and disappeared for a few minutes. Upon her return, she said: 'You have five minutes. Follow me.'

Mosley had been busy writing a letter when Kim had entered the room. He signed his name, blotted it and, rising to his feet, leaned over his metal desk to offer his hand to shake. The two men were about the same height and build. Mosley indicated that Kim should sit in the seat opposite, then asked: 'Come to join us, then?'

'I don't know anything about politics, sir,' Kim said. 'Only sport.'

'Same thing,' Mosley said with a trace of a laugh. 'Sport is politics by other means. So you're hoping to compete in the Berlin Olympics?'

'Yes, sir.'

'Your discipline?'

'Hurdles, relay and broad jump.'

'Did you know I fenced for Britain at the Olympics?'

'I did, sir, yes.'

Mosley, with his upright bearing, seemed to have around him a disturbing energy field, as if he buzzed with ungrounded electricity. He tilted his head back to study Kim. His nose was sharp and his gaze intense, with pupils that seemed as coal black as his eyebrows, moustache and slicked-back hair. He held his stare for a moment and then smiled. 'Yes, of course you did. That is why you are here.'

'Yes, sir.'

'You see this?' Mosley plucked at his uniform. 'Our shirts are modelled on my old fencing tunic. That's why they button across the shoulder.' He gave Kim another evaluating glance. 'Now, how can we help you, young man?'

Kim tried to find the right words. 'My work commitments are . . . I work as an apprentice clerk at an insurance firm and . . .'

'You're finding it a struggle to keep to your training routine?'

'Yes, sir.'

Mosley had pressed a finger and thumb together, raised them to his moustache and slowly smoothed down his whiskers. 'And you want financial support from us, so that you can give up work and dedicate yourself to your sport?'

Taken aback by how direct the BUF leader was being, Kim nodded. 'I don't want to give up work entirely, just take a . . .' He couldn't think of the word.

'Sabbatical?' Mosley helped.

'That's it. I need to have a career to go back to when I hang up my spikes.'

'And of course you must be careful not to compromise your status as an amateur,' Mosley said, tapping the table impatiently. 'Well, I'm sure there is something we can do. It's all a matter of wording. We would have to call it, I don't know, a bursary or something. Not sponsorship.' He was bouncing a curled knuckle against his mouth now. 'I like a man who takes responsibility for himself. You remind me of myself when I was your age.' He stood up and, as he paced around the room, launched into an account of what he called his 'political journey', from the Conservative Party to the Labour Party, and finally to setting up a new party of his own.

Kim creased his nose – a smell of stale cigar smoke hung in the air – but as he listened, he became increasingly engaged. Mosley seemed to have a genuine desire to create a fairer society and improve the lives of ordinary people by providing employment for all who wanted it. And certain words and phrases resonated. When Mosley spoke of the working man, Kim pictured his father sullenly unloading crates at the docks in Portsmouth.

The BUF leader stopped pacing and came to stand in front of him. 'I believe in protectionism, Mr Newlands. Protecting the economy from the fluctuations of the world market. Doesn't that sound like a good idea to you?'

'Yes it does, Sir Mosley,' Kim said, realizing too late he should have said Sir Oswald.

Mosley did not appear to notice. 'And I want to fill the House of Lords with elected executives, and replace parliamentary democracy with a system similar to what I call the corporatism of the Italian fascists.'

Coming from a nearby room was the clickety-clack sound of several typewriters working in unison.

'Where did you school?'

Momentarily confused by the way the question was worded, Kim nodded again.

'Where did you go to school?' Mosley rephrased.

'I went to a grammar school, sir. You won't have heard of it.'

'Bright, then. Good. And did you trouble the varsity?'

'Couldn't afford it.'

'I didn't go either. Straight from Winchester to Sandhurst and then into the Queen's Lancers.' He rubbed his hands. 'Anything else you want to ask me?'

'There is something.' Kim cleared his throat. 'What is your attitude towards Jewish people? I couldn't find anything on the subject in your leaflets, but I heard a rumour that . . .'

Mosley smoothed his moustache again. 'That what? The answer is we have absolutely nothing against Jews, unless they are also communist troublemakers. We have no prejudices – and Jew-baiting in any form is strictly forbidden within the BUF. We even admit Jewish members.' He clapped his hands. 'Right then, I propose we have a second meeting, once I've had a chance to check your credentials. Meanwhile, I'll look into setting up this bursary for you, and we'll make sure it won't get you into trouble with the Olympic authorities. We'd expect one or two things in return, of course – photographs of you wearing a black shirt, that sort of thing, for our newsletter and posters.' He took one of the badges showing the bundle of sticks from a bowl on his desk. 'And perhaps you could wear this when you go to Berlin.'

Kim put the badge in his pocket and the two men shook hands.

When Connie found out that Kim had joined the BUF despite his earlier protestations, she had insisted on joining too, concluding excitedly that it could be something they did together – 'our hobby'. Kim hadn't told her about the sponsorship money that he was supposed to call a bursary.

'*Sieg Heil*, darling,' she whispered now as the taxi approached the throng outside Earl's Court.

Her three words seemed to solidify in Kim's brain, each separated by a pulse of his heart. '*Sieg Heil*,' he whispered back. He could not bring himself to add the word 'darling'. It felt false. The word belonged to her class, not his.

The taxi now stopped, blocked by protesters. Some were waving red flags from side to side, others pumping placards up and down. The crowd seemed an odd mixture: whey-faced young men wearing cloth caps and red kerchiefs, older men in spongebag trousers, mothers with children. As half a dozen mounted policemen appeared and cleared a path for their car, Kim's thoughts turned to the evening ahead. All eyes would be on him and the Leader, in front of whom he had been instructed to walk. The thought of this induced a prickling wave across his chest.

Connie took a drag from her cigarette, nodding in the direction of the exhibition centre: 'Will it be dangerous in there?'

'I'll protect you,' Kim said.

'That's the spirit,' she said. 'Good boy.'

One of the cars behind them honked its horn, causing a police horse in front to start bucking. Kim wound down the window and heard the protesters singing a song about cowards and traitors. Feeling something wet on his cheek, he realized he had been spat upon. Connie seemed unconcerned as she tapped the ash off her cigarette and blew on the end until it glowed orange. Grace under pressure, Kim thought. Another of the things he liked about her.

'What are the Reds so cross about?' she asked. When Kim did not answer, she added: 'Perhaps it's all that football. Isn't that all they care about? Football and allotments?'

Kim searched her face to see if she was joking, but her expression yielded no hint of irony.

'For some people life is a struggle,' he said in a measured voice. 'They live in poverty and have no opportunities. Not everyone has life handed to them on a plate.'

'Like me, you mean?'

'Yes, like you.'

'Whereas your life has been full of hurdles, has it?' She laughed, pleased with her double entendre.

Most of the time Kim found Connie's glibness endearing, but there were occasions when her unthinking snobbery got to him. 'I'm being serious,' he said.

'Sorry,' she said, sensing his mood shift. 'But you never tell me anything about yourself. *Has* your life been full of hurdles?'

Kim fell silent, for he did not know how to answer that. Would Connie understand? *Could* she understand? He was feeling too tired to think of a way to explain. The training schedule he had set himself was leaving him mentally as well as physically exhausted. He was always the first to arrive at the track and the last to leave. The other athletes thought him mad, but winning an Olympic medal clearly mattered less to them. Most of his team-mates – at least those who hadn't inherited money – seemed to have high-paying professions, such as the law or medicine, to fall back on. That, he was sure, was why their hunger for success was not as sharp as his.

Another car had pulled in behind them as their driver was directed with urgent hand signals towards a ramp. Here a Blackshirt with a widow's peak approached and opened the door on Connie's side. Instead of getting out, she dipped down and hid her face as a man emerged from the car behind them, wearing a white silk scarf and a top hat.

'Who's that?' Kim asked.

'The Londonderry Herr,' Connie said. 'Lord Londonderry. Don't want him to see me. One of Daddy's friends.' She waited for the man in the top hat to walk past, then she sat up. 'Daddy doesn't know I'm here. Although heaven knows, he ought to approve. He's always going on about commies and Jews.'

'What does he say about them?'

'Oh, the usual things. And I have to say, they both sound perfectly ghastly.'

As they climbed out, the Blackshirt who had opened the door gave a tight salute and people in the crowd who noticed this jeered and surged forward. A photographer elbowed his way through them with an explanatory 'Duke of Bedford', and raised his camera to take a photograph of another top-hatted gentleman, this one stepping out of a plum-coloured Rolls-Royce.

Once inside, the heckling of the crowd fell away and the murmur of thousands of supporters in the main hall could be heard. Kim took Connie's hand as they were ushered up some stairs to a door that opened into what looked like an assembly area. A short man with a large forehead was marching towards them. He had questioning eyes and a scar running from his mouth to his cheekbone that made him look as if he was smiling. Kim recognized him from the Black House but could not recall his name.

'Ah, here's our Olympic star,' the man said in a refined drawl. 'I trust your journey was comfortable, Mr Newlands. You will be at the rear of the column as we enter, immediately in front of the Leader.' He turned to Connie. 'Lady Constance, so glad you could join us. You will be with twelve other distinguished lady members in the middle section of the column. We're running a little late, I'm afraid. Let me get you a drink while you are waiting.'

'I thought fascists were supposed to be sticklers for punctuality,' Kim whispered as the man turned and strutted away.

'No doubt "the Bleeder" wants to build up the suspense,' Connie said. 'I'm not a "Lady", by the way. In case you were wondering about the title our little friend used.'

'What are you, then?' Kim asked.

Connie looked up, her eyes glittering with amusement. 'Darling, I'm a victim of circumstance.'

'I heard you were an Hon.'

'Yes, I am an Hon. And my older sister will be a Lady one day, because Daddy failed to produce a male heir. But not me.'

A few minutes later, the short man returned holding two champagne flutes. He looked as though he was snarling and only gradually did it become apparent to Kim that this was how he looked when he was smiling. As he handed the glasses over, the snarl faded from his face. 'Britain is a sewer and we are the disinfectant,' he said. 'Cheers!' Then he clicked his heels in salute and disappeared again.

When Alun emerged from Earl's Court Station half an hour before the fascists were due to start their grotesque jamboree, he found his way blocked by people. As a man who normally walked quickly with a short stride, he found this frustrating, but then he realized that the crowd was formed of thousands of protesters who had also arrived early. He removed his glasses, cleaned them and put them back on with a strained smile as he recognized a few faces. Would they recognize him in turn, even without his Trotsky beard? He had shaved it off before visiting the Black House and paying seven shillings and sixpence for a uniform that came with a year's membership of the BUF. When asked if he was unemployed, and therefore eligible for the discounted monthly subscription of fourpence, he had decided, on balance, against telling them that he ran the Communist Party bookshop in Covent Garden.

It had been Alun's idea that the *Daily Worker* should publish the BUF's plans for a march on Olympia, as well as print a road map to show readers how to get there in order to heckle. And, as he surveyed the crowd now, he felt pleased with himself. Although the majority were probably communists, Labour Party activists, and fellow travelling anarchists and pacifists, they also looked to Alun like ordinary, decent, hard-working citizens – the people whose rights Alun was here to defend. He had come too far and sacrificed too much to worry about any personal danger he might be putting himself in. Something had to be done. The world order had to change. The violence of their oppressors had to be met with violence.

As more cars arrived, dropping off MPs, peers and other dignitaries, the chatter of the crowd turned to laughter and jeers. Around five hundred policemen, some on foot, some mounted, formed a cordon to prevent the crowds from obstructing the entrance to the building.

Alun checked his watch again. According to a report he had read in the *Manchester Guardian*, a thousand Blackshirts would soon be here, arrayed in five columns as they marched from their Chelsea barracks. He thought he could hear them approaching along the Hammersmith Road.

A demonstrator began yelling and was dragged off by the police. Alun used the diversion to slip away from the crowd. As he walked towards the entrance, he removed his mac to reveal the black uniform he was wearing underneath. With his heart stuttering, he extracted his ticket from the pocket of his jodhpurs, smoothed down his hair and looked neither to his left nor right.

The dozen or so Blackshirts who were forming a tunnel leading to the entrance gave him a brotherly nod as he passed through. He showed his ticket to a steward and felt relieved when he was ushered inside without being searched. The mac draped over his arm had a knuckleduster in one pocket and a heavy, King Edward potato studded with razor blades in the other. He could feel its weight dragging the coat down, and his courage, momentarily, also plunged with it.

Inside the hall most of the ticket holders who had already taken their seats were, like the comrades outside, wearing civilian rather than paramilitary clothing. His mouth went dry and he tried to swallow. The arena was enormous, much bigger than he'd expected, with blocks of tiered seating arranged like giant coffins awaiting burial. He'd need a box of hand grenades for this lot, he thought, not a single potato. Making his way to a gallery that ran along one side of the arena, he saw an empty seat and sat between two middle-aged men, both of whom had well-brushed trilbies resting on their knees like sleeping lapdogs.

Alun surveyed the hall for other communist infiltrators – Herzl was supposed to be here somewhere – but he could not see any close by. He knew there were hundreds of them, though, incognito. Comrades under cover, working behind enemy lines. With a nod of satisfaction, he folded his arms.

At 8 p.m., the time the meeting was due to commence, the murmuring of the crowd died away. When nothing happened, it rose again, people lit cigarettes and a cloud of smoke drifted up to the lights. At eight thirty, an orchestra played and a choir sang the 'Horst Wessel' song, set to English words. In response to this, a chorus of equally orchestrated chanting began outside, muffled, but loud enough to carry into the hall: 'Hitler and Mosley, what are they for? Thuggery, buggery, hunger and war!'

Alun ground his teeth, a habit of his, and felt a ripple of nerves. The evening seemed to be tightening around him.

In the room upstairs, Kim took up his place with the men; Connie, the women. A dark, lean, Byronic figure appeared in the doorway and the assembled Blackshirts turned as one, stood to attention, and raised their arms in salute. They then formed a line, with each person finding the correct distance by stretching out their left arm and placing their hand on the right shoulder of the man or woman next to them.

Sir Oswald walked along the line inspecting his followers, checking a button here, adjusting a belt there, stopping for a quick chat when he recognized someone. When he came to Kim, he said, 'Ah, young Mr Newlands, how is the training going?'

Kim normally found it hard to meet the Leader's eyes for long, but not on this occasion. 'Very good, sir.'

'I envy you. Nothing I have done since has compared to the thrill of competing in the Olympics. Now listen, young man,' Mosley continued, 'it could get a bit hairy in there, but don't be distracted by the crowd. Keep your eyes straight ahead. I want the world to see how disciplined we fascists can be.' He patted Kim on both shoulders and gave a flat smile. 'And of course I want everyone to see the peak of physical perfection a true Aryan can achieve.'

Mosley started to walk away but turned back when Kim said: 'I'm not a true Aryan.'

'We all doubt ourselves from time to time,' Mosley said. 'It's just nerves. You'll be fine when we get in there.'

At eight forty-five, three-quarters of an hour after the rally had been scheduled to start, the fifty Blackshirts in the room formed a column, three abreast, with the standard-bearers going first. The women followed and Connie turned as she marched past Kim and breathed: 'See you in there.' Mosley was standing between four bodyguards carrying truncheons at the end of the column. Kim took his place immediately in front of them as trumpets sounded in the distance.

He entered the main hall with a ragged intake of breath. Although he had competed in stadiums before, this was different. There was a haze of cigarette smoke above the multitude and, as giant arc lights swung around to focus on Mosley, they caught the smoke and formed theatrical shafts of light.

The trumpeters sounded another fanfare and Kim now saw that they were positioned in the smoky distance at the other end of the hall, on either side of a platform that was dwarfed by two enormous Union flags hanging down from the ceiling. As he marched down the central aisle, Kim could see that some in the crowd were raising their arms at the Leader, while others cheered 'Hail Mosley! Hail Mosley!' Above these chants, in the distance, could be heard the unmistakable sound of booing. Surely, Kim wondered, the stewards had not allowed any of the protesters inside?

When they reached the platform, the Blackshirts fanned out and took their allocated positions, with Kim standing directly in front of Connie. He gave her a speaking glance as he turned, but did not risk a smile for fear that she might get the giggles. Then, after a rousing chorus of 'God Save the King', Mosley took centre stage. He stood absolutely still for a moment, waiting for the silence to build, then spoke without notes, his voice amplified around the arena.

'From time to time, in the history of great nations, comes the moment of decision, the moment of destiny, the moment of action. And in that moment, a great nation must sweep aside the little men of convention and delay and follow instead men who dare go forward with courage, with conviction, with strength.'

Mosley stood back from the microphone, like a boxer sizing up an opponent, then he stepped forward again, jabbing at the audience with his voice. Some of those listening were so caught up in his performance that they got to their feet, only to look around, see no one else standing, and sit down again. Glancing sideways, Kim could see that the Blackshirts to his left and right were glaring challengingly at the audience. Noticing that they were standing with their hands folded behind their backs, he did the same. He felt Connie's fingers tickling his. Trying not to smile, he tapped them away.

A couple of protesters somewhere in the gallery tried to sing 'We'll keep the red flag flying here' but were drowned out by a chorus of 'Rule Britannia'. While this was going on, Mosley stopped speaking and waited again, arms folded. When a woman in the audience shouted 'You bastard!', others took this as their cue and began heckling. From his elevated position, Kim could see some of the scuffles that now ensued. He glanced over his shoulder at Connie and shaped the words: 'What's going on?'

Connie gave an amused shrug in reply. With her cheekbones carved by shadow, and a golden nimbus haloing her hair, she did not seem alarmed. On the contrary, she put her hand to her mouth as she pretended to stifle a yawn.

From his seat in the gallery, Alun recognized one of the figures who had marched in as part of the Mosley Freak Show: Kim Newlands, the Olympic contender whose image had repeatedly been pasted across the pages of *The Blackshirt*. Alun thought he looked ridiculous – a preening popinjay in a black shirt. Did the idiot not know that Mosley was using him?

Some in the menagerie below were raising their arms in salute while others, with less conviction, cheered. Yet booing could also be heard. Alun allowed himself a furtive smile and raised himself on the tips of his toes to look around for the source. Mosley continued with his rant, slowly at first before building up, impaling the crowd on his words. Then, to Alun's delight, the heckling started in earnest. 'Useless bastard!' 'Sit down, you bugger!' 'Mosley, you wanker!' Alun wanted to join in but knew he must bide his time. The Blackshirt leader stopped speaking again and there were more interruptions – chants of 'Fascism is murder!' answered by 'Hail Mosley!' – and more skirmishes as stewards armed with truncheons hurled themselves at the hecklers.

There was a sound of breaking glass and now chairs were being thrown while leaflets fluttered down from the ceiling. Alun looked up and saw a man in the rafters being pursued by Blackshirts who were edging their way towards him along the beams. Taking this as his cue, he extracted the sharp murphy, wrapped in a hessian rag, from his pocket. He had used a small hammer to tap the blades in, and it had felt like loading bullets into a rifle. They were on one side of the potato only, so that he could hold the other and get a clean throw. If he was lucky he would reach Mosley and do some damage, maybe rip his uniform or at least add to the general chaos. He dipped his shoulder so that the man to his left could not see what he was doing as he removed the rag.

As Alun was later to reflect, part of him knew in that preceding minute that other outcomes were still possible, that it was not too late to avoid either the chain of grief he was about to set in motion or his own eventual punishment.

The heat was like an extra layer of skin and Kim, feeling sweat pearling his brow, watched as a female protester in the gallery jumped on the back of one of the stewards and shrilled abuse at him, right in his ear. More stewards hustled around her and, knotting her arms behind her back, bundled her out into one of the side corridors. She broke free of them and, when she ran back into Olympia's main arena waving a red flag she had found somewhere, they gave chase, with chairs and shoes being thrown after them.

Kim was still standing with his legs apart and hands clasped behind his back. Despite the growing agitation, he noticed through a fug of cigarette smoke that a Pathé News cameraman, positioned on a platform to his left, was filming him. May as well give them value for money, he thought as he raised his chin and inflated his chest. It was no accident that the two men chosen to stand either side of Kim on the platform were shorter and heavier-set than he, thereby emphasizing his own impressive height and athletic build.

The Leader attempted to resume his speech, only to pause again, hands on hips, while searchlights scanned the roiling sea below the platform. Some of the crowd were standing on chairs and laughing excitedly as they watched the fighting through opera glasses. Others, looking frightened, were leaving their seats and making for the exits. A brittle voice, distorted through loudspeakers, was repeating: 'Keep your seats! Please, everyone, keep your seats!'

Realizing that the men to his left and right were no longer standing tightly to attention but were exchanging glances and nods with one another, their hands balling into fists, Kim felt a strange hollowness in his gut – not fear exactly, more uncertainty. When he looked over his shoulder at Connie and mouthed the words he had used earlier – 'I'll protect you' – she blew him a kiss, but her calm demeanour was slipping.

As leaflets continued to drift down from the rafters, Kim looked up. A voice sounded high in the girders – 'Murderers!' – and he saw a man clambering across them, balanced 150 feet above the crowd. From each side, stewards soon appeared treading the same precarious perch. Kim turned to Connie again, to check she was safe, and as he did so, he caught a glimpse of a projectile the size of a cricket ball bearing down towards his head. Instinctively he ducked. In the same moment, he heard a scream from behind him and spun around to see Connie folding at the knees, her hands clutching her face.

TEN

Even from his position high in the gallery, Alun could see blood pouring through the fingers of the Blackshirt girl who had fallen. The tall Aryan was supporting her head in his lap, while others milled about them.

Horrified and unsure what, if anything, he could do, Alun tried to get down to the stage, only to be winded and brought to the ground by a charging steward. There was a blur of arms and legs and then he was being dragged backwards by his hair. He scrambled to his feet but fell again. Four more stewards came and as they carried him into the corridor at the side of the hall, Alun tried to wrestle free, twisting left and right. Now he found himself tumbling down a metal staircase headfirst. When he reached the bottom, disorientated, half a dozen more black-uniformed figures appeared out of the shadows and, in an explosion of hot, white pain, they set upon him. He absorbed the kicks to his stomach and spine. Heard a crunch of cartilage. Felt nothing more.

As Kim carried Connie out of the arena, he could feel her fingers locked behind his neck. Her chest was pitching, but she was no longer crying, and he wondered whether she had passed out from the pain. It was hard to tell because a makeshift bandage was covering both her eyes, making her look like a blindfolded prisoner. Kim had momentarily gagged when he saw that her right eyeball had been sliced open, exposing spidery nerves and ligaments. He had torn a dressing from the slip Connie was wearing under her black skirt, and as he looked at it now, dark red clots were beginning to ooze out from beneath it.

Seeing an ambulance parked near the entrance gate, Kim hurried towards it, only vaguely aware of the gang of stewards who were punching and kicking someone on the ground at the foot of a metal staircase. The ambulance doors were open and Kim spotted a man inside wearing a Red Cross armband over his white coat. He was signalling to Kim with urgent rotations of his wrist.

'Been hit in the eye,' Kim said as he laid Connie on one of two trolleys inside the ambulance.

As the medic attempted to unwrap the soaked bandage, the patient screamed. 'Can you hold her steady?' he said to Kim. At least the bleeding seemed to have been partially staunched.

Making comforting shushing noises, Kim positioned himself at the head of the gurney and gently pressed Connie's shoulders down. Her chin was quivering as the medic replaced the bandage, before drawing some liquid from a small bottle into a syringe, and injecting her.

'What's that?' Kim asked between wheezy coughs. Though the night was hot, he was shivering and struggling for breath.

'Morphine. You all right?'

As Connie went limp, Kim felt his own shoulders droop. How pale and fragile she looked; her skin was almost translucent. 'I'm sorry,' he whispered, the words catching in his throat. 'You're being very brave. Can you hear me?'

'Here's another one!'

Kim looked up as two stretcher-bearers lifted a body on to the second gurney.

'You'll have to make room,' the medic said.

As Kim squeezed past them and jumped out of the ambulance, he registered that the man on the stretcher was the one he had seen being set upon by the Blackshirt stewards. The man was groaning and clutching his sides, and his face and hands were spattered with blood. Confusingly, he was wearing a black shirt.

'I'm afraid there's no room for you in the ambulance,' the medic said to Kim. 'We're taking them to St Stephen's Hospital, on the Fulham Road.'

'I'll meet you there,' Kim said, the words clotting again as he struggled to breathe.

The ambulance pulled away with a raucous clatter and Kim stood for a moment, his hand rubbing his neck. He started walking in the direction of the Underground station but then had to stop again. Feeling dizzy, he bent forward and stayed in this position for half a minute; then he straightened his back and wiped his mouth with his sleeve. If he had reacted quicker, he could have stopped the projectile with his hand, he thought. Perhaps even caught it. He inspected his hands now and realized they were bleeding. Remembering he had picked the rock-like object up and put it in his pocket, thinking vaguely that it might be needed as evidence at some point, he took it out and saw that it was a potato spliced with razor blades. He dropped it in shock and kicked it away, as if it were a hand grenade with the pin removed.

He was breathing rapidly now, and as he felt the muscles around his airways tightening, he realized that, for the first time in years, he was having an asthma attack.

ELEVEN

Nuremberg

'Well, they all look the same to me,' Leni said with a dismissive flick of her manicured fingers. She was wearing riding boots, jodhpurs and a leather trench coat over a white polo-neck. In her hand was a megaphone. On her head, covering what she called her 'seaweed hair', was a newsboy cap worn back-to-front so that she could use the viewfinder. She wanted no one to be in any doubt who was the director here.

Ernst Röhm, a portly, scar-faced figure in the braided brown uniform of a stormtrooper commander-in-chief, bulged his eyes at her in disbelief. 'How can you say that?' he said hotly. 'They are clearly different. Look. My SA ranks are down that side.' He jerked the peak of his kepi right. 'And Himmler's SS are down that side.' He made a gesture with his left arm. 'It must be obvious even to a woman that they are not the same.'

Leni pretended to think about this as she looked down at the troops milling below her. A thousand – two battalions – had been gathered, at her behest, for this rehearsal on the Zeppelinfeld, a parade ground so vast it reduced the assembled soldiers to painted lead toys. There would be 149,000 more of them parading on the day, and the rehearsals for that event would begin in earnest sometime in the next few weeks. There was to be no repeat of the previous year's fiasco. Adolf's orders. For now, these token troops would represent the whole rally, to give Leni a sense of how her establishing shot, as well as her subsequent tracking shots, should be framed.

It was a sultry, pink-and-grey afternoon, and the vigour of the sun could be felt above the thin, low-hanging clouds. As they awaited their orders to fall in, the soldiers stretched and walked about or stood around looking bored. Some were squatting on their haunches, their helmets or kepis removed in order to find relief from the humidity. Others were lying down, apparently asleep.

Those on the right were wearing brown uniforms, those on the left black, and Leni knew the difference between them. Apart from anything else, the SA looked as if they had come straight from a beerhall. They were beefier, scruffier and shorter than their SS counterparts, who seemed tall and stylish in their well-cut Hugo Boss uniforms.

'Wait,' Leni said. 'Let me see if my tiny female brain can grasp this. Your men are in the brown costumes, correct?' Röhm needed reminding of his place, and hers. While this tactic might have seemed risky to those outside Adolf's inner circle, she had heard rumours that Röhm's stock had fallen in recent months, while her own had risen. He was the one playing the dangerous game here.

'That is what I keep trying to tell you!' Röhm snapped. 'And they are wearing uniforms not costumes.'

'And will there be anyone wearing grey?'

'*No, no, no,* the Wehrmacht wear field grey and they will be having their own rally on a different day.'

'Then this might work,' she said.

'*Of course it will work, woman!*'

Leni stared at him coldly. 'May I remind you, Mr Röhm, that as the director of this film I am in charge here. My concerns take priority, and they are purely aesthetic. I believe the contrast of the colour brown moving in one direction and black in another, like two counterflowing rivers, may well, with the appropriate choreography, work.'

'This is not a film!' Röhm spluttered. 'This is the Sixth Party Congress. And it's called drill, not choreography!'

Leni allowed herself a cool, clear smile, pleased that she had provoked the pompous old buffoon. Being the only woman present was proving to be electrifying rather than unnerving. And being the only one of the twenty or so people on the grandstand who was not a member of the Nazi Party was making her feel not vulnerable but empowered, especially as everyone knew that, in Adolf's eyes, she could do no wrong. She was aware of the gossip that she and the Führer were more than friends, but she had not rushed to dismiss it, not least because she could see how it could be used to her advantage. By keeping in with her, people would think they were keeping in with him.

'I have no interest in who has the larger army, or the shiniest boots,' she said. 'And I care about neither rank nor decoration.' As she tapped the Iron Cross on Röhm's uniform, she noticed that Heinrich Himmler and Albert Speer, who were standing nearby, were trying and failing to suppress their smiles. 'My lack of interest in these things,' she added, playing up to her audience, 'is precisely why your friend the Führer asked me to make this film. He said to me, and I quote: "I don't want another boring old Party film. I don't want newsreels or propaganda. I want a timeless work of art."'

It was true that the Führer and Röhm had been through a great deal together, and he was allowed to address Adolf with the informal 'you' – the intimate *du* rather than the starchier pronoun *Sie*, which nearly everyone else had to use. But it was also true that Röhm had been making a lot of enemies in high places lately, and not only because of his overt homosexuality and his enthusiasm for appointing fellow travellers to positions of power within the SA. There were rumours that he was planning a coup.

Leni had used the words 'your friend the Führer' deliberately, and the implication that Röhm owed his position solely to his friendship with Adolf had clearly stung. Normally he had a habit, when challenged, of lowering his large, domed forehead as if about to charge, but as he did this now he was sweating, his face red, and he looked more as if he was about to have a stroke.

'He's your friend, too, miss,' Röhm said in a tone of low menace.

'I have many friends,' she countered lightly.

'Yes, I've heard that you bestow your affections liberally.'

'Do not worry, Mr Röhm, I have no intention of casting my intoxicating spell on you.'

'Be careful,' Röhm hissed. 'You don't want me as an enemy.'

'Nor do I want you as a friend,' Leni said with another dismissive flick of her hand. Friends, enemies. Enemies, friends. It struck her how pathetic these men in Adolf's gang could be. They were like boys in a playground, all trying to elbow each other out of the way so they could stand next to the school bully. 'Now, if you would be so kind, I would like browns on the left – my left, looking down – and blacks on the right. The opposite to where they are now.'

With whatever scraps of dignity he had left, the Brownshirt commander straightened his kepi, stuck out his chest and tried to pull in his paunch as he turned his back on Leni and descended the stone steps. When he reached the bottom, he began barking orders. The five hundred men wearing brown uniforms rose to their feet and shuffled into ranks on the left half of the square. The men in black uniforms watched them insolently, staying put.

Himmler sighed audibly as he surveyed the scene through his pince-nez. He then moved closer to Leni before whispering: 'Don't worry about that old queer. He won't be causing you any problems by the time of the rally.' Leni turned to face him as she tried to gauge what he meant by this, but his small eyes gave nothing away.

'Be that as it may,' she said, 'for the time being, would you mind accompanying him for your stroll up the path, as we discussed.' Himmler gave a teasing bow and followed the same route down taken by Röhm. Without being ordered, the men in black uniforms jumped to their feet and formed themselves into a long, smart column, five abreast, facing the rostrum – the one where Adolf would, in due course, stand to deliver his rallying speech to an audience of close to a million. As they came to attention, the whole ground echoed to the liquid slap of leather on stone.

There was a large gap between the SA and SS ranks, the width of the granite path that joined Albert's crescent-shaped grandstand and the arcaded Ehrenhalle, and the symbolism of the gap was not lost on Leni. The tension between the two battalions was palpable.

Leni sidled over to Albert, who had taken off his linen jacket, rolled up his sleeves and tucked his tie into his shirt. He was now studying plans he had spread out on a foldaway table. She liked him, not least because he was more urbane, tall and easy on the eye than the other members of the inner sanctum, most of whom seemed, to Leni, to resemble pigs, dwarfs or cadavers. Albert was not only ironic of manner but also gentlemanly. She liked the sophisticated way he always greeted her with a three-cheek kiss, in the Montpellier style. They shared a passion for skiing and mountaineering, were more or less the same age, and they understood each other. They were, indeed, fellow artists, and Adolf, who was older, was their patron – 'Adolfo de' Medici', as Albert had once mischievously called him . . . behind his back.

Although Adolf had failed to get into Vienna's art academy and had begun his career as a painter of picture postcards for tourists, he nevertheless considered himself to be a man of culture and he enjoyed the company of artists. And he had certainly demonstrated his good taste by commissioning Albert to transform Nuremberg into a vast film set for Leni where, all being well, she could create an artistic masterwork to rival Eisenstein's *Battleship Potemkin* or Fritz Lang's *Metropolis*.

'What are these going to be?' Leni said now, pointing to some drawings of what looked to be a series of gun towers lining the perimeter of the parade ground. 'Are we planning to shoot anyone who marches out of step?'

'No, they will house the lavatories,' Albert said.

Leni laughed and touched his arm. 'You think of everything, Albert.'

Leni considered mentioning that her father was a plumber specializing in public conveniences, but thought better of it. Albert probably imagined that he was a professor or a lawyer. Best to keep it that way. We all invent ourselves, one way or another.

'There is something I would like you to build for me,' she said.

'At your service,' Albert replied.

'I'd like some rails laid down for my cameras.'

'Of course. Where?'

Leni moved alongside him, so that their hips were touching, and tapped the plans on the table as she spoke: 'Here, here, here and . . .' She surveyed the parade ground; then she lowered her gaze to the plans and described an arc with her finger: '. . . all across here.'

Albert pulled out a pencil stub from behind his ear and shaded in the areas she had requested. While he was doing this, Leni turned her back to the parade ground and contemplated a small group of workmen who were removing graffiti – a hammer and sickle painted in red – from one of the sandstone blocks at the back of the grandstand. 'What will you have up there?'

Albert straightened his back, turned and followed her sightline. 'A giant swastika on a crown, I thought. Contained within a wreath.'

'Will there be the three vertical banners again?'

Albert nodded. 'Slightly taller than last year, I thought, maybe a hundred and fifty feet.' He stared at the grandstand, tapped his lips and nodded again. 'They could provide a visual echo of Adolf walking back to the grandstand with Röhm and Himmler, after saluting the wreath at the memorial hall.'

As she listened, Leni found herself wondering if Albert found her attractive. It was hard to tell. Having a certain useful power over certain useless men did not constitute objective beauty and she could never understand why the papers insisted on describing her as a 'femme fatale'. At certain angles she could look cross-eyed, despite her parents' laborious efforts to correct this during her childhood. She found small comfort in the assurances of cameramen that her slightly squinting gaze and 'determined' jawline were perfect for the two-dimensional medium of film. What did that even mean? As for the bird's nest that passed for her hair, well . . .

'I suspect you find the SA commander something of an aesthetic challenge,' Albert said insouciantly.

Leni let out a pointed sigh.

Albert gave a laugh. 'At least Göring won't be in the line-up,' he added.

'Yes, if Adolf had to walk sandwiched between Göring and Röhm . . .' She didn't finish the sentence. 'Albert, I'd like the chance to do some aerial footage. If you do go for the three flagpoles again, might you be able to build a small lift on one of them, so that I can get a rising, panoramic shot as the two armies part?'

'To hold one person or two?'

'One, plus a camera.'

'Consider it done. Are you OK with heights?'

She touched his arm again. 'You ask that of a fellow mountaineer?'

Albert smiled. Noticing that he was wearing a Golden Party Badge like hers, Leni asked in a confiding whisper: 'Has Adolf given you any presents lately?'

'Such as?'

'I don't know, a Mercedes sports car maybe?'

Albert grinned. 'You too?'

Leni nodded.

'I don't suppose our friend Mr Röhm will be getting one any time soon.'

When Leni pressed him to elaborate, Albert asked if she had heard about Heinrich Brüning and Kurt von Schleicher, two former Chancellors who had received warnings from friends in the Reichswehr that they should leave Germany as soon as possible because their lives were in danger. Brüning had already fled to Holland, Schleicher had chosen to dismiss the tip-off as nonsense. 'I think Schleicher may come to regret his choice,' Albert added.

'Has Röhm been given a tip-off, too?'

When Albert put his fingers to his lips, Leni felt a shock of heat course through her. She wanted to ask Albert more but, recognizing that there were some things she was better off not knowing, she tried instead to compose herself by becoming businesslike again, sharing with Albert the innovations that she was planning: the use of long-focus lenses so that the sea of flags would be foreshortened to create a blurred pattern as the standard-bearers marched in opposite directions. She also told him about an idea she'd had to make some of the cameramen wear roller skates to get smoother tracking shots and for others to wear uniforms, brown and black, so they could blend in with the soldiers without being caught in each other's shots. Could he arrange that? Albert nodded. 'And I'll need an arc of tracks below the podium,' Leni continued, 'so that the cameras can circle Adolf as he speaks. Would that be possible?'

'Good idea, film him from below, you mean, so that he looks monumental?'

'Exactly,' Leni said. 'The lone messiah facing the multitude. Being anointed by his people. Rudolph, Heinrich, Hermann and the others will be behind him, just in shot, but on a lower platform.'

'He'll love that,' Albert said. 'I will supervise it personally.'

Leni's gaze was focused on one of the workmen. Not only was he the same height and build as Hitler, he had a toothbrush moustache. 'Are these your men?'

'Yes,' Albert said, 'veterans from Verdun and Ypres. We like to find work for them.'

'You!' she called to the man, pointing at him. 'Come here.' The man looked surprised and his eyes moved to Albert for permission. The architect shrugged his consent.

'Now,' Leni said. 'I want you to go and join the Reichsführer-SS and the other one, the fat one, over by that hall. I want to film all three of you as you walk back towards us. Slowly. You will be in the middle, and a few paces in front.'

Again, the man looked at Albert, this time nervously. The architect said in a stage whisper: 'You're going to be the Führer for a day, my friend. Enjoy it while it lasts.'

With feline gentleness, Leni looped her arms through Albert's and asked: 'You have any cigarettes on you?'

Albert patted his pockets and produced a packet that was full. Leni took it from him, and slipped it in the worker's jacket. She then signalled for one of Himmler's SS adjutants to join them.

'May we borrow your cap?' Leni asked him when he arrived with a click of his heels.

Darting a look at the worker, who lowered his eyes, the SS officer glowered and said: 'I must respectfully decline your request, Miss Riefenstahl.'

Leni took a step closer and asked in a gentle voice: 'What's your name?'

'SS-Obersturmbannführer Franz.'

'Do you normally disobey orders, Franz?'

The officer looked straight ahead. He clearly felt confused, but equally he was not about to surrender his cap.

'I must mention your name to my "executive producer",' Leni continued, placing two fingers vertically under her nose.

There was panic in the officer's eyes now.

'I'd give it to her if I were you,' Albert said, his mouth on the edge of a smile.

Franz finally handed over his cap. Leni turned her back to the officer, approached the construction worker and removed his leather cap.

When she saw it was covering a Jewish skullcap, she froze for an instant before quickly placing the SS hat with its death's head badge over it. It was a good fit. She turned her head slightly to see whether Albert had noticed the yarmulke. She suspected he had but she was sure that Franz, who had now taken a few steps back, was in the wrong place to have seen it. Patting the bemused construction worker's arm, she said: 'Off you go. Remember now, slowly on the way back.'

As the man trotted down the steps, holding the SS cap in place, Albert leaned towards Leni and whispered: 'That was naughty.'

'Well-behaved girls don't make history.' She felt relieved that Albert was choosing to be amused by what she had done, rather than appalled. Although she knew it was risky to trust anyone in the Nazi hierarchy, she felt he was on her side.

Albert turned to Leni and asked: 'Why didn't you use the SS officer to stand in for Adolf?'

'He's all wrong. This will be the climax of my film,' Leni said. 'I have to get it right. There will be no chance of a second take.'

'There is a word for people like you,' Albert said.

'Perfectionist?'

'German.'

Leni smiled.

The construction worker had now caught up with the heads of the SS and the SA. She could see him explaining what he had been asked to do, pointing first at his SS cap then at Leni on the grandstand. Himmler looked up to see if this was correct. Leni, who was looking at them through a viewfinder, waved back.

When they set off walking back towards them, Leni signalled for one of her assistants to pass her loudhailer and then, putting it to her mouth, she shouted: 'Wait!' She raised her eyebrows at the cameraman next to her and he gave her a thumbs-up. 'Action!' she shouted, raising her viewfinder again. She was soon muttering to herself: 'No, no, no.' Again, she put the megaphone to her mouth: 'Slower!'

'We should film this in the late afternoon,' Albert said as he watched the scene. 'So that we get long, dramatic shadows.'

'What time does the sun set here in September?'

'Not sure,' Albert said. 'But if you want the sun to set at five fifteen p.m., I will make sure it sets at five fifteen p.m. I will even make it set in the east, if you think that would be better for your shot.'

With her mouth twitching into another smile, the director took a sideways step and kissed the architect lightly on the cheek, just once, in the German style. As she did this she wondered, almost in an abstract way, if they would work as well together on a personal level as they did on a professional. Could Albert be the man for her?

Probably not. Though she had often felt sexual desire, she did not think she had ever been in love. The Portuguese had a beautiful word, *saudade*, which meant the feeling of longing for someone you have lost. That was more how she felt – that she was always longing for someone she had lost.

TWELVE

London

When Alun came around in the hospital, the first image in his head was of the beautiful blonde girl in the black shirt. He opened his eyes with a gasp. It was daylight and he was lying on his back in a bed. Turning his head, he saw through the cracked lens of his glasses that there were other beds, occupied by men whose faces were bruised and crusted with dried cuts. When he tried to sit up, a pain across his chest caused him to wince. A broken rib. He now spotted the thickset man wearing a beret who was sitting in a chair beside his bed. Martin Herzl, reading the *Manchester Guardian*.

'Morning, Comrade Pryce,' Herzl said, lowering his paper and raising his fist in a half-hearted salute. 'You were out cold for a whole day.'

'Where am I?' Alun managed through cracked lips.

'St Stephen's Hospital. You look terrible, by the way.'

Alun groaned in response.

'We've won a great victory,' Herzl continued. 'The papers have been condemning the Blackshit brutality.' He picked up his paper again and read from it. '"The 150 MPs present at Olympia were unanimous in their condemnation of the Blackshirts' behaviour."' He folded the paper, lit a cigarette and looked around for an ashtray to drop his spent match in. 'There are dozens of comrades here and for once the press have been listening to our stories,' he said, leaning forward to hold the cigarette to Alun's lips so that he could have a drag without having to lift his arms. Alun inhaled, started coughing and shook his head to make Herzl take the cigarette away.

'There's some of the Blackshits here too,' Herzl continued. 'There's one of them in the next ward, a woman someone blinded with a razor.'

Picturing his victim as he remembered the blood streaming down her face, Alun felt sick and groaned again. He had imagined that his missile would inflict a minor cut on Mosley's arm or leg. That would have been more than justifiable in the struggle for a new Britain. But to cause a young woman to lose an eye? His limbs heavy with guilt, he sat up, this time ignoring the pain in his chest, and swung his legs over the side of the bed.

'Where are you going, Comrade Pryce?' Herzl asked. 'I don't think you're supposed to get out of bed.'

Alun struggled to his feet regardless, swayed, and then, with his teeth clamped together, tried a couple of steps. He was unable to put any weight on one of his legs – the kneecap felt knocked out of place. Seeing some crutches leaning against the end of the bed opposite, he made his way towards them.

'What about your breakfast?' Herzl called after him. 'They're about to come around with it; I heard the matron telling one of the nurses.'

'You can have it,' Alun said.

'Can I?' Herzl removed his beret and jumped into Alun's vacated bed, making the springs jangle. He pulled the sheets up around himself so that he looked like a patient. 'I'm starving,' he said. 'I just hope it's not strawberries and cream. I don't like strawberries and cream.'

Alun knew how the routine went. It was a favourite in communist circles. He was supposed to say 'You will when communism triumphs' but today he was not in the mood. Instead he turned his back on his comrade and, aided by the crutches, limped towards the door.

Catching his reflection in the window, he saw his head was covered with contusions. There was tape across his nose and both his eyes were blackened. He was still wearing his black shirt. Seeing some fresh flowers in a vase beside an unoccupied bed, he looked left and right, then, wincing in pain, he grabbed them.

With small, agonizing steps, he made his way down the corridor to the Ladies' Ward. By the time he leaned against the swing doors to open them, his brow was mantled with sweat. Seeing a blonde woman with a bandaged eye, he flinched and felt nauseous again. 'What have I done?' he said under his breath as he approached her.

There was a Blackshirt sitting in a chair beside her bed, his back to the door. He was holding the patient's hand.

'Heard you were injured at Olympia,' Alun said when he reached the bed. 'How are you feeling?'

The woman pointed with a limp finger to her bandaged eye and replied in a hoarse voice: 'I've felt better.' Noticing the flowers, she added slowly: 'Those for me?'

In that moment, with those words, Alun felt a pulse of intimacy pass between them, something innocent and pure that burned through to his heart. He shook himself and looked around for a vase. Finding a carafe half filled with water, he put the flowers in it and placed them on her bedside table next to an unemptied ashtray and a plate of untouched kippers.

'That accent,' Connie said. 'You're Welsh. My family have a house in Wales.'

'Whereabouts?'

'Vale of Glamorgan.'

'That's where I'm from,' Alun said. 'Rhondda.'

As the steady green gaze of her single eye met his, Alun felt as if they were almost in unconscious communion with one another, able to read each other's thoughts.

The other visitor now cleared his throat and stood up, making Alun feel small. The man looked as if he had not slept. His pupils were enlarged, his skin grey. Alun recognized him. 'You're that athlete, aren't you?' he said.

'Kim Newlands,' the athlete said, proffering his hand. 'I believe you and Connie' – he nodded at the bed – 'shared an ambulance here.'

'Those bastards, eh,' Alun said, leaving it ambiguous which bastards he was referring to. Drawing Kim to one side, he added in a whisper: 'Will she be OK?'

Kim's shoulders sagged. He glanced towards the bed, and when he looked back at Alun, his eyes were glistening. 'The doctor told me they can do wonders with glass eyes these days.'

Alun felt a thickness in his throat, his guilt driving him towards anger. Why had the Blackshits put a girl in harm's way? They should have known projectiles would be thrown. They should have expected violence to be met with violence. This was not his fault.

But then his own shoulders dropped, too. What had Kim called her? Connie? Connie did not deserve this. And it *was* his fault. With a deep, pained breath, Alun closed his eyes and said: 'I'm so sorry.' And those three words, though barely audible, were sincerely meant.

At that moment Alun heard someone cough behind him and looked up to see Herzl filling the doorway. The idiot was wearing his communist 'uniform' of red neckerchief and beret.

'It was kippers,' Herzl said. 'I don't like kippers. Aren't you going to introduce me to your friends?'

THIRTEEN

In the two weeks that Connie had been home from hospital she had not been receiving any visitors. Whether this was by choice, or an instruction from her doctors or parents, Kim could not determine, but when he had visited the address he had for her – it turned out to be a five-storey, white stucco townhouse in a Georgian square in Mayfair – a butler had passed on a message that she would see him soon, when she was feeling stronger.

The sense of frustration he felt had been heightened by the heart palpitations and shortness of breath he had been suffering. His waking thoughts churned with the knowledge that Connie had only joined the Blackshirts because he had – and even when he'd managed to get some sleep, his dreams had been haunted by images of her injured eye and by his broken promise to protect her. That night at the rally, as he had cradled her head in his arms, it had been a distressingly visceral reminder of his mother's death.

In the hope that it might help him feel calmer, he decided to visit his mother's grave once more, but on the train down to Portsmouth his thoughts kept returning to the financial support that had been coming his way since he became, as Sir Oswald had put it, 'the poster boy for the BUF'. In light of Connie's injuries, that money felt tarnished, yet he was in no position to pay it back. What would his mother have made of his situation? And would she have believed his assurances that the Blackshirts had nothing against the Jews?

He knew she would never have criticized him directly for doing what he felt he had to do, but he suspected her silence on the subject might have spoken for her.

He took out his copy of *The Blackshirt*, the one with the picture of him in his running vest on the cover. How he wished his mother could have seen this photograph. She would have covered her heart with her hand and said: 'My boy. You look so handsome.'

At the cemetery, Kim looked around to make sure no one could overhear him before crouching down in front of his mother's headstone and telling her about Connie – although he didn't mention her injury – and about his hopes of being selected for the British team that would compete at the Berlin Olympics. He could hear in his head his mother saying how proud she was of him; comparing him to 'the Jewish athlete Harold Abrahams'.

Upon returning to London in the afternoon, Kim went to the track to practise some hurdling but found it hard to concentrate. He kept thinking about his BUF 'bursary'. It meant he was able to work part-time and, on days when he wasn't at work, he could train for eight hours, but was it a betrayal of his mother and her background? Mosley had assured him that not only was his party not anti-Semitic, it was on the side of the working class, protecting their rights and tackling social injustice. And Kim wanted to believe him. Nevertheless, he wondered whether he should talk to Mr Riley about it.

As he weighed this option, he tried another run but he fell halfway round. Kim had always been willing to tolerate pain and carry on despite the inevitable bruising crashes and knee-scraping tumbles that came with hurdling, but today he worried that he might do himself a more serious injury if he continued. Instead he focused on some endurance training for the broad jump, quick movements involving the legs and trunk: back squat, front squat and hang cleans.

At the end of his session, Mr Riley came over with a message. Connie had telephoned to say she would like Kim to visit.

Rather than waste time waiting for a tram, Kim decided to jog the four miles or so to her house. After about a mile, as he was running along a street of shops, he passed a heavy-set man with a blond handlebar moustache. He stopped and turned. With his neck muscles constricting, he watched the man cross the road and saw his face again. It wasn't his father. Realizing he hadn't been breathing as he stared, Kim now took a deep lungful of air, regained his composure, and began running again.

It was stress, that was all. Whenever he felt he was losing control of events, he would imagine seeing his father.

When Kim arrived at Connie's house, slick with sweat, he was surprised to see Alun, the Welsh Blackshirt he had met at the hospital, emerging from its columned entrance wearing a suit and tie and with a walking stick in his hand.

On one of his visits to see Connie at the hospital, Kim had stopped by Alun's bed and they had chatted again about the rally. Kim had said he had seen someone filming the event for Pathé News that night and wondered if the footage would show who had thrown the sharp murphy. Alun had said that he knew some people in journalism and might be able to get hold of the film so they could check. When Kim asked him what he did, Alun had seemed vague, saying that he worked in publishing, political books mostly, but Kim had come away with the impression that Alun was hiding something, perhaps even involvement with MI5. It had been when the conversation had turned to his friend Herzl. Alun had implied that Herzl was some kind of communist who 'we are trying to turn'.

A look of puzzlement must have shown on Kim's face now as he stood outside Connie's house because Alun immediately said: 'The hospital gave me her address.'

'How is she?' Kim asked as they passed on the steps.

'Putting on a brave face. Poor thing.'

'Thanks for calling by,' Kim said over his shoulder as he reached the door. 'I'm sure she appreciated it.' Noticing Alun's limp as he walked away, he called after him: 'How's your knee?'

Alun gave a thumbs-up sign.

A housemaid wearing a headband trimmed with ruffles answered the door and directed Kim down a long hallway towards a drawing room with a chandelier hanging from its high ceiling. Connie was sitting at a table doing a jigsaw. She was wearing a dressing gown and a black patch with a wad of cotton wool covering one eye.

The sideboard behind her looked as though it belonged in a doctor's surgery, laden as it was with rolls of bandage, forceps and an enamel kidney dish, as well as pots of ointment and bottles of some tincture that gave off a chemical smell barely masked by the scent of flowers coming from a large bouquet. There was a note attached to the flowers and Kim read that they were from Sir Oswald Mosley, who had written 'Tom' after his name in brackets. He was sorry to hear about her injury, and he wished her a speedy recovery.

'My parents left for the country this morning,' Connie said. 'So you won't have the grisly ordeal of meeting them.'

'But I'd like to meet them,' Kim said. 'And it's nice finally to see where you live.' He took in the large oil paintings and tapestries, the marble busts, the grand fireplace. 'Cosy.' He walked over and kissed her carefully on the cheek.

'You'll have to come around this side,' Connie said with a flap of her fingers. 'I can't see you there.'

The absence of ambiguity in the comment momentarily shocked Kim into silence, then he said awkwardly: 'I came straight from the track. How are you feeling?'

'So-so,' Connie said, and then, pointing to the eyepatch, she added: 'What do you think?' Her speech was slow and slurred. 'Does it make me look like a pirate? You just missed Alun Pryce. I got to know him quite well in the hospital. We would walk down to the canteen for a cup of tea and a chat. He knew all about Dalton Hall. Told me he had friends who used to beat for my father on shooting days. He brought me a bottle of brandy.'

'How is it? The pain?'

'Much the same. There's a constant, dull ache. The specialist has given me some morphine. He wants me to come in for a fitting for a glass eye, but I can't bring myself to think about that just yet.'

'Is it hurting now?'

'I was feeling a bit weepy and fragile earlier, but the morphine has done the trick. You should try it.' Connie looked at the jigsaw piece in her hand as if unsure what it was. 'I keep waking up drenched in perspiration. My mind keeps replaying what happened that night but now I . . .' She looked confused as she lost her train of thought. 'It's the morphine. It leaves me foggy.'

'Is there anything I can do?'

'Could you deal with my BUF uniform for me? It's soaked in blood. I put it in a bag somewhere.'

'Of course. Do you want me to clean it?'

'No, I want you to get rid of it.'

Kim wondered what he would say if Connie asked him to leave the BUF. He would have to explain why he couldn't; he'd have to tell her about the bursary.

'You mustn't blame yourself,' she said.

'If I ever find out who threw that thing, I'm going to—'

'Don't do anything,' Connie said. 'You're not that sort of man. It's one of the things I admire about you. I'm sure whoever it was didn't mean to, you know . . .' She pointed to her eyepatch again, unable to say the words.

'But who would do that?' Kim asked. 'I mean, razor blades? What did they think would happen?'

'Did Alun tell you I looked hideous?'

'Course not.'

'People do think me hideous now, though, don't they?'

'No.'

Connie lowered her head. 'What about you, Kim?' she said, almost in a whisper.

Kim put a hand on her shoulder. 'To me, you are more beautiful than ever.'

'Darling Kim.' She felt for his hand. 'Where does your goodness come from?'

'Everything's going to be all right, you know,' he replied. 'You may not think it right now, but things will get better. I promise. We are all stronger than we think.'

Connie seemed to weigh this for a moment; then she said: 'Where does your strength come from, Kim? Is it your parents?'

Kim must have averted his eyes because Connie now asked: 'Why won't you ever talk about yourself, about your family? What are they like? When am I going to meet them?'

Kim shook his head.

'Something happened to you as a child,' Connie pressed. 'What was it, darling? What happened?'

With a sigh born of resignation, Kim decided it was time to tell her, if only to help her put her own ill fortune into some perspective.

'For my thirteenth birthday,' he began, 'my mother made me a fairy cake . . .'

FOURTEEN

Autumn, 1934

It had been three months since the rally in Olympia. After visiting Connie once or twice, Alun had been trying to avoid thinking about her injury by taking on extra work at the Communist Party building in Covent Garden. Then he had bumped into Kim in Leicester Square, who didn't recognize him at first, because he had grown back his Trotsky beard. When Alun had asked after Connie, Kim said she had been convalescing at her family seat in Wales and that he was soon going to be driving down there, in her sports car, to bring her back to London. At that moment, Alun's feelings of guilt came rushing back.

He was reminded of her again when Harry Pollitt summoned him to his office. Although the two men had bonded after being held in the same prison cell in Wales, the general secretary was a formal man who always addressed Alun, his junior by more than two decades, as 'Mr Pryce'. Alun felt nervous every time he knocked on his door.

'You asked to see me, Mr Pollitt.'

'Yes, come in, Mr Pryce. Take a seat.'

The general secretary, who was sturdily built, was sitting at his desk under a large and forbidding portrait of Lenin. As was his habit, he was wearing a three-piece suit that made him look serious. He always sounded serious, too, talking in a monotone that countered the musicality of his Lancastrian vowels. Harry Pollitt even had a serious way of being prematurely bald.

As Alun sat down, grateful to take the weight off a leg that still ached from the night he was attacked, Pollitt stood up and began pacing the room with his thumbs tucked into his waistcoat pockets. 'I keep thinking about that rally the Blackshirts held at Olympia,' he began. 'Are you still a paid-up member of the British Union of Fascists?'

'Yes, I suppose I am,' Alun said. 'Although I haven't been back to the Black House since the rally. I don't imagine they would be too pleased to see me.'

'But they wouldn't recognize you, would they? Not from that one night?'

Alun gripped the handle of his walking stick. 'I doubt it. There were thousands of people there and it was chaotic. Smoke bombs. Chairs being thrown. So many injuries. No one knew whose side anyone was on. And it was dark. I couldn't tell you what my attackers looked like, so I would be surprised if they could tell you what I looked like.'

'That's what I thought,' Pollitt said. He stopped his pacing and locked eyes with Alun. 'I want you to go back to the Black House. Infiltrate them. Try and get to know their leadership. You're an educated young man. You speak their language. We want to know everything they are planning, every march, every rally, every secret meeting they have with a politician. We especially want to know about the Prince of Wales. He's made no secret of his sympathy for Mussolini and Hitler, but we need to know how close he is to Mosley. There are rumours that he wants Mosley to accompany him on a goodwill mission to Germany. We need to find out more about that so that we can plan our response. In the coming months, every propaganda victory we can claim, big or small, will be vital to our cause. We need the British people to see these fascist thugs for what they are.'

Alun digested this. 'Why me?'

'Because they trust you. Mr Herzl was telling me about this Olympic hopeful they are putting on all their posters, Kim Newlands. If he considers you a friend, you can exploit that. I gather you know the aristocrat he is courting too, the daughter of Lord Dalton?'

Alun flinched and then nodded.

'It will mean you'll have to be careful about not being seen coming and going from this building,' Pollitt continued, raising his finger. 'MI5 keep too close an eye on us for that. We'll carry on paying your wages but it will have to be in cash, so we keep it off the books. Mr Herzl will be your point of contact. You'll have to arrange to meet him somewhere, in a café or a park. Somewhere inconspicuous.'

'I'm afraid Kim Newlands and Connie Dalton have already met Mr Herzl. He was with me at the hospital, wearing his red kerchief and a beret.'

'Did they ask about him?'

'I implied that I was doing some secret service work. Trying to recruit him as an informer against the Communist Party.'

'Did they believe you?'

'I don't know. Think so. Everyone knows MI5 is riddled with Mosley's supporters.'

Pollitt was pacing again. 'That's a good cover. Plausible. If anyone at the Black House says they saw you here, in this building, that's what you'll tell them. This will be a dangerous assignment, Mr Pryce, but in the fight for a new, fairer Britain we all have to take risks.'

Alun stared at the bronze bust of Marx in the corner of the room and gave a solemn nod. 'I won't let you down.'

His meeting over, Alun joined Herzl downstairs in the bookshop. A knowing nod from his friend indicated that he already knew what had been discussed. Though he was feeling anxious about the prospect of working undercover at the Black House, Alun tried to appear nonchalant.

'Looks like I'm going to have to keep a lower profile,' he said.

'I'll miss you,' Herzl replied.

Alun was so surprised by the apparent sincerity of this comment that he couldn't think of a cutting remark in response. 'We'll still be seeing one another,' he said. 'Just not here. You'll be my handler. What's that?' Alun had noticed what looked like a small wireless next to a headset and a small wire transmitter mast on the floor behind the counter.

'That's a Morse code machine,' Herzl said. 'Just arrived from Moscow. A gift from the Comintern. There are two sets. One for you, one for me. Harry wants us to learn how to use them.'

Alun picked it up to examine it, and then looked over his shoulder. 'We'd better keep this out of sight,' he said. 'Herzl?'

'What?'

'Do you think I'll be safe?'

'Probably not. I give it a week before I have to come and identify you at the morgue.'

Alun laughed; then he felt a strong urge to confess something, as if Herzl could offer him absolution. 'I can't stop thinking about that girl I injured. I have nightmares about it.'

'Maybe you weren't the one who hit her.'

'What do you mean?'

'Dozens of our comrades were hurling sharp murphies and other things at the stage. Any one of them could have done the deed. Besides, look at you, you're too puny to throw that far.'

Alun had to concede that, if his days playing cricket at school in Wales were anything to go by, Herzl had a point. As he was leaving the bookshop, Alun turned back to Herzl and gave him a fascist salute. Herzl clicked his heels together and returned the gesture.

En route to the Black House in Chelsea, Alun made three stops. The first was his home, so he could collect his black shirt and shave off his beard, keeping the moustache in the style favoured by the British military. He had been clean shaven on the night of the rally, so this, he thought, might help in terms of a disguise. The second stop was at a grocer's, to buy half a dozen heavy potatoes. The third was Olympia.

There were a couple of vans parked outside but otherwise the place seemed to be deserted. Alun closed his eyes momentarily when he realized a metal staircase he was approaching was the one he had been thrown down. After taking a steadying breath, he adjusted the position of the strap on the bag he was carrying and passed the stairs, checking for old bloodstains on the ground where he had been beaten. A few yards further on he came to a door, but it was locked. He continued walking around the outside of the building until he reached a service entrance that was being held ajar by a rusty metal bin. After looking left and right, he entered and headed to the second-floor gallery where he had been sitting during the rally.

Without a sea of people filling it, the exhibition space did not seem as big as it had that night. As he surveyed the scene, he pressed his fingers against his temples. What had he turned into? Had he really become so blinkered by ideology, so filled with hate for Tories, fascists and aristocrats, that he was capable of violence against a woman? The act felt like a contradiction of his socialist principles and this was why he had to know for sure whether he was the person responsible for what had happened to Connie.

Lifting the bag off his shoulder, he selected one of the potatoes it contained and weighed it in his hand. With another furtive glance around, he drew back his arm and threw it as hard as he could in the direction of the stage. It landed halfway. He threw another potato and this one landed even shorter. The next went about ten yards further, but still well short of the stage. With tears of relief now pricking his eyes, he emitted a short sudden breath. He was sure now that the sharp murphy that had blinded Connie could not have been thrown by him. Almost in celebration he threw another one and watched in appalled fascination as it moved in a high arc through the air and landed on the stage, before bouncing twice and falling off the opposite side.

Alun groped for the seat behind him, slowly sat back down and touched his hand to his head. He pictured again what he had witnessed that night and felt a trickle of winter run down his spine.

FIFTEEN

Nuremberg

Leni rolled her shoulders and neck as she waited for the small cage that Albert had built for her to begin its lurching ascent of the flagpole. She could see her assistant director in the crowd, disguised in the brown uniform of a stormtrooper. He was holding up five fingers – that meant five minutes to go. She gave him the thumbs-up sign and did one more check of her 35-mm camera. The Parvo held 390 feet of celluloid, yielding six minutes of filming. That would be long enough to cover the entire ascent, but there was no room for error, and if her timing was out by even a few seconds the shot would be ruined. That was why she had insisted on doing it herself.

The afternoon shadows were as deep as she'd hoped, and the flags and standards were billowing as they caught the breeze. She crouched down so that her eye was level with the viewfinder and focused the lens on a cluster of banners in the middle distance. Drawing in a breath and releasing it slowly to calm her nerves, she thought about how Adolf had promised her that this would be the last film she'd have to make about the Nazi Party. After this she would be free to choose her own projects. But could she trust him? Her thoughts returned to Röhm – all references to him had now been obliterated from the public records. Röhm had trusted Adolf, too.

Before she had heard from Albert about the circumstances of Röhm's execution a couple of months ago, she had assumed that Adolf could not have been aware of what had happened, and that when he heard the news he would have been appalled. It was, after all, becoming a characteristic of German life that whenever something ugly happened, people would say, 'If only the Führer knew.'

But on this occasion the Führer had known. According to Albert, Adolf, as a last act of kindness to his old comrade, had given Röhm the option of taking his own life. An SS officer had walked into his cell, laid a pistol on the table, told him he had ten minutes to use it and left. But Röhm had refused, stating, 'If I am to be killed, let Adolf do it himself.' The SS officer had returned to find Röhm standing with his chest puffed out in a gesture of defiance. The officer had fired at point-blank range.

Leni may not have liked Röhm – few did – but she was nevertheless shocked by the reports of his 'liquidation', the euphemism that it had lately become fashionable to use. How could things have come to this so quickly? Could he and Adolf not have tried to settle their differences like honourable men? She had been trying not to think about Röhm's fate in recent days, had been distracting herself with preparations for the rally, but she could not help returning to the fact that, although Adolf had accused Röhm of treason, there had been no trial. How had he got away with that? It was as if nothing Adolf did could shock the German people. They now accepted his will without question. Enveloped in the armour of his own self-belief, he simply shrugged everything off.

Leni felt her blood chill at the thought that Adolf had not only disposed of some seventy members of the 'Old Guard' but had also arrested Röhm personally. How could he have done that to one of his oldest friends? Could he do that to Leni, too, if she fell out of favour?

She had wanted to ask Adolf about the arrest when they had had dinner together two nights earlier, but when she had approached the subject indirectly, by asking about Röhm's replacement, Viktor Lutze, Adolf's glance had sliced through her and she had lost her nerve. A blue vein had throbbed at his temple and she had never before seen that burning look in his eyes. Albert, who had joined them, had flicked his fingernail at the crystal goblet from which he was drinking, to see if it rang. He had clearly meant it as the equivalent of a full stop.

'Enough about Röhm,' Leni said to herself now, with a nod of determination. What was done was done. Adolf must have acted in the Fatherland's best interests. He always did. As he kept saying, his only motivation was to make Germany great again. And though she did not want to admit it to herself, part of her willingness to put the former SA leader's death from her mind was self-interest. She felt relief that Adolf had subsequently ordered the destruction of every print of *The Victory of Faith*, the one in which the porcine Röhm had featured heavily. She did not want that film to be part of her legacy. It was unworthy of her talents. Except that Hitler had ordered that anyone caught with a copy was to be charged with treason. She thought about the illegal duplicate sitting in the storage room at the Ritz and bit her lip.

As she now saw the signal from her assistant director, she gripped her camera. The cage began to move. Adolf, Himmler and Lutze had returned to the grandstand after saluting the war memorial. Lutze and Himmler were about the same height and slim build, which made for a much more symmetrical shot than the previous year, when she had had to film 'Laurel and Hardy', as she thought of Adolf and Röhm, side by side.

Adolf was now ready to review the march-past. Leni focused her camera on his back and the cage she was in rose steadily above the multitude.

At twenty-five feet, as the whirring sound of the film blended with the hum of the pulleys, a profound sense of calm washed over her. Thanks in part to her, the choreography below looked not only meticulous but also beautiful, the ranks of flags parting like a biblical sea in front of the rostrum. Within the space of twelve months, the annual Party rally had gone from being a shambles to a precision-engineered machine. It was sublime. This shot will be my crowning glory, Leni thought. Film students will be analysing it a hundred years from now, perhaps a thousand, just as they will be studying Albert's architecture.

Over their dinner, Adolf had asked Albert to explain to Leni his concept of 'ruin value' – how he had been constructing the Zeppelinfeld grandstand in such a way that it would leave aesthetically pleasing ruins a thousand years in the future. Such ruins would be a testament to the greatness of the Third Reich, Albert had said as he sipped a fine

Burgundy. Like the ruins of Ancient Greece and Rome, they would last for thousands of years.

At this moment, one of the giant gilt eagles at the side of the grandstand came into Leni's line of sight. She looked down at the thousands of smaller eagles raised on standards below and the beauty of the scene was so transcendent she found her vision blurring. She was an eagle herself now, perched above the crowds on the Zeppelinfeld.

Her film would also be a record of Albert's masterpiece, before it became a ruin. The two of them were so alike. Neither interested in politics. Not really. Only art. She could trust him. In fact, she was considering taking him into her confidence about her future plans. She wanted to move to Hollywood, to join her old friend Marlene Dietrich. She had heard that American audiences could not get enough of Marlene's film *The Blue Angel* and that German actresses were all the rage there. As soon as she had edited *Triumph of the Will*, she would book herself a one-way passage. No more Adolf. No more Goebbels. No more Ministry of Propaganda.

She would miss Albert, of course. Perhaps she and Marlene could persuade him to come and visit them. As she filmed the marching columns below, she started humming Marlene's 'Falling in Love Again'.

She thought of the crew of five that had filmed the Fifth Party Congress. Now, one year on, her team was 170 strong, including cinematographers, lighting technicians and sound engineers, and she was their commander-in-chief. This film would go down in cinema history. It was her defining moment, a triumph not of Adolf Hitler's will but of Leni Riefenstahl's.

The thunder of the crowd below, a million Teutonic voices, arrived in a wave that made the air shudder. '*Sieg Heil! Sieg Heil! Sieg Heil!*'

The cage had reached 130 feet, almost the top of its climb, and it had begun vibrating in a way that it had not done in rehearsal. Was it the breeze? What if the pulleys snapped? Albert had calibrated their strength based on Leni's weight combined with that of the camera, but she realized now that he had not factored the tripod in as well. She chewed her lip. You cannot allow the vibrations to affect the shot, she thought. Not now. The skin of her knuckles went pale as she steadied the camera, hardly daring to breathe.

SIXTEEN

Although not signposted on the road, Dalton Hall was marked on the map that Kim had been following carefully since Merthyr Tydfil. A limestone gateway with round, lichen-covered pier caps and wrought-iron gates marked its entrance and then he was driving up an avenue of lime pollards with parkland on either side where small herds of fallow deer were grazing. He checked his watch. In her telegram Connie had been specific, which was unusual for her: 'WILL BE READY AT THREE STOP KEYS ON BACK TYRE STOP LONG TO SEE YOU STOP'.

Although the drive from London in Connie's open two-seater had taken eight hours, with the exhaust pipe complaining raspily whenever he accelerated, Kim was on time. He crossed a humpback bridge over the corner of a lake, drove past a boathouse and there it was. The hall stood on a balustraded terrace and had two wings and a central façade approached by a double flight of stone steps. Kim's first reaction was to put his foot on the brake pedal. He stopped the engine, took off his driving goggles and leather helmet and stared in awed silence. Did people really live in such places? Just one family? It seemed impossible.

He let out a whistle, shook his head, then checked his jacket pocket for the engagement ring. It looked like an emerald but was a cheap imitation he had found in a costume shop. Once he had put it on Connie's finger he would explain that he would buy her a real one later, as soon as he could afford it.

Kim had given his proposal a great deal of thought in the months Connie had been away, convalescing at Dalton Hall. Before the Blackshirt rally, he doubted she would have accepted it, but she might now. The injury had changed her, made her less frivolous, helped him see her more vulnerable side. In one of her letters she had written about how she appreciated his honesty in telling her about what had happened to his mother, about the poverty and hardship he had endured growing up. If anything, she had written, it had made her admire him even more.

There was only one secret that remained between them: Kim's Jewishness. He had wanted to tell Connie about it but every time he had tried he had heard in his head the occasional unthinking remarks she was given to making about Jews. He knew she didn't mean anything by them. He doubted that she had ever knowingly encountered a Jew. And yet the words had been spoken by her and listened to – without response – by him.

He started the engine again and saw a lone figure waving from one side of a large fountain. Once he had driven past a stable block and emerged at the front of the hall, Kim saw that the figure was Connie. There were two brown leather suitcases, a hatbox and a hamper at her feet, and she was wearing a knitted green twinset, along with her eyepatch. In another of her letters she had explained that although she had had a glass eye fitted, she had decided to carry on using the eyepatch because 'everyone thinks it suits me'. She had signed herself 'Pirate Connie'.

Kim could also see that she had let her hair grow since they last met – it was almost to her shoulders – and that, judging by her creamy skin, she had not spent much time outdoors. When he jumped out of the car and tried to hug her, Connie hunched her shoulders in awkward resistance, darting a glance up at the hall.

'You're looking well,' he said, feeling self-conscious now. He thought he could see someone standing at an upstairs window. 'How've you been?'

'Bored,' she said in a firm voice. 'Come on. Let's go.'

Kim had been hoping to have a rest after his long drive, as well as a cup of tea, but Connie had already got behind the wheel, so he loaded the cases into the pull-out rear luggage rack and strapped them on with rope. 'Should you be driving?' he asked. Even when her vision was perfect, she'd never given signals and had always blamed other drivers for her accidents.

'I'll be fine,' she said. 'I have to turn my head more than before, that's all.'

'Aren't you going to say goodbye to your family?'

'I've said my goodbyes. Now, let's get going before—' She checked herself.

'Before what?' Kim asked. He thought: Before someone sees me?

She seemed to read his mind. 'They're all away. Gone fishing in Scotland.'

Kim looked again at the window, but the figure had disappeared. Had it been a servant?

'My family have a place up there,' Connie continued. 'A cold and forbidding folly with turrets and gargoyles. It's the stuff of nightmares, frankly.' She put on a headscarf before pulling out the choke and trying the starter button. The engine remained silent. 'You've lost weight,' she said.

'I've been worried about you,' Kim said, leaning over to reach for the crank handle that was under the seat. In fact his weight loss was more a consequence of his intense training schedule. 'I wish you had let me visit,' he said as he walked to the front of the car, bent down to insert the handle and gave it a turn. The engine came throatily to life.

'I've missed my little car so much,' Connie shouted above the noise of its pistons and cylinders.

'And I've missed you,' Kim yelled back, lowering himself into the passenger seat.

She touched her eyepatch and asked: 'Do you think me monstrous?'

'You know I don't.'

'What have you been getting up to while I've been away?' Connie was now revving the engine more than was necessary. When she let out the clutch the car lurched forward.

'Training mostly,' he shouted. 'I bumped into Alun the other day. Sends his regards. Said he didn't have any luck tracking down that news footage of the rally.'

'Oh, well, it was jolly kind of him to try.'

Narrowly escaping collision with a delivery boy who was pedalling quietly towards the house, Connie honked her horn.

'I'm famished,' she said. 'I asked Cook to make us a picnic.' Connie nodded towards the hamper in the back seat, taking her eye off the road again. 'You hungry?'

As they crossed the stone bridge, she tried to reach back into the hamper and the car swerved off the road, narrowly missing one tree and heading straight for another before she pulled the handbrake violently, causing the engine to stall.

In the buzzing silence that followed, time seemed to slow and Kim became aware of the lazy droning of insects. He flicked back the lock of hair that had fallen over his eyes. As he did so, he directed a smile at Connie, who took a deep breath, blew out her cheeks and exhaled loudly before emitting a short laugh.

'Perhaps I should drive,' Kim said.

'Perhaps you should.'

He felt in his pocket for the ring, but did not take it out. 'This may not seem like the best moment to ask,' he said.

'Ask what?'

'We're happy together, aren't we?'

Further conversation was curtailed by Connie suddenly looping her arms around his neck. Her delicate scent – something like a mixture of lavender water, trampled thyme and freshly cooked bread – crowded his senses, overpowering the smell of engine oil and cut grass. And then she was pressing her lips to his. Her kisses were deep and feverish. Feeling light-headed, Kim pulled her towards him and ran his hands under her skirt. Her skin was as soft and cool, sending a tingle down his shoulders and arms as if he were caught in a smooth ocean swell.

Connie moved over and within a few fumbling seconds, he was inside her. The sudden heat of her body made him shudder.

Connie gasped at the same yielding moment. 'Do you still love me?' she said.

'Yes,' Kim said, his breath ragged. 'More than ever.'

In that moment, he realized that in all the time he had known her, Connie had never said those words to him.

SEVENTEEN

Winter, 1935. Munich

Tiny white flakes eddied in the morning air before settling on Leni's wolf-fur coat, another of Adolf's gifts. With a lit cigarette between the middle and ring finger of her gloved hand, she gathered the collar tighter around her neck and looked up at Prinzregentenplatz 16, an imposing nineteenth-century apartment block on the corner of a cobbled square.

She thought she could see Adolf standing in front of a glass door that opened on to a second-floor balcony. It was either him or someone impersonating him: waving his arms as if he were conducting an orchestra. No doubt he was practising his oratory, seeing how his clenched fists and flailing arms looked when reflected in the glass.

Leni had been in her villa in the Grunewald, packing her skiing clothes for Davos, when the summons came. Munich was on her way, or at least not that far out of her way, and as she had driven through the night she had thought about how she had grown to hate Christmas. Why did her fellow countrymen always have to make such a fuss about it? So many rituals, candles and mawkish carols.

Not that it was those things that bothered her especially. The reason she disliked Christmas was that it was a celebration of giving birth. To be a childless woman in her thirties at Christmas was to feel like an outcast. It was to have an unwelcome reminder of her shortcomings as an adult – because being an adult, at least to people like Magda, meant having a family of one's own. This was why Leni always liked to go skiing at Christmas. It was a distraction.

Adolf appeared to be wearing a dressing gown, which didn't seem like something he would want to be seen in, even if he did like to rise late. As she checked her watch, Leni could almost feel her bones cracking with the cold. The Führer had asked to see her at ten and she was early for once, hoping she could keep this visit short and continue with her drive to Davos before the snowfall became too heavy.

She put her cigarette in her mouth, then bent down, made a snowball and threw it up at the window to get his attention. It fell short. Nevertheless, Adolf stopped his wild gesturing and looked down at her, his arms drawn up to rest on his chest, fists touching. Remembering her boss's disapproval of smoking, she flicked her cigarette away before wafting a hesitant hand. She realized she was breathing quickly and, despite the cold, perspiring. Adolf always had this effect on her.

No, that was not quite true. There were times when she felt completely safe with him, at home, protected from the world. Not only that, there were times when she felt adored, as if she were the only woman in Germany, in the world, who mattered to him. He had once sent her a dozen red roses. From any other man, it would have appeared a crudely sentimental gesture. From him, it had seemed strangely dignified and tender, because it was so out of character.

What could she say? The man was full of surprises. He was not to know she couldn't stand flowers. She had given them to her maid to take home.

Questions were circulating in her head now. Why did Adolf want to see her? Was he planning a seduction? Or, worse, what if he was intending to break his promise that he would not commission her to do any more films for the Party?

With the snow making a crumping noise as it compacted under her boots, Leni walked up to a guard box marked with chevrons. The member of the Ordnungspolizei inside it, a fat-lipped man with a brass gorget around his neck, nodded to show she was expected. As she climbed the stairs – the apartment sprawled over nine rooms and took up the entire second floor – she stamped to get the snow off her boots and recalled the first time she had met Adolf.

It was back in 1932. He had asked to see her. She, feeling intrigued, had agreed and had caught a train to the coast, where Adolf was attending a Party rally. They had walked along a beach by the North Sea together, with a couple of his adjutants following at a discreet distance. The sea was calm, the air warm, and they had talked like old friends. When he told her his nickname was 'Herr Wolf', because the name Adolf was derived from the Old German for wolf, she wondered if that was true. Did people really call him that nickname or did he just want them to? He also said he had seen all her films and had especially enjoyed *The Blue Light*. She had said, as was her habit, that she had no interest in politics, only in art, and could never become a member of the Nazi Party, but that she had seen him give a speech in Berlin and had found it 'thrilling'. He had called her his 'muse' and his 'she-wolf' and had said: 'I wish everyone around me would be as uninhibited as you.'

Adolf had then gone off to his rally and later returned to the inn where Leni and the rest of his entourage were staying. After dinner, he had invited her for another stroll on the beach and this time the two adjutants had not accompanied them. At one point he had stopped and looked at her for a long time before slowly putting his arm around her and drawing her towards him. When she had not reciprocated, he had let go, turned away and said: 'No, I cannot allow myself to fall in love, not until my work for the Fatherland is completed.' Out of pride, it seemed, he had tried to make it look as if he were the one who had rejected her advances.

Much had happened since then. The balance of power between them had shifted. He had become a god to the German people, thanks in part to the way Leni had immortalized him on film. Would she still have the nerve to resist him if he tried to woo her now?

The door was opened by Adolf's housekeeper. She took Leni's coat and led the way along a dark corridor that was filled with the smell of furniture polish. As they walked, Leni could sense there were other people behind the closed doors: Adolf's usual retinue of bodyguards, personal physicians and secretaries. Yet the apartment seemed eerily silent.

Leni was shown into a drawing room and asked to wait. The memory of what had happened to Röhm still haunted her, and she could not think of Adolf without a flutter of nerves in her chest. But when she saw some half-eaten cream cake on a side table – his favourite food – she relaxed a little. She remembered now that she had bought him a large bar of Toblerone as a Christmas present but had left it in the car. There was a Christmas tree, which, in accordance with the latest Party decree, was topped with a swastika rather than a star or a fairy.

The fire in the grate had been laid but not lit. Above the fireplace was a large painting by an artist Leni knew well, Adolf Ziegler, whose nickname was 'the master of German pubic hair'. This piece was typical of his work: a triptych depicting four blonde naked women in various poses, two in the middle panel and one on each side panel.

The decoration of the apartment, along with the furnishing, followed the German heroic colour scheme of blue, gold and white, as favoured by Wagner in his operas. On the large bookcase she noticed the eight-volume first edition of the works of the philosopher Johann Gottlieb Fichte that she had given Adolf for his birthday. She took down volume one and reread the inscription she had penned: 'To my dear Adolf, with deepest devotion, Leni'. She replaced it and, seeing volume five was missing, looked around. At the end of the bookcase was a model of the Reich Chancellery that Albert was proposing to build in Berlin. Next to this, on a round table with a lace cloth, was a moustache brush and the missing book on which Adolf's reading glasses were resting. She picked it up and, marking his place with her finger, flicked through and saw that he had covered the text in a blizzard of underlinings, exclamation marks and marginalia. Had she been summoned so that they could discuss the book?

Putting it back as she had found it, she looked around again. As well as the hundreds of books on the shelves, there were, on various other tables and surfaces in this high-ceilinged drawing room, further neat piles of books. It was as if Adolf needed them to be within reach at all times, lifebuoys to a nervous swimmer.

Next to an uncomfortable-looking wooden chair, there was a wind-up gramophone. When Leni walked over to it she was surprised to see the name on the label of the 78 rpm was not that of Wagner, the tedious, self-important Teuton, but Mahler, the artistically sensitive

Semite. What else did Adolf do in private that he railed against in public? she wondered. Drink beer? Hunt foxes?

The colours in the room sharpened, the air grew thicker and Adolf came through the door wearing a navy-blue smoking jacket. She realized that this, rather than a dressing gown, was what he had been wearing when she saw him at the window. Instead of smiling, he acknowledged Leni with a nod. He was accompanied by two German shepherd dogs. They ignored Leni and went to lie down on the hearthrug.

'My dear Adolf,' she said as she offered both her hands.

He took them in his and raised the left one to his lips. 'Thank you for coming at short notice, Leni,' he said solemnly. 'Sorry about my cold.'

'Merry Christmas,' she said (and thought: Now I will have caught his cold in time for my skiing. Lucky me).

'Of course,' he said in a dry, whispering voice. 'It's today, isn't it? Merry Christmas. Magda gave me this.' He stroked the velvet sleeve of his jacket. 'I opened it this morning, but I'm not sure about it.'

Leni considered saying that it made him look like an English aristocrat, but thought better of it. 'It becomes you,' she said, flicking some imaginary dust from the lapel before tilting her head. 'Magda has exquisite taste.'

'It feels tight around the shoulders.'

'Just needs wearing in a bit.' Leni felt relieved now that she had left the chocolate bar in the car. She would have to get him a more impressive present.

'I was early for once,' she said, 'thanks to my alarm clock.'

The day after she had been late for her own premiere, a lavish affair organized by Adolf to mark the release of *Day of Freedom*, a Meissen porcelain alarm clock had been delivered to her house. It had been a good joke, but although he gave a cautious smile, there was an air of melancholy about him today.

'As you can see, I set little store by comfort or property,' he said, 'as long as I have my gramophone records and my library. I wish I had more time to read.' He interrupted himself to offer her a drink. 'Forgive my manners.'

Leni considered asking for a strong martini but, remembering the time, and his – alleged – views on drinking, she asked for apple juice instead.

As she sipped it, she studied his bookshelf. 'Who is your favourite?'

He seemed pleased to be asked, confirming a rumour Leni had heard that the corporal turned 'philosopher Führer' felt insecure about his lack of a formal university education. 'Schopenhauer.'

'Not Nietzsche?'

Another twitch of a smile. 'No, he's more of a poet than a philosopher. He writes perhaps the most beautiful prose to be found in German literature, but he does not inspire me in the way that Schopenhauer does. Schopenhauer believed in the will to power but did not approve of revolutionaries. In fact, he once offered his opera glasses for use as a rifle sight to guardsmen firing on protesters. I read him every night, even if I go to bed very late.'

Apparently noticing that the fire was not lit, Adolf got down on his knees and struck a match. There were two cracked circles in the soles of his shoes, where the leather had partially worn away.

'I don't spend much time here any more,' he said.

'Do you not?'

As he reached for some bellows to his left, he briefly broke wind. It was so unobtrusive a sound that Leni wondered if she might have imagined it, but then decided she hadn't. His flatulence was, after all, the subject of much speculation around the Reichstag – a consequence, it was rumoured, of his vegetarian diet.

'No,' he answered. 'I am always either in Berlin or at the Berghof. But I like to spend Christmas here, out of remembrance.'

'Of?'

But he seemed not to hear, or chose not to. She knew the answer anyway.

Leni stared again at the two worn circles on the soles of his shoes. They were like eyes. The sad eyes of old people, with crow's feet.

She tried again. 'How did you spend yesterday?'

His shoulders dropped and he spoke slowly, with sadness in his voice. 'I had my chauffeur drive me around, along highways and through villages, until I became tired. I do that every Christmas Eve.' Pause. 'I have no family.' Another pause. 'I am lonely.' He patted the head of his dog, then stood up and fed it a slice of cream cake. 'My dogs are my companions.' He looked at one of them and added: 'Aren't you? My only companions? Yes, you are.'

Leni wondered if this was a cue. Did he want to tell her about Eva Braun, 'the secretary'? She had heard that it was Magda's job to keep Eva out of the public eye, but everyone in Adolf's inner circle knew about her, even if they had not met her.

'I would have thought you did not lack for female companionship,' Leni said carefully.

'I'm married to Germany.'

'A wife might—'

He interrupted. 'It would be irresponsible of me to bind a woman to marriage.'

'Why?'

'What would she get from me?' Adolf said. 'She would have to be alone most of the time.'

'Would you not like to have children?'

The question seemed to make him uncomfortable and he checked his parting, smoothing it down. 'If I had children they would have to live up to me, and what would become of them if fate should turn against me?' He moved to the window and contemplated the snowy scene below. He then turned and, giving Leni a searching look, asked: 'What about you? What are your plans?'

Leni hesitated. Around Adolf there were always pockets of awed silence, but this felt more like the pressure that builds in the ears during a flight. 'I too am married to Germany,' she said.

'I meant in terms of your work.'

Her stomach lurched. 'Has Dr Goebbels not told you?'

Adolf shook his head slowly.

That snake, Leni thought. Goebbels had promised to keep Adolf informed. Well, two could play at that game. 'I've been invited by the International Olympic Committee to make a film about the Berlin Games. I agreed on the condition that the film would be independent.'

'Independent?'

'Independent in the sense of being free from interference from the Minister of Propaganda.' Minister not Ministry. She arched her eyebrows to show that she had chosen her word carefully.

Adolf seemed surprised. 'But I thought you didn't want to make any more documentaries; that you only wanted to be an actress from now on.'

'That is true,' she said, looking around for somewhere to set down her glass, 'and this will definitely be my last.'

'Do you still dance?' Adolf asked. 'I saw one of your moving pictures. You were dancing by the sea.'

This surprised her. In *The Holy Mountain*, the film to which he was alluding, she was wreathed in diaphanous veils of chiffon, dancing on a rock before crashing waves. What would Adolf have made of that? Did he find it exciting? Erotic?

'No,' she said. 'I injured my knee. The only exercise I do nowadays is skiing, with a brace, and, when I get the chance, mountaineering. How about you?'

'I enjoy walking,' he said with a half-smile. 'When I get the chance.'

'Are you looking forward to the winter Olympics?'

'Not particularly.' Adolf gave a dismissive waft of his hand.

'What about the summer ones?'

'I'd rather stay away.'

'Really? Why?'

'We have no chance of winning medals. The Americans will win most of them and I won't enjoy watching that.' He smiled, causing dimples to appear in his cheeks. She always found his smile disarming but it was his eyes that beguiled her. They were pale blue, almost grey, and when they were fixed on her she could not look away.

'But do not be discouraged,' he said. 'You are sure to make a good film. I have every confidence in you.'

'I'm surprised Dr Goebbels didn't mention it,' Leni said. Then, reading the moment and taking a chance, she added: 'He's always trying to undermine me.'

'Can a man who laughs as heartily as the doctor be so bad?' He answered his own question: 'No, a man who laughs like that cannot be so bad.'

'Just because someone laughs a great deal, it doesn't mean they have a sense of humour,' Leni replied.

Adolf was staring at the record on his gramophone.

'What have you been listening to?' Leni said.

He looked at her thoughtfully and said: 'I think you know that, do you not? I think you had a peek before I came in.'

Had he been watching her through the keyhole before he entered the room? She could feel the colour rising in her cheeks.

'I once saw Mahler conduct in Vienna,' Adolf said. 'When I was a young man. He had an extraordinary style. Most theatrical.'

Leni wondered whether it was Mahler who had inspired Adolf's own extraordinary style, when he was making his speeches. He was looking distracted, though, so Leni took this as her cue to leave.

'Anyway, Adolf,' she said, 'I should get going or the road up the mountain will be blocked.'

'Do you have to?'

For an instant, as he wrapped one arm around his upper body, he looked vulnerable, almost shy. Leni had never seen him like this before. Seeming to sense this dropping of his guard, he checked his hair parting once more, then squared his shoulders and cleared his throat with a cough. 'Before you go, there's something I want to show you,' he said. He led her down a corridor to a locked door, which he opened using a key from his pocket. In an alcove was a bronze bust of a girl on a marble plinth, decked with wilted flowers.

'I told you I would never marry,' he said, gesturing towards the bust. 'But there was someone.'

'Who is she?' Leni reached towards the bust, but then stopped herself. She knew perfectly well who it was: Adolf's niece Geli, the young woman in whose memory he returned to Munich each Christmas.

From Albert, Leni had heard all about Adolf's relationship with Geli, the daughter of his half-sister: how he had been so possessive of her that he had followed her whenever she went to the shops; how he had fired a chauffeur he thought she was sleeping with.

'She shot herself in this very room,' Adolf said, folding then unfolding his arms. 'Using my pistol.'

'I didn't know that,' Leni lied. She had heard that he was in Nuremberg at the time and had rushed back. He had been inconsolable and had shut himself away in this room for a week. The only member of the Nazi leadership he had invited to the funeral was Röhm. That was how close the two men had been.

'Four years ago.' His eyes were wet now, though the tears did not spill. 'I've kept the room as she left it.'

Leni took his hand and squeezed it. He covered hers with his and they remained like this, facing one another, for a full minute before she broke the silence: 'You mustn't blame yourself.'

'But I do.'

She held his hand to her cheek for a moment and, feeling a rush of tenderness, kissed his knuckles. 'I really do have to go,' she said.

'I understand,' he replied, withdrawing his hand. He turned away from her, walked to the window and stared out at the whirling snow.

EIGHTEEN

Spring, 1936. London

Although almost two years had passed since Connie lost her eye, she had yet to regain her social confidence. That, at least, was Kim's impression. She never seemed to want to meet any of their friends, apart from Alun whom she had seemingly come to depend upon as a conduit to the outside world. He was always running errands for her, or dropping by with books for her to read, or joining them when they visited museums or went to the pictures. But Kim worried that when he was training, which was most nights, and Alun was working late or attending meetings at the Black House, Connie was sitting at home on her own.

In an effort to help her, Kim had accepted on her behalf one of the stiff white invitation cards that filled her chimneypiece. She had said she would only go if he came with her, so here he was, in a dinner jacket she had paid for, with a cocktail glass in each hand, one for her, one for John, the friend Connie had gone off to look for when they arrived.

The townhouse in Belgravia where the party was being held had several large rooms leading off an equally large central hall dominated by a wide staircase. A jazz band was playing somewhere on the ground floor and Kim tried not to spill the cocktails as he navigated a path through the crowd towards the sound. Some of the guests were wearing masks over their eyes while others were dancing in a frenetic style Kim had never witnessed before.

He returned to the hall to see if he could locate Connie, but could not see her there. It didn't help that she had come dressed like a man, wearing white tie and tails, because several of the female guests had done the same. Marlene Dietrich had a lot to answer for.

Some of the guests who were dressed as women were, upon closer inspection, men with painted faces. Around their necks were strings of pearls and feather boas; between their fingers, long cigarette holders. Kim, whose acquaintance with bohemia was limited, had never seen anything like it.

'Haven't seen her, have you?'

Kim lowered his gaze and was surprised to see that it was Alun who had spoken.

'Connie asked me to come along,' Alun added, anticipating Kim's question. 'Said you would need moral support.' He was leaning in close and shouting to be heard above the raucous laughter and music. 'I don't know anyone here, do you?'

'You'd better have this,' Kim said, handing Alun one of the cocktail glasses. 'I hate parties,' he added. 'I only came because I'm worried about Connie. She used to come to these things all the time . . .'

Alun took a sip and grimaced. 'Whose house is this?'

'The invitation said Guy Milford-Hamilton. No idea who he is.'

'There's a man in there wearing a fez.' Alun pointed at one of the adjoining rooms. 'I think he might be a waiter because he was walking around with a tray full of small eggs. Said they were plover's eggs.'

'Did you try one?'

Alun shook his head and then did a double take. Kim followed his line of sight. A young woman with a chin-length bob was being carried through the crowd on a chair born aloft by four men. She was wearing a revealingly low-cut, backless gown and had in her arms a small black pug dog with a diamond necklace for a collar. A shirtless man was walking behind them, holding a feathered parasol over her head.

'Perhaps it's for the best.' Kim ran a finger around his collar. 'The plover's egg, I mean.' He watched the procession disappear into the next room then added: 'Bloody hot in here. Do you feel hot? Let's go upstairs. See if we can find somewhere less crowded.'

As Kim led the way, weaving between the guests sitting on the stairs, he saw that some of the women dressed as men were sniffing small mounds of white powder off their knuckles. He did not check to see if Alun was following; he knew he would be, like a shadow. Kim did not really mind because whenever Alun turned up he usually had something interesting to say, even if he did use words that Kim didn't fully understand.

Upstairs, they found a library with strange Eastern statues on tables and half a dozen guests sitting on silk cushions and divans on the floor. In the corner on his own was a bald man wearing a silk kimono and smoking from a hookah pipe that gurgled and bubbled. Kim thought he recognized him from the Black House.

They were joined by a young, slim-hipped woman who had sad, hooded eyes, an Eton crop and a cool and distant beauty. She was wearing a monocle, a white scarf and a black top hat. 'Isn't this the dullest party ever?' she said. Kim had learned from Connie that when fashionable young aristocrats said things were dull they didn't necessarily mean it. It was more an affectation, an attempt to appear bored and world-weary.

The woman pressed a finger to her lips and whispered: 'Did you see who was downstairs?'

Kim shook his head.

'Charles Lindbergh.' Her vowels were so soft and elongated, Kim had to replay the words in his head before they registered properly. 'Everyone was making such a fuss of him.'

'Who is this Guy Milford-Hamilton?' Alun asked suddenly.

'I love that voice.' The woman peered at Alun through her monocle. 'Do it again.'

'It's not a voice,' Kim said. 'He's Welsh.'

'Oh, I do apologize,' she said. 'You must think me terribly rude.'

Alun drew himself up. 'What does Guy Milford-Hamilton do exactly?'

'Miffy? He doesn't do anything.'

'How can he afford to live in this big house, then?'

'Belongs to his parents,' she said. 'They're away in Rhodesia. Are you being followed?'

Alun ground his teeth. 'What do you mean?'

'Connie was telling me that she seems to be followed everywhere she goes these days. She thinks it's because she was a Blackshirt. She's under. . .' The woman was struggling with the word.

'Surveillance,' Alun helped.

'That's the chap.'

'You know Connie?' Kim asked.

'Course I do,' the woman said. 'She's my oldest friend. We do everything together.'

'I'm Kim.' When the woman looked blank, he added: 'Kim Newlands?'

'Kim and Connie are courting,' Alun interjected.

The woman laughed at this. 'Oh, you're *him*. She said she'd met a fine, strapping young fellow from the . . .' She didn't finish the sentence and Kim wondered if her hesitation meant that Connie had described him as being from the lower orders.

'I'm John, by the way,' the woman said, holding out her hand. Kim was unsure whether he was supposed to shake it or kiss it. When he kissed it, 'John' made a snorting noise that sounded like a snigger.

'You're called John?' Alun asked.

'It's what everyone calls me. My real name is so boring you would faint.'

Kim handed her the other cocktail glass he had been holding. 'This is for you,' he said. 'In answer to your question: yes, we are followed everywhere. Men in plain clothes. Connie always shouts "goodnight" to them when we reach her house.'

'Well, it won't be MI5,' Alun said with a wink. 'They're too busy trying to infiltrate the Communist Party to bother with us Blackshirts.'

'If you see Connie, tell her we need her to make up the numbers,' John said, tapping Kim on the shoulder. 'We're going to hold a séance. She was hilarious at the last one. You should come too. We need more men. Thanks for the drink.'

When John went back downstairs, Kim opened a French window that led on to a balcony overlooking the square. Once outside, he felt in his jacket for the Fabergé cigarette case that Connie had bought him and, opening it, offered one to Alun.

'Thought athletes weren't supposed to smoke,' Alun said as he took one, lit it and exhaled a blue cloud of smoke into the night air.

'I don't,' Kim said, feeling put out by his encounter with, apparently, Connie's oldest friend. Why had they never been introduced? 'The case was a present from Connie. I keep it filled with her brand. Cork-tipped Craven's.' He was talking through a smile in the measured way the speech lady had taught him. She used to say it would help him cope with stress. 'Actually I know plenty of athletes who smoke,' he added. 'There's one sprinter who always hands his half-smoked gasper to the starting official before a race and then goes back to collect it at the end. Says these little courtesies "distinguish the gentleman".'

'Think you'll win any medals in Berlin, then?' Alun asked.

'Maybe,' Kim said. 'If I'm lucky.'

'Is Sir Oswald going?'

'No idea.'

'There's a rumour going around the Black House that he and the King are planning to go together. Have you heard anything?'

Kim shook his head. 'Won't the King be busy making plans for his coronation?'

'I've heard he wants to meet all his fellow heads of state before the coronation, especially Herr Hitler.'

'That's news to me.'

'You might get to meet the Führer too,' Alun said, 'if you win a gold.'

'The odds of my doing that have dropped considerably now that Jesse Owens has said he won't be joining the boycott. The Americans call him the Buckeye Bullet. Last year he set four world records, even though he had a back injury. Two of them were in my disciplines.'

'I don't suppose the Führer will be too thrilled if a Negro wins,' Alun said. 'You'd better win on behalf of the Aryan race.'

'I'll be competing for King and country. And for Connie.'

'Anyone from the British team considering joining in the boycott?'

Kim gave Alun a sideways glance. He sometimes got the impression that his Welsh friend was testing him. Had he been sent by Sir Oswald to check on his 'investment'?

'I don't know about the others, but I definitely still want to go to Berlin,' he said carefully. He then smiled as he imagined himself being presented with a gold medal by Hitler before turning to the assembled reporters from the world's press and announcing that he was Jewish.

He had been feeling uneasy lately about the Party's apparently changing attitude towards Jews. There hadn't been anything specific, more a sense that some senior Party members were now only pretending to be tolerant. Even Mosley had started making references to 'Jewish interests' in his speeches. Am I being a hypocrite in accepting BUF money? Kim wondered. Perhaps. But then what choice do I have?

'Anyway,' he said to Alun, 'I can't join the boycott because the BUF would withdraw my bursary. And they might demand that I return the payments I've already received.'

'I've been meaning to ask you about that,' Alun said. 'Are you sure it's allowed?'

'What do you mean?'

'I mean, don't you have to be an amateur to compete in the Olympics?'

'Of course.'

'So doesn't accepting sponsorship money from the BUF make you a professional?'

'It's not sponsorship. They've looked into it. It's more like an allowance. All above board.'

Alun gave his cocktail glass a thoughtful swirl.

'Look,' Kim said. 'You know me. I'm not very political.'

'Everyone is political. Life is political.'

'What I mean is, I don't have your education.'

'Let me teach you about politics. I think you'll find it fascinating. I really do.'

Kim thought for a moment and then offered his hand. 'Deal,' he said. 'What can I teach you about in return? Sport?'

Alun lowered his head. 'I'd rather you taught me about women.'

Kim laughed. 'What's there to teach? Just be yourself.'

'That's easy for you to say. They swoon whenever you walk into a room.' Alun shook his head. 'I've never felt comfortable around them. What did you make of Lady Witherington-Scornforth, then?'

'Who?'

'John.'

'I really don't know.' Kim said this with a laughter-edged voice. He was feeling grateful for the company of his inscrutable friend. He was sure they were the only two men at the party who did not own a top hat and a pair of Purdey shotguns – though he imagined that Alun had probably assumed he was on his own in that regard.

Kim checked his watch. It was a Cartier Tank with a rectangular face and a leather strap and it had come in a Harrods bag tied with a silk ribbon. Connie had given it to him as a birthday present and at first, when he realized it was made from eighteen-carat gold and wasn't just gold-plated, he had refused to accept it, but then she had shown him the initials inscribed on the back – his. 'It's a magic watch,' she had said, 'because whenever you look at it you will think of me.' And it was true, he did, although he had no need of a prompt. Connie was always at the front of his mind and whenever his limbs ached in training he pushed himself on with the incantation: 'Do it for Connie.' It had dawned on him recently that he could no longer imagine life without her.

The balcony was level with the branches of the trees in the square. One was a horse chestnut and white pyramids were starting to appear on its branches. Through narrowed eyes, Kim noticed a couple on a garden bench below. They seemed to be engrossed in each other's company, sharing a moment of intimacy away from the crowd. The woman was leaning forward to allow the young man to light her cigarette. When she leaned back and blew a puff of smoke out into the air, he saw that it was Connie.

NINETEEN

'You know your problem,' Alun said as he moved his rook down the board. 'You still don't know the difference between a tactic and a strategy.'

'What is the difference, then?' Herzl said, staring at the board.

'This.' Alun placed his finger on the crown of Herzl's king before toppling it over.

'Hey,' Herzl said. 'We haven't finished.'

'Yes, we have,' Alun said. 'It's checkmate.'

'Why didn't you say "checkmate", then?'

'Because I thought it was obvious, even to a donkey like you.' Alun looked out of the café window at an ashen London sky.

'Off to see your friend Newlands, then?' Herzl said.

Alun had been seeing a lot of Kim lately, Connie too, tagging along when the couple went to the pub or on a walk in the park. When he had offered to accompany Connie on her trips to a private practice in Harley Street, one that specialized in eye trauma, the couple had seemed grateful. Kim was often too busy either working or training and Connie seemed to appreciate the company. They didn't seem to question his friendship and, in truth, he had grown quite fond of them, especially Connie.

In fact, he had been spending more time with the couple than he had been spending at the Black House, partly because Kim rarely went there – preferring to train at White City – and partly because the BUF leadership tended to have their meetings behind closed doors and most of the information Alun gleaned from the ordinary members was nothing more than tittle-tattle. He also felt nervous each time he went there. Although – so far – none of the thugs who had attacked him so savagely in the dark that night at Olympia had identified him as an imposter, Alun knew he had to avoid attracting suspicion.

'Has Kim worked out you're not a fascist yet?' Herzl asked.

'Apparently not.'

'What about me?' Herzl said. 'Does he know I'm a communist?'

'I imagine so. You're far too scruffy to be a fascist. Also I told him you were a communist and that I'd befriended you in order to turn you. He thinks you're an informer.'

'Clever,' Herzl said. 'Was that a tactic or a strategy?'

The tactics or strategy question was a recurring theme. They had decided between them that Alun was using a tactic in exploiting his friendship with Kim in order to gather intelligence, but that what he was planning next would be a strategy. The BUF had been presenting Kim as their poster boy. The Amateur Athletic Association seemed to have no objection to this, but they might be interested to know that the BUF was sponsoring him. And how would it look if the press got hold of the story? It was all a question of timing. If he was right, the BUF's poster boy could be exposed as a cheat.

'Don't you feel sorry for him?' Herzl said. 'He's been training hard all his life for this and you're going to ruin it for him.'

'Would you rather the headlines read: "Blackshirt athlete wins Olympic gold!"?'

'No, but . . .'

'No but nothing. He picked the wrong side.'

'But he trusts you. And you said you liked him.'

'I do like him, but as Marx said, "The last capitalist we hang shall be the one who sold us the rope."'

'You're a cold one, you are.'

'Look, aristos like Kim have been exploiting our lot for years. Grinding us down, keeping us in poverty and degradation. It has to stop.' Alun tapped the table. 'And the end justifies the means. Always. One day, Comrade Herzl, I'm going to take you to Wales and show you where I grew up. You would be appalled. People who have no hope. No dignity. It doesn't have to be that way.'

'Here,' Herzl said, 'talking of the coming workers' paradise, you'll like this one. A man goes into a shop in Moscow, looks around the empty shelves and says to the assistant: "I see you have no bread." "No, comrade," comes the reply. "We have no fish. The shop with no bread is next door."'

'That's funny,' Alun said without smiling. 'Anyway, when Kim goes to Berlin, I'm going too.'

Herzl nodded in a philosophical way that was clearly intended to amuse. 'That's nice. What will you be competing in, then? The men's freestyle overthrow? The shot putsch?'

Alun ignored him. 'The rumour going around the Black House is that Mosley wants to attend the Games.' Alun leaned across the table and whispered: 'And guess who else . . . King Edward. He's desperate to have a meeting with his hero the Führer. I'm going to get myself invited to as many social functions in Berlin as I can. Keep my ears and eyes open. See if I can dig up some concrete evidence that Harry can use.'

'Are we paying for your trip, then?'

'No, Connie is paying.'

'Connie the one-eyed fascist?'

Alun winced. 'Don't call her that.'

'What would you like me to call her? Connie the one-eyed class enemy?'

Alun lowered his gaze. 'Connie isn't like that. She's all right. And don't keep going on about her eye. How would you like it if you lost an eye?'

Herzl raised his arms in mock surrender. 'Sorry. So why is she paying for you?'

'Because she doesn't want to travel on her own.'

Herzl gave Alun a chafed look. 'What about her boyfriend?'

'Kim is travelling with the Olympic team.'

'Doesn't she have any female friends she can travel with?'

'There's one who calls herself "John", but she's "summering in Cap Ferrat".'

'I have to say, Alun, your capitalist friends sound like a funny lot.'

'They are not my friends.' But that was only half true. Alun now considered Connie to be a close friend, and he was increasingly sure that was how she regarded him too.

'Doesn't she have a maid or something?' Herzl continued, interrupting his thoughts. 'A lady-in-waiting?'

'They don't count. She wants engaging company.'

'And you are engaging company, are you? Will she be expecting you to iron her copy of *The Times* before you bring it to her every morning? Warm her solid-gold lavatory seat before she pays a visit?'

'Shut up.' Alun stood, put on his coat, then checked the doorways opposite to see if there was anyone who looked like a Special Branch officer waiting to follow him. He had missed his encounters with Herzl and it made him want to linger. 'Do you think she's attractive?' he asked hesitantly.

'Who? Connie? I suppose so. If you like that English rose sort.'

'She still doesn't know it was me who blinded her,' Alun said.

'Best to keep it that way, I'd say. Women are funny about that sort of thing.' Herzl seemed to sense that Alun had more to say. 'You're not just going after Kim Newlands to get him out of the picture, are you?'

'Course not.'

'So you haven't fallen for this Connie girl, then?'

Alun avoided his question. 'I'd always imagined I'd meet a nice communist girl one day,' he said. 'Though obviously not one who was too nice. A blousy redhead, perhaps, who had no time for bourgeois morality and considered it her revolutionary duty to deflower me.'

'Me too,' Herzl said, a faraway look in his eyes. 'I figured my best chance was to meet a buxom Jewish girl who found the prospect of a socialist insurrection arousing.'

What Alun was about to say next would, he knew, sound sarcastic to his friend, and this was probably as well. 'I think it was providence that I injured her,' he said. 'I think it brought us together.'

'You think she might be secretly in love with you?'

'No, but whenever I look at her, my chest hurts.'

PART THREE

TWENTY

Summer, 1936

Amid a fanfare of skirling bagpipes, Kim and his team-mates stood waving behind a rope on the platform at Liverpool Street Station. About a hundred well-wishers, most of them holding small paper Union flags, had turned out to see the team off, and, among them, somewhere, would be Connie. As clouds of steam billowed around them, Kim shouldered his kitbag and climbed on to the step of the locomotive to get a better view.

He was wearing the blue British team blazer, white flannels and, at what he hoped was a jaunty angle, a straw boater. He had worn this uniform, as well as his Olympic tie, when he had gone to visit his mother's grave in Southsea two days earlier. He had talked to her headstone for half an hour, promising her that he was going to try his hardest to bring back some medals from Berlin. He had also confessed to her that he still hadn't summoned the courage to present Connie with the engagement ring he had bought. 'Somehow I never seem to find the right moment.'

As he recalled this now, he scanned the sea of ladies' bonnets before him. And there she was, about fifty yards away, easy to spot because of her eyepatch. She was waving a handkerchief and standing on something and when she saw that Kim had noticed her, she tapped Alun on the shoulder. Being lower than her, Alun had to remove his cap and wave it to be seen. Kim felt grateful that he was accompanying Connie on this trip to Berlin. He would look after her. Keep her safe.

The three of them had arranged to meet up at the Adlon Hotel the day after the opening ceremony.

At 8.30 p.m., the train's steam whistle sounded, giving Kim a rush of adrenaline. As he and the rest of the team climbed on board, a cheer rose from the crowd and then the pistons began to turn.

The air of excitement among the athletes was palpable as the train clattered out of London. While some gossiped and laughed, others arm-wrestled, played cards or threw dice. Kim found himself cringing when some mocked the Nazis who were soon to be their hosts. He was reasonably sure that few if any of his team-mates knew about his BUF connection, and he had tried to keep it that way.

The journey to Harwich seemed to take minutes rather than hours and it was not until Kim was on the ferry, standing at the stern listening to the squawk of seagulls as they circled overhead, that he had time to reflect on this moment in his life. Out of habit, he stretched and twisted the knots out of his neck as he contemplated the receding English coastline. He thought about how much better it was to be a sportsman representing his country than someone like his grandfather who had worked hard all his life in the shipyards for scarcely any reward. And then he thought about his father's humiliation, his endless attempts to find work after he came back from the Great War. He pictured his angry face. Recalled the smell of alcohol on his breath.

He did not hear Mr Riley approaching until he was by his side. The head coach, who was also wearing a boater, was having to hold it down because of the strong sea breeze. In his other hand was an unlit cigar.

'Quite a sight, is it not?' Mr Riley said.

Kim took a deep, salty breath and nodded.

'Just think,' Mr Riley added. 'The next time you see the English coast you might have a gold medal or two around your neck. Possibly three.'

'Why? Has Jesse Owens broken his leg?'

'No, but he's not competing in the hurdles any more. Only the hundred metres, two hundred metres and broad jump.'

Kim's heart accelerated. 'When was this announced?'

'It hasn't been.' Mr Riley lit his cigar and kept Kim in suspense as he puffed on it to get it going. 'But I have a friend in the American camp who tipped me off.' He handed Kim a telegram.

'Why?' Kim asked after reading it hungrily.

'Because four events in four days would finish him off. He's only human.'

'Is he, though?' Kim reread the telegram. 'And he's still not competing in the relay?'

'Not as far as we know.'

Mr Riley puffed on his cigar for a moment. The sight of it reminded Kim of the starting pistol Connie had stolen at the same time as she had stolen one of Mr Riley's cigars. Many had been the time that he had thought to return the pistol, but some superstitious instinct had always prevented him. In truth, the gun seemed to have become a lucky talisman for Kim, accompanying him to race meetings, and it was his ritual now to kiss its barrel before every event. He had not lost a hurdles or relay race in eighteen months, and, though it did not count, as it was wind assisted, he had already equalled the United Kingdom record for the broad jump. He was in the best form of his life and, while he did not want to tempt it by acknowledging it, fate seemed to be on his side.

The ferry arrived at the Hook of Holland at six the next morning, then the team caught the North German Express. A few hours later, as they crossed the border into Germany, one of the team managers came down the rattling wooden carriage distributing copies of a leaflet. Kim did not immediately realize that it was supposed to be satirical.

You will be shown

1) The Reichstag, partly 'burned out' in 1933
2) Happy workers cheering the National Leaders at popular demonstrations
3) Jews, sitting in their cafés unmolested (for the period of the Olympic Games), enjoying their glass of beer as well as any Aryan
4) Many new and magnificent buildings, such as the Air Ministry

5) Impressive libraries from which all literature of writers such as Heinrich Mann, Albert Einstein, Ernst Toller, has been removed

But ask to see

1) The oath, under penalty of treason, which every guide has been asked to take; the secret rules laid down to chambermaids, waiters, porters, etc., whom you will meet in Berlin
2) Columbia House, and other prisons with their torture chambers
3) The leaders of trade unions who have not yet been 'shot while attempting to escape'
4) The women and baby hostages still languishing in 'concentration camps', their only offence being the fact that their menfolk were pacifists, socialists and communists
5) Great leaders of the Catholic and Protestant Church whose sermons have been seized by secret police

Kim felt uneasy as he read the words. He knew there was propaganda on both sides but still, he wondered how close these were to the truth.

As the train blurred through the countryside, it made an hypnotic *diddley dee, diddley dah* sound, but as it approached the Berlin suburbs and slowed down it seemed to make a more clanking, industrial noise, like hammer blows on anvils. They crossed an immense latticed bridge and, amid snorting clouds of steam, they finally reached Friedrichstrasse Station. Kim, realizing he still had the leaflet in his hand, folded it into his pocket to show Connie and Alun later.

In truth, as he stepped out into the echoing terminus, under a canopy of glass and iron, Kim's main emotion was excitement at how new and strange Germany seemed. He had never been abroad before.

His feeling of exhilaration mounted as he and his team-mates threaded their way through the jostling crowds to a waiting omnibus. Everything about the place seemed to be exotic, from the unfamiliar smell of the air to the music being played by the Bavarian oompah band that had come to greet them. On the bus Kim pressed his face to the glass as he took in the fashion boutiques and emporiums selling strange-looking meats and cheeses as well as expensive bottles of wine. When they came to a halt because of crowds blocking the road ahead, word spread through the bus that the *Hindenburg* was about to fly overhead as part of a rehearsal for the opening ceremony. Despite the protests of the officials, everyone tumbled out for a look. The airship swung slowly overhead, its engines making the air vibrate, its tail fins adorned with swastikas. Kim wondered if Connie and Alun had arrived at their hotel in time to see this magnificent sight too. The airship came so low that he could see the faces of the crew peering from the gondola. The hands of the Germans around him stretched upwards. It took a few seconds before Kim realized that they were giving the Hitler salute.

TWENTY-ONE

When their taxi reached Unter den Linden, Alun and Connie found themselves having to talk more loudly to be heard. There were tram bells, car horns, buses and bicycles as well as loudspeakers playing music between announcements, which the crowds thronging the boulevard seemed determined to ignore.

'"The glittering showcase of the Third Reich",' Connie said, quoting an article they had read on the train. The buildings did indeed look freshly painted, their porticos festooned with giant banners and garlands, their window boxes brimming with fuchsias and geraniums. The Berliners bustling about their business seemed not only more energetic and healthy than their counterparts in London, but also more prosperous, the men dapper in well-cut suits, the women dressed in the latest fashions from Paris and Milan. But there was, for Alun at least, something unsettling about the red ribbons looped between the trees – they made the city look as if it had been clawed by a leviathan and was now trickling with blood.

The taxi stopped a few hundred yards short of the Brandenburg Gate and a liveried doorman cleared a path for them through the crowd. Standing at the end of a red carpet under an awning bearing the words 'Hotel Adlon' was a concierge. Connie had brought a shooting stick and she used it to point to the four leather suitcases still stacked in the boot of the taxi. The concierge signalled a porter with a click of his fingers.

Alun's gaze lingered on the shooting stick as he wondered whether it had ever been used on the Dalton estate. He presumed that Connie would not have been allowed to shoot pheasants, being a woman, but she would have witnessed the men doing it. He tried to imagine her reaction if he told her he had once been jailed for trying to distribute the dead birds among the poor of the Rhondda valleys.

'Are they all clothes?' Alun asked as he turned his eyes to Connie's suitcases.

'Heavens no,' Connie said. 'Most of the outfits I'll be wearing are still in Berlin's finest boutiques, waiting for me to purchase them. These cases contain only the essentials. An inkstand, wine cooler, telescope, that sort of thing.' She glanced at the dark bridle-hide suitcase in Alun's hand. 'Why, what have you packed?'

Alun weighed the case as he pictured the cans of peaches and apricots it contained, along with Bird's custard powder, because Herzl had told him that he should not trust foreign food. It would cause constipation, which was why his comrade had, as a parting gift, presented him with syrup of figs, milk of magnesia, castor oil and Eno's Salts ('for Mr Can and Mr Can't'). Alun had packed them all, along with his Morse code contact key, oscillator and headphones, and a three-shilling pack of Dreadnought condoms, even though he wasn't entirely sure how they were supposed to be used.

'Just the essentials,' he said. 'I'm really pleased with it, by the way.' He raised the case to indicate what he meant. 'It is officially the most luxurious object I have ever owned.' Connie had bought it for him from a shop he had never heard of before called Swaine Adeney Brigg. It had a solid brass lock, with all-round straps, protective corners and silk lining. She had also bought him an umbrella from the same shop and had then had it monogrammed and delivered to his home. As this doubled as a walking stick, it had rarely left his side since. Not only had she insisted on buying him these items, she had also fitted him out in the clothes he was wearing, the result of a bewildering shopping spree. He had a Jermyn Street shirt with a detachable collar, a hat from Lock & Co and hand-stitched leather shoes. His suit was from Savile Row.

Although Alun regarded all this as an appalling compromise of his socialist principles, he did not seem able to say no to Connie, and his empty offers to pay for everything had been airily dismissed. Alun suspected she wanted to buy him a new wardrobe so that he wouldn't keep wearing his Blackshirt uniform all the time. It must have been an unwelcome reminder of the night she lost her eye. Or perhaps it was simply that she wanted her travelling companion to be dressed appropriately in case any photographers from the society magazines pictured them together.

In any event, Alun found, despite his nature, that he wanted to win Connie's approval. She not only treated him as a social equal, she was kind to him, and no woman, certainly no woman described in the papers as a 'society beauty', had ever been kind to him before. When he pleased her he felt warm inside and as tall as one of the five-storey banners that seemed to hang from every building in Berlin. And far from feeling an imposter – the noble communist among a nest of fascist savages – he was enjoying the strange sense of camaraderie he felt with this spoilt, erratic, maddeningly pretty representative of the hated upper classes. He was especially amused by the way she pretended she thought that Nazi was pronounced Nasty.

Perhaps it was simply that she seemed to like him.

A couple of bored-looking photographers who were loitering nearby looked up and took photographs of them as they entered the revolving door of the Adlon, presumably as a precaution, in case Connie and Alun were later identified as B-movie stars, exiled revolutionaries or minor European royals.

The calm of the lobby came as a welcome contrast and it took Alun a few seconds to orientate himself before he realized that the sound of running water was coming from a fountain in the middle of the room. A pianist in the corner was playing a version of 'Lili Marleen'. At a nearby table there was a portly figure who had a neatly upturned moustache and a homburg with a small plume of feathers sticking out of it. With his eyes closed and a fist propping up his jaw, he gave a gentlemanly snore. As Alun took in the wrought-iron balconies with plush red handrails above him and the art deco lampshades in the shape of shells, he felt awed, again despite himself. Berlin seemed so luxurious and pristine.

Connie cleared her throat.

'I've booked you a room on the same floor as me,' she said, glancing at her watch. 'It's five now. Shall we meet for cocktails on the terrace at seven?'

When the bellboy showed Alun to his room, which had a thick carpet and an ensuite bathroom, he received a tip of a few pfennigs. The boy stared at it for a moment and Alun wondered whether he had given too much or too little. Capitalist decadence, he thought, was much harder than it looked.

At 7 p.m., Alun waited for Connie to join him at the bar, nervously smoothing his hair down from time to time. 'This is most generous of you,' he said when Connie arrived twenty minutes later wearing a pale blue wraparound frock edged with ermine. He replayed his words in his head – 'most generous' – and felt annoyed with himself for slipping into Connie's bourgeois way of talking. He'd be doing all those 'frightfullys' and 'quites' and 'simplys' of hers next.

'Piffle,' Connie said. 'I probably wouldn't have come to Berlin if I'd had to travel with a boring old chaperone. You're much more fun.'

'I've never been accused of being fun before.'

'Clever, then. Intriguing. Unusual.' She picked up his book and, holding it at arm's length, read the cover out loud. '*Down and Out in Paris and London*. Well, that sounds depressing.'

'What's yours, then?' Alun said as he pointed at her book. '*Mein Kampf*?'

'Baedeker's guide to Berlin, actually.' She opened it. 'It says we must try the beer gardens and cabarets. And schnapps. Ever tried schnapps?'

When Alun shook his head, Connie clicked her fingers at a passing waiter, who turned to Alun for the order.

'Two schnapps please,' Alun said.

'Two for me as well,' Connie added.

The waiter did not laugh, merely took down the order and checked that they were guests.

Connie leaned forward, putting her elbow on the table and framing her face with her hands. 'I've never asked if you have a girl.'

Alun drew in a breath as if to speak, but then closed his mouth and made a sighing sound instead. He felt strangely safe with Connie, as if she would somehow understand. Could he confess to her that he had never been with a woman? He wanted to tell her everything. She would not mock him. If only you knew who I really am, he thought.

When the schnapps arrived, they drank a toast: 'To Kim, and the three gold medals he is going to win'; then Connie pulled a face at the taste and ordered a bottle of champagne instead.

On the train journey to Berlin, Connie had done most of the talking and, as he listened to her, Alun had been both entranced by her and appalled by how shallow her gilded life appeared to be. It was not so much that her only terms of reference seemed to be parties, holidays and 'the season', which was what she and her debutante friends 'did' in order to land suitable husbands; more her lack of experience of the real world, of what it meant to live in poverty, to not know whether there would be food on your table, or a roof over your head, from one week to the next. She had never had to try in life, never had to better herself. She had even confided to him once that she had been told by a snooty aunt of hers to avoid getting a reputation for being intelligent, as it put off 'dim but eligible suitors'.

Although there had also been moments when, as she contemplated the scenery out of the window, Alun had seen a shadow passing across Connie's face. It was not a wistful look, exactly, more despondent, as if she was not only afraid of being bored but of being boring. This intrigued Alun. As he stared at her halo of crimped blonde hair, he smiled. Clearly she had a rebellious streak, for someone high-born. After all, Kim didn't seem to be landed gentry, despite his well-honed speech; more likely he came from the middle classes, from a family of doctors or solicitors perhaps. And perhaps that was the point. Maybe Connie was using him to punish her parents for not buying her a new pony on her fifteenth birthday, before doing what was expected of her and finding a more suitable match.

'What do you know about Kim's background?' Alun asked.

'I know that his mother died when he was thirteen and that it was all very sad. Why, what do you know?'

'Nothing at all,' Alun said. 'I've asked him but he won't talk about it. I don't get the impression he comes from a particularly moneyed background, otherwise he wouldn't need the sponsorship.'

'What sponsorship?'

Interesting, Alun thought. Kim hasn't told her.

'Do you think Kim still finds me attractive?' Connie pointed to her eyepatch. 'With this, I mean? He says he does but everyone is entitled to change their mind.'

'You can never tell with Kim . . .' Alun said cautiously. 'He's so wrapped up in his sport it's sometimes difficult to know what he thinks about anything.' He allowed this time to land before adding: 'But I like it. It makes you look sophisticated. Mysterious.' He knew he was being cruel, but it had to be done. If he could turn Connie against Kim, he might be in with a slight chance. They weren't right for each other. Not as right as Alun was for Connie.

Over the next hour and a half, as the two travelling companions shared an ashtray and listened to a barrel organ turning in front of the Brandenburg Gate, they finished the bottle, ordered a second and, when that was finished, a third. Alun was no longer surprised by how much alcohol Connie could consume. Kim had told him that, since her injury, she had come to regard it as a form of medication.

'He's so bloody perfect, isn't he?' Alun said suddenly.

'Who?'

'Kim. And so annoyingly attractive to women.'

Connie let out a bark of laughter and said: 'Oh, Alun, stop it.' She leaned forward and patted his hand. 'You'll find a girl.'

'I've seen the way they are around him.'

Connie tapped his hand again. 'Now, now. You're making me jealous.'

Alun ran his finger around the rim of his glass. 'Because he doesn't give much away, women see in him what they want to see. They see still waters running deep. With me they see a shallow, babbling brook. One who talks too quickly.'

'That's because you have a quick mind.'

'No, it's because I worry that people will stop listening to me if I slow down.'

'Sorry, what was that?'

Alun slow-clapped.

'Oddly enough,' Connie said, 'there is a vulnerability to Kim. I think that's the real reason women find him attractive. I feel quite protective towards him sometimes.'

'What about me?' Alun said. 'How do I make you feel?'

Connie thought for a moment. 'Smarter than I am. You know about politics and you talk to me as if I know about it, too, as if I'm your intellectual equal.'

'You *are* my intellectual equal.'

'We both know that's not true.'

'I also think that in your black, over-privileged, capitalist heart you are a decent person.'

'See?' Connie said, cupping her mouth as she laughed. 'You said that like you thought I would know what you meant.' She leaned forward and looked around before whispering: 'Tell me, are the Nasties capitalists?'

'Up to a point,' Alun said. 'But they're not what you would call free-market capitalists. Jews aren't allowed to be capitalists in Nazi Germany, for example.' Alun leaned in closer as well now. 'All the anti-Jewish graffiti daubed on shop windows has been cleaned off and all the signs on the outskirts of towns and villages across the country – "*Juden sind hier nicht erwünscht*", which translates as "Jews are not welcome here" – have been taken down. Berliners have been ordered to be on their best behaviour. It's all a façade.'

'I'm sure you know all about façades,' Connie said, finishing her glass.

Was she on to him? Alun wondered if he had said too much, or if this was retaliation for his earlier attempt to sow doubts in her mind about Kim.

'We should get some food,' Connie added, before Alun could ask what she meant by her comment. 'I'm feeling tipsy. Do you think everything here comes with sauerkraut?'

It was dark by the time they had finished eating and the food had done little to mitigate the effects of all the alcohol they had drunk. When the floodlights came on, illuminating the Brandenburg Gate, Connie contemplated it for a moment before saying: 'Beautiful.'

'Like you.' Realizing what he had said, Alun self-consciously repositioned the knife and fork on his plate.

'Hardly,' Connie said, pointing an ironic finger at her eyepatch again. 'You may not have noticed, but I have something wrong with one of my eyes.'

'Really?' Alun said. 'Which one?'

Connie smiled, consulted her guidebook, then rose from her chair. 'Follow me,' she said, picking up the half-empty bottle of champagne from the ice bucket and handing it to Alun. He looked around for the waiter to check this was allowed and when given a discreet nod he picked up the two flutes from their table and limped drunkenly after Connie, who was striding towards the Gate.

'Where to are we going?' he asked when he caught up with her.

'The Tiergarten.' Connie raised her arm and pointed left towards what looked like a wood.

There was a rubbery squeal as the tyres of a six-wheel, open-top Daimler-Benz that was directly ahead of them turned to the right. On its bonnet was a small flag with a swastika flapping and it was being driven by a soldier wearing a grey forage cap. Another soldier sat in the passenger seat, this one wearing a black uniform and a steel helmet, and in the back was a woman with frizzy dark hair and a camera around her neck. She was wearing a white polo-neck under a stylish leather coat and, though it was dusk, she still wore sunglasses. She lowered them down her nose and peered over them at Connie.

'Who was that?' Alun asked.

'Someone frightfully important, I should say,' Connie said, lowering her arm. 'A wife of a prominent Nasty perhaps. Frau Göring. Or Frau Hess. I think she thought I was giving her a Nasty salute.'

In the park, gas lamps lit the paths and there seemed to be dozens of people out for an evening stroll. Some were buying food from kiosks, others were walking dogs; drinking from water basins. One path led to a bridge over a pond and, as they headed towards it, Connie seemed to speed up. Her change of pace was only slight, but Alun discerned it and, with a look of amused reproach, he nudged her with his elbow. She pretended not to notice, but her stride was definitely lengthening. This was a race.

They reached a bandstand out of breath and laughing. Here they sat down on steps opposite one another, with their backs to the railings, and poured two more glasses.

'Chin chin,' Connie said.

'Chin chin,' Alun echoed.

Connie sipped and looked thoughtful. 'Do you know Fruity Metcalfe? The King's equerry?'

'Of course,' Alun said. 'How is old Fruity?'

Connie looked pleased and was about to continue when Alun gave her a patient look. 'No. I do not know "Fruity Metcalfe, the King's equerry".'

'Well, Fruity is married to Baba Blackshirt. She was at that party you came to in London. You must know her. Lady Alexandra Curzon? Sister of Cimmie?'

Alun shrugged playfully, but he thought he might be playing a dangerous game here. Connie clearly expected him to know all the aristocrats and 'Savile Row fascists' who swanned around the Black House. He had done his best to learn their titles but this conversation was baffling.

'Lady Cynthia?' Connie said. 'Married to Sir Oswald? Or was. She died a couple of years ago.'

While Alun listened to Connie gossip, he became transfixed by her lips. They were the texture and colour of pale pink rose petals. She would pout in between sentences and he felt the urge to kiss her.

Connie's words came back into focus: '. . . and apparently Fruity knows that Baba is sleeping with Sir Oswald, but he doesn't mind.'

'I thought Sir Oswald was having an affair with what's-her-name.'

'Mrs Guinness?'

'No, that's not it. Mitford,' Alun said. 'Diana Mitford.'

'Yes, that's her, we call her "Mrs Guinness", since she married into the Beerage. We're contemporaries, you know. Diana and I came out the same season.'

'So, wait a moment.' Alun could hear he was slurring his words. 'This "Baba" is sleeping with her sister's husband. What does the sister think about this?'

'You're not listening. The sister is dead. Although Baba and Tom—'

'Tom?'

'Sir Oswald. His friends call him Tom. Baba and Tom were sleeping together while Cimmie was still alive. He used to go around boasting that he slept with both his future mother-in-law and his sister-in-law before the wedding.'

Alun poured two more glasses then set the empty bottle down on the step and asked: 'What wedding?'

'The wedding to Cimmie.'

'Cimmie who is dead?'

Connie's brow knitted momentarily, then cleared. 'Yes. But when she was alive she didn't mind her sister sleeping with her husband because it kept him away from "the Horror".'

'The Horror?'

'That's what Cimmie called Diana. Baba was doing the decent thing, in a way. Nobly sacrificing her virtue for the sake of her sister's marriage.'

Alun opened his mouth to speak, but, feeling confused, closed it again. He tried to imagine what Comrade Herzl would make of all this decadent, aristocratic tittle-tattle and shook his head.

'And Fruity doesn't mind all this because . . .?'

'Because I think he finds Baba too much of a handful, frankly. She's seventeen years younger than him.' Connie wafted a hand in front of her face to disperse some midges. 'Besides, Fruity is too busy trying to keep an eye on Mrs Simpson, along with half of Special Branch.'

Alun sat up, suddenly feeling sober. Although it had been announced that Edward would not be attending the Olympics, on the advice of his prime minister, there were many of his circle who were coming to Berlin, and it was rumoured that Mrs Wallis Simpson, an American divorcee who was romantically linked to the King, might be among them. Harry Pollitt had asked Alun to find out as much about her as he could. He was particularly keen to know whether or not it was true that she was having an affair with the German diplomat Joachim von Ribbentrop. Harry had high hopes that Mrs Simpson could bring down the monarchy more or less single-handedly and thereby spare the Communist Party the job.

'Do you know Mrs Simpson?' Alun asked.

'Not really,' Connie said. 'Might have met her once. Looked like a man.'

'Is she here in Berlin?'

'No idea. Diana's here, though, and she would know. Why do you ask?'

'Just curious. Have you heard anything about Mrs Simpson and Ribbentrop?'

'Ribben who?'

'Doesn't matter. They sound a racy lot, these aristocrats. Everyone having affairs with everyone else. What would you do if Kim was unfaithful to you?'

'Could I forgive him, do you mean? I don't know. Possibly not.' Connie drained her glass. 'But I do love him, you know. I don't think I've ever told him that, but I do.' She nodded. 'We should head back while I can still walk.'

They took a different route, one which brought them to a café where three Berliners in working men's caps were sitting at a table drinking foaming beer from tankards. 'How about one more for the road?' Alun said. 'A proper drink this time, not this filthy bourgeois bathwater.' When Connie shrugged her assent, Alun ordered two shots of vodka and, momentarily letting down his guard, said: '*Zuh vahs!*' before downing his in one. He was by now entertaining a drunken fantasy that he might be able one day to convert Connie to communism. After all, her set seemed to swing between the two ideologies – fascism and communism – as fashion dictated. He knew for a fact that one of the Mitford sisters had been flirting with communism because Herzl had told him he had seen her browsing in the CPGB bookshop.

Connie repeated the toast before drinking her shot and asking what '*Zuh vahs!*' meant.

'It's Russian for "To you".'

The barman was running a rag around a wine glass and inclining it to the light. Seeing the still-wet shot glasses on the bar, he refilled them without being asked. Alun was now having to fight the urge to blow his own cover by confessing to Connie that he was a communist.

'What do you find upsetting?' he asked. 'Politically, I mean.'

'Not much.' Connie knocked back another shot and slammed it down on the bar. 'Keep up.'

Alun downed his and the barman refilled them again.

'I don't have your words,' Connie said, wagging a finger at Alun. 'I'm not educated like you.'

'There you go again,' Alun said. 'That's something to be upset about. Education for women. Why shouldn't you have had a decent education?'

'Don't ask me, women aren't allowed opinions.'

'See? That's clever. You're clever.'

'Oh, I was educated,' Connie said, 'just not like you. At my school we were taught good manners and how to make polite conversation at dinner, about art, gardens, horses and so forth. Never politics.'

'Did you want to learn about politics?'

'Good heavens, no. Then everyone would think I was a bluestocking and no one would want to marry me.'

'There isn't a man alive who wouldn't want to marry you, Connie.'

She wafted a dismissive hand. 'Nonsense. No one likes me.'

'I like you,' Alun said. 'In fact, I think I like you more than you like yourself.'

Connie looked puzzled. 'Yes, but . . .' She closed her eye. 'Why did you say that? Has Kim said something?'

Alun said nothing, allowing the thought to linger that Kim had been talking about her behind her back.

'Where were we?' Connie asked, opening her eye. 'I was about to say something witty.'

Alun had double vision now. 'Why should a woman's role in life be to marry?' he said. 'Why shouldn't you be prime minister?'

Connie laughed. 'A woman prime minister? As if.'

'Well, why not?'

'Because I'd make a complete bosh of it, that's why not.'

Time passed in a blur for Alun as he sat on the bar stool drinking shots and listening to his companion. He had a vague memory of them singing 'Me and My Shadow' as they staggered back to the Adlon.

And then he was lying on a bed in a room that was spinning.

And then another memory came to him, of having put his arm around Connie's waist to support her as they got into the lift, and again as they walked swaying down the corridor to her room. When she had draped an arm around his shoulder, he had smelled her flowery scent and had wanted to kiss her. And then he did kiss her, gently on her eyepatch, as a way of showing her he didn't mind it. She looked surprised and shook her head.

What happened next was lost to him, unrecoverable, but they must have reached her door because he had a mental image of her fumbling for her key before staggering towards her bed and passing out on it, still wearing her clothes.

And he remembered standing there at the end of her bed, staring at her helplessly, wanting to cry with the tenderness that troubled his blood.

TWENTY-TWO

'Who's that lady dressed like a man?' Kim said, pointing at a striking-looking woman in a white polo-neck and flared trousers who was striding around the track, barking out instructions in German to the three nervous-looking cameramen trying to keep up with her. 'I noticed her yesterday at the opening ceremony.'

'That's the Queen of Nuremberg.'

Kim pulled a questioning face at his interlocutor, a *Daily Express* photographer who had chatted to him on the crossing to the Hook of Holland.

'Leni Riefenstahl?' the reporter elaborated with a rising inflection. 'Don't you read the papers?'

'Never heard of her,' Kim said.

'You've heard of that ruddy great rally that the Nazis held at Nuremberg?'

'Yes.'

'Well, she organized it, pretty much. Made that film about it, *The Triumph of the Will.*' He jerked his head in Leni's direction. 'She's Hitler's favourite film-maker. And his mistress, according to the rumours. Now she's making a film about the Games. Look.' He pointed. 'Even has her own personal photographer in tow. None of us are allowed anywhere near her. She's treated like royalty in Germany. Some say she's the real dictator here.'

Kim gave a low whistle of appreciation.

The reporter caught his look. 'I've heard she likes athletes, though.'

He took from his pocket a rolled-up copy of *Time* magazine. On its cover was a portrait of a handsome if dishevelled-looking brunette in a figure-hugging bathing suit, facing up a ski slope. The caption read: 'Hitler's Leni Riefenstahl'.

Kim studied the magazine. It was dated 17 February 1936, and now looked dog-eared. 'Why is she trying to ski uphill in a swimming costume?' he asked.

'Why don't you go over and ask her?'

Leni was now shouting at a cowering sound engineer. 'No, thanks,' Kim said. 'She's terrifying.'

As the photographer now wound his camera on he asked: 'You and Lady Constance still courting?'

'We are, yes. And she's not a Lady, she's an Hon. She's here some . . . How did you know that?'

'My job to know.'

At that moment, the crowd let out a cheer. They then fell silent as two black athletes arrived together for the qualifying heat of the 100 metres: Jesse Owens and Ralph Metcalfe. Kim was transfixed as they bent over their marks in the semi-crouch favoured by the Americans. They looked like gods.

Owens seemed calm and loose. Metcalfe crossed himself. One of the other runners, fair-haired and thickset, rubbed his hands nervously on his shorts and took up the standard kneeling position. His legs were quivering. The next man in the line shifted in his footholes. An on-your-marks warning from the starter – '*Auf die Plätze*' – was followed by a crack from the pistol. As a small puff of smoke curled upwards, the sprinters exploded from their marks. For thirty yards, they bunched, then Owens drew ahead until, with a lead of a yard, he flashed first to the tape.

Kim was astonished by the power in Owens's legs. His style was as effortless as it was smooth. He had never seen an athlete move with such grace before. It was as if he were running on silken threads.

Later that day, Kim found himself training at the same time as Owens, who was now wearing a blue sweatshirt inscribed with blocky red letters spelling out 'USA'. As the American limbered up by the broad-jump pit, steam rising from his shoulders, the Englishman kept glancing across at him. The photographer from the *Express* had told him that Owens was the grandson of a slave and that this, according to the latest theories, was what gave him an advantage over white men. The plantation owners believed in selective breeding, the photographer had explained, only using the biggest and strongest 'bull slaves' as studs. As Kim studied Owens now he decided this theory was complete nonsense. Owens was average height and average build. Athletes were either good or bad, that's all there was to it. And Owens was good. Owens was the best. He'd trained to get where he was. The American track star looked up now and, noticing Kim staring at him, smiled – a disarmingly toothy expression that made his nose wrinkle, like a schoolboy.

Kim now experienced a prickly sensation at the back of his head, as if he was the one being stared at, and he turned to see that he was. Leni Riefenstahl was sizing him up blatantly, hands on hips, head cocked to one side. She seemed cool and clean, as if she had stepped out of an ice bath. Her hair was held off her brow by sunglasses. In front of her was a movie camera and when she put her eye to the viewfinder and smoothly turned its crank, Kim waved at her with an outstretched arm. The photographer from the *Express* was walking behind the director and captured Kim's gesture on his camera.

With a loose-gaited walk, Owens vacated the broad-jump pit, his head covered by a towel, as a couple of other jumpers arrived for a practice session. Leni now walked over to Kim, removed her sunglasses and studied him in a slightly cross-eyed way. She said in a reedy and heavily accented English: 'Did you watch Jesse Owens earlier?' She pronounced the name *Yaycee Ohvens*.

Kim nodded, feeling tongue-tied. He self-consciously hitched up the waistband of his shorts.

'I think we will see a lot of this Jesse Owens,' the film-maker said. 'He is beautifully proportioned, do you not say? Broad shoulders. Narrow hips. And those long legs. There is nothing . . .' She searched for the right word. 'Nothing "bulgy" about him.'

'I'm going to be competing against him later,' Kim said. 'In the broad jump. Worse luck.'

'What is your name?' She pronounced 'What' with a 'V'. It gave her voice a metallic quality, like a car door slamming shut.

'Kim Newlands.'

She did not offer her name, assuming, correctly, that he would know who she was. 'Then good luck, Herr Newlands. Do not let my cameras put you off. That' – she pointed to a thin but deep trench dug alongside the pit – 'is where we shall be lurking. Am I saying this word correctly? Lurking?'

'*Ja*.'

Leni looked pleased. '*Sprechen Sie Deutsch?*'

'No, that's about my limit, I'm afraid. *Ja, Nein, Danke, Bitte, Auf Wiedersehen* and *Sprechen Sie Deutsch*. Your English is good, by the way.'

'Perhaps you can teach me more of your tongue.'

'Well, I . . .' He felt lost for words again. 'I'd make sure you have plenty of film in your camera when Owens jumps. He's the current world-record holder.'

'What about you, Kim Newlands? Are you going to win a gold?'

'Against Owens?' He shook his head. 'He's jumping a foot further than the rest of us.'

'Silver, then? A big strong boy like you.'

Kim shook his head again and smiled. 'That will almost certainly go to your fellow countryman.' He nodded in the direction of Luz Long, who was, like Kim, tall, blond and blue-eyed. Long was not only the star of the German team, he was the European champion. 'I might come away with a bronze,' he added, shaking his arms and swivelling his hips to keep loose.

'You should be more positive,' Leni said. 'Winning is a frame of mind.'

'Were you filming me just now?'

'*Ja*, yes, I am using an experimental "blue filter" technique. You are my guinea pig. Is that how you say this?'

'Yes,' Kim said through a smile. 'Guinea pig.'

Leni looked up to see the sun had parted the grey clouds overhead. 'Can I ask a favour,' she said. 'I have been filming the shadows of the high jumpers. Can I film your shadow when you make a jump, while we have some sun?'

Kim did three jumps for her. For the first two Leni had her assistant set up his camera to film only his shadow then, on the third, she asked him to turn the camera to film Kim properly, from a low angle.

While the cameraman ran off to get more film, Leni sat down and patted the grass next to her. Kim came and sat down beside her, then winced and started rubbing his calf.

Leni looked concerned. 'Are you all right?'

'A little muscle cramp,' Kim said. 'It's nothing.'

Leni clicked her fingers twice and a minion came running over. She spoke to him in German. When he ran off again Leni stood up and said, 'Here, let me'. She took Kim's running spikes off before massaging the ball of his foot. She then placed the flat of it against her pelvic bone and leaned in so that he had to bend his leg at the knee. 'Push against me,' she said. 'Trust me, I know about this. I damaged my knee when I was a dancer.'

Kim was reluctant to push at first, fearing his own strength. The team's physios were all men and doing this with a woman felt shockingly intimate. But Leni, who was pushing at him and kneading his calf muscles, did not seem to mind. And she did know what she was doing. As he flexed and she stepped back, only to lunge forward again, he found it helped.

When he noticed the photographer from the *Express* hovering with his camera again, he said to Leni: 'It's gone now. Thank you.'

The minion returned with a glass of water which he handed to Kim. 'You are probably dehydrated,' Leni said, sitting down beside him once more. 'I've been to London, you know. The girls are very pretty there.'

Kim was not expecting this comment. 'I don't . . . I suppose so, yes.' As he studied her face it struck him that she had the air of one who had seen too much in life, its effects visible in the discrepancy between her beguiling looks and her hard voice.

'You have been to Berlin before?'

Kim shook his head.

'Do you like it?'

'I do, yes,' he said.

'What are they saying about Germany in the London newspapers?'

'They don't know what to make of your leader,' Kim said tactfully.

Leaning back to rest on her elbows, Leni looked up at the stand. 'Adolf is not so bad, you know. It is Goebbels who is the little *Fotze*.'

Kim found himself feeling disconcerted by her candour and direct manner. At this moment, the assistant ran up and, out of breath, said something to Leni in German.

'I have to go,' Leni said to Kim as she got to her feet. 'Remind me, when is the broad jump?'

'Not for a couple of days.'

Leni studied Kim and then said: 'Would you do me another favour, Kim Newlands? I want to do some night filming. I want to show how competitions like the high jump and broad jump continue until there is a winner. It should not take long, maybe half an hour. The sun sets close to nine, but the light will start to go down about eight fifteen. *Dämmerung*. How do you say this in English?'

'Twilight.'

'So, would you meet me here at the broad jump at twilight?'

'Why not?' Kim said, tilting his wrist to check the watch Connie had given him, only to remember he had taken it off and left it in his locker before training. 'I'm supposed to be meeting someone at nine-ish.' Seeing her puzzled look, he added, 'It means at around nine o'clock.'

'We Germans do not have this concept. When we say a time we arrive at that time. Well, we should be finished before nine-ish. I have to be somewhere later too. The International Olympic Committee is holding a reception.' She began walking away, but then stopped and turned back to him. 'Would you like to be introduced to Adolf? He will be at the reception. You must come along.'

Kim smiled at her and found himself shrugging and once more saying: 'Why not?'

'Good. I will ask my assistant to arrange the invitation for you.'

'What about my friends?'

'Bring them along,' Leni said, over her shoulder.

'Shall I give their names to your assistant?'

Still walking away, Leni gave a thumbs-up sign without looking back. She had known he would still be watching.

*

By the time Kim had gone back to the Olympic Village, showered, collected his blue blazer and white flannels and sent a message to Connie telling her about Leni and the film shoot, it was time to return to the stadium. After almost half an hour of filming in the cool night air, Kim found himself shivering between takes, but he felt flattered by the attention of this glamorous German star. With her hair ghosting in the arc-lights, she kept looking at him and saying '*Ja*, *ja*, good, perfect.' Then, inevitably, 'Just one more.' He could not help but admire her perfectionism, and her crew clearly held her in the highest regard.

'Frau Riefenstahl, I'm meeting my friends at nine fifteen,' he reminded her.

'Fräulein,' she corrected. 'But you can call me Leni. Now, I need one more. This will be the last, I promise. You look *wunderbar*.'

Kim walked twenty-two yards back, gathered himself with an arm across his midriff, rocked back on his heel and made his approach, lengthening his strides as he accelerated into the jump. And then he was in the air, wheeling his long legs and not looking down. His form held steady, his upper body straight and then, when his feet made land, he rolled to the side.

Leni shouted: '*Schnitt!*' – which Kim assumed meant 'Cut!' because the cameramen, seeming relieved, began to pack away their cables and lights.

Kim looked around and then, with a shrug aimed at Leni, stripped off his shorts and vest, opened his kitbag and took out his flannels, shirt and British team tie. As he dressed, Leni tilted her head and gave him an appraising look. 'That last one was perfect,' she said, walking over and giving him a hug. 'I cannot thank you enough. It may well be the best shot in the whole film. You had better win now, Kim Newlands!'

'I don't know about that,' Kim said, feeling gratified as he rubbed the back of his neck self-consciously.

'Of course you will,' Leni said. 'Now walk with me to the reception.'

'I'm supposed to be meeting my friends at the entrance gate.'

Leni gave the seat of Kim's trousers a pat. 'Then walk with me to the entrance gate.'

The floodlights had come on by the time they reached the twin clock towers at the east portal, but the crowds had gone and the concourse was almost empty apart from a few policemen and some race officials. Connie and Alun were nowhere in sight.

When a small, elderly man appeared carrying what looked like a placard, Kim nudged Leni and pointed in his direction. The man had a deeply lined face and a high forehead visible under a black felt hat. His back was hunched and there was a shawl around his shoulders, the ends of which were fringed. He moved past them; then he turned to face the clock towers and slowly went down on his knees, lowered his head as if in prayer and lifted his placard. It had German writing on it. One of the words was *Jude*.

'What does it say?' Kim whispered.

Leni was holding one elbow while the opposite hand cupped her mouth. 'Nothing that involves us,' she whispered back. 'Don't look at him. It is best not to look.'

Two policemen appeared and seemed to glower accusingly at Leni and Kim for a moment, before one of them grabbed the man's placard, snapped it over his leg and threw it on the ground. When the old man tried to pick it up again, the other policeman put his foot on it. The first then struck the man's face with the back of his hand, causing him to topple sideways. Kim stepped forward but Leni grabbed his arm. 'Don't,' she said. 'It won't help him.' Two more policemen ran over and, hooking their arms under his, dragged the old man off across the paving stones and out of sight inside the stadium.

'He was a protester,' Leni said.

'But there's no one here to protest to,' Kim said.

'He was waiting for him,' Leni replied, pointing at an open Mercedes that was gliding up the broad avenue towards the clock towers. There were two motorbike outriders in front of it and two behind.

It was Hitler. As the car slowed to pass through the towers, the passenger noticed Leni and gave a half-wave. She waved back and then the car disappeared from view.

'I'll see you in there,' Leni said before walking off briskly in the same direction.

TWENTY-THREE

While he waited for Connie and Alun, Kim felt a pulling sensation in his gut and he knew it was not from his exertions. The treatment of the old man, who he was sure had been Jewish, had been brutal, and witnessing it had left him feeling sunken and cowardly. Was he deluding himself in thinking that Mosley's British fascists were more tolerant than Hitler's German ones? He wished he had intervened and felt less of himself for not having done so.

Ten minutes later than the time they had arranged to meet, he saw Connie walking towards him, and felt an urge to tell her about what he had just seen. Perhaps now would be the moment to tell her that he was Jewish, too. She would need to know this if they were to get engaged. Or maybe she wouldn't? Was it even important? He wasn't a practising Jew, after all.

As Connie greeted him with a kiss on the cheek she asked: 'Why are you frowning?' She was wearing a scarlet cocktail dress and a black feathered headband that complemented her eyepatch.

'You look lovely,' Kim said, forcing a smile in the hope that it would clear his thoughts. 'I will be the proudest man in there. No Alun?'

'Said he'd meet us inside.' Connie looked Kim up and down and gave an appreciative nod. 'You don't look so bad yourself.' She took out a holder, slipped a cigarette into it and waited for Kim to light it for her. 'I mean it, you know,' she added. 'I turn to jelly when I look at you.'

Kim rolled his eyes, but he was pleased. 'I wish Jesse Owens would turn to jelly whenever he looked at me. And Luz Long.'

Connie linked her arm through his as they walked towards the marquee where the reception was being held. It had been set up in an area of parkland near the diving pool and was decorated with fairy lights. Torches lined the path leading up to it and there were huge butterfly lanterns glowing in the surrounding trees.

Kim became lost in his thoughts again. What if he told Connie about the old Jewish man and she made one of her facetious comments? Where would that leave him?

'You're nervous about the broad jump, aren't you?' Connie said, tapping her cigarette holder to deposit some ash on the path. 'I can tell. You go quiet when you're nervous.'

'I'm fine,' he said.

'Of course you are. You're better than fine. You'll be the best. Owens and Long don't have a chance.'

Kim closed his eyes momentarily and took a deep and calming breath.

Connie kissed him again, this time on the lips.

'Have I ever told you I love you?' she asked, leaning back to look him in the eye.

Kim gave a small shake of the head.

'Well, I do. With all my heart.'

'Thank you for saying it.'

She gave his arm a punch. 'Are you going to say it back?'

'I love you too, Connie, with all my heart.'

Holding hands now, they continued walking. 'Do you think you'll be able to sleep tomorrow night?' Connie asked.

'I think our German hosts might have given us lumpy mattresses deliberately. I'll sleep better when the broad jump is out of the way, then I can concentrate on the hurdles and the relay. Do we have to go to this thing?'

'It was you who wanted to.'

'I know but . . . let's not go in. Why don't we go back to your hotel?'

'Darling, it'll be fun. Besides, your girlfriend will be expecting you to come.'

'My girlfriend?'

'Leni what's-her-name.'

'Very funny,' Kim said; then he added: 'I suppose we can't leave Alun in there on his own.'

After a few moments, Connie said in a distant voice, as though half remembering something: 'What do you make of him?'

'Alun? He's certainly intense.'

'And enigmatic,' Connie added. 'I'm not sure I really know what makes him tick. He says such odd things. I do enjoy his company, though. That reminds me . . .' She took a badge from her purse and fastened it to Kim's lapel. 'He asked me to give you this. For luck.'

'I'm glad he's here to look after you,' Kim said, glancing at the badge. It was the BUF symbol of a bundle of sticks.

'I don't need looking after.'

Kim thought of all the social engagements he had tried to persuade her to accept as a way of rebuilding her confidence. 'You know what I mean. I was relieved when he said he was thinking of coming with you to the Games.'

'He got me dreadfully drunk the other night. I was a disgrace. Made an absolute fool of myself. I've no idea how I even got back to the hotel. I woke up the next morning with a thumping headache wishing someone would just shoot me.'

'Drinking sounds great.' Kim smiled. 'I must try it sometime.'

'Alun drinks vodka. Filthy stuff.' The silk of Connie's dress whispered as they continued in the direction of the marquee. 'What was that thing he said when we knocked back our shots?' She didn't finish the thought, distracted by the colourful merry-go-round they had reached. No one was riding on it but the sound of its organ was adding to the carnival atmosphere.

They showed their invitations to a steward who checked their names against a list. Inside, men in lederhosen were pouring beer from jugs while pretzels were served by girls dressed up as eighteenth-century pages. Connie pointed out Magda Goebbels talking to two men in uniform. With a surreptitious wag of her finger, she then pointed out two men in suits and whispered: 'Beaverbrook and Chips Channon.'

Leni was standing behind them. 'That's Leni Riefenstahl,' Kim said out of the corner of his mouth.

Connie turned to Kim and arched a plucked eyebrow. 'You didn't tell me she was so beautiful.'

'I hadn't noticed.'

'And young-looking . . . For her age. What is she, mid thirties?'

'No idea.'

'Well? Aren't you going to introduce us?'

'Fräulein Riefenstahl,' Kim said when they approached her. 'I'd like you to meet the Honourable Constance Dalton.' As the title and full name left his mouth, Kim wondered why he had used them. Was he trying to impress the film director?

Leni held out her hand as if half expecting Connie to kiss it. They shook lightly, with fingers only.

'I hear you're making a film of the Games,' Connie said.

'Yes, I am going to immortalize young Kim here.' Leni gave the athlete a wink and patted him on the hip. She cocked her head to one side. 'Have we not met before?'

'You were in a car driving past the Brandenburg Gate the other night,' Connie said.

'That was it! I never forget a pretty face. Come and meet Adolf.'

Because he was surrounded by tall bodyguards and acolytes, they had not noticed the Führer holding court in the corner of the marquee. When Kim shook hands with him, a photographer stepped forward and recorded the moment. Leni said something to Hitler and he looked at Connie and gave her a tight smile. He then took her hand and kissed it, before indicating that his guests should help themselves to one of the glasses of champagne that were being passed around by a waiter. He turned back to Leni and the encounter was over.

'Taller than I imagined,' Connie said when they were out of earshot. 'Did you notice his eyes?'

'Rather a damp handshake, I thought,' Kim replied. 'Not quite the electrifying presence I'd been told to expect.'

'His moustache was tickly when he kissed my hand,' Connie said. 'Look out, here come the English Rhine Maidens.'

Two striking women – tall and blonde, clearly sisters – were in stately progress towards Hitler, turning heads as they went. Diana and Unity Mitford.

'The rumour is that Diana has come to the Games to ask Hitler for more money for the Blackshirts,' Connie whispered, 'on behalf of Tom.' She tilted her head as she stared. 'Don't you think she has the most beautiful face? Poor Unity. There's a joke that she is like Diana reflected in one of those wobbly mirrors at a fairground. Oh, look.' She waved. 'He came. I didn't think he would.'

Kim followed her gaze and saw Alun standing at the entrance to the marquee talking to the photographer from the *Express*.

'We'd better go and rescue him,' Connie said.

As they were crossing the floor, Leni intercepted Kim. 'There's something I want to show you.' She turned to Connie. 'May I borrow him for a moment?'

'Be my guest,' Connie said with a stiff smile.

Leni led Kim out of the marquee, over some grass and up a short flight of steps towards the diving-pool area. From there they climbed to a platform where they could see across to the floodlit bell tower on the Maifeld. As they contemplated it, Leni slipped her arm through his and leaned her head on his shoulder.

'This whole place was built on the site of an old racecourse,' she said.

'Impressive.' Kim looked around to see if Connie had followed them. Leni's casual familiarity was making him feel self-conscious. He did not know what to make of her. She was attractive, certainly, but there was something androgynous about her, more to do with her bearing than her features. And he could feel the muscles in her arm, as if she were pushing him away at the same time as drawing him near. He noticed her scent, too – gardenia, he thought, the same as Connie's, but mixed with something foreign. Her skin seemed hard and soft at the same time, like the surface tension of water.

'We Germans are great believers in rebuilding things,' Leni continued. 'My friend Albert helped design this. It is part of his plan to build a new capital on the site of the old one.'

'Albert is an architect?'

Leni looked at Kim and he noticed again that one eye seemed to be listing slightly. 'You deduce correctly. I am thinking you are not just a pretty face.'

Kim smiled. There was something endearing about the way she spoke.

'I heard that your Führer wanted to come to the Games. Do you know when he will arrive?'

'We don't have a Führer.'

'King Edward,' Leni said. 'What is this rumour we are hearing about him?'

'Rumour?'

'That he has been hypnotized by an American woman who treats him as her sex slave.'

'You're asking the wrong person,' Kim said. 'Connie is the one who is in with that crowd.'

'Your friend with the eyepatch? Connie is her nickname, *ja*? I am right in this word?'

'Yes, nickname.'

'My friends call me Du-Du.'

'Does Adolf call you that?'

Leni scowled at him in a playful way. 'Be careful. Adolf only allows his closest friends to call him by his first name.' She looked away. 'Did Connie enjoy meeting him?'

'I think so, though it's always hard to tell with her. People of her background are not easily impressed.'

'Adolf has a strong effect on women. They get sexual excitement at his rallies. Young girls weep tears of joy. I have seen them.'

'What about you, Fräulein? Do his speeches excite you?'

Leni lowered her eyes and then raised them again. 'No, Adolf is not my type. I like actors.' She stroked his hand and dipped her head so that it was resting against his shoulder once more. 'And athletes.'

Kim extricated himself and moved one step away. 'What's he like?'

'Adolf? Not as bad as his opponents would make you believe. He has an excellent memory and much broader taste than people imagine. His favourite film is Marlene's *The Blue Angel* but he likes also *King Kong* and Mickey Mouse. And he loves his dogs. I've heard him talking to them.'

Kim felt a frisson at being taken into Leni's confidence in this way. He couldn't quite believe he was here talking to someone so famous. 'What about Göring? Are you friends with him, too?'

'Of course. Hermann is fun. A man of great appetite. Not just food and Dom Pérignon, he likes the Fräuleins too . . . You have a smile. Have I said something funny?'

Kim liked the way she pronounced the 'th' of 'something' as a 'z'. 'Is it true that he wears jewels and bearskin coats?' he asked.

'I expect so.' Leni laughed as a memory came to her. 'It was from Hermann that I heard that Hindenburg had named Adolf chancellor. I was naked, in a hotel sauna in Davos with my assistant Hans and a few other high-spirited young men. We were having a party!'

Kim felt his own inhibitions slipping away. He now had a mental image of Leni naked, which was perhaps precisely what she, in her flirtatious way, had intended. In all his twenty-four years, he had never met anyone like her and he was finding her openness quietly intoxicating.

'What about Goebbels?' he asked. He thought he heard someone on the steps and glanced behind Leni to try to see who it was.

Leni shook her head, causing a wisp of dark hair to cover her eye. 'The He-goat of Babelsberg. A complete hypocrite. He listens to jazz and sleeps with his starlets then tells everyone else they must not do the same.'

'But presumably—'

Before Kim could finish his sentence, Leni turned and kissed him on the lips, softly at first and then with more pressure. He was too surprised to reciprocate, or resist. Suddenly a flashbulb popped, startling them both, and momentarily blinding Kim. He rubbed his eyes but saw only the back of a man hurrying down the stairs. The taste of Leni's lipstick was on his tongue.

She lit two cigarettes and offered him one.

'I don't smoke,' Kim said.

'The bastards follow me everywhere,' Leni said.

'We should go back inside. Connie will be looking for me.'

Leni linked her arm with his. 'I am sorry,' she said. 'I should not have done that.'

'No, don't be sorry,' Kim said. 'I'm flattered. You are a very . . . Look, I must get back to Connie. She and I are . . .'

Leni let go of his arm, raised and lowered her shoulders and said again: 'I hope you can forgive me. We should probably go back separately.'

Inside, Kim found Connie chatting to Diana Mitford. Alun, who was standing next to her, looked relieved to see him, then quizzical. Kim wondered if there was lipstick on his face and wiped his mouth with his hand. As they chatted, he tried to spot the photographer, who he assumed was the man from the *Express*. He wanted to have an unfriendly word with him, but he seemed to have disappeared.

There was a subtle change in the atmosphere as Hitler walked past, with an entourage of four, apparently en route to the exit. He stopped to kiss Diana's hand and then kissed Connie's as well. Then, as if moving down a reception line, he shook hands with Alun and Kim, and was gone.

Twenty minutes later, Kim checked his watch and announced that he had better get back to the Olympic Village. Connie and Alun left with him and wished him good luck in case they didn't see him again before his first event. As they parted, a firework display began like an artillery barrage, the explosions turning the night sky blood red and then, in a tumbling rain of sparks, orange and gold.

TWENTY-FOUR

Even before she had reached the entrance gate of her villa, Leni could see the beams of light being cast by the cars waiting in her driveway. An actress is used to spotlights, but these felt more like searchlights. She parked, turned off her engine and stepped out of the car in the elegant manner her friend Marlene had taught her.

There were two cars and five men in plain clothes standing next to them. One man, in a double-breasted suit, was shorter than the others, his diminutive stature exaggerated by the considerable height of the figure standing next to him. She recognized them both.

'May we come in?' Goebbels said.

Leni tried to sound more nonchalant than she was feeling: 'If I'd known you were coming I'd have hidden the silver.'

'You know Reinhard Heydrich, I presume?' Goebbels's voice was flat, unamused.

Everyone knew Heydrich. As Himmler's deputy he had engineered the Night of the Long Knives. Barely two months had passed since he had started his new job, running the Sicherheitspolizei, the Security Police, and in that short time he had acquired a reputation – in what was a competitive field – for having the coldest heart in Berlin.

Though he had, incongruously, been put in charge of 'public relations' for the Olympics – the 'no public acts of violence against Jews for the duration of the Games' order had been his – Leni had never met him and had only seen him from a distance across a room. Unlike many of the hierarchy, he avoided cameras and social gatherings. Even Goebbels seemed intimidated by him.

Leni nodded and extended her hand in his direction but when the unsmiling Heydrich did not offer his in return, she turned this into an open-palmed gesture and suggested they go inside. Mariechen, her maid, must have been watching because she now opened the door and bobbed a curtsy.

'May I offer any of you gentlemen a drink?' Leni asked over her shoulder.

Again, Heydrich ignored her. He walked over to a polished walnut partners' desk in the hall and, without being invited, sat down, opened a briefcase and pulled out some papers. 'Sit,' he said in a disconcertingly dainty voice, without looking up. As Leni sank into the chair opposite, she looked over her shoulder and felt a fluttering sensation in her belly. Goebbels and the thick-necked, slash-eyed man she now recognized as his regular bodyguard remained standing, positioning themselves behind her. The other two men were guarding the door.

Alert and leaning forward, Leni studied Heydrich. He had a long, lupine face and blond eyebrows, blond eyelashes and blond hair that was swept back and shaved at the sides. 'Our records show you are not a member of the Party,' he said, still not looking up.

Leni could feel her heart rocking and tried not to let it show. 'Is that a question?' she said, keeping her tone light. She knew that Heydrich was not only a womanizer, he was a man of culture and an accomplished violinist. Perhaps he had seen her movies. They were about the same age. Flirtation might work.

He said nothing but continued to read. She could see what was written on the document: *Abstammungsnachweis*, Proof of Descent. 'Three years ago you signed a genealogical record of ancestry stating that you had no Jewish blood and that your grandparents were Protestants,' he said.

Leni's mouth had gone dry and she was blinking too much. 'If that is also a question,' she said, clearing her throat, 'the answer is yes, I did.' She sat up straighter. 'Is there a problem?'

'You declared that your mother . . .' Heydrich paused as he consulted the papers again. 'Bertha Ida Scherlach Riefenstahl was born in Poland in 1880, the daughter of Ottilie Bois.'

'That is correct.'

'How many children did Ottilie Bois have?'

Leni laughed, but it came out sounding false. 'Eighteen,' she said. 'They had big families in those days. She died while giving birth to the last one, my mother.'

'When was your grandmother born?'

Thinking about how she had had her real grandmother's birth certificate destroyed because she was possibly Jewish, Leni hesitated for a moment before answering. 'I don't recall.'

'She was born in 1863. That means that she must have been . . .' He paused for dramatic effect, as if trying to work out the age in his head. '. . . seventeen when she died giving birth to her eighteenth child.'

Leni now cursed herself for not having taken more care with the birth and death dates when filling out the Proof of Descent forms, but she had never imagined that she, the great Leni Riefenstahl, icon of the Third Reich, would ever have her records scrutinized in this way. 'I may have got the number of children wrong.'

'No, you got the number correct.' Heydrich now looked up and fixed his gaze upon her. His eyes – small, blue and wintry – were too close together. 'But you may have been confusing your mother's stepmother for your grandmother.'

'I believe my grandmother was born out of wedlock. That would explain the missing records.'

'What missing records?'

Leni looked behind her. Goebbels had his arms folded. 'Oh, I thought you said there was a missing record.'

'We have a marriage certificate,' Heydrich continued. 'When your grandfather's first wife died giving birth to her eighteenth child, he married his children's nanny in the Silesian town of Woldenberg and had three more children, making a total of twenty-one. I imagine you know the nanny's name?'

'I don't recall.'

'Her name was Ottilie Bois. Why did you pretend your mother's stepmother was your grandmother?'

Leni could feel her leg muscles tightening, ready to run. 'Look, I've been through all this with the authorities. There was an administrative mix-up, that's all.' A heavy silence settled on the room. 'If there is nothing else,' Leni continued in as strong a voice as she could manage, 'I must ask you to leave. I have a busy day tomorrow.'

More silence.

It was time for her to gamble; play the Adolf card. 'Does the Führer know you are here? I was with him at the reception just now and he didn't mention that you would be calling.'

'Your Proof of Aryan Descent is not what we have come here to discuss,' Heydrich said, the prettiness of his tone making his words seem uglier. 'Two years ago the Führer entrusted me with the task of destroying every copy of a Ministry of Propaganda film that featured the traitor Ernst Röhm.'

Leni's heart thrummed again. Why had he called *The Victory of Faith* a Ministry of Propaganda film and not 'her' film? Technically the Ministry owned the copyright and distribution rights but . . . Her thoughts were interrupted by Heydrich's next comment.

'He was insistent that anyone found in possession of a copy be charged with treason.'

Heydrich leaned back. The narrow set of his eyes intensified his obsidian gaze. 'Is there anything you want to tell us?'

'No,' Leni said, lifting her chin defiantly, 'why?'

'Did you make a duplicate negative of the film?'

'No.'

'Did you ask your assistant' – Heydrich consulted his notes – 'Friedrich Wilhelm Klein, to make a duplicate negative?'

'No.' Noticing her hands were shaking, Leni tried to put them under the table, but they would not move.

She thought of her eager young assistant, a student who had worked for her for a couple of months in the spring of 1934. She had a soft spot for him and did not want to get him into trouble. 'Is he claiming otherwise?'

'Not any more.'

'What do you mean?'

'He was shot while trying to escape from Number Eight Prinz-Albrecht-Strasse.'

Leni pictured the grand if grey building, a former hotel that was now the most terrifying address in Berlin. She opened her mouth but said nothing.

'Before he died, he confessed to making a copy of the film on your orders. Is the copy in London?'

Leni glanced behind her again, half hoping that Goebbels might help her, for old times' sake. He was staring at his feet.

'Look, stop playing games with me,' she said, returning to face her interrogator.

'You think this is a game?'

Leni hesitated then gave a slight shake of her head.

'Is the copy still in London?' Heydrich pressed.

A disturbing realization now: almost certainly these men would have searched her house before she arrived home. 'You obviously know there was a copy made and that I screened it to students at London University,' she said. 'What's wrong with that? I was the director. It was my film. This was months before the Führer gave his order that all copies of it were to be destroyed.'

'So where is it now?'

'As soon as he gave that order, I acted upon it. My copy went on a bonfire. Poor young Friedrich wouldn't have known that.'

Heydrich rode the silence that followed for a full minute as he stared at her across the table. Leni could hear herself breathing too loudly but held his gaze as best she could.

'You will remain here until this matter can be investigated,' Heydrich said, looking behind Leni at the two men by the door, signalling that he wanted them to go outside and guard the gate.

'You're putting me under house arrest?' She wanted to point out that she was the Führer's favourite film-maker, but they already knew that and were here anyway. And Heydrich would have sought, and must have been given, Adolf's permission before daring to take this action.

'This is ridiculous!' she said. 'How am I expected to direct *Olympia* from my home?'

Heydrich closed his briefcase, snapping the clasps, scraped back his chair and made his way to the door, followed by Goebbels and his bodyguard. As if possessed by an afterthought, he turned back and asked: 'Where did you stay in London on your trip two years ago?'

Leni thought quickly. Like all famous people she never travelled under her own name, but Heydrich's agents in London would know the dates of her trip and, when they looked through the registers of the five-star hotels, the name 'Lotte Richter' would make them sit up. Why had she used a German name when she had booked into the Ritz? And why had she used a name with the same initials as her own? Such vanity. Such stupidity. 'I stayed at the Dorchester,' she answered. 'Why do you ask?'

Heydrich left the house without answering. When she followed him to the front door she saw that Goebbels was looking in the glove compartment of her Mercedes. Unable to find what he was looking for – his lost Luger presumably – he got into the back seat of his own car and tapped his driver on the shoulder. As she watched the cars leave, Leni balled up her fists to keep them from shaking. The two remaining men lit cigarettes and eyed her insolently.

For a minute, Leni couldn't think what to do; then she went back inside, whispered an instruction to Mariechen, and collected a notebook. She marched back outside and went up to the men and asked them their names. They looked at one another before shrugging and answering. When Leni wrote the names in her notebook one of them smirked. Mariechen then came to the door and called out. 'Miss Riefenstahl, the Führer is on the telephone.'

Leni arched an eyebrow at the men, walked back inside and closed the door. Two minutes later she emerged again, rattling her car keys in their direction. They watched her as she started the engine and, when she drove towards the entrance gate, one of them stepped forward to block her path.

Leni wound down her window and said: 'The Führer has asked to see me. You'd better get out of my way.'

The men exchanged glances again, but seemed less certain of themselves now. When Leni honked her horn, the one blocking her path stood his ground for a moment and then moved to the side. As she drove out between them, she kept her eyes fixed on the road ahead. She didn't have much time.

TWENTY-FIVE

In his cottage in the Olympic Village, Kim sat on his bed thinking about his strange encounter with Leni Riefenstahl. He wondered whether all German women were as forward as she. Or perhaps the whole evening had been an hallucination.

He tried to think instead about the upcoming broad jump, but this set adrenaline coursing through his body. It was after midnight, which meant that the event was only one more day away. It seemed impossible. It was no longer next year, next month or next week, it was tomorrow. Taking a few calming breaths, he looked out behind the curtain. Only a couple of lights were still on in the surrounding cottages. Most of the other athletes would be asleep by now. To make himself tired enough to do the same, he tried some sit-ups. When that didn't work, he did something he had not tried since he was a teenager – he knelt beside his bed and prayed to Yahweh, his mother's God. He felt better after that and, to distract himself further, he read a few pages of his book, *The Thirty-Nine Steps*.

A knock at the door made him look up.

Kim slipped on his trousers as he got off the bed, but his hand hovered over the doorknob. No, it was too late to pretend he was not in.

'Who is it?' he asked.

'It's me,' Leni said in a loud whisper. 'I am sorry to disturb you,' she added as she marched in with a backward glance, 'but you have to help me.' She turned to face him, and then put a finger to her lips. 'I don't think I was followed. Is there anyone in London you can trust to do something for me?'

'Slow down,' Kim said. 'What is this about?'

'I . . . They . . .' Leni couldn't seem to find the words. Her eyes were bulging and wet and she looked frightened. Instinctively, Kim gave her a hug and, making shushing noises, rubbed her back. 'You need a cup of tea,' he said. 'Would you like a cup of tea?'

'Do you have anything stronger?' Leni said with a sniff.

'Afraid not.'

'Thank you, then. Tea. Plenty of sugar. I feel very shaky.'

As Kim put the kettle on, Leni tipped the contents of her handbag out over the bed. There was a leather-bound notebook, two pencils, a small camera, a wallet, a hairbrush, a packet of French cigarettes, an American Zippo lighter and a German Luger pistol. She lit a cigarette with unsteady hands, holding it between her middle and ring fingers.

Kim's eyes kept returning to the gun. She followed his gaze and said: 'Do you know how to use one? I think I will have to learn. I had some visitors at my villa tonight. Goebbels was one of them. He brought Sturmbannführer Heydrich with him. Do you know him?'

Kim shook his head. Leni seemed a different person to the one he had met at the reception earlier. Less flamboyant. As if her façade of confidence had been scraped away. 'He is an animal. You have heard of something called *Schutzhaft*?'

Kim shook his head again.

'It means something like protective custody. When Heydrich puts you in *Schutzhaft* it means the courts are no longer involved. You are on your own.'

'He's done that to you?'

'Not yet. But he has put two guards by my door.' She raised an eyebrow. 'I escaped. I said I was going to see Adolf. I came here instead.'

Kim poured the tea, added three spoons of sugar and, as he handed it to her, put his hand on her shoulder. She covered it with her hand. Her skin was cold. Clearly she was in shock.

At the same moment, they both heard footsteps outside. Kim went to the door and peered out into the darkness but couldn't see anyone. The night sky was dark and deep.

'Close the door,' Leni said. 'No one can know I am here.'

'What's happened?' Kim said. 'Why are you asking about London?'

'I need someone to collect something for me from the Ritz Hotel. Four film reels in a suitcase. If Heydrich's men find them, I will be dead.'

'I don't understand.'

'It's a documentary I made. The Führer ordered every copy to be destroyed. I wasn't supposed to have a copy and now . . .' She trailed off. 'Can you help me? I don't have much time.'

'Of course. When I get back to London I'll . . .'

'*Nein*. It has to be done now. Today. I can't ask anyone I know in London because Heydrich's agents will be watching them. Is there anyone in your family who might collect them?'

'I don't have any family. I could ask someone from the Black House, that's the headquarters of the British Union of Fascists.'

'No, von Ribbentrop will hear about it.'

'I might be able to find someone at White City, that's the stadium where I train, but most of the people I know there are over here for the Games.'

Leni lay on the bed and curled up into a foetal position. She looked as though she was on the verge of tears.

Kim suddenly clapped his hands. 'Alun will know someone.'

'Who is Alun?'

'One of my guests at the reception tonight.'

'Can we trust him?'

'I think so, yes.'

Leni wrote down her telephone number. 'Where is your friend staying?'

'The Adlon.'

'I'll drive you there. Come on.'

'I was asleep,' Alun said with a yawn as he opened his door. 'What do you want?'

'I need a favour,' Kim said. 'Can you think of anyone in London who could do an important errand?'

'What, now? What time is it?'

'It has to be today. It's urgent.'

'I suppose Herzl could do it. Why?'

Kim looked over his shoulder, then stepped into the hotel room. 'The communist?'

'Yes, but it's fine. Like I said, he's working for us now, a double agent.'

'Is he reliable?'

'Well, he's annoying,' Alun said, 'and lazy, but I suppose so, yes. What is it you want him to do?'

When Kim had finished his explanation, Alun raised an eyebrow: 'Leni Riefenstahl?'

'Yes, she's waiting for me in a car outside. But remember, the suitcase has been stored under the name "Lotte Richter". That's important. And once he's collected the case, Herzl must get rid of the film reels inside it. They have to be destroyed.'

Alun went to the window, opened the curtain and, signalling Kim over, pointed to a Mercedes sports car parked across the road. 'That her?'

The light was watery. It was almost dawn and the birds on the trees along Unter den Linden had started singing. 'Yes,' Kim said. 'That's her. You have to help. The poor thing seemed terrified.'

Alun was looking more awake now, as if his skidding thoughts were gaining traction.

'I must warn you,' Kim said. 'This could be dangerous, for both of us.'

'I'll ask the night manager to book a trunk call for me to London,' Alun said. 'Herzl won't be in the bookshop before nine. What time is it now?'

'You can't call, they'll be listening in.'

'Telegram?'

'Same.'

Alun looked momentarily lost in thought and then nodded before pulling out a suitcase from under his bed. He opened it and took out a contraption that looked like a metal coat hanger with wires attached to it and a Morse code machine. It seemed to confirm what Kim had suspected: that Alun worked for MI5.

TWENTY-SIX

London

'Sorry sir,' the liveried doorman in the top hat said, 'but you can't come in.'

'I have every right!' Herzl countered. 'Just because—'

'You need a tie, sir,' the doorman interrupted in an affable tone. 'We can lend you one, if you like.'

Herzl touched his shirt collar. His top button was done up, as he thought this made him look tidier, but he was not in the habit of wearing ties, because he considered them to be symbols of bourgeois hegemony. 'Thank you,' he said with more dignity than he was feeling.

Before he had set off for Berlin, 'Comrade Pryce' had given Herzl a Vigenère cipher, essentially a cryptographic slide rule with a 'fixed' alphabet on the bottom and a 'moving' alphabet on the top, and he had then shown him how to use it. Even though it had been straightforward enough for Herzl to decipher Alun's message – once he had found each letter of their agreed keyword, 'Stakhanovite' – it had taken him almost an hour to do so and the message, when he read it back, had unnerved him. He had then come straight here by Tube. It was now 10.30 a.m.

He slipped the borrowed tie on and asked the doorman for directions to the hotel's storage room. As he lumbered down the stairs, a couple of elegantly attired female guests glanced at him. Even though he was wearing a jacket, and now a tie, his scruffy figure clearly did not look as if it belonged in the Ritz. The beret he was wearing probably did not help.

When he reached the basement level, he followed signs to the lost property office. The storage room was next to it. There was a bespectacled porter at the desk there who did not notice him approach and, startled, tried to hide the newspaper he was reading.

'I've come to collect some film reels for Leni Riefenstahl,' he said.

The porter looked puzzled as he peered over the glasses sitting on the bridge of his nose. 'Like I told the other gentlemen, we don't have them here.'

'What other gentlemen?'

'Two of them. One sounded foreign. You just missed them.'

Herzl thought for a moment. 'Could you have another look?'

The porter blew out his cheeks and, looking slightly peeved, said, 'Certainly, sir,' before disappearing into a back room for half a minute in what was clearly a token gesture.

'Sorry sir,' he said, shaking his head. 'Was there anything else you wanted?'

Herzl drummed his fingers on the counter and contemplated, in a distracted way, the glass of milk next to a small plate that was empty apart from a few biscuit crumbs. 'Got a friend whose father delivers milk,' he said, not looking up. 'They call him the Pryce of Milk.' He frowned. 'No, that's not it. Pryce the Milk. Yes. He's Welsh, you see. That's what they do in Wales. Pryce the Milk. Jones the Bread. Owens the Death. That's the undertaker.'

'Was there anything else you wanted, sir?'

'Here's one for you,' Herzl said, now meeting the porter's eye. 'A man comes home and tells his wife: "Have you heard? Apparently, the milkman has slept with every woman on this street, bar one." And the wife says: "I bet it's that stuck-up cow at Number Forty-three."'

The porter laughed and, in a friendlier voice, said: 'Do you work for her as well, then?'

'Who?'

'Leni Riefenstahl?'

'Oh, right, yes. I'm one of her cameramen.'

'She uses English cameramen?'

Herzl adjusted his tie. 'Only works with the best.'

'I remember when she stayed here. People kept asking for her autograph.'

Herzl frowned again as he remembered a note in his pocket. He took it out, examined it, then said: 'Could you have one more look and see if anything has been left here under the name "Lotte Richter"?'

The porter returned to the back room and, a minute later, emerged with a suitcase. 'We've got this.'

Herzl opened it. It contained four metal canisters, each the size of a wheel hub.

The porter took a clipboard, filled in some details and asked for Herzl's signature. With an illegible flourish, Herzl signed it 'Leon Trotsky' and was relieved when the porter did not inspect the signature too closely. Instead the man stared pointedly at a saucer on the counter which had a few coins in it. Herzl twigged and rummaged around in his pocket but, unable to find any change, said: 'You know, in revolutionary Spain they have stopped giving tips to waiters because everyone there is considered equal.'

'I'll bear that in mind, Mr . . .' The porter now gave the signature a glance and said in a deadpan voice: '. . . Trotsky.'

The lobby was almost empty as Herzl passed through it on his way out. Seeing a couple of men in dark blue suits at the check-in desk going through a ledger with the concierge, he wondered if they might be the ones who had been asking for the film reels. When one of them looked up and noticed Herzl noticing them, he nudged the other.

After squeezing through the revolving entrance door with the case, Herzl was outside once more, breathing in the polluted air of Western capitalism.

'Excuse me, sir!'

He stiffened before turning slowly. Behind him the doorman was pointing to his tie. Once he had handed over the borrowed item, he crossed the road and walked in the direction of Piccadilly Circus. Looking over his shoulder once more he saw that the two men were now standing on the pavement outside the hotel. One of them spotted him and pointed.

Herzl quickened his pace. As a red double decker bus approached and stopped, he considered jumping on it but then realized he was at the entrance of the Royal Academy. He slipped through the front door, then turned left and entered a building he half registered as the Geological Society. He clumped as quickly as he could up a flight of stairs, then stopped and panted for a moment, before entering a room he saw was a library arranged over two floors with an ornate iron balcony. He headed to a window and looked down at the street below. One of the besuited men was jumping on the bus as it moved off, while the other weaved in and out of the pedestrians passing by on Piccadilly.

The library was empty and, as Herzl walked between the columns on its balcony, his footsteps echoed around the room. He needed to find somewhere to hide the suitcase, at least temporarily. There was a door that opened on to a corridor with lavatories on one side and what looked to be an office on the other. When he felt for a light switch and flicked it on, Herzl saw the space was dominated by four green cabinets, each with a dozen wide but narrow drawers. He opened one of the lower ones and saw it was full of large, topographical maps laid out flat. After trying a couple more drawers he found one that was only half full. This might be a good place to hide the canisters of film, he thought, if he slid them under the maps and pushed them all the way to the back. The drawer was deep; at least four feet. Unless someone pulled it all the way out, they were unlikely to find the reels.

Thinking he had heard footsteps, Herzl peered around the side of the door. He could see the shadow of someone in the library. As quietly as he could, he padded across the corridor, opened the door to the lavatory, headed for the furthest cubicle and sat down. He heard someone enter and stand still. Though he was out of breath, Herzl stilled his lungs and gritted his teeth. With a creak of his leather shoes, the man started moving slowly down the line of cubicles, pausing at each. Was he checking underneath the doors? He could hear the man breathing heavily now, as if he had been running. Herzl lifted the suitcase silently off the floor.

TWENTY-SEVEN

In the colourless morning, Kim lay on his hard mattress trying to get back to sleep. Today was his first event, the broad jump, and he had woken up too early. It didn't help that he kept thinking about his strange visit from Leni the night before last. Had that really happened or had he dreamt it? He still didn't know if Alun's friend Herzl had been successful in retrieving Leni's films in London.

Giving up on sleep, he swung his legs over the side of the bed, opened his bedside table drawer to get his book and saw Leni's Luger pistol lying there. She had said she couldn't be found with it in her possession as it would give Heydrich another excuse to arrest her. When she had added that she would miss the feeling of security it afforded her, Kim had suggested she swap it for the starting pistol he had brought with him to Berlin – from a distance, it looked real.

He now felt a prickle of anxiety as he realized he could no longer perform his lucky ritual, kissing the starting pistol before each of his events. He also felt a flutter of panic at the thought of what the German authorities might do to him, a Jew, if they found him in possession of a pistol that Leni had apparently stolen from Goebbels – she had shown him where it was engraved with his initials. He determined to get rid of it straight after breakfast.

A few minutes later, as cold rain bounced off the paved paths of the Olympic Village, Kim made his way to the dining block. There was a picture of Hitler hanging on the wall and a group of American athletes were amusing themselves by throwing rolled-up bread pellets at it. After complaints about the endless sauerkraut and boiled vegetables, the caterers had started providing a breakfast of bacon, eggs, tomatoes, mushrooms and toast. Kim piled his plate high, but his appetite deserted him when he received a summons from Mr Riley. All he was told was that it was 'urgent'.

As he entered the coach's office, Kim heard the scratch of pen on paper. Mr Riley lowered a curved blotter over fresh ink and peered up over half-moon glasses. He took the glasses off and blew on the lenses before polishing them with a handkerchief. 'The *Daily Express* is running a story about you,' he said. 'They've asked me for a comment.'

'About me? Why?'

'They reckon you're a member of the British Union of Fascists.'

'But my membership has never been a secret,' Kim protested. 'Quite the contrary. I was on the cover of *The Blackshirt*. Where's the story in that?'

'It says they were sponsoring you. You know that's not allowed.'

'It's not like that.'

'If you needed money you should have come to me.' The coach pulled a watch from his waistcoat pocket and clicked it open and closed. 'As for the photographs . . .'

'What photographs?'

'Apparently, there's one of you shaking hands with Hitler while wearing your British blazer with a BUF sponsorship badge on it.'

'That wasn't—'

'And another one of you giving a Nazi salute by the broad-jump pit. What the hell were you thinking?'

Kim scowled. 'I didn't give . . .' He thought for a moment and then pinched the bridge of his nose. 'No, I remember now. I was waving. At Leni Riefenstahl.'

'Yes, that's the other thing. There's a photograph of you kissing her.'

Kim stared at him with his mouth half open. The coach was asking a question but all Kim could hear was the music of the rainstorm outside.

'Well?' the coach was asking. '*Did* you kiss her?'

'That bugger,' Kim said. 'There was a photographer from the *Express* at a reception I went to.'

Mr Riley let out a sigh of exasperation. 'What did I tell you about avoiding women before an event?'

'Nothing happened between us.'

The coach checked his watch again. 'We can decide what to do later. Some of the British Olympic Committee want to have you suspended straight away, but they've not had their meeting yet so, if I were you, I'd get over to the broad jump as quickly as you can.'

On the bus to the Olympic stadium, Kim sat next to a young woman with an Australian accent who had introduced herself with a perfunctory 'Pat Norton, backstroke', but he had been too absorbed in his thoughts to talk to her and he had little recollection of changing into his kit at the journey's end and walking to the broad-jump pit where almost fifty competitors were warming up. It had stopped raining but the sky was still cloudy and the air was cool.

Only when he was the next but one to jump in the qualifying round did Kim start to feel a familiar fluttering sensation in his stomach. He scanned the crowds, hoping to see Connie's face. And then he stiffened.

His father was sitting two rows from the front and was staring at him.

Feeling as if he had been punched in the solar plexus, Kim looked away. His lungs began to burn and tighten and he felt as if he was struggling to breathe. With his eyes bulging in panic, Kim looked for his father again and this time realized it wasn't him. It was just a man who looked like him.

Kim's sense of relief was instant and, as the breath returned to his loosening airways, he looked up at the sky.

Jesse Owens must have sensed his tension because he sidled over and, with a pat on his shoulder, said: 'I'd wait a few minutes for this headwind to drop, if I were you.'

Kim tried to regain his poise. 'Thanks,' he said, before adding more formally than he intended, 'You're such an impressive athlete – everyone is talking about you.'

Owens smiled. 'Thanks. You're Kim Newlands, aren't you? Our German friend Miss Riefenstahl has told me all about you.' He nodded at one of Leni's cameramen, but the director herself was nowhere to be seen. 'Good luck. Know what my coach always says to me?'

Kim shook his head.

'Jump like you don't care about the outcome. It's good advice.'

Buoyed by this friendly gesture, Kim could feel his composure and confidence returning. This time it was excitement he felt rather than nerves. Instead of his father, he pictured his mother smiling at him and, in that moment, he knew in his heart that he could win and, more importantly, that he wanted to win. Not only that, he was going to enjoy winning. Winning was the only thing that mattered to him now.

Blocking out the noise from the crowd and narrowing his peripheral vision to the length of the path ahead of him, he waited for the head-wind to drop, as Owens had advised. He checked his run-up mark then set off, running faster and faster until he hit the take-off board at precisely the right point and leapt through the air with his long legs folded beneath him.

As he left the pit, with sand clinging to his calves, he gave Owens a thumbs-up, then looked across to the indicator board in the centre of the stadium. It gave his distance as 24 feet 11 inches, only three inches off his personal best, and more than enough to get him through to the finals later that day.

Owens was the last to jump. He jogged down the runway and through the landing pit in a gentle practice run, as American broad jumpers tended to do. But then a German official in a white jacket ran up waving a red flag and shouted 'Foul'. Three American coaches immediately approached the official and started arguing with him, but the decision stood. The warm-up jog was marked down as Owens's first attempt. All the athletes who had witnessed this looked at one another with the same thought: the German official was, in effect, trying to sabotage the favourite.

Owens now looked unsettled and his second jump seemed wobbly – his rhythm was off and his strides choppy – and he fouled again, this time genuinely, by overstepping the take-off board.

Kim could not believe it. Owens could jump the qualifying distance – 23 feet 5½ inches – in his sleep. After all, his personal best, set the previous year, was 26 feet 8 inches.

The world record holder sat down on the field, looking dejected. Then Luz Long, the German champion, approached his American rival and, draping an arm around his shoulder, said something to him in a voice too low for Kim to hear. Long, who was wearing a white vest emblazoned with a swastika over an eagle, lined up a white towel a couple of inches before the take-off board and nodded at Owens. Owens nodded back, composed himself and started his third and final jump. This time his strides were more evenly spaced, his gait less hesitant and, a couple of inches before he reached the board, he propelled himself into the air. It worked, and from the parallel trench, shooting from a low angle, Leni's cameraman captured Owens in mid-flight.

Long came over to congratulate him with a pat on the back. 'See?' he said. 'Easy.'

'*Danke*,' Owens said, one of the few German words the foreign athletes had learned.

As Owens walked away with measured steps, Kim was joined by Long.

'What did you say to him?' Kim asked.

'I said: "What has taken your goat, Jesse Owens?" I told him I thought he was afraid he would foul again so he should begin his jump a few inches behind the take-off board, that way he would not be over-concentrating when hitting it and should still make the qualifying distance, but without risking a foul.'

'Good advice,' Kim said. 'That was sporting of you.'

'Thank you. Perhaps in the final tonight I should advise him to jump with his shoelaces tied together!'

Both men laughed briefly, then seemed to be struck by the same thought: that a few minutes earlier the bookies would have been shortening the odds on Long winning gold and Newlands, silver.

That evening, with Hitler rubbing his knees in excitement as he watched, Kim felt strangely calm. He looked for Connie in the crowd but could not see her. Nor could he see Leni. Was she still under house arrest?

Only sixteen of the jumpers had made the qualifying distance and his turn soon came around. After stretching his hamstrings, he began his approach slowly before accelerating into a sprint. His penultimate stride was longer than his last, as it should be, and then, placing his foot flat on the take-off board, he entered the jump with his torso upright and his hips well forward. With his legs cycling in the air, he found himself following a perfect parabolic path, rising to the height of a man at its peak, so high he felt as though he might clear the pit altogether. The stadium seemed to fall silent and then he was down and conscious of the crowd cheering. When he turned to the board, he could scarcely believe what he was reading: 25 feet 5 inches, a personal best by three inches. It was also a new British record.

Like the others he would have five more attempts, but Kim knew in his gut that he would not be able to improve on this first jump. Owens beat him with his second jump and Long with his third, as expected, but as he stared at the leader board, Kim's heart pummelled his ribs. It was looking as if his first jump might be enough to secure the bronze.

On his fifth attempt, Long set a new European record with a jump of 25 feet 8 inches, but Owens made a jump of 26 feet 5½ inches in his final attempt, beating the previous Olympic best by three and a half inches.

The stadium erupted. Long was the first to congratulate Owens, running over to him and throwing an arm around his shoulder. Then, turning to the side of the stadium where Hitler's rostrum was located, he grabbed Owens's right hand with his left and flung their arms in the air. The crowd seemingly turned as one to see Hitler's reaction, but he looked on impassively. As the blond, Aryan *Übermensch* and the black grandson of a slave paraded across the infield, hand in hand, tens of thousands of German voices chanted '*Yaycee Ohvens! Yaycee Ohvens!*'

Kim looked back at the board. Owens had won gold, Long had taken silver but the bronze slot was still empty. He could see a huddle of white-coated officials. When one of them, a short man with a crooked mouth and a jutting lower lip, looked across at Kim, his heart tripped, a stumbling double beat.

A hush settled on the crowd as, with pointed fingers and whispers, more people became aware of the blank space where the name of the bronze-medal winner should be.

TWENTY-EIGHT

Kim could feel his heart rate mounting and, though he was trying to control it through his nose, his breathing was ragged once more. And then time slackened as a series of random letters appeared on the board. Was it broken? They spelled out 'Naoto Tajima'. This was not possible. The Japanese jumper had recorded 25 feet 4 inches, one inch less than Kim's distance.

He closed his eyes and then opened them again. The name was still there. People in the crowd were rising to their feet. Kim gave another slow blink and looked at their faces. Some were contorted. Mouths were open as if they were shouting – accusations of cheating? – but he could not hear their words.

And now Mr Riley was standing in front of him saying something. Kim could hear a ringing in his ears before the coach's words slammed into focus. 'You've been disqualified.'

'Why? What for?'

'It's this damned report in the newspaper. The officials are saying it means your amateur status has been compromised. I'm sorry. Are you all right, lad?'

Mr Riley put a hand on his shoulder and Kim felt himself staggering slightly under its weight. 'But that's not fair,' he gasped. 'It's not true.'

He pushed the hand away and walked off to be on his own. What could he do? If he was disqualified from this event, did that mean he would be disqualified from the others too? He looked around for Mr

Riley. Surely he would be allowed to appeal the decision? But when he could not see the coach, he lowered his head again. He was feeling faint now and thought he might pass out.

It was over. Everything he had dared to dream of, everything he had worked for, everything he had made sacrifices for: over. He took the towel from his neck and covered his head with it.

And then he felt an arm around his shoulder and looked up to see Mr Riley sitting on the ground beside him. The coach gave him a sympathetic smile, unscrewed the top from a hip flask and took a sip from it before passing it to him. When Kim waved it away, he gave a little frown of insistence before proffering it again. This time Kim took it, had a sip and coughed. The alcohol was raw against the back of his throat, but its sudden warmth in his belly felt pleasant and it seemed to help numb the pain he was feeling. He took another sip, swallowed hard and tried not to show how close he was to tears.

TWENTY-NINE

The following morning, in her studio, Leni tapped a pen against her teeth as she stared at the telephone on her desk. She was still under house arrest but if everything had gone to plan she would soon be back working at the Olympic stadium. Kim was supposed to call her as soon as he heard any news from London. She had explained that he must not mention the films over the telephone or give his name. If the mission had been successful, he was simply to say 'Wrong number' and then hang up. To distract herself as she waited, she watched some rushes that her cameramen had brought her from the previous day.

She wished she had thought to instruct them to use filters for the medal ceremony following the broad jump. The footage of the Stars and Stripes being run up the tallest flagpole, with the swastika and the circle of the sun on the flagpoles either side, would have looked more dramatic if they had used a red filter to turn the blue sky behind them black. Owens, with the Olympic laurels on his head, and his red, white and blue striped shirt flecked with sand, was smiling toothily as he waved from the dais. She marked this clip with a wax crayon, draped it around her neck and threaded the next clip into the reel.

This one showed the winners receiving their medals and laurels on the podium: Owens gold for America, Long silver for Germany, and Naoto Tajima bronze for Japan – but only after a stewards' enquiry. As the flags were raised, Long, in a white roll-neck, stretched his arm out in front of him in the Nazi salute, Tajima, also in white, stood to attention and Owens, in his baggy blue sweatshirt with a towel wrapped around his neck, gave a US army-style salute. This was a better clip and Leni used a chinograph pencil to mark it with a small cross before draping it on top of the one already around her neck.

Next she looked at some earlier footage her cameraman had taken of Kim finding out his bad news. There was a close-up of his face screwed up in anguish and then the lens zoomed out as his hands clenched into fists. He laced his fingers behind his head, opened his eyes, noticed the camera pointing at him and turned away. It was a moving piece of footage, a vivid expression of what losing meant to an athlete who had trained for four years for this one moment. It would definitely make the final cut of her film.

The camera kept rolling as a man in a straw boater, the British coach presumably, went over to comfort her English friend, who was sitting on the ground looking miserable. The coach got down beside Kim, put an arm around his shoulders and offered him a sip of something from his hip flask.

She checked her watch and stared at the telephone again. Drawn from her reverie by the sound of the film strip flapping as the reel continued to spin, she turned the projector off and picked up the *Daily Express* that her assistant had brought her, copies of it having arrived on the overnight train from London.

The story on the front page alleged that Kim had been receiving sponsorship money from the British Union of Fascists, and noted that, if this were true, it would mean he no longer had amateur status and would therefore be unable to compete in the Olympics. Under the headline 'British athlete is Nazi sympathizer' there was a photograph of Kim doing what did, in truth, look like a Nazi salute, but which Leni knew to be a wave, because it was directed at her. That Jesse Owens was in the background made the image seem all the more symbolic. There was also a photograph of Kim in London wearing a black BUF uniform, marching behind Sir Oswald Mosley, and another of him lying on his back on the track in Berlin, with Leni holding his leg and pressing herself against him. He looked good in that one, but it was not a flattering one of her. The one of them kissing was better. And she liked that the newspaper had described her as a 'German film-maker considered by many of her fellow countrymen to be a genius'.

It occurred to Leni now that a shot of this newspaper might make a good 'sub-plot' in her film. It would give a romantic twist to the 'story' of the broad-jump final. Like Alfred Hitchcock, she could have a cameo in her own film, the equivalent of a great artist signing a canvas.

When the telephone rang, she flinched.

Before picking up the receiver she wriggled her body as if to compose herself. 'This is Leni Riefenstahl,' she said in German. 'Hello?'

There was a pause and then an English voice said: 'Wrong number.'

THIRTY

So far during the Games, a number of Kim's team-mates had been amusing themselves by saying 'Hail King Edward' whenever a uniformed German greeted them with 'Heil Hitler'. Kim had joined in a couple of times, throwing in a sloppy salute for good measure. But he was not in the mood to do it now as he encountered a guard outside the changing room. He had come to collect his watch and his running shoes as he would no longer be needing them for the qualifying races for the hurdles today.

When he entered, already feeling self-conscious because he was wearing a suit and tie, those of his team-mates who looked up made matters worse by stopping their conversations mid-sentence. He got the impression that they had been talking about him. No one made eye contact as he walked to his locker, and a javelin-thrower he had considered a friend pointedly refused to move out of his way. Another team-mate who was getting dressed leaned down to adjust his gaiters, thereby avoiding an acknowledgement.

Ten minutes later, once he had found an empty telephone booth in the main reception area, Kim tried Connie's room at the Adlon Hotel again. He had been trying to reach her since the previous night, but she had not been picking up. When he managed to get through now and Alun answered, he assumed the switchboard must have put him through to the wrong room.

'Is Connie there?' he said. 'I need to speak to her.'

'She's gone for a walk,' Alun said. 'To the Tiergarten.' There was a long pause before he added: 'I'm afraid she's heard about the story in the *Express*.'

Kim closed his eyes and tapped the telephone against his forehead. 'How?'

'My fault. I assumed someone had already told her.'

'I'm coming to the hotel,' Kim said. 'Can you meet me in the lobby in half an hour?'

'There's a fountain,' Alun said. 'You can't miss it. I'll be waiting there.'

A chemical smell was being carried on the easterly wind as Kim's taxi drove past a gasworks en route to Unter den Linden. He found Alun sitting alone amid the square pillars of marble.

'She's not back yet.'

Kim chewed his lip. 'How did she seem?'

'Distracted.'

'So tell me again: you overheard an English couple talking about the article at breakfast?'

'Yes. The hotel probably has all the foreign papers delivered.'

Kim thought about this for a moment. 'But I still don't know how the *Express* found out about my bursary. That night when we went to the reception and were introduced to Hitler, I saw you talking to their photographer. Did you tip him off?'

'Course not. Look, I don't know what happened, Kim, and I feel devastated for you, but as your friend I have to say I think you are worrying about the wrong thing here. Connie knows now and that's that.' Pause. 'I watched the broad jump yesterday. You must feel cheated.'

Kim was rubbing the back of his neck.

Alun looked over his shoulder and whispered: 'Did you give your German friend the news from London?'

'Yes,' Kim said in a distracted voice. 'Yes, thank you for that. And please thank your friend Martin Herzl for me. You both did a kind thing. I won't forget it.'

'Well, tell Miss Riefenstahl she has nothing more to worry about. Herzl said he was followed by a couple of men but he managed to give them the slip. The films are in a place now where no one will find them.'

'Didn't he destroy them?'

'No need. No one will find them where he has hidden them.'

Kim fell silent as he stared at the fountain.

'Why did you have to tell Connie about the story in the *Express*, Alun?' he said suddenly.

'I thought she already knew. I said I was sorry.'

'No . . . No, you didn't.'

After jogging the short distance from the Adlon to the Brandenburg Gate, Kim asked a policeman for directions to the Tiergarten, or rather he said 'Tiergarten?' and gave a shrug. When the policeman made a sweeping gesture towards the wooded parkland across the road in front of them, Kim walked briskly along its tree-lined edge for a few hundred yards, alternately crouching and standing on his toes looking for a bandstand. Alun had said he thought that was where Connie had headed.

Seeing a woman who was about the same height as Connie, Kim followed her along a gravel path that led deeper into the park. It wasn't her, though. Looking left and right, Kim crossed a wooden bridge that spanned a pond on which two swans were poised motionless, facing one another. They seemed oblivious to the paddle boats nearby.

His whole body seemed to be over-sensitized, as if every step was vibrating up from his feet and jarring his brain. Finally he spotted the bandstand. Connie was sitting on a bench in front of it, her back to him. He approached her, stopping to compose himself before quietly sitting down. She turned her head when she became aware of him but then, wordlessly, turned it back. He could see from the smudged tracks below her intact eye that she had been crying. She smoothed out her skirt and rested her hands on her knees, staring down at them.

'Thought I might find you here,' Kim said in as airy a tone as he could manage. 'Did you see the swans?'

Connie said nothing.

'I didn't see you at the broad jump yesterday,' Kim continued.

Connie held the silence for a beat and then, still looking down at her hands, she said in a distant, almost trance-like voice: 'You know, when I lost my eye, I thought my life was over. No one would find me attractive.'

'I did,' Kim said. 'I still do.'

'Let me finish, Kim. I'm not good at this and there is something I need to say, something I want you to know. I . . .' She let out a long breath and her shoulders drooped. 'I know *you* still found me attractive. That was what gave me the strength to carry on. As long as I had *you* by my side, loving me, supporting me, I felt I could do anything. I felt normal. I felt . . .' She sighed again. 'I know you think I am just a spoilt and frivolous girl . . .'

'I don't.'

'Yes, you do, everyone does. But I . . .'

Connie seemed to lose the sequence of her thoughts and the curtain of silence between them thickened. After what seemed like a minute, she turned, met his gaze and said with a sudden heat in her voice: '*How could you?*'

Kim leaned back. 'How could I what?'

Connie turned her whole body now so that she was facing him, squaring up for a fight. 'You know what.'

'That photograph with Leni Riefenstahl? It was nothing. I was set up.'

'I'm not talking about the photograph. I'm talking about what happened after the photograph was taken.'

'Nothing happened.'

Connie fell into an accusing silence.

'Nothing happened,' Kim repeated; then he added, 'Why, what do you *think* happened?'

'That woman came to see you at the Olympic Village. Later that night.'

Kim was trying to keep his tone light but a raised note of concern was colouring his voice. 'You're being ridiculous.'

Connie said nothing, simply let his words hang between them like a toxic cloud. Then she said: 'Don't I mean anything to you?'

Kim frowned. 'Of course you do.' For a moment, he wondered if he could regain some lost ground. 'Though I'm not sure what I mean to you as you haven't even told your—'

Connie raised her hand as if she was about to slap his face. '*Don't you dare . . .*' Her hand remained suspended in the air for a moment; then she clenched it into a fist and lowered it. In a quieter voice, she added: 'Don't make this about me and my family.'

'What makes you think she came back to the Olympic Village?'

'I was told.'

Kim was shocked by this. He wanted to ask who had told her but he could sense that now was not the right moment. He did consider telling Connie about the reels of film Leni had wanted collecting from the Ritz, but an instinct stopped him. He didn't want Connie implicated in any way – and it was safer for her if she knew nothing. The fear that Leni had displayed had alarmed him. What if Connie was stopped and questioned – it wouldn't be fair to put her at risk. He decided to give her a version of the truth.

'OK, she did visit me but look, honestly,' he said, 'she didn't stay long.'

'Liar.'

'I'm not lying. She was in trouble. She needed help from someone with connections in London so she came to me.' He reached for her fingers. 'Nothing has changed.'

'Please don't.' Connie withdrew her hand. 'Everything has changed. I'm going back to London on the next train.'

'Leni came to ask me for a favour,' Kim replied. 'That was all. Nothing else happened.' He felt dry-mouthed and breathless now. Why was Connie being so unreasonable? Why was she not leaving him room for manoeuvre? He had never seen her so angry before. 'I'll come with you,' he said in a taut voice. 'Back to London.'

She allowed his words to settle across the park like falling ash before saying: 'No.' With that she got to her feet and walked with tight steps and raised head in the direction of the bridge.

Later that afternoon, Kim received a message from Alun saying, 'Meet me at the diving pool at three.'

'What do you want?' Kim asked tonelessly.

'I wanted to see you before we left,' Alun said, patting the bench beside him.

'Where is she?' Kim said, sitting down.

'Back at the hotel. Our train doesn't leave until this evening. It's a sleeper. The only one we could get.'

Alun was staring in the direction of the pool. Leni was standing with her hands on her hips barking orders at one of her cameramen in the water. She then marched off in the direction of another cameraman, who looked as though he was trying to escape from her by climbing the ladder to the diving boards. As she passed a white-gloved soldier, he snapped to attention.

'Is she as relaxed as this in private?' Alun asked.

Kim acknowledged the question with a distracted murmur. He could not order his thoughts. All he could hear, over and again, was Connie's crisp final word to him: 'No.'

Alun cocked his head to one side as he turned to face Kim. 'So what are your plans now?'

'I'm going to try and talk to Connie again.'

'I wouldn't,' Alun said. 'You'll only make things worse.'

Kim did not try to disguise the irritation in his voice. 'How could things be worse?'

'She needs time to think. Time to forgive you.'

'For what? I didn't do anything.'

'You and I both know what happened that night,' Alun said, 'but Connie doesn't, and she can't, not while she is still here in Berlin. I can tell her the truth when we get back to London and then, in a few days, when she's had time to calm down, you can talk to her on the telephone and sort everything out between you.'

Kim watched the diver on the 5-metre board launch himself off the platform and perform a graceful backward somersault. 'No,' Kim said with a shake of his head. 'I'm going to come back with you both.'

'What about your other events? I thought your coach was going to appeal against your disqualification.'

'He is.'

'So you might still be able to compete?'

'I suppose it's possible, but it looks unlikely.'

'You're going to have to stay, then. You can't miss this opportunity. They might reinstate your bronze medal.'

Kim swivelled around in his seat and studied Alun's face. He could feel anger contracting the muscles in his neck. He trusted Alun as a friend, especially after he'd helped get Leni's film, but there was something about his behaviour that didn't add up. 'Were you the one who told Connie that Leni had been to see me in the Olympic Village?'

Alun held Kim's stare and said: 'Yes.'

Kim had not been expecting this answer and lapsed back into silence.

'It was before you came to see me,' Alun added.

'I don't understand,' Kim said. 'How did you know I'd had a visit from Leni before I told you?'

'Connie sent me back to look for you after we left the reception that night and I saw her with you in your cottage.'

'What do you mean "Connie sent you"? What are you talking about?'

'When we got back to the Adlon, Connie went to her room and collected a bottle of sleeping pills. She put me in a taxi and asked me to take them to you, so that you could get some sleep before your events. She said you'd be feeling nervous. But when I saw you with Leni, I didn't want to interrupt.'

Kim pursed his lips. This sounded plausible. He remembered that at one point that night he and Leni thought they had heard someone prowling around outside his cottage. 'Why didn't you mention it when I came to see you?'

'It was the middle of the night. I wasn't thinking straight.'

There was a cheer from the crowd as a diver emerged from the water and raised his arms in the air.

'But later I told you that Leni only came to visit me that night because she needed help getting her films back, so why did you let Connie believe that there was more to it than that?'

'Connie is my friend. When I went back to the hotel that night and returned the sleeping pills, she kept asking me why I hadn't delivered them and I ended up telling her what I'd seen. And then, when I found out the truth, I didn't tell for the same reason you didn't. Neither of us want her to get caught up in it all.'

'And what did you say to her when she asked why you . . .' Feeling as though he was going around in circles, Kim trailed off and made a dismissive gesture, his hand pushing the thought away.

'I didn't mean to get you into trouble,' Alun said.

Kim raised his eyes and exhaled loudly. 'Didn't you?' He was no longer bothering to disguise his suspicions. 'If she doesn't know me well enough to trust me . . .'

Alun looked up at the diving boards, where Leni was now standing with the cameraman, giving instructions to a female diver in a swimsuit and cap. 'I'm sorry,' he said.

'Not as sorry as me,' Kim said with a hard swallow.

'She'll come around, once she realizes she's overreacted. I mean, nothing happened between you and Scary Eyes, did it? There was that photo . . .' He nodded in Leni's direction. There was a throbbing sound as the diver leapt from the board.

'No, nothing happened,' Kim said. 'As I tried telling Connie.' He looked up at the sky. It was overcast again. 'Know what her last word to me was? "No". Not "Let me think this over" or "I need some time". Just "No".'

'She can be very decisive, when she's made up her mind.' Alun pulled a sympathetic face. 'She said to me . . .' He trailed off. 'No, it doesn't matter.'

'Said what?'

'I wasn't going to mention it.'

'Tell me.'

'She said that she didn't care whether you slept with "that woman" or not. That it was over between you two.'

Kim didn't think that it sounded like something Connie would say – yet she had used the expression 'that woman' in reference to Leni when they had spoken at the Tiergarten.

'I guess things haven't exactly worked out as you planned,' Alun continued, his tone supportive.

'I think my athletics career is over,' Kim said. 'And it's my fault. I've brought this on myself. I was being naïve about my bursary.'

'I don't understand why you needed the money anyway. Don't you have a private income?'

Kim gave a cynical laugh. 'You think I'm some kind of toff?'

'Well, aren't you?'

'My father was a docker. My mother was a charlady. I was given elocution lessons.'

Alun fell silent as he took this in. When he next spoke it was in a more subdued voice. 'Was it about trying to impress Connie? Wanting to win the medals?'

Kim puffed out his cheeks. 'Partly, I suppose.'

'I don't think a medal or two would have made much difference.'

'What do you mean?'

'Lord Dalton was never going to give permission for you to marry his daughter.'

Kim sat back and closed his eyes momentarily. He was feeling angry with Alun again, even though he couldn't work out why. After a long pause, he said: 'Who said anything about marriage?'

'You did just now, with your silence.'

'We wouldn't need his permission.'

'So you were planning to elope? Off up to Gretna Green. Because she'd never agree to that.'

'Why not?'

'Her family would disinherit her.'

'She doesn't care about money.'

'Only because she's never had to. We are all prisoners of our class, even Connie.' Alun looked over his shoulder and then, leaning in closer to Kim, he said in a low voice: 'As you know, I despise the Bolsheviks, but there is one thing they are right about.'

'What's that?'

'That there is the bourgeoisie – the capitalists who own the means of production, like Lord Dalton – and there is the proletariat, people like me and you, who sell their labour. How did Connie's ancestors make their money? I'll tell you how,' Alun continued. 'By exploiting workers in their coal mines.' He made a chopping motion, the side of one hand against the flat of the other. 'The point is, there is a class war and Connie and her family are on one side and we are on the other.'

Kim felt a flush of indignation at this, not least because he suspected Alun might be right. 'Why?' he said. 'Because I didn't go to Eton? I could be part of the bourgeoisie one day. I could start my own insurance company.'

'Where would you get the capital? No one is going to lend you any money because you don't have the right connections, apart from Connie.'

'I never thought of Connie as "a connection".'

'Did you ever meet her family?'

Kim felt a coldness in his gut. 'I don't want her money,' he said. 'I don't need it.'

'No,' Alun said, 'but she does. Look, she's an aristocrat. Coronets and caviar. You're claiming to be a commoner like me. Flat caps and pies.'

Again, Kim suspected that Alun might be right. Connie was never going to marry him. He was merely her plaything before she settled down with someone more suitable.

At that moment, a photographer spotted Kim in the crowd and took his picture.

'You all right?' Alun said, glancing at Kim's clenching fists.

Kim looked at them, too; then he slowly unfurled them. 'I don't seem to have had much luck lately,' he said. 'I really thought the bronze was mine in the broad jump. And with Jesse Owens not taking part in the hurdles and relay . . .' He trailed off again. 'Did Connie come and watch me yesterday?'

Perhaps deliberately, Alun hesitated before saying: 'I'm sure she did.'

Kim lowered his head. 'I can't believe she didn't come.'

Alun put his arm around Kim's shoulder and gave it a brotherly pat.

'Perhaps you're looking at this the wrong way,' Alun said. 'You didn't do anything wrong, did you?'

'No.'

'Yet she stormed off without believing you, without even giving you the benefit of the doubt?'

'I suppose.'

'Then she is being unreasonable. I'm sure that once she realizes this she will be the one knocking on your door with the bunch of flowers and the "I'm sorry" face.'

Kim sighed. He could see Alun was trying to cheer him up.

'I suppose as far as her parents are concerned, it could be worse. You could be Jewish.'

Kim winced as he thought of all the flippant, anti-Semitic asides he had heard Connie utter but that he had chosen to ignore.

'What?' Alun asked, picking up on his reaction.

'I *am* Jewish,' Kim said.

It was Alun's turn to flinch, though Kim could see it was more out of embarrassment than prejudice. 'Since when?'

'Since I was born. My mother was Jewish.'

'I had no idea,' Alun said, almost in a whisper. 'Why didn't you tell me sooner? If I had known . . .' But he didn't finish the thought.

Kim fell silent; then he said: 'Will you give her a message?'

'Of course,' Alun said.

'Tell her I love her.'

Alun stubbed his cigarette out against his heel and got to his feet. 'Consider it done.'

THIRTY-ONE

Leni reread the handwritten invitation from the American track and field coach and then tapped it against the back of her hand as she thought. Jesse Owens had won a third gold medal – in the 200 metres, his final event – and his coach was hosting a cocktail party in his honour to celebrate. Inexplicably, the two sentries had disappeared from her gates that morning, but Leni knew not to let down her guard. This was what Heydrich did.

Still, it meant she could go about her work again, and part of that meant spending time with the athletes. Leni also hoped Kim might have been invited to the party. She was intrigued by him. Apart from being a fine physical specimen, he had a certain nobility that seemed almost Germanic. Yet there was also an air of innocence to him, a purity almost, and it was this that set him apart from the other men she knew. He seemed more of a challenge.

When she walked across the Olympic Village to the coach's brick-and-stucco cottage, one of the ubiquitous flower girls, dressed in a dirndl and with her blonde hair in plaits, handed Leni a posy, which she sniffed and then, when the girl was out of sight, dropped in a bin. She saw Owens was standing outside his cottage, wearing sunglasses and his three gold medals. He was posing for photographs and signing autographs for a huddle of about thirty fans. One was holding a placard with words written in English: 'Henry Ford was right, any color as long as it's black!'

She slipped past the crowd and, seeing Luz Long talking to Kim, picked up a glass of champagne from a passing tray and joined them. Kim's face was drawn, as if he hadn't slept in weeks.

'Congratulations on your silver,' Leni said to Long in German.

'The best man won,' Long said in English. 'And here he is.'

'They want a photograph of us together, Luz,' Owens said. 'Hello, Kim. Leni.'

'Hello, Jesse,' Kim said. 'Congratulations.'

'Thanks. You did well too. I hope next time you'll get to keep your medal.'

'Please excuse us,' Long said to Leni and Kim, clicking his heels.

Leni waited for Owens and Long to be out of earshot before she leaned towards Kim and said in a low voice: 'I haven't thanked you properly for saving my neck.'

'I was glad to help,' Kim said. 'Everything all right now?'

'I think so, yes.'

Leni put the back of her hand to her brow in a gesture of relief. 'No Connie tonight?'

Kim lowered his eyes. 'She and Alun have gone back to London.'

Leni thought for a moment and then said: 'I see.' She took a puff from her cigarette. 'So how do you feel about what happened?'

'Humiliated.'

'Yet you came tonight.'

'Thought it might help take my mind off things. My coach wants me to stick around while he appeals against the disqualification.'

Leni took a sip from her champagne flute; then, noticing that Kim didn't have one, she clicked her fingers and offered him hers.

'No, thanks,' he said. 'I don't drink.'

'I saw some footage of you having a sip from your coach's hip flask,' Leni said, holding the glass to his mouth. When Kim took a sip and pulled a face that suggested he found the taste sourer than he was expecting, Leni laughed. 'Sorry about that story in your English newspaper,' she said, taking a fresh glass from a waiter and handing it to Kim. 'I am feeling partly responsible. The best way to deal with the press is to ignore them. They are animals. Absolute pigs. Have you seen what they are saying about me today?'

Kim seemed to be finding it hard to concentrate. He shook his head and watched as Leni flicked the bottom of her packet of cigarettes to propel one up, then asked Kim to light it for her.

'The papers are saying my maternal grandmother was a Polish Jew,' she said after inhaling and exhaling a jab of smoke. She removed a shred of tobacco from her lip and added: 'It will be that snake Goebbels's doing.'

Kim sighed. He did not seem to be in the mood for conversation. 'If your grandmother was Jewish,' he said, taking a sip from his glass, 'would that be so terrible?'

Leni cast a surreptitious glance at the Golden Party Badge in her lapel and then levelled her eyes at him. 'I have never been a member of the Nazi Party, if that is what you're thinking.'

'But you do work for them. Isn't Goebbels your boss?'

'*Nein*. He wishes.' She rubbed her earlobe, looked over at the door and said in a quieter voice: 'I am completely independent, and I refuse to allow him to use my film *Olympia* for propaganda purposes.'

'So you won't be showing the footage of Hitler, then?' Kim said in a sarcastic tone Leni had not heard before. 'By the way, there is something I wanted to ask you. Why didn't Hitler shake Jesse's hand after he won his first race? I saw him shaking hands with the German medal-winners the day before.'

'The Olympic Committee have decided that Adolf should no longer shake hands with the winners in his box,' Leni said. 'Instead he is doing it away from the cameras, in his private suite below the stadium. Then there can be no accusations of bias.'

Kim said: 'So he and Owens *did* shake hands?'

By way of an answer Leni held an imaginary camera to her eye and made a clicking gesture.

They fell silent for a moment; then Leni leaned closer to Kim and said: 'Has Connie gone back to London because of us?'

Kim blinked, sighed, took another sip and then nodded.

'But nothing happened.'

'That's not what she thinks. Can you recommend a cheap hotel? The IOC has said I will have to move out of the Olympic Village, but my coach wants me to stay in Berlin for the time being.'

Leni blew a smoke ring as she considered this. 'You can stay with me. I have a spare room.' Seeing Owens approaching with Long, she said in a louder, more businesslike voice: 'Ah, here comes the man of the hour.' She signalled to a waiter who was hovering with a bottle of champagne. Taking the bottle from him, she topped up the glasses of the three broad jumpers. 'I wish to propose a toast to the star of my film,' she said. 'To the great Jesse Owens.'

'I am outraged that the Führer would not shake your hand, Jesse,' Long said in a hushed tone.

Leni gave Owens a significant look. The others did not appear to notice. Kim was staring at his gold medals. What was he thinking? Leni wondered. That could have been me?

Owens held up his glass: 'To equality,' he said.

Long said: 'To freedom.'

Kim said: 'To sportsmanship.'

They looked at Leni.

'To truth,' she said. 'And beauty.'

The American coach joined them and when Long and Owens turned to talk to him, Leni tugged Kim's sleeve and drew him to a quiet corner. 'You are the reason I came here tonight,' she said. She leaned towards his ear so that he would feel the warmth of her breath. 'Do you want to see the rushes? The footage of you doing the broad jump? It has come out well. I have the projector set up back at my villa in the Grunewald. It's not far.'

As they watched the rushes, sitting together on a chaise longue, Leni felt for Kim's hand. 'I think the broad jump is my favourite discipline,' she said. 'There is something about the combination of grace, speed and energy that is so . . .' She searched for the right word. 'Mesmerizing.'

She turned in her seat so that she was looking at Kim's profile, illuminated by the flickering images. 'Tell me about yourself,' she said.

'Nothing to tell. All I think about is sport.'

'We are not so different, then,' she said. 'All I think about is making films.'

Kim turned to face her and, as he opened his mouth to speak, Leni leaned towards him and silenced him with a kiss.

Kim pulled back and raised the backs of his fingers to his lips, as if to wipe the kiss away. 'I don't think we should.'

'You are putting up a fight,' Leni said. 'I like that in a man. There is no point, though. I always get what I want.'

Kim gave a short laugh. 'Do you?'

'*Ja.* And I do not believe in playing hard to get,' Leni added. 'With me you just have to ask nicely.' She lowered her eyes for a moment and when she raised them once more to meet his, Kim seemed unable to look away.

'Look,' Kim said. 'I really like you, but my heart belongs to someone else. I shouldn't be here.'

'And yet here you are,' Leni said. 'Another drink?'

Kim hesitated for a moment before nodding and watching in a detached way as his glass of champagne was refilled. The drinking seemed to be making him feel more relaxed. It was also helping to pull his thoughts away from Connie and his disqualification. Somewhere at the back of his mind, he believed he could put things right, that there was still hope.

'Are you at least planning to stay until the end of the Games?' Leni asked.

'Don't know yet,' Kim said as he reached for his glass. His coordination was a little off.

'I would like it if you did. You are my muse, after all. And I could do with some . . .' She searched for the right word again. 'Support. Yes, support. I feel safe with you around. I haven't heard any more from Heydrich, but men like that do not give up easily. He will find something else to accuse me of.' She finished her glass and recharged it. 'And Goebbels is being a swine. He wants my film to fail, because he is jealous. I sometimes feel like I am running this whole damn show on my own. There are times when . . .' She trailed off. 'I worry about the direction we are taking. The Reich, I mean. It frightens me.' She took hold of Kim's hand and stroked it. 'Please do not go back to the Olympic Village tonight.'

'Part of me wants to stay with you,' Kim admitted, his voice slurring slightly.

'Which part?' Leni said with a suggestive flick of her eyebrow. 'Please.' She ran a hand through his hair. 'I do not want to be alone.'

'All right,' he said, 'I'll stay tonight. You mentioned a spare room.'

'*Wunderbar*,' Leni said. 'I will ask Mariechen to get it ready for you.'

THIRTY-TWO

When Kim opened his eyes the following morning it was with a start. Leni was looking back at him in her slightly misaligned way, her face filling his field of vision. She was kneeling by the side of his bed in the spare room.

'Were you watching me while I was sleeping?' he said.

'I was.' She stroked his cheek. 'You are beautiful, yet you do not know this.'

Kim yawned without opening his mouth. He then touched her hair only to withdraw his hand guiltily. He felt confused. Leni seemed such an exotic and glamorous woman and yet here she was flirting with him. Even though he had never seen any of her films, he felt awed by the thought that she was an international star. He didn't know whether he wanted to kiss her or ask for her autograph. 'I imagine actresses get tired of being told all the time that they are beautiful.'

'Trust me, darling, that you could never tire of, especially when your hair is like a bird's nest. I'm like Medusa. And I have a squint. They tried to correct it when I was a child. I had an operation.'

'I had what is called a lazy eye as a child,' Kim said as he stretched out his arms and then put his hands behind his head. 'I had to wear a patch on one eye to strengthen the other one.'

'Me too!' Leni said excitedly. 'This is something else we have in common.' They locked eyes for a moment and then she added: 'An attractive woman is a powerful woman. I have no power.'

'You're joking,' Kim said, sitting up and feeling more awake. 'You have more power than any woman I've ever met. You have the leadership of the Third Reich eating out of your hand. You have an army of cameramen awaiting your orders. You even have journalists describing you as a genius, even though they're all bastards.'

'I have no power over you,' Leni said, getting to her feet in one fluid movement. 'You are still in love with Connie.'

Kim opened his mouth to speak and then looked away. It was true. Although he felt hurt by Connie's overreaction, and though he agreed with Alun that she was being unreasonable, he was certainly in no mood to retaliate by having an affair. 'She filled the silence in my heart,' he said. 'I just don't understand her right now.'

'Women are born with a thousand years of experience,' Leni said. 'Men can never catch up.'

Kim could feel a knot of apprehension in his gut. He couldn't think what to say.

'You were shouting in your sleep,' Leni continued. 'That is why I came into your room. Were you having a bad dream?'

Kim heaved a sigh. 'I've always had bad dreams,' he said. 'Ever since I was a child.'

While Leni had a bath, Kim went out into the garden and his thoughts turned to what Alun had said about Connie and him being from different social classes. It was true, of course. Connie's family crest was stitched on her crêpe-de-Chine sheets and pillowcases. It was on her notepaper and embossed on her luggage, too. Was he wasting his time, thinking he could bridge the vast chasm between them?

When he headed back inside he met Mariechen, whom Leni had earlier introduced as her 'loyal maid and helpmeet'. She seemed to be about the same age as Leni, only shorter and, with her tightly braided hair pinned in a bun, more homely. The two smiled at one another. She was coming out of the study and left the door open. Kim could see a candlestick telephone in there on the desk.

Hearing Leni upstairs singing a Marlene Dietrich song slightly out of tune, Kim stepped into the study and had a look around. On the wall were two large framed photographs presumably taken during Leni's acting days – one of her looking sultry in a fur coat, the other of her wearing a bejewelled head-dress. The desk was littered with notebooks, telegrams and pink slips. He lifted the earpiece on the phone, clicked the switch hook up and down to get a tone and dialled 0. There was a delay and then he heard an operator at the local exchange say: '*Guten Tag. Nummer, bitte.*'

The woman understood enough English to book a call through to London. Kim then hung up and paced the room until the phone rang again, making him flinch. As the connection was made there was a click and then came a repeated purr as the number rang. Kim twiddled the plaited cord around his finger, then heard a familiar crisp voice reciting the number: 'Mayfair 1524.'

'It's Kim. Can you hear me?'

'What do you want?' Connie said.

Disconcerted by this curt response, he said: 'To hear your voice.'

'Well, you've heard it now.'

'And I wanted to check you got home safely. We need to talk. Hello? It's not a good line . . . I don't know whether you heard what happened. It's the qualifiers for the hurdles tomorrow. But I still don't—'

'Who are you talking to, darling?' Kim turned to see Leni in a silk dressing gown, a towel wrapped around her head.

'Is that her?' Connie asked down the line.

Kim said nothing, but his grip tightened on the receiver.

'Don't call me again,' Connie said. 'And don't write to me. I hate you. I never want to see you again.'

Kim heard a click followed by a burring sound as Connie hung up.

For the rest of that day, as Kim waited to hear whether a decision had been reached about his appeal, he watched Leni at work, following her around the various Olympic events she wanted to film. And, all the while, he tried not to think about Connie. When he did, he felt a stabbing indignation about the way she was treating him; the way she would not listen; the way she assumed he had been unfaithful to her when he had not.

In the evening Leni came to sit on the grass beside Kim as they watched the tracks laid in front of the main podium being packed away.

'I am exhausted,' she said. 'When this is over, I will have a holiday. Have you visited the Tyrolean mountains? They are beautiful and dangerous. You can escape there. I made a film there once. *Das blaue Licht. The Blue Light*. Have you seen it?'

'No,' Kim said. 'I haven't been to the mountains and I haven't seen your film.'

'It is about a young woman who lives apart from her village in a mountain cave surrounded by blue crystals. Because she is strange, the villagers think that she is a witch who lures young men to their death with her blue light . . .' Noticing an engineer drop a piece of lighting equipment, she shouted: '*Vorsichtig damit!*' and then resumed her normal volume. 'Sometimes I feel like a witch. I feel I have these powers, that I can perform magic. I feel it most strongly when I'm in the Tyrol. I am thinking of buying a ski lodge there, if I ever come back from America.'

'You're moving to America?'

Leni put her fingers to her lips. 'Not so loud. It has always been my ambition to work in Hollywood.'

'Will you miss Germany?'

Leni shook her head. 'Things will turn ugly here now the Olympics are over. Things will be worse for the Jews. There will be new laws . . .'

'Leni.' Kim lowered his eyes. 'There is something you should know about me.'

'You are Jewish.'

'How did you know?'

'A guess. I do not care. My grandmother was Jewish.'

Kim's eyes widened. 'But you said . . .'

'Not everything Goebbels says is a lie.' She lit a cigarette, holding it between her middle and ring finger and cupping her hand to shield the flame against the breeze. 'So now we know each other's little secret. Both your parents, or just your mother?'

'Just my mother.'

'Is she involved in athletics?'

'She was a charlady.' Her look of puzzlement prompted Kim to add: 'A cleaner. She cleaned other people's houses.'

Leni's hand came to rest on Kim's abdomen, fingers outstretched. 'Again, we are not so different,' she said. 'We have had to make our own way in this world. Earn our privileges. And we are good at what we do, we are among the best. And we did it without a helping hand.'

Kim smiled through his words. 'I bet your mother wasn't a charlady.'

'I let people think I'm of noble birth,' Leni said, 'but I'm not. My mother, she sewed clothes for other people. My father was a plumber. You remind me of him. He was tall and fair like you. When I told him I wanted to be a dancer he shouted at me and said that dancing was for whores. But he could also be gentle. He once lost his temper and threw some china at my mother but later I found him trying to glue it back together.' She paused for a moment at this memory, then added: 'They divorced.' A shrug now. 'I think we want the same things, Kim Newlands. We want people to see our achievements, not where we came from. I see it in your eyes. There is hurt in them. You feel like you aren't good enough. You feel like an . . . an imposter, *ja*?'

Kim smiled. 'Two imposters, balancing on a high wire.'

'Wearing masks. Is your mother still living?'

Kim shook his head.

'Oh, I am sorry,' Leni said.

'It was a long time ago. I was thirteen.'

'What was the cause?'

'I'd rather not talk about it.'

Leni lifted his chin gently with a finger and looked him in the eyes. 'Are you afraid of dying?'

'Yes.'

'Why? It is not a thing you will ever experience.'

Kim furrowed his brow.

'You can only experience a thing if you are conscious,' Leni elaborated, 'and, by definition, the moment you die you will no longer be conscious. So there is nothing to be frightened of.'

Kim pulled a face. 'It's the nothing part that frightens me.'

Leni laughed. 'We come from nothing and we return to nothing. All we can do in between is try and enjoy ourselves. Have you read any Schopenhauer?'

'Was he a philosopher?'

'Much more than that. He was known as "the great bachelor", a man who never married but rarely slept alone, sometimes with a different woman every night. We are all animals, he believed, driven by our bodily needs. Hunger, fear, sex.'

'She had an asthma attack,' Kim said, turning away. 'My mother. Her lips went blue. She died in my arms. I still talk to her sometimes, when I think no one is listening.'

'That is sad,' Leni said, moving closer and stroking his hair. 'My poor, beautiful boy.'

'She was trying to protect me from my drunken father. I had tried to fight him, but it was hopeless.'

'A mother will do anything to protect her cubs.'

'As she lay on the floor she was trying to say something to me, but the words . . .' Kim's voice caught and he gulped. 'I couldn't hear them.'

THIRTY-THREE

The following day, Leni made a point of keeping Kim by her side. It was partly because, as she kept telling him, he made her feel safer after her ordeal with Heydrich, partly because he had been robbed of a bronze medal one day and his English girlfriend had walked out on him the next, so she felt sorry for him. When they heard that evening that his appeal had been rejected and his disqualification was going to stand, Leni hugged him and stroked his hair while they stood in the kitchen rocking from side to side. But that was as far as their intimacy went. Kim was still sleeping in the guest room. When she asked if he would now return to England, he said he had nothing to go back to.

Over the next couple of days, Leni came to suspect that Kim found her a consoling presence, even if he was clearly still in love with Connie. While she inferred that this might be a temporary consequence of his ill fortune – the loss of control over his own life – she nevertheless felt the two of them were making a connection and she had shown him that, contrary to her intimidating public image, she could be warm, funny and tender in private.

Was he falling under her spell? Perhaps. He seemed intrigued by the way she could switch from playful nonchalance when they were at home in the Grunewald to ruthless efficiency when going about her work at the stadium. Clearly, he liked strong women. And he seemed to trust her. One morning, as they drove to the stadium, she asked him why he was being so quiet and he confided in her that he had once, when he was a teenager, gone for almost a year without talking. And he had also suffered from a chronic stammer as a child.

'He left the stage eventually,' Kim added, 'but I know he is still waiting in the wings.'

'He?' Leni asked.

'I think of my stammer as a he, not sure why. I try not to let him interfere with my life. I won't let him stop me doing things just because they are stressful.'

Leni then started talking about the next Olympic Games in four years' time in Tokyo, suggesting that perhaps Kim would return in triumph and equal Jesse Owens's haul of three gold medals.

'Actually,' Kim said, 'Jesse might have four gold medals before these Games are over.'

Kim had heard from Mr Riley that Owens and Metcalfe had been selected at the last moment to run in the 4 × 100 men's relay. There were two theories about why this was, Mr Riley had said: the first was that the American team was bowing to pressure to drop Stoller and Glickman, their two Jewish runners, because Hitler did not want to see them on the winners' podium. The second, more plausible, theory was that the American team had heard that the German team – knowing they did not have anyone who could win against Owens and Metcalfe in the 100 metres – had been keeping their best sprinters under wraps for the relay, allowing the Americans to think they would win easily.

The event was held on the second Sunday of the Games and overnight rain had slowed the red clay of the track. As she set up her shots, Leni could sense Kim's eyes on her and it made her feel more energetic and focused. Moving from camera to camera before the starting pistol went off, she felt in complete control of her environment. She was a maestra. A martinet. And Kim seemed impressed. 'Even the gentlemen of the press seem to respect you,' he noted.

'It's because I have the power to revoke their passes,' she replied.

There were six teams. The Americans, the favourites, were drawn in lane four; the Germans, the only other serious contenders, were in lane two. Owens got off to an explosive start as he ran the first leg. His handover of the baton from his left hand to Metcalfe's right was smooth.

Metcalfe's handover did not go as well and, from where Leni was filming, it looked as if it might have been outside the box, but he passed it on cleanly enough and the American who was running the final leg finished 12 yards ahead of the German in a new record time of 39.8 seconds.

The crowd fell silent while one of the judges walked on to the track and studied the spike marks where Metcalfe had handed over. He then scrubbed out the marks, apparently satisfied it had been fair, and a cheer went up. Owens had his fourth gold.

Upon their return to the villa, Leni went to the kitchen to give instructions to Mariechen while Kim looked at the paintings hanging in the hall. They were of distorted, almost primitive figures painted in bright, unnatural colours and he did not understand them. Also in the hall was a white baby grand piano with the word Blüthner in gold letters on its lid. As he touched one of the keys, Leni reappeared and asked: 'Do you play?'

Kim smiled and shook his head. 'You?'

Leni sat on the piano stool and said: 'A little. All nice German girls are expected to learn.' She began playing something which sounded good to Kim's ears but then she stopped after a minute, lowered the lid and said: 'I'm out of practice.'

Later, at a table in the garden, Mariechen brought them two dishes that Kim had never tried before: rabbit served with marinated scallops and cinnamon butter followed by a venison stew. They were served with a claret, something else he had never tried before. He liked the taste.

As they put their knives and forks together on their emptied plates, Leni asked Kim who his favourite composers were. When he said he didn't have any, she affected shock, led him indoors, gathered a handful of records and fanned them out on a table.

'With the exception of Verdi and Puccini, all the great composers are German and Austrian,' she said, giving him a playfully schoolmarmish frown. 'Boring old Beethoven and Wagner are the most popular with our Party leaders, but my favourites are Bach, Mozart and Schubert. Do you know the "Trout" Quintet?'

When Kim said that he wasn't sure, Leni poured two glasses of cognac, handed one to Kim and then took a 78 from its sleeve. Holding it between two fingers, she placed it on the gramophone player before turning the handle and lowering the needle. After a tense spasm of concentration, the orchestra began to play.

As Kim listened, Leni reached for her Leica camera and started taking pictures of him, some from above, some from the side. Each time she wound her film on she studied him, her head on a tilt. Then she lit candles, turned out the lights and excused herself. When she returned, her hair was down, a dark chestnut cloud loose around her shoulders, and she was wearing her silk dressing gown, the belt untied, revealing she was naked underneath. She began to sway in time to the music and walked *en pointe* in her bare feet, before becoming more fluid and uninhibited as she half skipped in a circle while making sweeping movements with her arms.

'In Germany we call this *Ausdruckstanz*,' she said as she turned and carved shapes in the air with her body. In the candlelight, her gown rippling silkily, she seemed to flow between upward soaring gestures and contracting ones that left her kneeling, before rising again like a fish caught on a line.

Kim looked on in a state of helpless captivation, stirred by the answering tension of his own body.

When he awoke in the morning, Leni was staring at him again, but this time she wasn't kneeling by the bed but lying in it, her head resting on a pillow.

Kim thought of Connie. He pictured her hurt face that day not long ago as he tried to convince her that he had not slept with Leni. It had been true at the time. He wished she had believed him.

'You were shouting in your sleep again, darling,' Leni whispered.

'What was I shouting?' he asked.

'You were shouting, "I'm in love with that crazy bitch Leni Riefenstahl."'

As Kim laughed and moved across the bed to kiss her neck, he noticed an empty cognac bottle on the bedside table. Feeling an ache across his brow, he assumed he was experiencing his first proper hangover. Yet it was Leni who had intoxicated him. There was something magnetic about her. He knew that whatever was going on between them would be short-lived, that he could not live with a woman like her, or envisage a future with her in the way that he could with Connie, and yet here he was, in her bed, and his feelings for her, however they might be defined, were strong.

With a gratified murmur, she insinuated an arm underneath his bare flank, and then, rolling on to her back, pulled him on top of her.

THIRTY-FOUR

Leni didn't think she had ever felt this way about a man before. Kim was calm, gentle and strong. He was a good lover, too, considerate and athletic. For the first time in years, she felt content. There was nowhere else she wanted to be and no one else she wanted to be with. That he was ten years her junior was also good, she thought, because women live longer than men.

That evening, after her crew had packed their cameras away and the crowd had left the stadium, Leni took Kim's hand and led him to the diving pool, the place where she had stolen their first kiss. When she lifted a rope that was cordoning off the swimming-pool area, Kim asked: 'Isn't this *verboten*?' Endearingly, he seemed pleased to demonstrate the new German word he had learned.

'Do not worry,' Leni said. 'You are with the boss.'

They sat on the 5-metre diving board as they watched the sun set over the stadium until all that was left to compromise the darkness was a thin crescent moon and the flickering gas lamps in the alcoves of the stadium wall. Apart from the brief angry bark of a distant guard dog, the night was silent.

'I feel so happy at this moment,' Leni whispered. 'Here. With you, Kim Newlands.' She looked down at the water below them. It was like black ink. Not even a ripple disturbed its surface. 'You know, you can come and work for me after this is over,' she added. 'If you like.'

'I don't know anything about the film world,' Kim replied, seeming uncomfortable.

'I could teach you. You could be my assistant director.'

'I don't speak German.'

'No need. I told you, I am going to move to Hollywood. We can buy a mansion in Beverly Hills with palm trees and a pool.'

'That seems like quite a big step . . .' Kim said slowly. 'We hardly know each other.'

'We will have a lifetime to know one another.'

'Will that be long enough?' Kim said, stroking her hair. 'You seem pretty unknowable to me.'

There was something in his tone that suggested he wasn't being serious, or rather that he thought she was joking. It was something she could never quite fathom about the English. They spoke in riddles and with understatement, and never quite seemed to say what they meant.

'*Ja*,' Leni said with a soft laugh. 'I'm unknowable. Behind my mask there is another mask. That is what makes me so fascinating.'

Suddenly she stood up and stripped off her clothes. 'Come on,' she said. 'Let's have our own diving competition.' Without hesitating, she performed a deft swallow dive into the black void below.

From the water, she looked up to see Kim in silhouette, looking down at her, the stars glittering behind him. He looked around to see if anyone was watching before stripping off his clothes and standing naked on the edge of the board. She wondered for a moment if it bothered him that there was a decade between them; then, as she followed his long and tightly muscled form falling through the air before he plunged into the water, she dismissed the idea. When he came to the surface he swam over to where she was waiting by the side with his easy, boyish smile.

'Mine was better,' she said. Not only did Kim make her feel younger, he seemed to bring out the best in her. Funny Leni. Honest Leni. Good Leni. She tried not to think about the other Leni who saw only what she wanted to see.

As Kim kissed her, she felt a rush of desire of a sort she had rarely felt before. Under the water, she wrapped her legs around him. He was hers now and she was never going to let him go.

*

Leni awoke with her head on Kim's chest and her waist under his arm. After extracting herself without disturbing him, she got to her feet and smiled in recollection as she saw that the enormous swastika flag they had stolen the night before was draped on the bed like a counterpane. It had been on a flagpole next to the diving pool and Leni had handed it to Kim with the words: 'This is for you, my honorary German friend.'

But now she remembered the look of consternation on his face as he'd tried to hide the swastika under his shirt, and she became aware of a pressing silence in the room. She realized she could not hear the sound of Kim breathing. He seemed too still. When she touched his neck he jumped, making her jump, and she laughed.

Wrapping the flag around herself, she crossed the room on the tips of her toes, stood at the window and asked over her shoulder: 'Did you sleep well, darling?'

'We hardly slept at all.'

She heard Kim rise from the bed and then she felt his strong hands stroking her arms as he stood behind her. Outside the villa, dawn was breaking and the deep, velvety indigo that had enveloped the surrounding trees was melting into shades of copper.

After a couple of minutes, Leni noticed how withdrawn and silent Kim seemed. 'You are thinking about Connie, are you not?'

'No,' Kim said. Then: 'Well, maybe. I feel guilty.'

'But she left you, *ja*?'

Kim sighed. 'Yes, but . . .'

'Then you do not have to feel guilty. It was over.'

'I know . . . but . . . it didn't *feel* over. And . . . I don't know how to explain this but . . . She's vulnerable. Connie needs me.'

Leni turned to face him, opened the flag and, wrapping Kim in it with her, said: 'I need you.'

Kim closed his eyes. 'Leni,' he said, 'you are making this so hard for me.'

'No, darling,' she whispered as she pressed herself closer. 'I think it is you who is making it hard for me.'

*

By the time of the closing ceremony a week later, the weather had finally improved. The flags came down, the Olympic flame went out and the crowd sang '*Deutschland über alles*'. Although Jesse Owens with his four gold medals was the undoubted star, Germany was the overall winner with a total of 89 medals, including 33 gold. America was second with 56 medals, 24 of which were gold. Britain came tenth with 14 medals.

As they listened to this tally being announced, Leni turned to Kim and whispered: 'It should have been seventeen for Britain.'

That night there was a banquet at the Kaiserhof Hotel organized by the German Olympic Committee. Most of the disciples – Göring, Hess, von Ribbentrop and Goebbels – were going to be there, but not the messiah, and no members of the British team, at least as far as Leni could see.

She wore a diamond and sapphire necklace that had been a present from Adolf and a navy-blue ballgown that shimmered as she walked. She was in a mischievous mood. Earlier, indeed, when she had come down the stairs at the villa, she had had a cushion stuffed under the gown, over her belly, and she had joked: '*Mein Gott*, Kim Newlands, why did you not warn me you have Olympian seed!'

Her joke had fallen flat. Kim had been reluctant to attend the banquet, and he kept questioning why she would even want to be in the same room as Goebbels and the other Party officials.

'I don't understand, Leni – aren't these the same people you were so afraid of a couple of weeks ago?' he'd said petulantly.

'My darling,' Leni said, putting her hand on his arm. 'Everyone will be there. And I must continue as before. I must not show them I am afraid. It is important to me.'

Kim was wearing tails and a winged collar that Leni had hired and a white tie which she tied for him, standing behind him as they faced a mirror. In his lapel was Leni's *Bonbon*, her Golden Party Badge. As she attached it, she had whispered: 'This is precious to me. I want you to have it. It will keep you safe.'

Kim had turned to her, with a look in his eyes she had not seen before. 'You really think that?' he asked. 'Have you forgotten that old man we saw outside the stadium?'

Leni found she had no answer.

At the party they ate lobster thermidor and grilled suckling pig, drank 1918 Mouton Rothschild and, when the orchestra played, they danced to a Viennese waltz. Of the Germans to whom Leni introduced Kim, only Albert Speer spoke a little English. He made a joke about not knowing that Leni had a son.

'He is only ten years younger than me,' she said, tapping Speer's arm, feeling a little hurt.

Throughout the evening, Kim seemed detached and whenever a photographer came up wanting to take their photograph, Leni linked her arm with his, but he half turned away, clearly worried that the photographs might be reproduced in the British press and Connie would see them. He seemed so distant, she thought. Had he decided to return to London? She didn't want to lose him.

As they drove back to her villa, the tyres of her Mercedes making a thumping sound on the cobbles, Leni turned to him and almost whispered, 'I've never said this to anyone before . . .' There was hesitation in her voice. 'Because I don't think I have ever felt this way about anyone before . . .'

There was a tight silence before Kim said: 'Don't say it. Don't squander those words.'

The next morning, Leni was sitting in a rocking chair by the open window when Kim appeared in the doorway wearing his coat and trilby, his suitcase in his hand. She stared at it for a moment before covering herself up with her dressing gown. She inhaled deeply on her cigarette, holding the smoke down for three beats of her heart before exhaling, directing into the garden a tumbling shaft of blue-grey that caught the morning sunlight.

'Please do not,' she said, lowering her gaze.

Kim cleared his throat. 'I'm sorry.'

Part of her wanted to pretend that she didn't care, that he was of no consequence to her. Yet she now found herself crossing the room, lifting his hand to her lips and kissing it. 'I can change,' she said. 'I can be whatever you want me to be.' She looked up now and it was Kim's turn to avert his eyes. 'I act like a strong woman,' she said, 'but I'm not. I need you.' She kissed his hand again. 'Please don't make me beg.'

Kim swallowed but said nothing. There was a soft look in his eyes.

'I won't help you to leave me,' Leni continued. 'I won't tell you I'm going to be fine.'

'But you don't need me,' Kim said, now with a crack in his voice. 'And you will be fine.'

She could feel that her eyes, as they searched for his, were wet. 'I won't help you to leave me,' she repeated, 'but you can help me let you go.'

'How?'

'Tell me you don't love me.'

Kim closed his eyes. For a few seconds the only sound was their breathing; then Kim opened his mouth to speak and Leni stopped him with a finger gently placed on his lips.

'No,' she said with a sigh of resignation. 'My heart will not be able to stand the truth. Let us part with lies . . . I do not love you, Kim Newlands.'

Kim nodded. 'And I don't love you, Leni Riefenstahl.'

For several minutes after the front door closed, Leni waited for it to open again. Her thoughts were liquid, refusing to solidify into an effective plan. She stood up, sat down and then, after standing again, crossed to the door, opened it and looked out. There was still time.

But there was indecision in her movements and instead of driving after Kim she returned indoors and stared at her reflection in the hall mirror. The woman staring back at her looked older than she had been the last time their eyes had met.

He did love you, she thought. He loved you, but not enough.

After a further ten minutes had passed, she nodded to herself, went to get dressed and noticed a watch on the floor by her bed. When she picked it up she saw it was a gold Cartier Tank watch. Engraved on the back were the initials 'KN'. She momentarily pictured herself turning up on his doorstep in London, waving the watch in front of him and saying in her usual flirtatious manner: 'I think you forgot something.' Then she collected her car keys.

She arrived at the station with a yelp of rubber, parked at an angle across two bays marked for postal vans and left the engine running as she ran down a ramp to the platform. A group of people were coming the other way and, as she weaved between them, some, having recognized her, pointed and whispered. She tried to read the information boards, then she stopped, looked at the empty track next to her, and realized that the train to London via Paris and Calais had already departed.

On another platform, a locomotive clattered slowly in under a cloud of steam and Leni stared at it for a moment imagining that Kim would step off it.

Once she was back behind the steering wheel of her car she stared at the passenger seat and, picturing where Kim had been sitting the night before, leaned over and kissed the leather.

She knew in that moment that, though other lovers would come and go in her life, she would always feel alone.

PART FOUR

THIRTY-FIVE

Almost two weeks had passed since Kim's return to London and, from what Alun could determine, he still had not had a chance to talk to Connie. When Kim had visited her house in Mayfair he had been told by a housekeeper that she was not there. The servant did not know where she was or when she would return. A telephone call had met with the same response. Kim wondered whether she had gone to the country but Alun, who had taken on the role of go-between, had assured him that she was in residence at her London townhouse and that Kim needed to be patient. She would speak to him soon, when she was ready. He offered to hand-deliver a letter from Kim and then returned it to him unopened, claiming that Connie had declined to receive it.

In fact, as well Alun knew, Connie was in Wales where the grouse-shooting season – a high point of the social calendar, apparently – was under way. He had known this because she had contacted him by telephone to find out how Kim was and had asked his advice about arranging a meeting with him upon her return to London. As subtly as he could, Alun had implied that it would be better for her to wait, because Kim needed more time. His feelings had been hurt by the way she had left him in Berlin.

Alun knew he was playing a dangerous game, but it seemed to be working. Frustration and resentment, each for the other, seemed to be building in their respective hearts, especially as Alun had omitted to tell Connie the truth about what had happened with Leni that first night. Connie had now decided to stay on at Dalton Hall until the start of the pheasant-shooting season in October.

In the meantime, Kim had returned to his job as a clerk at Pickering, Turnbull & McCann. If his bosses had seen the story in the *Express* they had not, apparently, taken much notice of it. He had not returned to his training, however, and the only exercise he had been doing lately had been sits-up, push-ups, and the occasional run around the park.

Alun was with him one chilly morning in early September when a summons arrived from Sir Oswald Mosley's secretary. It asked Kim to come to the Black House the following day for a meeting, the subject of which was not specified. Kim declared that he would go and that he would take his uniform along with him, because he wanted to resign his BUF membership. He told Alun that he thought that this was probably the reason Sir Oswald wanted to see him, and that what he felt about this prospect was, above all, relief. He also felt ashamed for not having resigned before now and was minded to tell Sir Oswald the truth: that he was Jewish and that the BUF's increasingly unambiguous anti-Semitism was an affront not only to him but to the memory of his mother. One problem remained for Kim, however: he was in no position to repay the bursary he had received.

Alun had offered, in what he called a 'gesture of solidarity', to meet Kim at the Black House. As he contemplated his reflection in the window of the tram on the way to Sloane Square, he sucked in his cheeks and ran a hand through his hair, noticing that the boy sitting opposite him was staring. From his pocket he retrieved his Blackshirt cigarettes, put one in the corner of his mouth and made as if to offer one to the boy.

The boy's mother, who was wearing a headscarf, pulled her child towards her and hissed: '*Don't stare.*' Other passengers were now digging each other in the ribs and pointing in Alun's direction. When a bell announced that the tram was approaching his stop, he took a last drag and jumped off in one fluid movement.

As he turned the corner he saw a commotion going on near the entrance of the Black House. Three Blackshirts were jeering as they circled a gangly teenager who was carrying a bulging shoulder bag and wearing dungarees and a baggy cap. When one knocked the cap off and the others started pushing him, Alun came to a halt. He recognized the youth as one of Herzl's paper boys.

He also recognized one of the Blackshirts, a short and stocky man with slit eyes and a flattened nose. His name was Higgins. When the lad went to pick his cap up, a second Blackshirt, older and leaner, kicked him on the backside so that he fell forward on to the ground. The victim instinctively curled up, holding up an arm to protect himself. His nose was bleeding and, from where he was standing, Alun could see tears glistening in his eyes. The third Blackshirt ripped the shoulder bag away from him and, tipping out some of its contents, shouted: 'Red scum!' The bag contained copies of the *Daily Worker*.

Higgins picked up one of the papers and, grabbing him by the hair, forced the boy to look at it. 'What's this, then? What do you think you're doing handing out this communist filth here, eh?'

A crowd was forming, but they were staying well back – all except for an elderly lady with hair as compact and white as a cauliflower. She pushed her way through them and shouted in a cockney accent: 'Why don't you bullies pick on someone your own size?' Noticing Alun's black shirt, she turned to him and said: 'They're your lot, can't you stop them?'

Alun felt sorry for the boy and could see that the Blackshirts were working themselves up now; that they had a taste for blood. But what could he do on his own? He studied the handle of the furled umbrella he was using as a walking stick but then shook his head and took a step back to make himself less conspicuous.

The men were spitting and laughing now. 'Jew boy!' one shouted. 'Yiddish scum!' Higgins got the youth back on his feet by pulling at his ear. Another cuffed him across the head, while the third pushed him to the ground again. He began screaming for help as the Blackshirt who had tipped the newspapers out dragged him by his hair along the pavement. When the Blackshirt lost his grip and let go, the boy scrambled to find his footing but fell again, his arms cradling his head as he waited for the boots.

At this moment Kim emerged from the entrance of the Black House wearing a suit and tie. When he registered what was happening, he strode towards the boy and placed himself between him and the three Blackshirts. As Kim drew himself up to his full height, Higgins said: 'This doesn't concern you, Newlands.'

Kim folded his arms. 'Yes, it does.'

The Blackshirts were weighing their options, clearly trying to decide whether they should rush Kim and try to overpower him. The tallest made a feint but when Kim did not flinch, the Blackshirts seemed to lose their confidence. Kim turned his back on them before helping the teenager to his feet and draping the strap of his newspaper bag across his shoulder. As he handed the youth a handkerchief for his bleeding nose, he must have heard Higgins barrelling towards him from behind because he turned and sidestepped like a matador evading a charging bull. In the same supple movement, he stuck out his foot to trip Higgins up and pushed the back of his head forward and down. Caught off balance, Higgins crashed to the ground, landing on his face.

The other two Blackshirts looked at one another and then at the crowd, who had fallen silent. Their sense of humiliation was palpable. Kim helped Higgins, who seemed concussed, to his feet; then the other two men came to support him, helping him to walk unsteadily through the entrance of the Black House. The moment they disappeared, a cheer went up.

'That was a good thing you did there,' Alun said as they walked side by side towards the Lyons Corner House. 'I would have intervened, but I arrived at the same time as you.'

Alun then asked Kim what Mosley had wanted.

'He isn't expecting me to repay the bursary.'

'That was it?'

'And that I am free to leave, after . . .'

'After what?'

They reached the Corner House, found a table and ordered tea.

'After what?' Alun repeated, now in a low voice.

'He has one last propaganda job for me,' Kim said, adopting a similarly hushed tone. 'He wants me by his side for a big march he's planning. He's going to get the press to run a story about how I was the victim of a communist slur and how I am going to go back and win medals in the Tokyo Olympics in 1940. He says if I do that, he'll forget about the money.'

Alun rolled his wrist impatiently. 'Where are we planning to have the march?'

'Through the heart of the East End.'

The tea arrived. Alun waited for the waitress to pour it and then said: 'So Sir Oswald wants to target the Jewish area?'

'Yes, from Royal Mint Street along Cable Street to Stepney.'

'Did he say when the march is going to be held?'

'Start of next month.'

'How big?'

'About ten thousand Blackshirts.'

Alun let out a whistle, causing a customer at a nearby table to turn and glower at him.

'He is expecting the residents will petition the Home Office to have the march banned,' Kim said, taking a sip of tea.

'The Home Secretary will never agree to that,' Alun said. 'He's practically a member of the BUF himself, along with half of Special Branch and MI5. Is Mosley expecting any counter-protests?'

'Yes, that's the thing . . .' Kim trailed off.

'What?'

'No, I can't say. He swore me to secrecy.'

'You can tell me.'

As the two men eyed one another, Alun wondered whether he could detect a hint of suspicion in Kim's eyes, but decided he was being oversensitive.

'All right,' Kim said, 'but promise me this won't go any further.'

THIRTY-SIX

Wearing his Blackshirt uniform, but with a mackintosh tied around his waist, Alun ran his binoculars towards the bottom of Royal Mint Street, where more Blackshirts were arriving, then back to the ranks of female Blackshirts. With her blonde hair, willowy figure and eyepatch, Connie would be easy to spot if she was among them but, to his relief, she was nowhere in sight. When she had returned to London three days earlier Alun had gone to see her. Even though she had left the Blackshirts after her injury, when Alun had mentioned that Kim was planning on attending the march, she had said she might come along too, as there was something she needed to tell him. Something that could not wait. Forced to think quickly, Alun had suggested she write him a letter, one that he would deliver to Kim by hand. As he took it from her he warned her to stay away from the march because even if the BUF managed a turnout of five or ten thousand, as they boasted they would, they would be heavily outnumbered by the anti-fascists, twenty or thirty thousand of whom were expected to turn up, not including all the residents.

Alun did not add that he knew this to be true because he had helped organize them.

All morning the anti-fascists had been arriving by the busload, armed with coshes and knuckledusters. Some of them were not even committed communists, anarchists or pacifists – they were ordinary tradesmen, labourers, shopkeepers, members of co-ops and dockers organized by their unions. On Cable Street nearly every household had put up a red flag of support.

When he heard the thrum of motorbike engines, Alun turned towards the sound and saw two outriders followed by Mosley's open-topped Bentley. His knuckles whitened as he gripped the binoculars tighter and then he looked around for Kim.

His 'friend' had not only unwittingly supplied Alun with Mosley's intended route through Shoreditch, Limehouse, Bow and Bethnal Green, but had also given him the exact timings, the various assembly points and the expected head count. Most usefully of all, Kim had revealed Mosley's arrangement with the Commissioner of Police, namely that at an agreed time Mosley would telephone the Home Secretary for 'permission' to cancel the march on the grounds of public safety. The Commissioner would formally 'request' that Mosley reroute his march back down Queen Victoria Street towards the Embankment and, in a gesture intended to demonstrate how disciplined, law-abiding and opposed to unnecessary violence the Blackshirts were, Mosley would 'comply'. This, the Blackshirt leader imagined, would give him a propaganda victory.

Alun had his own propaganda officers ready to counter this version of events. If all went according to plan, the headlines in Monday's papers would be about the way the cowardly Blackshirts had run away from a fight with the Reds. But in return for this scoop about Mosley's planned route, Alun's photographer friend at the *Express* had shared some disturbing information he had uncovered about Kim's background. Kim's father was a docker by trade, but had been unemployed most of the time. He was also an alcoholic, a violent one who not only beat his wife but also his son. As with the revelation that Kim was Jewish, Alun found that this news clouded his plans with unwelcome guilt.

He couldn't see Kim at the moment but he could spot Mosley. Surrounded by his usual phalanx of tall bodyguards clicking their heels and giving the fascist salute, the Leader appeared agitated. Wearing the newly introduced BUF uniform of black military jacket with a red and white armband, grey jodhpurs and a black cap, Mosley began inspecting his troops, marching briskly down the line, holding one arm at his side, thumb in leather belt, while the other flapped occasionally in casual salute. When he reached a tall man in the front rank, he stopped for a word. Alun was sure it was Kim, but the cap obscured his face.

Alun lowered his binoculars and walked as briskly as his limp would allow in the direction of the Embankment. Even before he saw the hundreds of mounted police assembling by the Thames, he could hear the clatter of horseshoes and smell the grassy odour of manure. Some of the beasts were proving hard to control. They were snorting and pawing the ground, as if they sensed the looming danger.

According to Alun's sources, some six thousand constables would be deployed and the anti-fascists knew that if they were to win the propaganda war, they would have to take them on. They had to show the general public that they, unlike the Blackshirts, were not afraid of a fight in the name of democracy. Moreover, they had to show the country that the left outnumbered the right; that they represented the will of the people.

When Alun came level with one of the police horses, which was standing swishing its tail, the policeman in the saddle said: 'I wouldn't hang around here if I were you, son.'

'Expecting trouble, officer?' Alun asked. As he limped away in the direction of Cable Street, he put on his mac, removed a red kerchief from its pocket, tied it around his neck and, when he had gone twenty yards, added over his shoulder: 'Because you're going to get it, fascist!' He gave a clenched-fist salute before turning and breaking into an uneven run. His undercover days were over. This was a fight he wasn't going to miss out on.

Near the junction with Christian Street, towards the west end of Cable Street, a van had been turned on its side and tables, chairs, lamps, metal bins, bikes and even a bed had been built up around it to act as a barricade. Veterans of the Great War were there wearing their medals alongside comrades in cloth caps and trilbies. Some were singing the 'Internationale' as they dug up paving stones with picks. Clearly struggling to recall the lyrics, they began to chant instead 'Madrid today, London tomorrow' and 'Praise Marx, and pass the ammunition! Praise Marx and smash imperialism!'

Many were waving placards daubed with the phrase that their republican brothers in Spain had been using: '*¡No pasarán!*' Alun doubted that many of the anti-fascists knew Spanish but he felt moved by the care that had been taken to imitate faithfully the accent and upside-down exclamation mark. Red flags were draped from the windows and volunteers were handing out communist leaflets. A scuffle broke out when a couple of young men who were quickly identified as fascist sympathizers came out of a side road. Firecrackers that sounded like guns were let off, making everyone scatter.

Sensing the tension, Alun grabbed a loudhailer and, assuming the role of leader, climbed up on to the van. He had not prepared a speech but could see that one was needed.

'Comrades!' Alun shouted. 'Remember today. It will live on in history as the date on which fascism was defeated in this land. Years from now your grandchildren will ask you if you were here, if you fought in the Battle of Cable Street. Brothers, sisters, tell them you *were* here, and tell them you fought bravely. Tell them you did it for England. Tell them that today, the fourth of October, 1936, was the day the fascists did not pass.' This was met with a cheer. Alun raised a clenched-fist salute, which was mirrored by many in the crowd. He dismounted the barricade to echoes of 'They shall not pass! They shall not pass!'

'Not a bad speech, Comrade Pryce,' Herzl said, lumbering alongside. 'Did you know I was born on this street?'

Alun turned and looked back up Cable Street. 'Well, let's man the barricade and defend it then, shall we, comrade?'

The jubilant mood was short-lived as mounted police appeared at the other end of the street and, at a signal, began trotting towards them, batons raised. As the clatter of horseshoes on concrete grew louder, there was another signal, this time from the anti-fascists, and children's marbles were scattered across the road. The charging horses panicked and whinnied as they lost their footing and stumbled. From the surrounding windows, chamber pots were emptied on to the mounted police and rotten vegetables thrown. Over the top of the barricade came a hail of bottles, bricks and chairs wrapped in barbed wire. A running battle ensued, with anti-fascists wielding iron bars, followed by a counter-charge from police on foot. Punches were thrown, skulls cracked and the wounded dragged off to the sides and left in doorways. The air filled with the sound of ambulances, breaking glass, shouts and screams.

Through the maelstrom, Alun glimpsed Herzl sitting against a lamp post holding his head. There was blood on his fingers and, when he looked up, Alun saw there was a fat-lipped gash on the side of his brow.

'You all right?' he asked when he reached him.

Herzl groaned. His eyes looked unfocused.

'What happened?' Alun asked, sitting down beside his friend. He wanted to keep Herzl conscious. 'Comrade. Talk to me. Isn't this the street where you grew up? Cable Street? What number was your house? What was it your mother used to bake? You always talk about it. Strudel? Was it strudel?'

Herzl had gone limp. His breathing was shallow.

'Stretcher!' Alun shouted this to no one in particular as an ambulance went by. Anti-fascists were running in every direction, scattered by mounted police who were lashing out indiscriminately. Where they charged, people in front of them parted before closing around behind them. The mounted police regrouped into another ragged line and dug their heels into their horses' flanks. Some of the anti-fascists were now retreating to a second barricade further down Cable Street. A stationary tram had been abandoned by its driver but a brass band was still playing somewhere and, combined with the shrill of police whistles, the noise rose in a cacophonous crescendo. Glass from a smashed shop window was now being thrown at the police and smoke bombs added to the confusion.

Alun lowered Herzl, so that he was lying on his side, stood up and, covered in his comrade's blood, ran to the first barricade. There he searched for a door he had seen earlier, wrenched it free and dragged it back along the pavement. He rolled his fallen friend on to it, grunting with the effort, then looked around for help. Because people were hurrying past to get away from the police, it took several minutes before he found four volunteers to lift the door. Then, half running, half walking as they pushed their way through the crowds, it took almost half an hour to reach the first-aid post in Whitechapel Library. There they lifted Herzl on to a table and a doctor came over and tested his pulse. Slowly he shook his head.

Herzl's eyes had caps of frost on them. When Alun took his hand, he recoiled at the cool skin.

He noticed two policemen smoking cigarettes and drinking mugs of tea. 'What are they doing here?' he asked hotly.

'It's all right,' one of the stretcher-bearers said. 'They're comrades. They've surrendered to us.'

Alun walked up to the nearest of the policemen and punched him in the stomach.

THIRTY-SEVEN

Although Alun always talked with pride of the time he shared a prison cell with Harry Pollitt, he had been more unnerved by the experience than he cared to admit. He was reminded of it now as he stared at the door of his cell in Wandsworth Prison.

He heard footsteps, a rattle of keys and a metallic groan as the door was pulled open. Then a rasping voice said: 'Come on, you.'

Harry had paid his bail. Alun had to sign a form in return for his laces, belt and the half-crown he'd had in his pocket at the time of his arrest for assaulting a police officer.

Moments later he was standing outside the prison looking up and thinking bitterly that Martin Herzl would never see the sky again. He turned up his collar against a fine rain and slowly made his way to Earlsfield Station. There he handed over elevenpence for twenty cigarettes. Realizing he didn't have enough money left to buy the *Manchester Guardian* as well as a pint of beer – his next stop – he stood and read a copy of the paper in the kiosk instead. He then looked around for a telephone box. The beer could wait.

Connie answered after five rings.

'It's me,' Alun said. He was going to have to play the role of sympathetic intermediary carefully.

'Hello, Alun.' Distorted by the crackly line, Connie's voice sounded flat, almost hollow. 'I've had some Blackshirts round here asking me where Kim is,' she said slowly. 'Is he in trouble?'

'Yes. Serious trouble. If they come around again, tell them Kim is somewhere they won't find him. It's best that you don't know where. Is everything all right? You don't sound your usual self.'

'No,' Connie said, 'everything is not all right.'

'What's wrong?'

There was a long silence.

'Hello? Connie? Are you still there?'

'Did you give him my letter?'

'Yes. But I don't know whether he's read it or not.'

Connie fell silent again; then she said: 'I need to talk to him. When can I see him?'

'That's what I was ringing about. Kim is going away for a while.'

'Where?'

'I can't say. Not over the telephone. Your line may be tapped. He's told me he'll write to you when he gets there.'

'Is it abroad?'

'Not over the telephone, Connie.'

'Is it Berlin?' Connie asked. 'Is he going to stay with that Riefenstahl woman?'

Alun allowed the silence to balloon around them, long enough to make Connie suspect that Berlin was exactly where Kim was headed. The line hissed, then Connie coughed twice to clear her throat and said: 'No . . . he's going to Spain, isn't he?'

Alun made a quick calculation. Spain might be better. Spain was dangerous at the moment. British volunteers were going to Spain and not coming back.

'It is Spain, isn't it?' Alun could hear stifled sobbing coming from Connie now. 'Isn't he even going to say goodbye to me?'

It was Alun's turn to feel his throat tighten, but he had to remain strong. This was a means that would be justified by its end. If he could convince Connie that Kim had gone to Spain, he could step in and have his chance to win her heart. 'It's not safe for you to see him,' he said. 'You're under surveillance. We all are. And MI5 is full of BUF sympathizers. They'd be on to him in a shot.'

'I don't understand,' Connie said. 'What do they think he's done?'

'The Blackshirts think Kim betrayed them. Tipped off the anti-fascists about Mosley's plans to call off the march.'

Connie seemed to regain her composure. 'Well, you tell him,' she said in a firmer voice, 'you tell him that if he goes to Germany, or Spain, or wherever, he needn't come back.'

Alun bruised the air with a punch but said nothing.

Connie blew her nose. 'Alun?'

'Yes?'

'You've been a good friend to us, to Kim and me. Can you pass on a message to Kim before he goes?'

'Course.'

Another long pause, then: 'Tell him I love him.'

Alun shook his head. He thought about the message Kim had asked him to pass on to Connie when they were in Berlin, the one he had never delivered.

'And tell him I want him to bring me back a souvenir from wherever he is going . . .' She sniffed, trying to find a lighter tone. 'And tell him . . .' She fell silent again. 'Yes. Tell him . . . Tell him I think I'm in the family way.'

THIRTY-EIGHT

The Royal Oak pub was a five-minute walk from Vauxhall Station. When Alun reached the door, he hesitated before knocking. His thoughts were still spiralling from the news of Connie's pregnancy. Where did this leave him? Having achieved his aim of driving a wedge between Connie and Kim, it now looked as if his efforts had been in vain. A baby would change everything, and he would have to tell Kim.

Possibly . . .

As he calculated his next move, Alun began pacing around outside the pub. What if, he thought, this could be turned into an opportunity rather than a setback? What if he said to Connie that he was willing to spare her the stigma of being an unmarried mother? No, that would sound wrong. 'Don't worry,' he could say. 'I'm here. I can look after you and the baby.'

But before he could become a husband and stepfather, he would have to appear in court to answer charges of assaulting a police officer. In all likelihood he would be convicted and would have to serve time, possibly as much as a year, in prison. He couldn't face that. In fact he thought it might just kill him. Perhaps he had an alternative, which was to skip bail and head for Spain to join the fight against fascism there. Once the civil war was over, he could arrange for Connie to come and join him with the baby. That might work. But there was still the problem of what to do about Kim.

Taking several deep breaths in quick succession, he marched up to the door and gave two sharp knocks three times. There would be no going back now. 'The end justifies the means,' he said under his breath. A moment later he heard the clunk of a bolt sliding back and Jackson, a publican with a wide mouth and uneven, brown-looking teeth, put his head around the door, looked left and right and then stood aside to let Alun in.

'He's upstairs,' Jackson said in a low and scratchy voice.

'Pour me a pint of mild, would you?' Alun said, slamming fourpence down on the counter. 'I have a feeling I'm going to need it.'

'We're not open,' Jackson said.

'I know, but your small act of kindness will be rewarded. I'll get your unwelcome guest out of your hair.'

Jackson began to pour.

'And I'll need to borrow your paper,' Alun said, nodding at a copy of the *Guardian* he had spotted on a nearby table.

When he had finished the beer, Alun lifted the counter to the bar and opened what looked like a heavily varnished cupboard. It led to some narrow stairs at the top of which was another door. Alun gave the same knock as before and a voice from inside said: 'That you, Mr Jackson?'

'It's Alun.'

The door opened but there was no one on the other side. Alun stepped into the room only to discover that Kim was behind the door, pointing a pistol at him. He stiffened. 'Good to see you, too.'

With a flick of the gun, Kim signalled for Alun to move over to the bed.

'Where did you get it?' Alun asked.

'Leni,' Kim replied.

'Well, would you mind putting it down, please? You might hurt someone.'

Kim was wearing a vest and, judging by the sweat on his brow, he had been exercising. Or perhaps his appearance was a reflection of the stress he was feeling. He looked as if he had lost weight and his skin was grey. Alun presumed there had been death threats.

Taking the rolled-up copy of the newspaper from his pocket, Alun opened it and said: 'See this? The BUF is a laughing stock. It says here Mosley "lost his nerve" and that "his reputation as a credible leader is damaged irreparably".'

Kim did not seem unduly concerned. 'And listen to this,' Alun went on. '"Harry Pollitt, the General Secretary of the Communist Party of Great Britain, called it the most humiliating defeat ever suffered by any figure in English politics."' Alun looked at Kim and felt puzzled. 'You don't seem too worried.'

'I'm not. I was hoping this would happen. That's why I told you what Mosley told me. I knew you would tip the papers off.'

'What are you . . .?' Alun felt disconcerted now. Was this a bluff? Had Kim been using him?

'I'm no more of a fascist than you are,' Kim said. 'Not any more. Mosley had to be stopped.'

'I wouldn't worry about Mosley,' Alun said, trying to shift the subject, 'he's got other things on his mind. He's gone to Berlin to get married to Diana Mitford. The ceremony is being held in Goebbels's drawing room, apparently.' Alun sat down on the bed. 'No, I wouldn't worry about Mosley. Mosley's men, on the other hand . . .'

'What do you mean?'

'They think you betrayed them.'

'I wonder who gave them that impression.'

'No idea,' Alun said. 'I've been in prison, remember.'

'Have they set a trial date?'

'Not yet. And I don't plan on being around when they do. I'm going to Barcelona.'

Kim blinked. 'Spain?'

'No, Barcelona in Wales.' Alun lit a cigarette. 'I'm going to buy a weekend return to Paris. I have a contact who can meet me at the Gare du Nord and escort me to the Pyrenees where I can cross over the border at night. Takes three days, four at most. You don't even need a passport. You could come with me.'

'What are you talking about?'

Alun stood up. Walked over to the window. 'Well, you can't stay here.'

'In case you hadn't noticed,' Kim said, 'there's a war going on in Spain.'

'That will make it easier to disappear,' Alun countered. 'It would only be for a few weeks. By the time you get back, the dust will have settled here. Connie will have forgiven you and forgotten what happened in Berlin.'

'And which side will you be fighting on?'

Alun could hear the cynicism in Kim's voice. 'I'm not going there to fight. I'm going there to disappear. Like you.'

'I'm not as naïve as you think,' Kim said. 'I know you're a communist. What were you doing at Earl's Court the night Connie was blinded?'

'I was attending the rally,' Alun said. 'Same as you.'

'But you weren't like me, were you?'

'If you've got something to say, come out and say it. You reckon I had something to do with Connie being blinded?'

'I know you did.'

Alun shrugged. 'I swear I didn't.'

There was a blur of movement and Alun felt himself being lifted by his jacket lapels. Their eyes were level now and Kim was breathing rapidly, his nostrils flaring with anger. They remained like this for a few seconds before Alun was tossed aside like a kitbag.

'You've been trying to turn her against me!' Kim shouted. 'Trying to sabotage me! It was you who sold me out to the press when we were in Berlin, wasn't it? You wanted to score a propaganda victory against the Blackshirts by exposing their poster boy.'

Alun felt trapped. What if Kim was able to turn the tables and prove to the Blackshirts that it was Alun who had betrayed them? What if the thugs came for him instead? He could not allow that to happen.

'You've poisoned my life,' Kim said. 'Why? Where does all this hatred come from?' His hands were balled into fists.

If he hits me, Alun thought, I can show Connie the bruises. Show her what her poster boy is really like. 'Go on,' he said, getting to his feet. 'Do it.'

Kim drew his fist back in line with his shoulder, but it remained there.

'You can't, can you?' Alun said with an incredulous laugh. 'You want to hit me but you can't.'

'How have I wronged you?' Kim asked in a softer voice, lowering his fist.

'Listen to yourself,' Alun said. 'You're being irrational.' He adjusted his tie and smoothed down his hair, then he made a lunge for the pistol, grabbed it and pointed it at Kim. 'Whatever you think has come between us you have to put it from your mind,' he said. 'I'm your friend and I would never do anything to hurt you. You have to trust me.'

Kim was staring at the gun. 'Trust you? I don't even know who you are.'

'I'll tell you who I am, Kim. I'm your only chance. I can get you away from here.'

'I'm not going anywhere. I'll find somewhere else to stay.'

'Where? With your family?'

Kim's shoulders dropped and he shook his head. 'Don't have any family.'

Alun's eyes narrowed and a smile crept across his face. 'That's not entirely true. There's your father. He's been looking for you.' This was a gamble. If Kim questioned him he would soon realize that Alun didn't really know anything about his father.

Kim's face was contorting as he tried to push out the words. His chin was quivering and he was taking little sips of air like a drowning man. It was as if he had lost the ability to speak.

Alun made another calculation. He needed to make sure that Kim did not have any contact with Connie before he left the country; did not ruin everything by sharing with her his suspicion that Alun was the one who had blinded her. But it was getting harder to keep the two apart. He needed to arrange a warning shot that would persuade Kim that it was not safe for him to stay in London. Higgins, the Blackshirt thug whom Kim had humiliated outside the Black House, would be the man to do it, along with his sidekicks. As the fighting in Cable Street had been between the anti-fascists and the police, Alun was sure that the Blackshirts would still believe he was one of their number.

'Look,' he said. 'Here's what I'll do. I'm going to arrange for you to meet Connie. Tomorrow night.'

*

Kim was wearing a trilby when he emerged from the Royal Oak at 7.30 p.m. the following evening. The collar of his overcoat was turned up and there was a scarf covering his chin.

'Over here,' Alun said, emerging from the shadows. He was wearing a donkey jacket and Breton cap.

They did not talk as they made their way across Vauxhall Bridge, with Alun limping as he tried to keep up with Kim. The Thames below them was dark and silent. When they reached the north side, Alun said: 'She's looking forward to seeing you.'

Alun was sure that Kim no longer trusted him, but he was also sure that Kim would be so excited by the prospect of meeting Connie that he would ignore his own reservations.

With their shoes loud against the pavement, they continued along Vauxhall Bridge Road until they reached Rampayne Street and turned. Alun checked his watch, then led the way along Lupus Street towards St George's Square. When they reached the railings, he checked his watch again. 'She should be in there,' he said, pointing. 'On a bench at the far end by those trees. I'll keep watch. Don't be too long.'

Kim set off, but then stopped, turned and came back, his hand outstretched. As they shook he gave a kinked smile and, swallowing his emotions, tried to say something, but gave up and nodded instead.

The garden was long and narrow, its sides partly illuminated by light from the surrounding houses. Alun checked the time again and watched Kim stride away from him, quickly covering the distance to the end of the lawn.

When he reached it, Kim turned and gave an exaggerated shrug. At the same moment, three black-clothed figures loomed up out of the darkness behind him.

Alun looked down at his feet for a moment; then he turned away. 'The end justifies the means,' he whispered to himself. As he walked back in the direction of Vauxhall Bridge Road, he lit a cigarette with hands that were shaking.

PART FIVE

THIRTY-NINE

Winter, 2005. Frankfurt

Twenty minutes before the movie was due to end, Sigrun patted Dieter's knee, directed a thumb over her shoulder and whispered: 'Meet you outside.'

Dieter raised his hands to the level of his shoulders and frowned as Sigrun edged past him. Although, at thirty-one, her boyfriend was a year younger than her, he looked older, and he dressed in a less youthful way too, this evening wearing the kind of fleece-lined zip-up jacket and rubber-soled, slip-on shoes a pensioner might wear. Why, Sigrun thought as she left, can he not make more of an effort when we go out?

Instead of waiting in the foyer, with its harsh fluorescent lighting and heaters billowing hot breath, Sigrun stood on Dreieichstrasse, looking up at the clear night sky for signs of snow. She could almost taste it. There was electricity in the air. A lorry with rotating orange lights spat salt at her as it passed and then a taxi slowed to see if she wanted a lift. She shook her head, checked her watch and wondered if the driver thought she had been stood up.

She gripped her shoulder bag and shivered. The film clip she had stolen the previous day on her trip to Leni's house in Pöcking was in there. One of the reasons she had left the cinema early was that she had been struggling to concentrate, her thoughts returning constantly to the British athlete who featured on the clip. Who was he? Why had Leni kept the clip all these years? Kept it hidden?

Figuring that Dieter would stay watching the film for a further five minutes, out of male pride, she checked her watch. When he emerged after six minutes and shivered in an exaggerated way, she registered her gratitude to him with a smile and thought: I know you better than you know yourself.

They were silent as they made their way to the car park; then, as they approached the barrier and looked around for their car, Sigrun broke the spell. 'Told you we should have gone to see *Downfall*.'

Dieter stopped walking and turned to her, examining her face in the amber glow of the streetlights. 'You've already seen it!'

'I know, but you haven't.'

'How many more times?' Dieter said. 'I can't face another film about the fucking Nazis.'

'There haven't been any others, not like *Downfall*.'

'I'm sure if it's any good there'll be a sequel. Perhaps the bunker scenes will turn out to be a dream and Hitler will have retired to Miami to work as a second-hand car salesman who tampers with the mileage. I'll watch that instead.'

At home, she was the first to go to bed – as usual – because she had to read to make herself tired, and he could not sleep with her bedside light on. When Dieter joined her, he slipped off his jeans and briefs in the same action, before closing the window.

Sigrun's pulse slowed as she watched him in the low light. 'Can you leave that open?'

'It's freezing out there.' But this was not said as a stand-off. He opened the window, with a rattle of complaint. 'In fact . . .' He paused as he peered harder into the night. 'Yeah . . . It's starting to snow.'

'Really?' Sigrun took off her reading glasses, pulled back the duvet and crossed the room to stand by his side. As she contemplated the downy flakes caught in the street lighting below, her hand felt for his. Snow always made her think of Leni, who had been at her happiest in the Alps. 'I love it when it snows,' she whispered. They stood like this for a minute, neither wanting to leave the moment, then Sigrun shivered, hastened back under the duvet and took up her book once more.

Reaching over to take it from her hands, Dieter examined the cover before handing it back with a reproving stare. 'Goebbels's diaries? Seriously? What's wrong with you?'

'It's research. I've only ever read extracts from them before, and I had no idea how detailed . . .' She trailed off, sensing she was losing her audience. 'Have you read the reviews for *Downfall*, by the way? They are incredible. It's a proper piece of film-making.'

Dieter rolled over, turning his back on her and drawing the duvet tight to his shoulder. 'Are we allowed to show the monster as a human being?' he said to the wall, quoting a review from *Bild*.

'It is more dangerous to pretend the monster never existed,' Sigrun countered.

He rolled over again, this time to face her. 'Why are you so obsessed with the Nazis?'

'I'm not.'

Dieter sat up now and made a two-handed gesture at a framed poster of Leni Riefenstahl's *The Blue Light* hanging on the wall. It was a signed original from 1932 and it had cost Sigrun 750 euros on eBay – 750 euros she could ill afford.

'Leni was not a Nazi,' Sigrun said. 'She merely hung out with Nazis.'

'And she was only obeying orders, right? Like Hitler.' Dieter allowed himself a chuckle at his own joke; then he asked: 'I wonder how much she really knew. Didn't she have it off with Goebbels? Or am I thinking of someone else?'

'I believe she was the only actress in Germany who *didn't* have it off with Goebbels, though there were rumours.' Sigrun put her glasses back on and raised her book to eye level before adding: 'In her memoirs she made out that she hated him, though this doesn't tally with what he wrote in his diaries. To be honest, I hadn't appreciated how much her version of events differed from his. It's hard to know whom to believe.'

Dieter's eyes were closed now and his speech was muffled by the pillow. 'Goebbels wrote his diary at the end of every day, right? It was contemporaneous. Whereas hers . . . when did she write her autobiography?'

'Late eighties.'

'Well then, fifty years or so after he wrote his. And she would have seen what he had written. So it would make sense to go with Goebbels.'

'Except he *is* Goebbels.'

'Yeah, there is that.'

'It's funny,' Sigrun said. 'I can always tell when Leni is lying in her memoirs; it's whenever her account of a conversation – with Goebbels, say, or Hitler – reflects too well on her. She always seems to be complaining to Hitler about his treatment of the Jews, for example. As if.'

'Are we talking about this now?'

'But she was honest about her sex life. She was so much more sexually liberated than other women of her generation. She enjoyed sex. Efficient German sex. She reckoned every man she met fancied her . . . Don't get me wrong, she was fussy about whom she slept with. She always went for young, handsome, athletic types. Nearly all her cameramen fitted that description. They were like her harem. Went through them like a . . . Dieter?'

Silence.

Taking off her reading glasses once more, Sigrun marked her page and turned out the light, only to find her thoughts were spinning too violently for sleep. Dieter was right. She *was* obsessed with the Nazis, or rather the rise of the Nazis in the 1930s. But not in an unhealthy way, surely? It was professional. As a film historian, this was the period Sigrun taught. Or at least it was at the moment. The faculty would be meeting to discuss her tenure any day now and if she didn't get it, she was not sure how much longer they could manage financially. She thought about how Dieter kept saying the firm of architects he was working for part-time, while he finished his PhD, was about to offer him a full-time job. They needed to talk about that.

'Dieter?'

But he was asleep.

The following night, in the Chinese restaurant opposite their apartment, Dieter opened a soft pack of Gauloises and offered one to Sigrun. When she took one with a I-don't-normally-do-this look, he lit it for her before lighting one for himself. 'They're thinking of banning smoking in restaurants,' he said.

'It was only a matter of time.'

As the first course was being cleared away, they ordered two more bottles of beer from a bad-tempered waitress.

'When I was a student I used to live off Chinese takeaways,' Dieter said.

'You still are a student,' Sigrun replied.

More plates of food arrived and they put out their cigarettes before Dieter snapped apart some fresh chopsticks and picked up a dumpling. Sigrun rubbed her chopsticks together and picked unenthusiastically at some noodles. A woman came up to their table with a bunch of roses individually wrapped in brown paper and offered one to Dieter, indicating with a gesture that he might like to proffer it to his dining companion. Sigrun waved her away. 'Leni hated flowers,' she said.

'I remember when you first mentioned her to me, you said there had been a book or something. That that was the reason you got into her.'

Sigrun pushed her plate away. 'My mother bought me a book about the Berlin Olympics for my tenth birthday. It had a chapter on Leni.'

'Well, you know what they say,' Dieter said. 'There are no accidents in Germany. No coincidences.'

'I suppose I just find her fascinating,' Sigrun said. 'She was the most aloof, intoxicating, ballsy German woman of her generation. A feminist icon, in her way. And I think what intrigues me most about her is that she was an unreliable narrator. She fictionalized her own life. Living on the border between her truth and her lies, so that even she no longer knew the difference. She would reverse cause and effect. I think she knew exactly what she was up to.'

'Lies like what?'

'Well, she would selectively edit her film reviews to compensate for the shortsightedness of her critics.' Out of the corner of her eye, Sigrun watched a man with a ponytail at a nearby table. He was covering his mouth with his hand as he used a toothpick.

'That doesn't sound so bad,' Dieter said.

'OK, how about this? She claimed that her Olympic film was independently funded, but it wasn't. Goebbels's Ministry of Propaganda bankrolled Leni's whole *Olympia* project. And paid her a fortune. She had it written into her contract that she would get twenty per cent of the net profits.'

'Clever woman.'

'It was the little things, too. She would always claim that *Olympia* won the Golden Lion at Venice, but it didn't. It won the Mussolini Cup. And when she went to New York in 1938 she stayed at the Hotel Pierre on Fifth Avenue, not the Waldorf Astoria as she claimed. And when she went to London she stayed at the Ritz but wrote in her memoir that it was the Dorchester.'

'We all do a bit of that.'

Sigrun pursed her mouth. 'OK then, this is not a lie exactly but it is typical of what she did. In her memoirs, she wrote that she went to the opera in Berlin one night in 1934, with Goebbels and his wife Magda and the Italian ambassador. She described how a photograph was taken of them all that appeared in the papers the next day. That photograph was published in the papers in 1933. A year earlier. I checked.'

'So she wasn't very good with dates.'

'It was more than that. It would have been so easy for her to check the papers. She could have corrected the date in her memoir – but she chose not to. And she was good with numbers, so the mix-up with dates makes no sense. With Leni things were never straightforward. She would reveal the truth by flying close to it and doing something like changing a name to throw the reader off the scent. You have to be a detective to understand her memoirs. They are full of evasions, omissions and half-truths. Here's another example. She described a bizarre incident in which Glenn Morris, an American decathlete she was sleeping with during the Berlin Olympics, won a gold medal and when he came off the podium he marched straight up to her, ripped open her blouse and kissed her breasts. Ridiculous, right?' Sigrun raised her hands, palms open. 'This was supposedly in front of a hundred thousand spectators yet not one of them, not even the journalists present, thought to mention that moment. Only Leni did, in her autobiography written half a century later.'

More dishes arrived and Dieter took hold of a fried squid with his chopsticks and held it up for Sigrun to try. 'So she was a fantasist?'

'No, you're not listening to me,' Sigrun said, leaning forward to take the squid. 'It was more misdirection with her. Smoke and mirrors, as if she was covering up a secret. She would bury the truth in carefully chosen words. I think she *did* have a fling with an athlete during the Games, but I think the athlete was British not American. There's a strange film clip I saw at her house. I think it's of the athlete.'

With her foot under the table, Sigrun touched her shoulder bag. She didn't want the film clip she had stolen to leave her side. 'Leni had to operate in a man's world,' she continued. 'In fact, she was probably the only woman who came anywhere close to having power in the Third Reich. To do that she had to learn to think and behave like a man. That included her love life. She was insatiable.'

Dieter leaned in. 'And you don't think it's a coincidence that it was her express wish, as declared in her will, that you and no one else should open the film canisters?'

Sigrun puckered her brow. 'What do you mean?'

'Like I said, we Germans don't do coincidences.'

'But that . . .' Sigrun lit a cigarette, took a couple of thoughtful drags and flicked ash over her uneaten food. Realizing what she had done, she said: 'Sorry.' The meal was not going to plan. She had something to tell Dieter, something that was going to annoy him, and she was missing her moment.

'I wish you'd talk as much about your family as you do about Leni,' Dieter said. 'It's been over a year now and I hardly know a thing.'

'Too boring.'

'That's what you always say.'

Sigrun sighed. 'I told you about my father – the industrialist in Düsseldorf? I barely see him – after he remarried, we drifted apart. I don't get along with my stepmother, and my stepmother doesn't get along with me.'

'You said your mother died when you were ten but what did she die of?'

'Brain tumour. It was shortly after she gave me that book. The only other thing she gave me was this.' She waggled the little finger on her right hand to show the ring on it. It was an unusual design, a plain and angular black sapphire that looked like a small slab of coal set in a band of white gold. 'Told me it was a family heirloom.'

'What about your grandparents?' Dieter asked, scooping some egg-fried rice into a bowl and pouring the last of the sweet and sour sauce on top of it.

'From what I can gather my mother was adopted, but records about adoption during the war years are unreliable, partly because of the "Lebensborn" houses.'

'The what?'

'The SS-run centres where Aryan babies were taken to be raised and indoctrinated as Nazis.'

'What does your mother's birth certificate say?'

'Never been able to track it down. I don't even know what year she was born.' Sigrun took a sip of beer and swallowed with a tight jaw. 'I have no proof, but it's possible my grandmother, whoever she was, was one of the two million German women raped by Red Army soldiers in the final weeks of the war.'

'Wow,' Dieter said. 'That's . . . heavy.'

'It's just a theory,' Sigrun said with a shrug. 'You see, a lot of the Red Army babies ended up either aborted, in orphanages or adopted.'

The waitress came to clear their plates and looked in disgust at the stubbed-out cigarettes. She muttered to herself as she took them away.

Dieter reached across the table and touched Sigrun's hand. 'That's more than you've ever said before. It's OK to talk about this stuff, you know,' he said in a gentle voice.

'Is it OK, though?' Sigrun asked, withdrawing her hand. 'Do you know anyone, any of your friends who talk about what their grandparents did in the war? It doesn't really help.'

Dieter looked lost in thought, as if trying to arrive at a decision. He reached into his jacket pocket and brought out a small black leather box which he slid across the table towards her. 'Sigrun?' he said, without meeting her eye. 'I have another question for you.' He opened the box to reveal a diamond ring.

Sigrun found herself blinking as she contemplated it. She had not been prepared for this. With a cough to clear her throat she said: 'I'm flattered, Dieter. But the answer is no.'

FORTY

The gurgle of the percolator, the sound of breakfast eggs tap-dancing in a boiling pan, the rasping clunk as two halves of a bagel were launched from the toaster – with each new noise the silence between Dieter and Sigrun seemed to deepen. When, having loudly scraped a butter knife over her bagel, Sigrun took a bite, her chewing seemed too loud as well.

The tension between them did not diminish as he carried her suitcase out to the VW. The morning was hard and grey and a cold wind was blowing. When he gathered up his architect's drawings, they flapped around dangerously, and when he dropped them into the boot to make space for her suitcase on the back seat, Sigrun wondered why he had not put the case in the boot instead. Was he making a point about how there was room in there for two cases, his as well as hers?

'Are you going to London because I asked you to marry me?' he said.

'No. I told you, as far as I'm concerned nothing has changed between us.'

But she could see that to Dieter it might not look that way. Her trip to London, to do some work for the British Film Institute, had been scheduled for a month's time and Dieter had planned to come with her.

'Why didn't you tell them you'd already made arrangements that you couldn't change?'

'Because,' she said, 'I was the one who asked if I could bring the trip forward.' She did not want to say why, because it sounded ridiculous, but the truth was she couldn't wait a month to visit the National Archives at Kew to see if she could find out the identity of the British athlete she had seen in the film clip she had stolen. It was hard to explain even to herself, but it was as if when the British long jumper looked at Leni behind the lens, he was looking at her, Sigrun. If he was still alive the man would be in his late eighties by now, possibly older, but if she could just talk to him . . .

Dieter misinterpreted her silence. 'If you want to leave me,' he said, 'you should have the guts to come out and say it.'

'No,' she said. 'That's not it. Look, we haven't been together that long. It's complicated and I'm not sure I can explain it to you. Not yet.'

Once Sigrun had boarded the Lufthansa Airbus and fastened her seat-belt, a flight attendant handed her a complimentary copy of *Der Spiegel*. As she flicked through it, she came to a short article in which her name was mentioned in the final paragraph. The headline read: 'Footage found of Hitler shaking hands with Jesse Owens?' It was only in the second paragraph that the qualification came: 'According to unofficial sources, film footage may have been found showing Adolf Hitler shaking hands with the American gold-medal winner Jesse Owens at the 1936 Berlin Olympics.'

Sigrun imagined that the 'unofficial source' was Becker, the lawyer, wanting to generate publicity at the behest of 'the family' for the forthcoming auction of the Riefenstahl estate. There had been a message from him on her answering machine when she got back from Pöcking. It reminded her that she had signed a non-disclosure agreement – and that under no circumstances was she allowed to talk to anyone about what she had, or had not, found. If reporters approached her, she was to say that she could neither confirm nor deny any details.

'Oh God, Dieter,' Sigrun muttered to herself as the plane reached its cruising altitude. She pressed her forehead against the warm Perspex of the porthole. 'What am I getting into here?'

The shadow cast by the plane on the clouds below reminded Sigrun of the opening scene of *Triumph of the Will*. She thought about how Leni had flown to England herself a few months before making it, taking with her what would become the only surviving copy of her previous film, *The Victory of Faith*. The BFI thought they had found the missing copy in a drawer in the Geological Society building in Piccadilly, of all places. They wanted her to come to London to authenticate it, restore it and transfer it to digital. It was an exciting assignment, but added to that was the thought that she might also be able to identify the mysterious British athlete. She had given herself a few extra days to do some research at the National Archives before she headed over to the BFI.

After she had checked into her modest hotel close to Covent Garden, Sigrun lay on the bed, pointed the remote at the television, and flicked through the channels before picking up the phone to call Dieter. Realizing what she was doing, she put it down again. It was habit, that was all. Was their relationship really over after only one mostly happy, if sexually underwhelming, year? Could it be that simple?

She crossed the room and began to unpack her small, portable reel-to-reel projector. Once she had focused it against a blank wall, she threaded the stolen film clip, having spliced it to a few feet of unexposed film so that she could play it on a loop. Sigrun now felt a tingle of anticipation. As before, when the film was reversed and the athlete retraced his steps, he seemed to come to life. And again it happened, that electrifying effect as he stared directly down the lens at her.

As she contemplated the athlete she wondered if the illusion that he was coming to life might be one of Leni's tricks, like the much-imitated opening sequence of *Olympia* in which the statue of the discus thrower of Myron 'comes alive' and starts to swing the discus in slow motion. For that effect she had superimposed footage of a flesh-and-blood athlete over the marble statue of an athlete.

But with this clip of the long jumper, it seemed to have more to do with the film being played backwards. Leni had used this technique for her acclaimed diving sequences – by filming from above and below, and running film backwards as well as forwards, she was able to make the divers look like swooping birds. So subtle was her use of backward film, many viewers did not realize they were, at times, watching divers rising up from the water and returning to the board.

What seemed like a few minutes later, Sigrun checked her watch and saw that half an hour had passed. Feeling slightly dazed, she retrieved a brush from her shoulder bag and began brushing her hair. She looked in the mirror and almost, but not quite, saw Leni reflected back at her. It was something she'd noticed many times before, but the hair colouring was wrong.

Ten minutes later she found herself out in Covent Garden looking around for a chemist. Once she had bought the correct brunette colouring in a branch of Boots, she browsed a few clothes shops. She wasn't sure what she was looking for until, on her way back to the hotel, she wandered into a charity shop and found it: a cream-coloured polo-neck made of lambswool. The Leni Riefenstahl look. It was a good fit.

Back in her hotel room she used the hair dye and applied ruby lipstick and studied herself in the mirror once more. She looked at the planes and contours of her face, the shape of her eyes. Surely this was a coincidence, but as Dieter had said, the Germans didn't believe in coincidences. She realized with a shock that although she still resembled Leni, she also looked strikingly similar to the British athlete, even though he was blond. With quickened pulse and skittish fingers she replayed the film clip. It was true. The curves of his cheekbones and mouth had the same sculptural quality as hers. Why had she not been able to see it before?

She switched the projector off and went to splash cold water on her face and clean her teeth. Then, like an addict, she returned to the room and switched the projector back on. Without taking her eyes off the wall, she took a couple of steps backwards to the bed, lay down and fell asleep.

She was woken next morning by the sound of the film slapping against the desk like a bird trapped in a room, trying to escape through a closed window. The splice had come undone. She switched the projector off and cursed herself for her own stupidity. Film on reels was a notorious fire risk. The projector could easily have combusted in the night as she slept.

She thought about the film all the way to Kew Gardens. The day was unseasonably warm as she walked past benches surrounding a pond with ducks and coots bobbing on its surface. A faint green dust was starting to cover the leafless trees. The first buds of spring, she thought as she continued on up a path towards the modern stone and glass building that housed the National Archives.

She made her way up a curving staircase to the main lobby and here she keyed 'British/long jump/Olympics/1936' into one of the computers. When no results came up, she frowned. Her subject seemed reluctant to emerge from the shadows.

She scanned the room for an assistant and, seeing a bespectacled man with thinning, greasy hair and a name badge on a lanyard, raised her hand to catch his attention. Then she saw a younger, more attractive assistant with gelled hair and a carefully trimmed beard. As he drew nearer, she could see the name on his badge – Nathan.

In her hesitant English, she said she was looking for anything he might have on the British long-jump team for the 1936 Olympics. 'How do I go about that?'

Nathan led her over to a computer, placed his fingers over the keyboard and began tapping. Sigrun did not tell him she had tried this search already. 'Been here before?' he asked over his shoulder. There was a nasal quality to his voice, a raised inflection that suggested he was Australian.

'Once,' she said, opening her mouth to add something, but then closing it again.

'Getting one file number here,' he said. 'Would you like me to order it?'

Wondering why that information had not come up for her, she blinked in assent.

'Where will you be sitting?'

Sigrun pointed to an octagonal table bearing several green-shaded lamps. It was numbered sixteen. Nathan typed this in and pressed the return key. After a moment, a message appeared on the screen: 'Approved'. She touched his shoulder and whispered, '*Danke*.'

'Might take half an hour or so,' Nathan said. 'Someone will bring it to your table.'

While Sigrun waited, she opened her laptop and checked her emails. There was one from Dieter, which she saved for later, one from Becker repeating his message about her not talking to the press, and three from her head of faculty at the university informing her about forthcoming 'budget meetings'. What did that mean? Was she about to be made redundant?

When the file arrived twenty-five minutes later, it was empty. She held it open for a moment, as if waiting for the contents to materialize, then she stood up, closed her laptop and slid it into its case.

'Any luck?'

She turned to find Nathan standing at her shoulder.

'It's completely empty,' she said.

'Oh. Sorry about that.' He chewed his cheek. 'Did you want to search for a specific name?'

'That's the trouble – I do not know his name.'

'So, a British long jumper competing in the Berlin Olympics, is that it? We must have something. Wait here and I'll see what I can find. Something might have ended up in the wrong file.'

Sigrun was beginning to think the young archivist had forgotten about her, when, after a quarter of an hour, he came back smiling, holding a manuscript box tied with string. He placed it in front of her. 'According to one of my colleagues, "long jump" was called "broad jump" back then, so I searched again and found this.' Theatrically, he unwound the string fastening the cardboard box, ran his fingers over its waxy surface and lifted its lid like a waiter revealing the chef's special. On the top was a photograph showing four athletes in British vests sitting in a row.

Sigrun picked it up and examined it hungrily, then frowned again. 'He's not here.'

'I know,' the archivist said. 'But look at the right side. There's no white border.'

'So?'

'So someone has taken a pair of scissors to it. Also, look on the back.'

She turned the photograph over. Written across the top were the words: 'British track and field team, 1936 Berlin Olympics.' Underneath this were five names, followed by their discipline in brackets: javelin, discus, shotput, high jump and broad jump. 'There are five names here,' Sigrun said. 'Not four.'

'See? And the names are ordered left to right.' Nathan tapped the letters 'L to R' on the photograph. 'That means the broad jumper is the one who is missing.'

Sigrun read the broad jumper's name out loud. 'Kim Newlands.'

'Ta-dah!'

Sigrun covered her smile with her hand. 'You are like Sherlock Holmes.'

'Guess that's how they got rid of people from photographs before the days of airbrushing. Shall we look him up?'

They went back to the computer and, after keying in the words 'Kim Newlands', Nathan swivelled the screen towards her. 'Doesn't tell us much. Well, it does and it doesn't. It says he was a hurdler and relay runner first, before he took up the broad jump. And it says there is a file on him covering the period 1934 to 1936, but I'm afraid it's coming up as "Document unavailable".'

'What does that mean?'

'Government papers are normally closed to the public for thirty years, but some documents, especially criminal ones, are closed for fifty, to protect the families.'

'But this was almost seventy years ago.'

Nathan chewed his cheek again and said: 'Good point.' His fingers moved across the keyboard and then he paused and tilted his head to one side. 'That's odd. This file is coming up as classified.'

Sigrun pursed her lips. 'Does it say why?'

'No, only that the closed file is not a criminal file. It's an HO file. That's Home Office. Did he have anything to do with MI5?'

'I have no idea.'

'Normally documents are closed only for matters of national security. It might be that this has been filed incorrectly and it should have been declassified after fifty years, or thirty. They sometimes don't get around to declassifying files until someone puts in a request to see them.'

'How do I put in the request?'

'It can take a while.'

'I'm in no hurry. There are things I have to do in London.'

'I mean . . .' Nathan said, '. . . it could take days or even weeks.'

'Oh.' Sigrun gripped her shoulder bag.

'But don't worry,' he added. 'There are other methods.'

'What do you mean?'

'It depends who you know.' He jiggled his eyebrows.

'*You* could get them for me?'

Nathan made a shushing gesture. 'It wouldn't be anything illegal. There's a new Freedom of Information Act that has just come into effect. It has opened up all sorts of new avenues . . . Hang on, there's a cross reference to another file here, on his girlfriend.'

'His girlfriend?' Sigrun felt a coldness running down her flanks. 'Was it Leni Riefenstahl by any chance?'

'No, it says here her name was Constance Dalton. Would you like to see it?'

When Sigrun nodded, Nathan typed the code for the file, pressed 'Enter' and after a moment the words 'Document ordered' appeared on the screen. 'Great,' he said. 'This one seems to be declassified. I'm afraid it could take a while as well, though. If you fancy a coffee . . .' He plucked at his hair self-consciously. 'I'm coming up to my break – I can show you where to go.'

Sigrun smiled and indicated for him to lead the way.

When they returned to the main lobby, Nathan sat at a computer terminal and checked on the progress of the file. As he did this, Sigrun stood close by his side. When he leaned away, she said: 'I'm sorry, I was invading your personal space.'

He looked up at her and smiled good-naturedly, then studied the screen. 'It's not going to get here until tomorrow, I'm afraid. Stored off-site. Look,' he added in a low voice. 'As I said, I might be able to get hold of the classified file you're after, but it probably wouldn't be a good idea for me to be seen handing it over to you here so perhaps I could photocopy it for you. I could drop both of them off at your hotel if you like. Where are you staying?'

Sigrun knew it. This guy was coming on to her. A favour for a favour. She weighed whether he really could get hold of the file, or whether this was just a ruse to get her to go on a date with him. She asked herself: What would Leni do? 'Sure,' she said, writing down her mobile number. 'Why not?'

Nathan wrote down his own number and handed it to her. 'I'm curious,' he said. 'Why are you so interested in this Kim Newlands guy anyway?'

Sigrun thought for a moment, then surprised herself with her answer: 'This will sound crazy, and it's a long shot, but I think it's just possible he might be my grandfather.'

FORTY-ONE

Wearing a white hotel dressing gown and with her hair still wet from the shower, Sigrun projected the film clip on to the wall and felt once more a rush of warmth as it breathed into her. She also noticed something she had not seen before. The film no longer seemed to be monochrome. The shades of grey now had a bluish tinge. She knew that Leni had experimented with filters on her mountaineering films in the early 1930s but this was different.

She checked her emails. There was one from her friend at the university saying that the results of the DNA test she had done for her would soon be back from the lab. There would be one result for the strand of hair Sigrun had found at Leni's house and another for a strand of hair that Sigrun had plucked from her own head.

It had been a whim at the time, yet in an almost subliminal way she had always wondered about her affinity to Leni, as well as her resemblance to her. Then, when she'd been selected to view the 'lost' Leni film reels, her imagination had taken flight and she'd allowed herself to think: What if there really is a connection?

When the phone rang it made her jump.

'Hi, it's Nathan from the National Archives. I'm downstairs in the lobby. I've managed to get hold of that classified file you were after.'

They found an empty sofa in the corner furthest away from the reception area and sat down. When Nathan passed the file to Sigrun, it was warm from his hands, its seal of red wax still intact. About two inches across and imprinted with a coat of arms, the seal seemed incongruously large. Stamped in capital letters below it were the words 'CLASSIFIED DOCUMENT: NOT TO BE OPENED UNTIL . . .' But there was no date.

'Thank you,' Sigrun said in a low voice. 'I hope this doesn't get you into trouble. Why didn't you just take a photocopy and put it back?'

'Dunno! There was something about that seal.'

Sigrun ran her fingers over the red wax and then shook her head.

Nathan asked: 'Aren't you going to open it?'

'Not here.'

'You may as well keep hold of it for now,' he said. 'Files go missing or are misplaced all the time.'

'I'm going to be here for a few more weeks so I can give it back to you soon. Perhaps I could buy you lunch to say thank you.'

'I'd like that. I hope it helps you find the answers you're looking for.'

'You know,' Sigrun said, 'part of me wants to open it and see if it tells me who my grandparents are, but part of me doesn't. We have this thing in Germany called *Familienaufstellung*. I'm not sure how you would translate it. Families getting together to try to talk about the past. We had no *Familienaufstellung* in my family. I was raised in a fog of silence and collective German guilt.'

Nathan nodded thoughtfully. 'Oh, I almost forgot,' he said, reaching into a carrier bag. 'Here is the file on his girlfriend. I was able to photocopy this one for you.' He handed over an A4 manila envelope.

On the train to Wales, Sigrun shifted her eyes from the sealed file on the table in front of her to her reflection in the window, a fixed point against a background of blurring green. She thought she could see a fall of half-melted snow on the tops of the brambles as they flew past; then she realized that the bushes were covered with early spring buds that were a watery white, creating the illusion of snow. She picked up the file and weighed it in her hand. It seemed too light.

'What am I doing, Leni?' she said out loud, causing one of the passengers opposite to look up and stare at her.

Why could she not bring herself to open the file? Something about it filled her with dread, as if the act would be like a desecration of Kim's grave.

A crack and the hiss of a can being opened nearby made Sigrun jump. A young man put his mouth to the can to stop it foaming over, then took out an iPod, put in earphones and began a mime of playing drums as he listened.

Sigrun reread the photocopied file on Constance, Lady Dalton. It included an entry from a book she had never heard of before called *Burke's Peerage*. The entry for Lady Dalton said she was born in 1912, which would mean she was ninety-three if still alive. There was no mention of a marriage to Kim, but there were three other marriages recorded in the decades following the war: the second had ended with her husband's death, the others in divorce. Constance had clearly been unlucky in love, or perhaps careless.

There was an address: Dalton Hall, Tonypandy, South Wales. The file also revealed that she had inherited the place, along with the title of Baroness – there being no male heir – when her older sister had died in 1973. The entry had included a phone number for the baronial hall and Sigrun had tried ringing it, but all she got was a recorded message saying the number was no longer in use. She was going to have to pay Lady Dalton a visit in person.

There was also a two-page, MI5 profile of her ladyship, with background and character notes that revealed she had been expelled from school for cheating in an exam; that she had moved to London for her 'coming-out season' and that, in the early 1930s, she had featured regularly in the gossip pages of *Tatler* and had acquired a reputation as a 'bolter': that is, a woman who often got engaged but did not marry. She had had her portrait painted by Sir John Lavery RA and her photograph taken by Cecil Beaton; also, it was rumoured, she had been the muse for a Noël Coward play, though the profile did not specify which one. But then, in 1934, this socialite, whom everyone had called Connie, had swapped her A-line dresses for a black shirt. Section B5(b), a semi-autonomous division of MI5 responsible for monitoring potentially subversive groups, had put her under surveillance for the next six years. It was suggested in the dossier that she had been persuaded to join the British Union of Fascists by Kim Newlands. Sigrun presumed that Kim's fascist allegiance was the reason he had been cut from the 1936 British Olympic team photograph.

The MI5 officer who had compiled the dossier had been blunt in his assessment of Connie, describing her as 'not committed ideologically', 'the black sheep of an aristocratic family' and 'tall and coltish'. He also mentioned that she had been 'injured' at a BUF rally, but did not specify what that injury was. His summation that 'part of her attraction to Newlands seems to be his social inferiority' struck Sigrun as being especially brutal. How dare this anonymous officer presume to know the secrets of her heart?

The last paragraph covered 1940, the year Connie had been interned in Holloway Prison under Defence Regulation 18, along with other active or former British fascists.

Sigrun fanned out the photocopied pages on the table and re-examined a page from the *Daily Express* dating back to August 1936. As she took in the images of Kim, she shook her head. Here was one of him kissing Leni. She'd done so much research – how had she never seen this before? There was a much-reproduced photograph of Leni frolicking with the American athlete she was said to have seduced during the Berlin Olympics, but she must have used her influence to make sure this one with Kim was never printed in the German papers.

On the last of the pages there was a cross reference to a friend of Connie's, a young Welsh communist called Alun Pryce whom MI5 had also had under surveillance in the 1930s. He seemed to have worked for both sides because there was also a reference to him having been a member of the British Union of Fascists. His address, presumably long out of date, was given as 17 Berw Terrace, Tonypandy, Rhondda. Sigrun planned to stay a couple of days and if she had time, after her visit to Dalton Hall, she thought she might have a wander around the town and see if she could locate the house. The file noted that Alun was born in 1911, a year before Connie. The chances of either of them still being alive seemed remote.

*

When Sigrun arrived at Rhondda, its grey pavements were wet from a recent shower. She tapped on the window of a taxi and a tattooed bodybuilder in a brimless cap looked up. 'Do you know Dalton Hall?' she asked. The man seemed resentful at having his afternoon disturbed. Or perhaps it was her German accent that had annoyed him.

'That's in the middle of nowhere, love,' he said. 'I'll never get a fare back from there. And I'll lose my place in the line.'

Sigrun straightened her back, looked along the rank and, seeing that his was the only cab, raised an eyebrow at him.

Twenty minutes later, the taxi drove over a humpback bridge, and there it was. The hall looked imposing but also mellow and listless, as if it had somehow grown tired of its own beauty. When the car came to a stop, Sigrun looked up. She had not expected Connie's family seat to be so neglected. In fact, it looked abandoned, as if it were slowly being strangled by the ivy that had overtaken its gutters and pipes. Behind the mullioned windows the shutters were closed and some of the glass had visible cracks.

When she asked the taxi driver if he could wait, he shook his head and then gave her a card with a number on it. They would send someone when she was ready to be collected. As the taxi drove off, Sigrun looked up again at the hall and shivered. She tried an iron bell-pull to one side of the entrance arch. When she did not hear it sounding, she peered in through a window, brushing the cobwebs aside and trying to see past the gaps in the shutters.

'Hello?' Though she shouted this, it was more by way of letting anyone who might be listening know that her intentions were not criminal.

Seeing a large fountain in the centre of the lawn, she strode over to it. Carved from Portland stone, it featured four recumbent tritons, which Sigrun presumed were meant to be blowing water over their scallop-shell basins into the main bowl. But velvety moss, lichen and dead leaves were all the fountain contained now. Apart from a distant plane, the countryside was quiet, as though the weak winter sun had sapped the day of its vigour.

Sigrun continued across the lawn, towards an ancient cedar of Lebanon, and saw that where the formal lawn ended there was a ha-ha keeping out the sheep that grazed the parkland. Not that it would have mattered if they had grazed the lawn; it clearly had not been mown in a while. She came to a stone terrace with empty plinths where she presumed urns or statuary had once stood. There was also a wall of knapped flint, which seemed to have contained the kitchen garden, but the ground inside it was now overgrown with brambles, dead nettles and ragwort. Behind this there was a rusting metal door in an alcove leading into the house. This was ajar.

'Hello?' she called out again.

The door led on to a scullery with peeling white walls. In the kitchen was a butler's sink, an Aga which was hot to the touch, and a panel of bells. Sigrun's rubber soles seemed raucous on the floorboards as she passed down a corridor and opened another door. This one led to a hallway and a floor laid with black and white marble tiles. The ceiling was much higher here and, though her eyes were finding it hard to adjust to the gloom, Sigrun could see the hallway opened on to a circular central hall with a large and dusty chandelier at its centre. On the walls were old masters and tapestries that looked as if they had not been cleaned in years. A pigeon swooped from its nest in the ceiling and the clap of its wings startled her. Seeing now that there were bird droppings spattered over the floor, Sigrun stepped around them cautiously and made her way towards the foot of the stairs.

'Hello?' she called out once more. 'Is there anyone home?'

When no answer came, she tried another door leading off the central hall and, finding it locked, tried another. This one opened and she found herself in a drawing room dominated by an elaborate plaster chimneypiece on top of which was a large mirror. The room smelled musty and damp. In the bay of a shuttered window was a figure sitting in a high-backed armchair, half in shadow. Next to her was a small decorative table with an empty wine bottle and glass on it.

'Hello?' Sigrun repeated in a gentler voice, but the figure did not stir. 'The door was open.'

As Sigrun approached, she realized the person was a woman and she was asleep. She appeared to be of middle years, with fair hair set in a finger wave, and buttery soft skin. Over her right eye was a black leather patch and she was wearing a shirt and tie, a tweed waistcoat, breeches and riding boots. At her feet was an old wire-haired lurcher with cloudy eyes. Its hackles were raised but it was not growling.

Sigrun took hold of a freckled hand, which was as light as paper, and gave it a little pat. 'Hello?'

When there was no response Sigrun backed out of the room, followed slowly by the old lurcher, its long claws making clicking sounds on the marble floor as they reached the central hall. There was one more door leading off it and when Sigrun opened it she saw it was a study lined with ancient, leather-bound books. On a desk there was an empty vase and an old Corolla typewriter. Next to it she noticed a framed black and white photograph of four people: two men in the foreground, two women behind them. When she picked it up, she realized that one of the men was Kim Newlands; the man he was shaking hands with was Hitler. Between them, standing a few yards back, were two women who appeared to be sharing a joke. She identified the one on the right as Leni Riefenstahl. Sigrun recognized the other woman by her eyepatch.

Suddenly, seeing someone behind her reflected in the glass of the frame, Sigrun jumped. The picture fell from her hands and broke on the floor. She turned but there was no one there. She picked up the frame and removed the shards of broken glass before slipping the photograph into her shoulder bag. She then retraced her steps to the drawing room. The woman was sitting in the same chair as before, her visible eye now open. She seemed older than before.

Sigrun cleared her throat as she approached. 'Are you Lady Dalton?'

The woman with the eyepatch gave a slow blink as she tried to focus on her guest. 'I wondered when you would turn up,' she said, her voice as fragile as her skin.

Sigrun felt confounded by this comment. 'Excuse me for intruding,' she went on. 'I did try ringing the bell but . . . I am looking for Lady Dalton. Is she . . . Are you?'

The woman frowned slightly, as if searching her memory, then nodded her head. 'I don't look my age,' she said.

But Sigrun did not feel reassured by this response. It didn't seem possible that this woman was ninety-three. There were hardly any lines around her eyes and mouth, and while her cheekbones were prominent, the skin over them seemed as soft and blousy as rose petals. Her forehead was high and smooth and Sigrun wondered whether she had had plastic surgery.

'*You* are Constance, Lady Dalton?'

'Connie. Call me Connie. And I don't use the title.' Her voice seemed firmer now. 'Are you my new housemaid?' she asked. 'You're younger than the last one . . . You speak in a peculiar way. What's wrong with you, girl?'

'I'm German. My name is Sigrun Meier.' Without being invited, she sat down.

Connie assumed a more upright position, her spine locking into place. 'I knew a German woman once. Who sent you?'

'No one sent me. I have come to ask you about Kim Newlands. I am a film historian. Doing research about Kim. I believe you knew him in the nineteen thirties?'

'He's not here.'

Sigrun felt thrown again. 'No, you don't understand, I did not think he . . .' But then she thought this moment of confusion might offer a profitable line of inquiry. 'Where is he, then?'

'He was going to go off to Spain.' The old lady pronounced 'off' as 'orf' and Sigrun was having difficulty tuning into her crisp, clipped speech patterns. The only other person she had heard speak in this way was the Queen.

'What was he going to do in—'

'I told Alun to tell him not to go,' Connie said, swallowing the interruption with a gulp. 'I said: "Tell him if he goes to Spain I won't be waiting for him when he gets back." You can go and ask him.'

'Ask Alun? Your friend Alun Pryce? Is he still alive?'

Connie looked momentarily confused. 'He was. I don't know whether he still is. It's been a while.'

Sigrun took both of Connie's hands in hers and asked: 'Who is the Prime Minister, Connie?'

Connie reflected upon this for a moment. 'Tony Blair?' she said, and then a look of determination stole across the old woman's face. 'That's right, isn't it? Tony Blair has been the prime minister for . . .' She counted on her fingers. 'Eight years. Did you think I was going to say Stanley Baldwin?' She stared at her bony knees for a moment; then she looked up and gave a curt nod. Holding Sigrun's gaze once more, she reached for an ivory-handled cane next to her chair and, using it for balance, rose in one fluid movement. 'I don't need any help, you know,' she said. 'Not since I had my hip done. I mean, look.' She planted her feet in a wide stance and thrust her chest out. 'And I haven't got dementia, if that's what you're thinking. I was asleep. It takes me a while to wake up, that's all. How do you know about Kim?'

Smelling the alcohol on Connie's breath, Sigrun glanced at the empty wine bottle by her chair. 'I saw some film of him at the Berlin Olympics. You were there too, were you not?'

'Yes, I was.'

'And you said you knew a German woman once?'

'Did I? How extraordinary of me.'

'Was it Leni Riefenstahl?'

Connie turned her head and stared at the mirror for a full minute before facing Sigrun again. 'You remind me of someone.'

'Who? Leni?' Sigrun touched the back of her dyed hair, momentarily pleased, then she remembered she was wearing a white polo-neck. It was probably that.

Connie was studying her face again. 'It's your eyes. They are just like Kim's.'

'Did Kim have an affair with Leni in Berlin? Was that the reason you and he did not get married?'

Connie raised an admonitory finger to forestall further questioning.

After a long silence, Sigrun got to her feet, walked towards the chimneypiece and ran a finger over its dusty mantel. There were more photographs here of Connie with various men: her husbands, presumably. She tried to work out her age in them by the clothes she was wearing: a 1960s maxi skirt; 1970s flares and floppy-brimmed hat; one photograph, likely from the 1980s, showed her with shoulder pads talking to Margaret Thatcher.

'It was Alun who told me Kim had gone to Spain,' said a voice nearby.

Sigrun shied. She'd had her back to Connie and hadn't heard her approaching.

'For months I believed him,' Connie continued, leaning on her cane. 'I had no reason not to. But Kim never went to Spain. They eventually found his remains in mudflats near the mouth of the Thames Estuary. He'd been missing for more than a year.'

Sigrun felt a falling sensation in her chest.

'The coroner recorded a verdict of death by misadventure,' Connie went on. 'Everyone said he had killed himself. I arranged for him to be buried down in Southsea,' she continued, 'next to his mother. A Jewish cemetery. I don't know why he never told me he was Jewish – I couldn't have cared less – but he didn't, so that's that. I go down there once a year and clean his headstone. I tell him all my news and sometimes, as I'm leaving, I give him a kick for breaking my heart.'

Connie fell silent for almost a minute, blinking occasionally, then she shook herself and returned to her seat in the bay of the window.

Sigrun didn't know quite what to say. 'Do you live here alone?'

Connie wafted a dismissive hand. 'There were some husbands. All dead now. Useless, the lot of them. And my friend John lived with me for a while. We were like an old married couple in the end, each waiting to see who died first, and neither of us really caring which one of us it would be. It was she as it turned out.'

'She.'

'She liked to be called John.' Connie now tapped her own little finger to indicate the ring on Sigrun's hand. 'Unusual ring.'

'This?' Sigrun said, splaying her fingers to look at them. 'It's just something my mother left me. I don't think it's worth much.'

'Your mother is dead?'

'She died when I was ten. A tumour.'

Connie lowered her head and shook it slightly as she took this in. 'That is sad,' she said. 'Very sad. You should treasure that ring.' She seemed lost in her thoughts for a moment then suddenly pointed her cane at Sigrun's bag. 'You can keep it, by the way,' she said. 'The photograph you stole. I have a copy.'

Feeling embarrassed about her petty crime, Sigrun took the photograph from her bag. 'I wanted to ask you about this. Did you know Leni well?'

'I did and I didn't. She came to visit me once. I was pregnant at the time. It was just after Kim disappeared.'

'Leni came to London?'

'She was looking for Kim. I was supposed to be keeping a low profile – Daddy's orders. It was all rather tiresome but no one was allowed to know about the baby.' She gave a thin smile. 'There would have been such a scandal.'

'What year was that?'

'Must have been in 1937. February or March. The funny thing was, we actually got on. I liked Leni. She told me what had happened in Berlin during the Games, how she had tried to seduce Kim and he had rejected her, at least until I had given him nothing to lose by telling him I hated him and never wanted to see him again. I was young and hot-headed.' Connie pushed her shoulders back, raised her chin. 'Perhaps I even felt sorry for Leni. She was clearly besotted with Kim. I think she saw him as an antidote to all those ghastly Nasties she used to spend time with. There was a certain unworldliness to Kim, you see. He had a good heart. A sweet nature.'

'Leni never mentioned Kim in her memoir.'

Connie allowed herself another smile at this. 'Well, she wouldn't, would she? It didn't fit with her image. She always had to put on the strong woman act. Always had to be the one breaking men's hearts. Did you ever meet her?'

Sigrun studied the ring on her little finger and shook her head. 'But I did go along to a press conference she once gave, at the Frankfurt Book Fair. It must have been five years ago now. When the questions came, she just gave the same self-justifying answers she'd repeated so many times before: that she was never a member of the Nazi Party; never a propagandist; that she'd had no idea what happened to the Jews until she was told by her American interrogators at the end of the war. At one point I remember she said: "Look, I am ninety-eight years old, but in my entire life I only did seven months' work for Hitler."'

'Were there protesters there?'

'Some, outside, but mostly the audience seemed to be in awe of her. They even laughed when she was asked how she would describe her life and she replied: "Far too fucking eventful. Next!"'

'And did you get to ask her any questions?'

'I did, yes. Just one. I asked her if she regretted not having any children.'

FORTY-TWO

When Sigrun got back to her hotel in Tonypandy, she stripped off her clothes, cleaned her teeth, and felt the spin of sleep soon after getting under the duvet. Less than three hours later she was awake and checking the time. She had been having a feverish dream that featured Kim, Leni and Connie and she wanted to return to it, but after a few minutes of turning and pillow-plumping it was gone so she switched on the bedside light and contemplated the photograph of Kim shaking the hand of Hitler, with Connie and Leni in the background. The news of Kim's death had left her feeling off balance, even though she should have expected it after all these years. It was not so much the fact of it as the manner, and the realization that he had only been in his twenties.

She now focused her gaze on Leni. Someone had once described her as being 'as pretty as a swastika' but Sigrun thought this unfair. Even if Leni had obviously been lying when she claimed she had had nothing to do with the organization of the Nuremberg rally in 1934 – that it was all down to Speer and Hitler – as far as Sigrun could determine, Leni had been telling the truth about never having been a member of the Nazi Party. There was certainly no record of her membership. All Sigrun had been able to find was a reference to Goebbels saying that Leni was 'the only one of the stars that understands us'. It was a damning phrase, on one level. But on another, perhaps it meant that Leni was the only star who understood how dangerous the Nazis were;

understood what dark forces she had helped unleash with *Triumph of the Will.*

Feeling disorientated, Sigrun took her projector from her case and threaded the clip of Kim once more. Her hand flicked the on-switch and she turned the rewind dial.

'Why did Leni keep you locked away in her safe all these years?' she asked as the familiar image of Kim appeared.

In the morning, Sigrun decided to try the address she had for Alun Pryce. If he was still alive, she thought, he might be able to shed some light on what had happened to Kim. She followed a steep alleyway and, detecting the wet tang of fish, came to a covered market where she asked for directions to Berw Terrace.

Alun's house was not difficult to find. It was small – a two-up, two-down – and had a pebbledashed exterior. Next to it was an identical one, only this one's windows had been boarded over. The faint outline of graffiti was visible on its walls: an anarchy sign and the words 'Coal not Dole'. When Sigrun knocked on the door, she caused flakes of red paint to fall from it. There was no answer, so she cupped her eyes and put her face up against the grimy window. Sitting on a chair inside, she could see a small old man staring at a television that was not switched on.

She was about to knock on the glass when the old man looked up in surprise and blinked at her from behind his thick glasses. His cheeks looked drawn, as if he wasn't wearing his false teeth. He got to his feet with the aid of a rolled-up umbrella, then tucked in his shirt. Sigrun smiled and waved, hoping that she had not alarmed him too much. A short while later, she heard a bolt being pulled back and a lock turning. The door opened, but only as far as the security chain would allow.

'What you selling?' the old man asked in a thin and gummy voice. 'There's nothing I want.'

'Are you Alun Pryce?'

'Why? Who sent you?'

'No one sent me.' Sigrun leaned closer so he could hear. 'I have come about Kim Newlands.'

There was a pause before he said: 'Are you from the police?'

'No. I'm . . . just a friend. I need your help.'

She could see his watery eyes looking her up and down. 'Wait there,' he said, closing the door. The bolt slid back into place.

Ten minutes passed and Sigrun began to wonder if the old man had forgotten she was there. She went back to the window but he was no longer in the sitting room. There was a cat litter tray in the corner, and a pile of newspapers beside it. With a glance at her watch, she went back to the door and finally heard the bolt and chain rattle once more. The door creaked open.

The old man was more animated than before. He had put in his teeth, combed his hair and was wearing a tie. He held out his hand and, as they shook, he said in a voice that was high in pitch and wheezy: 'You have now shaken hands with someone who shook hands with Hitler.'

Sigrun surreptitiously wiped her hand on her jacket as Alun stood to one side and indicated that she should head along the narrow hallway, which was partially blocked by a folding wheelchair. 'No one ever believes me when I say that,' he said, sliding the bolt into place once more. 'I don't need that damn thing,' he added when he saw Sigrun squeezing past the wheelchair. 'Social services offered me one so I said yes.'

Sigrun could hear a kettle gently singing on a hob. Hanging on a hat stand in the hallway was a brown duffle coat with a CND badge on it. On other pegs were a Russian-style astrakhan fur hat and a black Breton cap of the sort Lenin used to wear, with a red metal star pinned above its peak.

'I was making a cup of tea,' Alun said over his shoulder. 'Want one?'

Sigrun was in the front room now. 'Thank you.'

'Take a pew.' The old man pointed at an armchair before disappearing into the kitchen.

Sigrun noticed there was a chess set laid out for a game but it was covered in a film of dust. The curtains were gaudy, a brown and red swirling pattern; the lampshade was plastic, the walls were covered in woodchip, and the only picture hanging on them was one of Trotsky.

Along one wall was a flimsy-looking bookcase laden with volumes that had bleached in the sun so that the titles were barely readable: *The Open Society and its Enemies* by K. R. Popper and *Pre-Capitalist Economic Formations* by Eric Hobsbawm. In front of the bookcase was a pair of slippers and a brass music stand with sheet music, but no instrument. She noticed the newspapers around the cat litter tray were copies of the *Morning Star.*

'Cat died,' Alun said when he returned a few minutes later, carrying a tray with cups and saucers, a teapot, sugar bowl, milk jug and four custard cream biscuits on a plate. 'Been meaning to throw that tray out. Stinks, it does.'

Sigrun smiled at him as, with arthritically crooked hands, he poured the tea unsteadily. She had the strange feeling that, despite appearing to have been caught unawares by her arrival, he had been expecting her. It was the same feeling she'd had when she met Connie.

'You're German, aren't you?'

She nodded, realizing that she had not told him her name, or what she did for a living – and also that he had not asked.

As he handed over a cup that rattled in its saucer, he stared into her eyes. 'That's a name I haven't heard in a while. Kim Newlands.'

Sigrun took the cup and put it on the table beside the file from the National Archives. Alun leaned forward and placed his hand on it, before looking up at Sigrun. He too seemed slightly spooked by the unbroken seal.

'Where did you get this?' He ran his bony fingers over the red wax. 'Are you with MI5?'

'No, I am a film historian. My name is Dr Sigrun Meier and I am doing some research into Leni Riefenstahl.'

'I met her, too, you know. Leni Riefenstahl. Same time as I met Hitler. But that's all . . .' He picked up his rolled umbrella. 'So you know what happened to Kim, then?'

'Only that his body was found on the banks of the Thames. I thought maybe this file might shed some more light on the circumstances of his death.'

'But you still haven't opened it?' Alun asked.

'No. I don't really know why,' Sigrun said, giving a wary smile. 'It's the seal, I guess. It's like it does not want to be opened.' She sat back in her chair and took a sip of tea. It was stewed.

Alun must have seen her pull a face because he said: 'I'm sorry. I don't know how strong other people like it. I don't get many visitors. In fact, you're the first I've had since . . .' He trailed off as he tried to recall. 'How did you get hold of the file?'

'It has just been declassified,' she lied. 'Can you think of any reason why a file on Kim would be classified until now?'

'No idea. Sometimes it's best to leave the past undisturbed.'

'When did you last see him?'

Alun thought for a moment then nodded. 'Autumn of 1936, shortly before I went to Spain. I fought for the International Brigades in the civil war. Have you ever been to Catalonia? It's a lot like Wales – an occupied country clinging on to its own language and culture.'

Reaching for a custard cream, Alun indicated that Sigrun should do the same. 'When I got back from Spain, in 1939, I was arrested.' He took a bite from the biscuit and chewed slowly. 'It was for something petty that had happened before I left in '36. I'd punched a police constable. But I wasn't sent for trial because by then the authorities were distracted, what with the coming . . .' Apparently remembering he was talking to a German, Alun paused.

'It is OK,' Sigrun said. 'You can say it.'

'The coming war with the Nazis. The authorities said I wouldn't be prosecuted if I joined up, so I did. But I would have fought anyway. I joined the Sappers. Royal Engineers. Served in Africa and Italy.' He nodded at a frame on the dresser that contained four medals. 'Campaign medals. Nothing special.'

'Did you stay in the army after the war?'

'No, I put my training to good use and became an electrician in a white goods factory for thirty years, until my retirement. Was on the executive of my trade union for most of that time. In charge of arbitration agreements.'

'And is there a Mrs Pryce?' Sigrun asked.

Alun adjusted a discreet, transparent hearing aid in his ear which Sigrun had not noticed before.

'Is there a Mrs Pryce?' she repeated.

'No,' he said this time. 'I never married.'

Sigrun took another sip of tea and placed the cup back on the table. Without meeting Alun's eye she tapped the file and asked: 'What sort of a man was he?'

'Kim? Everyone liked him, especially women. I don't think he was ever a committed fascist.' He nodded. 'I have some of his things upstairs. Do you want to see them?'

After watching Alun shuffle towards the stairs, Sigrun was relieved to see him sit on a stairlift. 'I don't really need it,' he said as he pressed a button and began to ascend. 'It just makes things easier and the council was giving them away.' At the top, he stood up and paused before opening the door to a bedroom.

The room was small, with barely enough space for a single bed. It smelled of dust and mothballs. There was a chest of drawers with a vase containing faded plastic flowers and a framed photograph of a bulky, unsmiling man in a beret giving a clenched-fist salute.

'Who is he?' Sigrun asked.

Alun picked up the photo and studied it for a moment before shaking his head. 'This is Herzl,' he said. 'A comrade of mine. I don't think I've met anyone more annoying in my life.'

'Why do you keep his photo on display if he was so annoying?'

'Because I miss him, I suppose.' He pointed at the bed with his umbrella. 'He was my best friend, the old bastard. You'll have to move that.'

The bed was blocking a cupboard door. Sigrun pushed it to one side, noticing the deep indentation its castors had made in the carpet.

'His things are up there,' Alun said, indicating a high shelf. 'In that suitcase. You'll have to reach up for it. I'm too short.'

Like the umbrella, the suitcase was incongruously elegant. It had solid brass locks and protective corners.

'May I?' Sigrun asked.

Alun nodded his assent.

Inside was a shoebox tied with hairy string. It had the name 'Kim Newlands' written on it. Sigrun pulled the bow then lifted the lid. It contained a lock of blonde hair tied with a ribbon, what looked like a running vest, and, on top of that, a tarnished garden trowel.

'Kim used to take that with him wherever he went,' Alun said, nodding at the trowel. 'He told me it was for digging footholes before a race. It was what they used back then, before the days of starting blocks.'

'Where did this box come from?'

'He'd been staying with a friend of mine, a pub landlord, before he disappeared. After the war I bumped into this friend and he asked me if I wanted the box. He was going to throw it out so I said yes.'

Sigrun removed the trowel and the lock of hair and placed them carefully on the bed; then she picked up the running vest and saw that it was covering another object. When she realized the object was a rusty pistol she flinched and it slipped from her hands, landing on the bed.

'Don't worry,' Alun said. 'I doubt it would still work.'

'Was this Kim's too?'

Alun nodded. 'He said he was given it by Leni Riefenstahl. It's probably worth a bob or two. You can have it if you like. I've got no one to leave it to. In fact, you can take the whole box, if you want. I don't know why I've kept it all these years.'

'Thank you,' Sigrun said, examining the weapon and recalling a passage in Leni's memoirs in which she described Goebbels putting a pistol in the glove compartment of her Mercedes. This was a Luger P08, with the Nazi eagle insignia on its side, as well as some ornately engraved initials. She peered into the box again and saw a silver-and-gold-ribbed cigarette case. A cursory examination revealed a Fabergé hallmark. 'I think you should keep this,' she said. 'It's worth a lot of money.'

Alun shook his head. 'I'll be glad to be rid of it. It just brings back memories.'

Below the cigarette case was a Golden Party Badge. Sigrun picked it up and turned it to catch the light.

'Riefenstahl gave him that too,' Alun said. 'She got off lightly at the end of the war. Claimed she wasn't a fascist, but she clearly was.'

'Like you?' Sigrun said.

'I only pretended I was a Blackshirt,' the old man said, looking affronted. 'To infiltrate them. I was always a communist.'

'And are you one still?'

Alun patted her shoulder. 'It's complicated. I wasn't one of these misty-eyed, left-wing romantics. You know, labourers harvesting during the day and ballet in the evening. I was a realist. A true internationalist. I didn't just chant the slogans, I lived my life by them. The workers united can never be divided. All property is theft.'

'So you do not condemn Stalin?'

'I was never a Stalinist. I was always a Trot. I don't think Trotsky's form of communism has ever truly been tested. Our day will come.'

Sigrun now noticed that at the bottom of the shoebox there was a letter. It smelled musty, the paper had yellowed and the ink had turned brown but Sigrun's heart thumped when she saw it bore a German postmark. '*Ach, mein Gott*,' she said in a whisper, putting her hand to her mouth. 'I recognize this handwriting.'

Alun shrugged again and coughed. 'I never opened it,' he said. 'Neither did Kim. It arrived long after he disappeared.'

Sigrun could not decide whether she believed Alun or not. The glue on the envelope seal had discoloured but it opened at the slightest touch, as if wanting to be read.

It was from Leni to Kim and was dated 18 October 1938. As she read it, the background chatter in Sigrun's head, which she had been hearing since she was a ten-year-old child, fell silent.

'Anything interesting in it?' Alun asked.

'The answer to something that has puzzled me for years,' Sigrun said. 'I could never understand why Leni, who was a fast editor, had taken two years to edit her film *Olympia*. But now I think I know. She needed to disappear from public view for at least nine months.'

'Nine months?'

'I think she had a baby with Kim. And when she came to accept that she would forever be regarded as toxic because of her association with Hitler, she decided the best way for her to protect her child was to have someone else raise it as their own.'

'Who?'

'Her maid Mariechen, according to this letter. Leni wrote it shortly before she sailed to New York for the premiere of *Olympia*. Mariechen stayed behind in Germany with the baby. The plan was that they would follow her to Hollywood and start a new life there. I think Leni was still hoping she could persuade Kim to join them.' Sigrun sighed. 'But there's one thing that still doesn't quite make sense to me.'

Sigrun rummaged in her shoulder bag for her copy of Goebbels's *Diaries* and found between its pages the photograph of Hitler and Kim shaking hands, with Connie and Leni in the background. 'You said you met Hitler,' she said, tapping the photograph. 'Was it on this night?'

Alun adjusted his glasses, studied the photograph for a long time, then nodded slowly. He looked shocked, as if unable to believe his own memory.

Sigrun put a hand on his arm. 'You recognize the woman Leni is talking to, yes?'

Alun looked up and stared at Sigrun with rheumy eyes but did not answer. He then returned his gaze to the photograph, extended a finger and ran it down the image of Connie, as if stroking her hair.

As she watched him, Sigrun felt moved. She cleared her throat and in a gentle voice asked: 'Shall we go and see her?'

FORTY-THREE

Those who live into extreme old age tend not to lead sociable lives; instead they work deep in the fabric of the every day. Constance, Lady Dalton, who wanted neither to be remembered nor forgotten, was an exception.

As she sat waiting in her armchair, wearing a thick-knit woollen jumper that emphasized the smallness of her wrists, she stared out along the drive and wondered how much longer she had left. Weeks? Months? Probably not years. Sometimes she awoke in the night and listened in fear to the beating of her heart, knowing that one day soon this pulsation would cease. Yet even at her grand age, the end of her life seemed to her an intellectual impossibility.

Though Connie had not seen Alun since they were in their twenties, she had thought about him often and had always known that they would have to see each other again one day and settle their accounts; and that they would not be allowed to rest, or die, until they did.

Alun had tried to contact her on several occasions but she had not wanted to see him, not after what the photographer from the *Express* had told her when he came to visit with a reporter, shortly before she was interned at the start of the war. Alun, the photographer claimed, had been a communist, not a Blackshirt, and he was the one who had given the *Express* the story about Kim's BUF sponsorship in 1936. When she had heard this, Connie had realized that all the time Alun had claimed to be acting as go-between for her and Kim, he had been doing no such thing. He had betrayed both of them.

There was a car driving over the bridge. A taxi. With Oswald, her old lurcher, by her side, she made her way to the front door. When she opened it, she saw that the gamekeeper had hung a brace of pheasants from the bell-pull. How long had they been there? They looked fresh enough. With her ivory-handled cane she gave them a prod.

Connie recognized Alun as soon as he got out of the car. But he looked old, his face a crumpled envelope. Though he still carried his rolled-up umbrella, the one she had given him before they went to Berlin, he accepted the offer of Sigrun's arm and they mounted the worn stone steps together. He was staring at the pheasants as if they were ghosts.

'Hello,' Sigrun said. 'You remember Alun, don't you?'

Connie looked down at the old man. Their height difference was considerable. Alun seemed to flinch when he saw her eyepatch.

'Yes, I remember Alun,' Connie said, gesturing with a flick of her cane. 'Come in. I want to show you something.' She led the way across the gloomy central hall to the drawing room.

'How old is this place?' Alun asked.

'God knows. Seventeenth century, I think.' She opened the door and pointed at a table on which there was a yellowing copy of *The Blackshirt* newspaper featuring Kim on its front page. There was a magnifying glass on top of it and it showed what looked like a faded lipstick mark where the paper had once been kissed. 'I was just looking at it,' she said.

The floorboards creaked as Alun crossed the room. When he sat down, Connie pulled up a chair next to him and, reaching for his mottled hand, revealed the knucklebones beneath her loose, dry skin. There was a crowded silence and an exchange of glances, then Connie said firmly: 'Do you think all this excitement will finish us off, Alun?'

He shrugged. 'Probably.'

'Do you remember that night in Berlin? I don't think I've ever been so drunk in my life.'

'It was a good night.'

Connie narrowed her eyes. 'I was listening to some music just now,' she said, standing up again and leaning over a gramophone as she wound its handle before placing a needle on a 78-rpm record. There was a crackling sound, then, when a man's voice began singing 'Who stole my heart away . . .', she began swaying to the music. 'Jack Buchanan. Such a lovely voice.' As she danced she removed the pins from her finger wave and shook her hair loose. 'Who would like a glass of wine? I'm trying to get through my cellar before I croak. I found a case of 1961 claret down there the other day.' Connie pointed at a dusty bottle of Château Margaux on the side table with three crystal wine glasses lined up next to it. 'Would you?' she said to Sigrun.

'To absent friends,' Sigrun said when the glasses were poured.

'Absent friends,' Connie echoed.

Alun remained silent.

Sigrun had brought a suitcase and she now retrieved from it a shoebox tied with string. She placed the box on the table and pushed it towards Connie. Seeing Kim's name written on the top, Connie untied the string, removed the lid and took out the trowel; she smiled, shook her head and placed it on the table. She did the same with the Golden Party Badge and the Luger, and when she came to the lock of hair she held it up to her head and smiled again to show she knew its provenance. Upon discovering the cigarette case, she gave a small, almost inaudible gasp before kissing it tenderly and closing her eye momentarily. 'He didn't smoke, you know. He carried them around for me, because he was a gentleman.' The running vest was next and this she held to her face and inhaled its musk.

'You know the way tribespeople used to think the camera captured the soul?' Sigrun said now. 'Well, there is a clip of film I want to show you both.' She rummaged in her case again and retrieved a portable projector. 'May I take down one of these paintings for a moment?'

Connie waved her cane in a 'help yourself' gesture.

Sigrun carefully removed a portrait, turned off the lights, plugged in her projector and focused the beam of light on to the area of white wall where it had been hanging.

Connie put her hand to her mouth in shock. The film clip was of Kim. As he looked directly into the lens and smiled his off-centre smile it was as if he had come back to life. She could sense Kim's presence in the room like the ticking of a clock. As she peered over the edge of her life, whole decades shrank to seconds and she felt herself caught in a rush of vertigo.

When the clip came to an end, Connie dabbed at her eye with a handkerchief. 'Can you leave those off for the moment, please,' she said when she saw Sigrun reaching for the wall switch. 'Light the candles instead.' She pointed at a silver candelabra on a side table laden with five tall candles. Sigrun lit them then carefully carried the candelabra back to the table.

'He left his life too early,' Connie said.

'I know,' Sigrun said.

Alun stood up and began looking around the room. Connie tapped her cane on the floor and said: 'You all right over there?'

'I was seeing if you had any pictures of . . .'

'Children?' Connie said this with a harder edge to her voice. 'Someone to leave this millstone to?' She spread her arms and looked up at the ornate cornicing. 'I know it's a bit run-down, but I believe there are grants one can get if one wants to have an old pile like this restored. I could never be bothered with all the paperwork. There's also a townhouse in Mayfair and a ghastly hunting lodge in Scotland. I did consider leaving them all to the National Trust, but they are such a bunch of wet blankets.'

'What about leaving them to another charity?' Alun asked. 'Like the NSPCC.'

'Frankly I'd rather leave them to the RSPCA. And I hate the RSPCA. Lefties, the lot of them. I was even thinking of leaving them to old Oswald here.' She patted the head of her lurcher. 'But then my granddaughter turned up.' Her eye snapped towards Sigrun. 'Didn't you?'

At first Sigrun couldn't take in Connie's words; then she frowned and pointed to herself. 'Me? But . . . I thought perhaps Leni was my grandmother, wasn't she?'

'That's almost right,' Connie said, raising a finger to acknowledge the point. 'I told you she came to London looking for Kim while I was pregnant. At that time, as far as I knew, Kim was in Spain and wasn't coming back.' Connie took a sip of wine and nodded in appreciation at the taste. 'I think I was still angry with him. Leni offered to help. After I gave birth I sent a telegram to her in Berlin and she sent Mariechen, her maid, to me in London. Mariechen took my daughter back with her to Germany and raised her as her own, using a trust fund I had set up in her name. It was supposed to be a temporary arrangement, until I could find a way to look after the child myself.' She shook her head. 'You have to remember, I was devastated when Kim left me; I thought I was on my own. I knew where my daughter was and that she was being looked after properly. It also meant she was far enough away from England that my father's circle would never find out. Scandal averted.' Pause. 'But then the war broke out, communication ceased and I heard nothing more about her after that. No correspondence. No Christmas cards. No phone calls. I think Mariechen had nothing more to do with Leni, or she was killed. I just don't know.'

'That's really sad,' Sigrun said, overwhelmed. 'So you last saw her in 1937?'

'Yes. When it was time to say goodbye I kissed my baby girl on the forehead and put a little gold chain around her neck. Her head was so small I didn't even need to undo the clasp to get it on. Attached to it was a ring. A black sapphire in an unusual setting and so dark it absorbed all the light around it. It wasn't worth much, but it was one my mother had given me.' She pointed at Sigrun's hand with her cane. 'That was how I knew who you were.'

Sigrun opened her mouth to speak but no words came. Instead she wiped her eyes with the heels of her hand, stood up, took a step towards Connie and kissed her on the cheek. She then returned to her side of the table, took a document from her bag and pushed it across the table to Connie. 'I think the truth about what happened to Kim is in this file,' she said. 'You can do with it what you want. Open it. Don't open it. It is up to you. I don't want it any more.' She glanced over at Alun; then, with a tight nod, she looked back at Connie and said: 'You don't believe he committed suicide, do you?'

Connie shook her head, picked up the file and frowned as she ran a stiff hand over the seal.

'Is this the MI5 file on Kim?'

'It is.'

'I requested to see this several times,' Connie said, 'but they always said it was classified. They had one on me as well, you know. Though God knows why they bothered.' She tapped the file on the table in front of her, turned to Alun and asked: 'Do *you* think I should open it?'

Alun looked away and cleared his throat. 'I think whatever secrets it contains belong to Kim.'

Connie studied her glass for a moment before saying carefully: 'We all do things we regret.'

Alun blew out his cheeks. 'I know what you're thinking. There are things I regret, too.' He looked at Connie with eyes that were watery, as if he were leaning into a gale. 'I've always regretted not saying sorry to you.' His voice was becoming hoarse. He stood up and shuffled away from the table towards the door; then he stopped and turned his head, but did not seem to see them. He was staring through them into the deep past. 'Please don't open that file,' he said. 'It won't change anything.'

To Connie it seemed logical, inevitable even, that the three of them were here, assembled like family members for the reading of a will. She put down the file, levered herself up using the table and moved towards Alun. Then she took his hand and led him back to the table. When he sat down in the light of the guttering candles, Sigrun took his other hand as well as Connie's. They remained like this for a moment, before Connie picked up the file again and handed it to Sigrun. 'I don't need to know what's in it,' she said, 'but I think you do. You must open it.'

Sigrun inhaled deeply before finally breaking the seal. After taking out a single sheet of thin paper she looked in the envelope to check there was nothing more. She then read it, pressed her lips together and handed the sheet of paper to Connie, who felt for her reading glasses with clumsy fingers.

Connie looked on the back of the sheet first and, seeing it was blank, turned it over. Here there were two paragraphs typed by an MI5 officer who was identifiable by his rank and number only. They gave an account of how Alun had arranged for Kim to meet three members of the British Union of Fascists one night in a park in Pimlico. One of the Blackshirts had been identified by name: Higgins. Kim had been reported missing the following day. 'It seems likely', the report concluded drily, 'that the two events were not unrelated.'

When she had read the paragraphs twice, to make sure she understood, Connie took off her glasses and offered the piece of paper to Alun, who was still slumped in his chair. He gave a faint shake of his head and said in a voice that was thin and cracked: 'I know what it says.'

Connie saw him now for what he was: a small and frightened old man. There was a pause and then her questions to Alun came. 'Did Kim try to see me in London when he got back from Berlin?'

Alun held Connie's gaze as best he could, and then gave a single dip of his head.

'Did he think he was coming to meet me in the park the night he died? Is that what you told him?'

Another nod from Alun.

'Were you there when the Blackshirts attacked him?'

'Yes!' The word rang through the room like the sustained note from a piano. Alun lowered his eyes. A tremor in his shoulders showed his anguish. 'But they were only supposed to rough him up. Not . . .'

Connie tapped the table with her cane. 'Why?'

Alun looked as though he was struggling for breath. 'Because I loved you, Connie, that's why. Because you were supposed to be with me.'

With this he stood up once more, apparently eager to leave. As he shuffled towards the door, Connie stuck out her cane and the old man tripped. Falling forward, he landed with a soft clap of bone like the snapping of a stick.

Sigrun got up to help him but Connie raised her cane to block her path.

Alun had turned on to his side now and, his face contorted in pain, was holding out his arm for help. Sigrun rocked on her feet in indecision. Connie looked down at Alun. A deadly silence filled every crack in the room, and then she shook her head and mouthed the word 'No'.

PART SIX

FORTY-FOUR

Autumn, 1938. New York

A ghost casts a shadow that only other ghosts can see. As Leni held the roll of celluloid up to the cabin light, she thought she could discern the hint of one, granular and indistinct, visible only to her. Then the shadow flitted away, disturbed by a noise.

The knock on the door was tentative and muffled. Coiling up the strip of film carefully, she returned it to its canister and picked up her brush. This she ran through her hair several times before she stopped, raking the bristles with her fingernails, then started again. It was no use. The more she tried to straighten her hair, the more it frizzed and tangled. Sea air. It always had this effect. And for the past five days, the ship's hairdresser had been useless.

Leni gave a determined nod at her reflection. The first thing she would do when they disembarked was make an appointment with a proper hairdresser. Based on the pictures she had seen in *Vogue*, she was convinced Manhattan would have one on every street corner.

And there it was again, the knocking. This time it was joined by an uncertain voice: '*Fräulein Richter. Guten Tag.*' In her head Leni translated this into English. She needed to practise. 'Miss Richter. Good day.'

Her *nom de voyage* was 'Lotte Richter' – that, at least, was the name on the passenger manifest alongside cabin 142, the most luxurious address on the SS *Europa*. But such was Leni's celebrity, her fellow passengers – those on Deck A at least – had been greeting her as 'Miss Riefenstahl' within hours of setting sail.

She got to her feet. Took a step to the door. Hesitated. Once she opened it, there would be no going back. She had long fantasized about starting a new life in America, but now that fantasy was becoming a reality, she felt apprehensive, disloyal even. Germany had been good to her. The German people adored her. Adolf adored her. Could she, at the age of thirty-six, turn her back on them? On him?

From the other side of the door: 'Hello?'

The steward could wait. She needed more time to think. Could she really stay in America? She thought of Goebbels back in Germany, and her resolution returned. No more unwanted sexual advances, no more nights spent worrying about his plots against her, no more interference with her film-making. And no more terrifying visits from Heydrich. She would arrange for her villa in the Grunewald to be sold and, once the proceeds had been cabled to her, she would buy a place in Beverly Hills with a swimming pool. And once she was settled in Hollywood she would send for Mariechen, who would bring the baby with her. She would then try again to persuade Kim to join them. Surely he would be back from Spain by now? He hadn't replied to her last letter but she hoped that the baby, his baby with Connie, would be the incentive he needed. She would send him an invitation he would find hard to refuse: a first-class ticket to New York on the *Queen Mary*; financial support that meant he didn't have to worry about money and could retain his amateur status; and, with a little string-pulling, a chance for him to train with the top American coaches. Of course there was the question of Connie, but Leni would find a way. She always found a way.

'Miss Richter? Hello? The captain has asked me to collect you.'

Leni did not look over at the door but instead held out an open palm in its direction, as if to silence her interlocutor. She put down the brush and flicked, for the third time that morning, through the newspaper cuttings her press chief Ernst Jäger had pasted into a scrapbook for her. They were all to do with *Olympia*. Her magnum opus had taken her two years to edit, but judging by the reception so far, it had been worth the time and effort.

She knew all the Reich ministers, not only Goebbels, thought it outrageous of her to take so long to complete the editing process, but so what? What did they know about art? More than 250 kilometres of film had been exposed during the making of *Olympia* and the speed at which her cameramen had had to work meant that they had not had time to use a clapperboard before each take, so there were no identifying numbers. That was the reason it had taken two years.

The world premiere had been held in Berlin on 20 April, the date chosen to mark the forty-ninth birthday of the guest of honour, Adolf. It had been a glittering occasion, with Albert designing a new façade for the Universum Filmpalast on Auguste-Viktoria-Platz. The entire front of the building had been floodlit and covered with golden ribbons and giant flags bearing the five linked rings of the Olympics. Twin towers, meanwhile, represented the entrance to the Olympic stadium, with laurel wreaths suspended between them. The name 'Leni Riefenstahl' was lit up in electric light bulbs across the entrance. In addition to the usual ambassadors, industrialists and financiers, plus their wives and mistresses, the guests had included Himmler and von Ribbentrop, as well as the Little Doctor. And all had to walk under her name in lights when they arrived.

The champagne corks had popped all night and, afterwards, Adolf had presented her with a bouquet of white lilacs, kissed her hand and declared her film: 'Wonderful, wonderful.'

The critics had agreed, and not just in Germany. In the scrapbook, Jäger had underlined some of his favourite quotes – 'Technically dazzling', 'a lavish hymn to physical beauty and strength', 'visually ravishing'. As Leni reread them now, she felt her confidence returning like a tingling rush of heat through icy veins. Once more she felt invigorated and optimistic about her future in America. Though German modesty meant that she could not say it out loud, she thought she might just be, at this moment in time, the greatest film-maker in the world.

In the months since the world premiere, her progress through the capitals of Europe had been that of an all-conquering heroine: Vienna, Paris, Copenhagen, Helsinki, Oslo, Rome. At each premiere there had been banquets, welcoming speeches and bouquets of flowers. So many flowers. Why did people always assume she liked flowers?

In Graz, hundreds of young girls in Styrian costumes had formed a guard of honour from her hotel to the cinema. In Stockholm, members of the audience had risen spontaneously to their feet and sung

'*Deutschland über alles*'. In Brussels, the Belgian King himself, Leopold III, had attended and at the Venice Biennale, *Olympia* had been awarded the Mussolini Cup, beating the bookies' favourite, Walt Disney's *Snow White*. She liked to tell people it was the Golden Lion she won, because who has heard of the Mussolini Cup?

'The captain has asked me to collect you, Miss Richter,' the steward said through the closed door, a rising note of impatience in his words. 'I'm to escort you to the bridge.'

Leni sighed as she closed the scrapbook, got to her feet and opened the door with one hand. The steward was young and was standing with his mouth open as if caught in mid speech, his white-gloved hand raised as he prepared to knock again. She gave him a considering look. He had narrow shoulders, a prominent Adam's apple and thick black eyebrows that met in the middle. Not her type.

She reached behind the door for her wolf-fur coat. There would be photographers waiting for her on the quayside, no doubt, and they would expect a sophisticated German woman to be wearing fur. She handed it to the steward so that he could hold it open for her and then she lifted up her hair in order to fan it out over her up-turned collar. When she checked her reflection a final time, a shadow of a frown passed across her brow.

The steward coughed discreetly. Leni looked in his direction but her focus was elsewhere. She could see in her memory her old friend Marlene waving goodbye as she left Berlin. Now *there* was a real femme fatale. Leni had several meetings arranged for the second half of her trip, including one with Walt Disney, who was going to give her a guided tour of his studio, and another with the matinee idol Gary Cooper, who had invited her to lunch at the Beverly Hills Hotel. But it was her reunion with Marlene that she was looking forward to the most. The two had lived so close to one another in Berlin in the 1920s that Leni had been able to see into her apartment. As actresses, they had compared notes about where they wanted their key light placed. Marlene liked it almost directly above her, so that it emphasized her cheekbones and made the broad planes of her face look more gaunt. Leni's features were angular enough already, so she could afford to have a softer light at a lower angle.

Marlene had not only made the transition from life in Germany to America look easy, she had also managed to woo Hollywood with her smouldering looks and become one of its biggest stars. Leni was hoping she could persuade her to take the lead in her directorial debut there, perhaps with Gary Cooper as her co-star. In any event, Marlene had shown how it could be done. Leni had many questions to ask her. Many.

She was about to follow the steward when she remembered her handbag. Inside it was the small canister containing the roll of film that she always kept close to hand. Once she had collected it, she held it to her chest momentarily, took a deep breath and caught up with the steward.

'My friends bet me that I would not get two words of conversation out of you,' the steward said as they reached the top of the stairs.

'You lost,' Leni replied as she stepped past him.

Although the sun had risen, a rolling fog meant visibility was poor, and the duty officers on the bridge were little more than outlines. Leni gave a small bow of acknowledgement when she saw the captain signalling to her to join him. 'We are here,' he said, jabbing a finger at the chart in front of him, 'and we expect to dock in half an hour, though I am afraid there will not be much to see.' He looked out of the window and pointed. 'The Manhattan skyline is over there, but you will have to take my word for it.'

Somewhere above the bridge the foghorn groaned, a mournful note that exaggerated the silence it disturbed and left behind. As the ship sliced in a slow curve towards the port, Leni thought she glimpsed Liberty's giant green face for a moment, looming out of the fog like an omen.

Jäger suddenly appeared by her side, wearing an overcoat with an astrakhan collar. 'You might want to see this. I think your welcoming committee has arrived.'

She followed him out on to the upper deck and coughed as she tasted the cold, salty air. Seagulls were piercing the sky with their squawks. Hearing the resonant boom of another foghorn, she looked down over the handrail and saw, emerging from the swirling whiteness, two high-bridged tugs and a puffing ferryboat along with a small flotilla of water taxis, half a dozen of them bobbing along in the ship's wake like ducklings trying to keep up with their mother. She heard an American voice over a megaphone shout: 'Miss Riefenstahl? Is it true you are *Aydolf* Hitler's mistress?'

Leni looked at Jäger, raised her eyebrows and said with a brittle laugh: 'Did he ask what I think he asked?'

Jäger gave an amused twitch of his moustache by way of reply.

Another voice carried up towards them: 'Are you the Führer's honey?'

'You have to admire their ingenuity,' Leni said, ignoring their questions and leaning over the handrail to take a photograph of them.

At the same moment, she heard the *pfuf* sound of a magnesium filament flashbulb going off and turned to see one of the crew taking a photograph of her rear. 'I'll take a dozen of those,' she said nonchalantly as she resumed her own photographic endeavours.

They disembarked down a narrow gangway. The shouted questions from the press were drowned out by the sound of a brass band playing American folk tunes. Mounted policemen in peaked caps were holding back a small crowd of spectators and there was a dais with microphones set up in front of them. A huddle of reporters in macs and trilbies were waiting around it in an expectant semi-circle. As she was guided towards the platform, Leni put on a pair of sunglasses, knowing from experience how blinding flashbulbs could be.

'What do you think of America, Miss Riefenstahl?' a reporter shouted from the back.

'I have not had the chance to see your country yet, but I am thinking it is *wunderbar*,' she answered.

From somewhere in the middle: 'Is it true you are Hitler's mistress?'

Clearly they were not going to let this one go. 'No,' she said with a strained laugh. 'These are false rumours. We are good friends only. I made a couple of documentaries with him, that is all.'

A barrage of flashbulbs popped in unison as if to capture this exact moment of clarification, and the sound was followed by that of broken glass as the used bulbs were discarded on the ground.

'What do you say to the reports that your government is systematically burning down all the synagogues in Germany, and destroying all the Jewish shops?'

The crowd fell silent and turned as one to stare at the reporter who had asked the question. He was tall and sinewy with a shock of peppery hair.

'That cannot possibly be true,' Leni said, waving a dismissive hand.

Jäger, who had been pitching back and forth on the balls of his feet, now intervened. 'That is all the questions we have time for,' he said. 'Fräulein Riefenstahl has had a long journey and would like to check into her hotel now. Please be understanding.' With this he cupped her elbow and led her away.

The brittle crunching of glass beneath her heels followed her all the way to her waiting limousine.

FORTY-FIVE

Leni was gratified to see that she had been given the penthouse suite at the Hotel Pierre, which she had decided she would later tell people was the Waldorf Astoria, because no one has heard of the Hotel Pierre. She was less pleased to note that its art deco interior was filled with fresh flowers. They gave off a scent so strong it was almost visible. The cards that came with them were reassuring, though. She kept touching her chest and emitting little snorts of incredulity as she read them. They were from people wishing her luck with the premiere: Walt Disney, Henry Ford, Humphrey Bogart and Charlie Chaplin, who added that he had been a fan of her film *The Blue Light*. There was one from Adolf, too, attached to a bunch of red roses.

After breakfast, Leni hailed a cab to do some sightseeing with her camera and when the driver asked her where she wanted to go she said: 'Anywhere.' Then she added: 'On second thoughts, Mac . . .' She had learned from the movies that all New York cab drivers like to be called Mac. '. . . let us go to the Radio City Music Hall.'

When they reached Radio City, which had the biggest cinema in the world and was the venue for her upcoming premiere, Leni was disappointed to see that instead of her name up in lights outside it, they were advertising 'The Ziegfeld Girls'. She saw her name in much smaller letters chalked on a board by the entrance and frowned. It was misspelled.

'You getting out, lady?' the cab driver asked.

Only now did Leni realize they had been parked for a while. She shook her head and indicated with a flick of her fingers that he should continue. 'Just drive,' she said.

'Central Park?' he suggested.

'Why not.'

Along Madison Avenue, everyone appeared to be in a hurry to get somewhere else. Then, where the avenue met East 56th Street, she did a double take as she recognized a tall and athletic young white man sitting on the sidewalk, limp like a puppet with his strings cut, a look of mournful reproof in his eyes. She turned in her seat for a better look at him, but he was gone.

What was Kim doing in New York? She felt in her handbag for the canister. Had she imagined him? She sometimes had premonitions – nothing dramatic, but small, unexplainable things, such as an urge to pick up the phone a second before it rang.

In the afternoon, Leni and Jäger visited the Museum of Modern Art and the Empire State Building and, now that the fog had lifted, they found the views spectacular. Leni asked Jäger to take a photograph of her with her back to the skyscrapers, wearing her fur coat again. Before he clicked, she took hold of her collar and blew a kiss at the lens. Perhaps it was the height of the building, but she felt exalted, as if she might at any moment take wing and soar above Manhattan like a Valkyrie.

This was her moment, she thought.

Although *Triumph of the Will* had won prizes and been critically acclaimed in America for its cinematography, composition and creativity, it had also been much criticized for being a propaganda film. Her protests that it could not have been, since it did not have a voice-over, had been ignored. But the reception for *Olympia*, she felt sure, would be different. If she had portrayed Hitler as a Wagnerian deity in *Triumph of the Will*, as her critics claimed, in *Olympia* it was Jesse Owens who had been given the heroic treatment – and Jesse Owens was a black American. Surely that would go down well with the critics?

That night Leni slept soundly, despite the air still being heavy with the scent of the flowers she had stored in the bathroom. In the morning, she was already awake when she heard a commotion outside on the street below. Wrapping herself in one of the dressing gowns provided by the hotel, she went to the window to see what the noise was about. On Fifth Avenue, she could see a small crowd, no more than twenty strong. They were waving placards. She opened the window to hear what they were saying, but was distracted by a knock on the door. Jäger.

When he saw the window was open, he marched across the room and closed it. 'Ignore that rabble,' he said, his face uncharacteristically solemn. 'Some attention-seeking writer has organized them. Dorothy Barker.'

'Parker?' Leni suggested.

'Yes, Parker. Have you seen the papers?'

Leni felt a tightness in her chest. When she shook her head, Jäger held up the front page of the *New York Times*. She could usually get by in English, but the only words she could recognize in the headline were her own name.

'Want me to translate?' Jäger asked, fingering his tie. Without waiting for an answer, he read the headline: '"Leni Riefenstahl dismisses reports of Crystal Night as 'pack of lies'".'

She gave Jäger a wordless glare, looked away, then asked in a voice that was sharp but unsure: 'I said no such thing. What is this "crystal night" anyway?'

'It's what they are calling the burning of the synagogues. The night of broken glass. The papers are full of it. Jewish shopkeepers have been attacked, at least according to this.' He tapped the paper. 'Their shop windows smashed. Thousands of them. Right across Germany. And Jewish cemeteries have been desecrated everywhere. Heydrich's orders. They are calling it a pogrom.'

'It can't be true.'

'There are pictures, look. The situation is serious. Roosevelt has recalled his ambassador from Berlin.'

Leni took the newspaper and flicked through the reports. 'But . . . Does the Führer know about this?'

Jäger gave her a patient look. 'Would you like me to put out a statement?'

'No. Let us wait.' She drummed her fingers on the table. 'I feel such a fool for answering that reporter's question. Should we contact him and explain that I did not know?'

'There's a story in the *Los Angeles Times* you should see as well,' Jäger said, ignoring her question and handing her another front page.

Leni read the headline out loud: '"No place in Hollywood for Leni Riefenstahl".'

'And I'm afraid Gary Cooper's agent has sent a telegram cancelling lunch.' Jäger took it from his pocket and unfolded it slowly, as if enjoying the suspense. '"MR COOPER LEAVING FOR MEXICO UNEXPECTEDLY STOP REGRETS CAN NO LONGER MEET MISS RIEFENSTAHL STOP".'

The words reached her through a lifting numbness. She asked him how to say '*Scheisskerl*' in English.

'Son of a bitch?' Jäger suggested.

'Yes, send Mr Cooper a reply saying "Son of a bitch",' Leni muttered.

Jäger returned to the window and opened it. The chants of the crowd could be heard clearly now: 'Leni go home! Leni go home!' He closed it again and said quietly: 'If you do go home . . .'

'What?'

'My wife. Might you be able to arrange for her to . . .'

Leni recalled how Goebbels had told her she had to fire Jäger, because he was married to a Jewess. She had ignored the order, but her press chief would have to stay in America. 'Of course,' she said. 'Leave it to me.'

Leni did not go home, not straight away. For the rest of that morning she did not even leave her room, accepted no calls and declined to open the door to visitors. She tried to read but, unable to concentrate, she took a long bath instead.

After that, almost in a trance she reached into her handbag, retrieved the canister she always carried with her, opened it and held the roll of film to the window. Whatever fate had in store for her in America now, at least she still had this. It was her safety net. Her lifeline. Filmed two years earlier, shortly before Jesse Owens won his gold medal in the broad jump, this clip had not made it into the final edit of *Olympia*, mainly because she had filmed it as an experiment, using a higher definition film stock of her own invention, one that could be used with a combination of blue and red filters.

She had heard about the development in America of a new technique for making films seem three-dimensional, but she had yet to see an example of it. From what she had heard, though, it only worked with colour film. What she had created with this roll of film was something akin to a 3-D effect using black and white. It was partly to do with the dramatic contrast. Blue filmed on black and white stock through a red filter is a perfect black. But this went beyond that. The white was perfect, too, and so was the grey. Each was in dramatic contrast to the other, and the image not only advanced from the picture plane like a *trompe l'oeil*, but also receded into it.

When she got to Hollywood, she was going to show it to some directors, producers and studio heads. She had not decided which ones yet, but possibly Cecil B. de Mille, Frank Capra and Walt Disney, depending on their availability. She thought of it not so much as her calling card but her insurance policy. Whatever the critical response to *Olympia* now, this clip would surely open doors for her in California.

A dull ache in her lower back distracted her so she put the film back in the canister and went to lie on her bed with a pillow over her face. She drifted off and, when woken by a knock on the door, the thin winter light was fading.

It was Jäger again. 'There's been a development,' he said, not meeting her gaze. 'The manager of Radio City Music Hall has telephoned. The premiere has been cancelled. He says he's sorry.'

Leni sat down and placed both her hands flat on the table in front of her.

'Walt Disney still wants to see you,' Jäger offered.

'Walt Disney does not count!' Leni snapped. 'He is more fascist than Rudolf Hess!'

'And there's someone downstairs in the lobby,' Jäger continued calmly. 'He has come in from Chicago on the train, for the premiere. You might want to tell him in person that it has been cancelled.'

'Jesse?'

'Jesse.'

Still feeling dazed, Leni said in a distant voice: 'Of course, of course, send him up.'

'There is a problem. He's not allowed to use the lift.'

Leni blinked. 'Why ever not?'

Jäger gave her another one of his patient looks.

Leni had heard of segregation but had given little thought to what it meant in practical terms. 'I see,' she said. 'Well, I'll go down to meet him.'

'That's not advisable. The lobby is full of press. And there has been some trouble with the protesters outside. A group of pro-Nazis from Long Island has turned up in support of your visit.'

'Lucky me,' she said flatly.

'I know,' Jäger said. 'I'll go down to the lobby and collect our friend. Perhaps I can disguise him in some way.'

Ten minutes later Jesse Owens appeared, unwrapping a scarf that was covering his face. When he looked up he gave her a toothy smile.

'We used the freight elevator,' he said, taking off the fedora he had borrowed from Jäger. He looked as though he had lost some of his muscle tone since they had last met two years earlier. His collar was frayed and his jacket threadbare and he seemed shorter than she remembered. And yet, for all this, an edge of his former elegance nicked Leni like a papercut.

'Mr Owens,' Leni said, holding out her hand for the athlete to kiss. 'It is good to see you again.'

'And it sure is good to see you,' Jesse said. 'My train got in an hour ago.' As with their previous encounters, Leni had difficulty understanding his Midwestern vowels. 'I can't wait to see your film.'

'*Ja*, you must see it,' she said. 'You are the star, after all. But there has been a . . . The premiere has been . . . postponed. Come and have a drink. Champagne?'

'Is the postponement to do with those protesters outside?' Jesse asked.

Leni nodded. 'Let us not talk about that.'

They clinked glasses.

'To *Olympia*,' Jesse said. 'I've heard great things about it.'

'The reception in Europe has been overwhelming,' Leni confirmed. 'But its success has . . .' She trailed off. Then, with a shake of her head, she snapped back into the moment: 'I only hope American audiences eventually get a chance to see it and judge for themselves.'

'I'm hoping that too,' Jesse said. 'I could use some of its limelight at the moment.'

'Why do you say that?'

The athlete looked over his shoulder at Jäger. Leni, reading his mood, signalled with a click of her fingers for Jäger to leave them alone.

'Things haven't worked out so well for me since Berlin,' Jesse said in a low voice.

'But I heard you were treated as a hero here?'

'Sure, when I first came back I was. They held a ticker-tape parade for me down Fifth Avenue, and there were promises of sponsorship, and jobs, and advertising, but nothing came of it. I don't think America is ready for . . .' It was his turn to trail off. 'The truth is, I've had to go back to pumping gas.'

Leni was shocked. 'You do not compete any more?'

'I race against horses at country fairs.' Jesse averted his eyes as he said this. 'They bet on me. Or the horse.'

'Perhaps our fates are not so dissimilar,' she said, pulling up a chair and indicating for Jesse to do the same. 'My association with the Nazis has tainted me. Look at this.' She reached for a newspaper and held it up. 'A scandal sheet from Hollywood is claiming I am not only the mistress of Hitler but also the playmate of Goebbels. Can you believe it? They call me "the Nazi pin-up girl".' She tossed the paper on the floor.

'Don't pay them no heed,' Jesse said. 'They'll be picking on someone else tomorrow and will have forgotten all about you, like they forgot about me.' He cleared his throat. 'What will you do now?'

Leni thought of Mariechen and the baby. 'Return to Germany. I can do no other.'

They sat in a silence that bloomed uncomfortably. Then Leni asked: 'Have you stayed in touch with anyone from the Olympics?'

'You remember the English broad jumper I competed against in Berlin?' Owens said, his fingertips chattering in his lap. 'Kim Newlands?'

Leni's heart dilated. In the past two years, she had thought about Kim so often he had almost become an abstraction.

Jesse carried on talking but Leni had turned her head away from him, unable to concentrate on his words. 'A newspaper had the idea I should get together with some of the athletes I competed against in '36,' he was saying. 'A sort of reunion. Luz Long. Kim Newlands. I wrote to him in England but got no reply, so I wrote to his coach. The coach wrote back to say that Kim was dead.'

Leni was distracted, finding it unnerving to hear Kim's name on someone else's lips. It was almost as if he were a tangible person made of tissue and bone, not just a strip of celluloid, half-man, half-shade. When she next saw Kim, she thought now, she was going to present him with the clip of film and explain that, as she had recorded him through her lens that day in Berlin, it had felt as if her heart were beating in his life. She pictured him now, running towards the take-off board, then lifting, soaring into the sky.

'*Ja, ja,*' she said, regaining her focus. 'I remember Kim.' Her eyes slowly panned back to Jesse. 'You mentioned a letter. How is he?'

'He's dead,' Jesse said, with a look of confusion. 'Didn't you hear what I said? He died.'

As she finally took in the news, Leni could hear her blood thumping, feel its pressure on her inner ear. Several seconds passed before she could find any words.

'*Er ist gestorben,*' she muttered. 'What happened?'

'I don't know. The letter didn't say.' Jesse shook his head. 'He was only a year older than me.'

Leni swallowed, her throat dry. 'There's something I want to show you,' she said, standing up and pinning a white sheet to the wall before unpacking her portable Bolex projector. Granular images of Jesse Owens soon flickered on the screen, but he was not the star of this clip. Behind him, on the edge of the frame, was Kim. And as he directed his gaze towards her and gave his lopsided smile, Leni felt as if she were rising a finger's breadth above the floor, remaining in suspension, defying gravity.

Acknowledgements

I am grateful to Kirsty Dunseath, my editor at Doubleday, and Jon Wood, my agent at Rogers, Coleridge & White, for their wise counsel. Such has been the long incubation period of this novel there is also an earlier, now retired editor to thank – Marianne Velmans – as well as my previous agent and much missed friend David Miller, who died on 30 December 2016. I would also like to thank Gill Coleridge, Emma Howard, Craig Simpson, Natasha Fairweather, Matthew Marland, Suzanne Bridson and Michael Carlisle for their close reading of earlier drafts, as well as for their astute comments. Above all, for her forbearance, encouragement and good humour, I would like to thank my wife Mary.

Nigel Farndale is the author of *The Blasphemer*, which was shortlisted for the Costa Novel Award. His previous books include *Haw-Haw: The Tragedy of William and Margaret Joyce*, which was a finalist for the Whitbread Biography Award and the James Tait Black Memorial Prize. He lives on the Hampshire–Sussex border with his wife and their three sons. www.nigelfarndale.com